Close Contact

Close Contact

Tales of Erotica

SEAN WOLFE

KENSINGTON BOOKS
http://www.kensingtonbooks.com

KENSINGTON BOOKS are published by

Kensington Publishing Corp.
850 Third Avenue
New York, NY 10022

ISBN 0-7582-0850-2

First Kensington Trade Paperback Printing: August 2005
10 9 8 7 6 5 4 3 2 1

Printed in the United States of America

This book is dedicated to Gustavo Paredes-Wolfe, the first real love of my life. All of these stories, with the exception of "Truth or Dare," were written while we were loving partners. Gustavo never belittled me for my flair for porn, and read everything I wrote. His insight was valuable in editing the stories, and his pride in my writing talent was immense. Gustavo passed away September 4, 2003. I miss him very much, and thank him for showing me what love means and how to do it right.

Gustavo, siempre vas a estar en mi corazón.
Te amo y te extraño mucho.

Acknowledgments

Thanks to the guys in my writers' group: Matt Kailey, Jerry Wheeler, Drew Wilson, and Peter Clark. Your critical eyes (and constant amazement at my fascination with nine-inch uncut cocks) and constructive criticism is much appreciated.

Thanks to my earthly angel, Jane, for loving me and encouraging my love for writing . . . even when I write stuff she would never read. Your unconditional love and encouragement mean the world to me.

Thanks to my editor, John Scognamiglio, for your relentless pursuit of excellence, and your persistence in getting this anthology published. Your support of my writing career is appreciated very much.

Contents

Author's Note

I've been interested in writing for as far back as my memory al-
lows. But it was my senior year in high school when I realized
that I wanted to be a writer. My English teacher, Mrs.
Knighton, was a loving and inspiring soul who encouraged me
to pursue my dream of becoming the next Stephen King, John
Grisham, or if I preferred . . . Anne Rice.

 Though not intentionally, it was also in Mrs. Knighton's
class that I first expressed myself sexually through the art of the
written word. My assignment was to write a short story about
a car accident. Simple enough. The story was good, but I
wanted to make it brilliant. So I embarked upon a quest to re-
place simple, common, and mundane words with ones that
would take the reader's breath away. I believe I succeeded.

   The old Chevrolet Impala skidded only slightly as it
rounded the treacherous curve. Then Brian lost control of
the car, and watched in horror as the road disappeared and
he became airborne, tumbling down the jagged edge of the
cliff. He began to pray as the car looped and dove closer to
the rocky beach of the shore ahead and behind and below
him. Then, the miracle he'd cried so desperately for was
granted, and he was ejaculated through the open window
just moments before the car smashed into the boulders
below and burst into flames.

 There were several more pages to the story, and I received
an A for the assignment. Mrs. Knighton's praise of my flair
for description and detail was endless. Except for one little

comment: "Though I appreciate your attempt at finding just the right words to express the emotional impact of this scene, I encourage you to make sure that certain expressions are really the right choice. Specifically, the word "ejaculate." Though it does mean to be released with a surge of power . . . I don't believe it is really the proper word for what you are trying to get across. Excellent effort, however. And a very good story. Keep up the good work!"

I looked the word up in several different dictionaries, and then I cried. I curtailed my enthusiasm for writing erotica for many years. It wasn't until 1998 that I actually used the word again, this time intentionally, for the purpose of igniting arousal in my reader.

In the last six years I have written fifty-two erotic stories, and two full-length erotic novels. Most of them have been published previously (some several times), and are included in this book. I am often asked by readers if the stories you are about to read are based upon true experiences or if they are all made up and entirely fantasy.

Though I did not graduate with valedictorian honors, I also do not consider myself stupid. So, I always smile mischievously, and reply with the same answer: "It's purely fiction. That's my story, and I'm sticking to it." I am not sure that everyone believes me. But I am in a committed, loving relationship with a wonderful man, and I wish to remain so. His one minor flaw is that he tends to get a little jealous sometimes. Therefore, whenever I am asked about my stories, I stand firm with my reply: *It's purely fiction: That's my story and I'm sticking to it.*

Read on, and read into the stories what you will about their origins. But please, if you are ever around my partner, be kind. Watch my back . . . and I'll wash . . . I mean, watch yours.

Badlands Bad Boy

I grew up in a very small town called Booker, Texas. In the extreme northern panhandle, only seven miles from the Oklahoma panhandle border, it boasted a population of approximately 600 people. One school. One stoplight. One post office and one bank and one supermarket (which is actually a stretch for even the most vivid imagination). There were, however, nine churches to meet the spiritual needs of the farmers who lived there.

Ninety percent of Booker was white. And not just plain old white, but Clorox Bleach, Wonder Bread, Macy's White Sale White. The other ten percent were Mexican immigrants who provided the majority of the work done on the farms that occupied most of the surrounding area. There was not a single Black, Asian or Other person living in our town.

There were a few Mexican students in our school, and for that I am grateful. It was my only glimpse of the diversity of the world we live in. If not for those few friends of Mexican and Mexican-American heritage, I'd have been completely deprived. Back then there weren't even any TV shows with people of color on them! When I moved away from Booker to go to college, I figured I would be exposed to lots of people of diverse background and skin colors. I was wrong. I attended a Quaker university in Wichita, Kansas, and their idea of diversity was to offer two kinds of sauce for the spaghetti served in the school cafeteria . . . one with ground beef and one vegetarian.

So you can imagine the culture shock I experienced when I moved to San Francisco right after I graduated. The epitome of the term diverse, The City by the Bay was overflowing with Latinos, Asians, Blacks and everyone in between. I almost felt intimidated by my own whiteness, and was anxious to soak up as much of the exotic cultures of my new neighbors as possible.

My mother was great when I told her I was gay. No big shock. When I told her I had a boyfriend she was ecstatic. When I told her he was Latino she tried to control the twitch in her eye and the quiver in her voice as she squeaked out, "That's nice, sweetie." Though not an overly enthusiastic endorsement of approval, Ruben was glad that she didn't come right out and faint or ask for an exorcism. She tried to appear interested as she asked Ruben where he was from. She looked confused when he said he was born and raised in San Jose, California.

"His grandparents came to the U.S. from Guadalajara, Mexico," I told her proudly.

"Oh," she replied in a tone that was intended to convey that she understood perfectly.

I later found out that she told my sister that my boyfriend was from Guatamala. Apparently the all-white Catholic school education she'd had as a teenager hadn't taught her the difference between Mexico and Central America.

Needless to say, she was less than thrilled with the fact that I was perhaps a little too enthusiastically attracted to Latino guys. Ruben and I broke up after a couple of years, when I met Andy. Mom was noticeably relieved when I told her his name. Then I told her his last name which was unpronounceable for her, and that he was Portuguese. After Andy was Richard, who was half Filipino and half Puerto Rican. Next was Victor, who was full-blooded Puerto Rican, and by then mom was convinced she'd have to learn Spanish in order to communicate with the grandchildren she was still bravely holding out for.

Though I would loved to have seen the look on her face, taking my mother to The Badlands would not have been the best way to impress upon her just how "normal" and "respectable" gay people are. Located between a Laundromat and a pastry shop on San Francisco's famous Castro Street, the bar has a reputation even for this city of being seedy, smoky, and cruisy.

I'd been there a couple of times with Victor, and we'd both been overwhelmed with the intense atmosphere. When we broke up I was devastated and desperate to make new friends and have new experiences. How dare he walk out on me and call me a prude? So what that I'd never been drunk or touched a cigarette to my lips? So what that I'd never used any drugs and felt not the least bit self-conscious about preaching to others about the dangers of doing so? So what that my idea of living dangerously was to sneak into the express lane at my local Safeway when I quite obviously had at least twelve items in my basket rather than the boldly advertised ten or less?

I'll show him, I thought to myself as I took a deep breath and walked into the front door of the bar. The heavy curtain of smoke and strong odor of stale alcohol assaulted my nose at once, and I began coughing melodramatically as I forced one foot in front of the other and advanced into the dark room. I covered my ears to shield them from the music that was several decibels too loud.

People were drinking and laughing all around me, and I quickly became convinced that their chuckles were aimed at me. I walked past the bar on my right and to the back of the dark room, where a large crowd pressed themselves onto a tiny dance floor and gyrated just a little too suggestively for my comfort. Several men were sitting on top of stereo speakers and unopened boxes of beer. It was all I could do not to remind them that certain items were not structurally safe nor specifically designed to be used as furniture.

Instead I walked to the bar and ordered a drink. The bartender looked at me with stunned disbelief when I asked for a Midori Melonball. Though I was two months shy of my twenty-seventh birthday, I still looked much younger and was often carded. Was he going to embarrass me by asking me for my ID? I had just had the tips of my normally brown hair bleached and it looked great. So that couldn't have been the problem. I'd also left my glasses at home, opting instead to wear my contacts, so I didn't look too much like a nerd. Granted, I was not tattooed, and I was a little paler than anyone living in sunny California should be, but did I really stand out that much? I cursed myself for not having pierced any body parts before coming into the bar, but at least I was well-muscled from my daily trips to the gym.

I opened my mouth to change my order to something more mature and very butch, like a Bud Light or a Long Island Iced Tea, but then decided against it. No reason to go overboard, at least not yet. When I didn't change my order, the bartender smiled, winked at me and left to fix my drink. I was well on my way now, I thought, and decided to throw caution to the wind. I tipped him a whole dollar and walked toward the pool tables as I sipped my Melonball through the tiny red stirrer stick.

The pool tables were located on the other side of the bar, directly in front of the rest rooms. The smell was even worse here, a mixture of sweat and alcohol and pee pee from the men's room. But it was not as crowded as the rest of the bar, and the fog of cigarette smoke was not quite as thick here, since there was a window that opened onto the street and the entrance door was only a few feet away. So I decided I would stay and watch the hunky guys playing pool. Money was being exchanged and not very discreetly, I might add, but I bit my tongue and didn't say anything. The guys who were playing pool and betting their hard earned money were all quite a bit bigger than me.

I was amazed (and a little ashamed) at how quickly I finished my drink. I never could hold my liquor very well, and less than thirty minutes after I'd walked into the bar, I found myself needing to visit the little boys' room.

Though I'd been inside the bar a couple of times before, I'd always carefully planned out my bladder relief so that I would not find occasion to enter the room beyond the pool tables. Once inside, I realized I'd made the right choice in doing so. Though it was far less smoky inside the small rest room, and the music was at a blessedly more tolerant level, I was much more frightened inside there than I had been out in the open next to the pool tables. The walls were painted black and littered with graffiti. The two toilet stalls didn't even have doors on them, for crying out loud. I toyed with the possibility of changing my mind and waiting until I got back home, but my car was a good four blocks away, and then the drive was at least fifteen minutes, so I decided to be brave and go ahead and pee right there.

I walked up to the urinal and nearly stopped breathing. Could I have had too much to drink with just the one Melonball? Was this really an open, long trough these people tinkled into? Yes, it was, and I made up my mind then and there to turn around and walk back to my car after all. But the pressure in my bladder was unbearable, and I knew there was no way I would make it all the way back to my Taurus.

Taking a deep breath might not have been the wisest move I could have made, but I was a little buzzed, and so I did so anyway as I hurried to the trough and began to unbuckle my belt and unbutton my jeans. Spit flew from my mouth as I coughed and gagged. I reached forward with my left hand and braced myself on the wall in front of me as my right hand hurriedly pulled my penis out of my pants. The pee was flowing even before I was able to steady myself.

My eyes were closed and the music from the dance floor located behind the rest rooms pounded through my head. I'm not exactly sure how long I'd been standing there peeing like some animal in a barn before I realized that I was no longer alone. I opened my eyes and quickly noticed that there was a guy on either side of me.

Oh, no, this can't be happening, I thought to myself. But it was. I looked to my right, careful to make sure my eyes stayed on the face of the guy next to me. It was pretty easy to do, because he was about my height. And he was beautiful. His mocha colored skin was smooth as marble, as was his shiny shaved head. Twin dimples graced both sides of his thin, yet sensuously full lips. He smiled at me, and I nearly fainted with his beauty. I forced myself to look away from his hypnotic smile and gaze into his eyes. Big mistake. They were even more gorgeous. Long, thick eyelashes blinked to reveal Elizabeth Taylor–like lavender eyes. They were obviously contact lenses with no prescriptive value, but it didn't matter. They worked.

I was so engrossed in taking in this stranger's beauty that it took me several seconds to realize that there was an extra hand squeezing my exposed penis. My heart skipped several beats as I quickly looked away from the black guy to my right and glanced down at my penis. I was equally grateful and mortified at the same time. Grateful that sometime during my drunken stand at the trough I had actually finished peeing. Mortified that there was indeed a strange hand tugging and squeezing my manhood, and that my brain had decided it liked the stranger's touch very much. Swollen to well past its halfway mark of arousal, it was quickly filling the warm hand that was not attached to my own body.

I knew that a protest was in order, but instead moaned with animal lust as the guy to my left slid his experienced hand up and down the length of my now fully hard cock.

"You like this, man?"

"Uh-huh," I whispered as I turned to look into his face.

He was definitely Latino. The copper-colored skin and jet-black hair and eyes gave him away immediately. The goatee and thin mustache that framed his very sexy mouth told me he was probably around twenty-three or twenty-four years old. He was several inches taller than me and built like a bodybuilder. His chest was powerfully muscular and dusted with a light coating of black wavy hair. The mountains he called pecs flexed teasingly as he tugged and squeezed my fully hard dick. Clad in nothing but a ripped pair of denim shorts, his legs were smooth and tightly muscled. His own dick stood hard and throbbing directly in front of him. I gasped as I looked at it. At least nine or ten inches long, it looked as thick as my wrists.

"Look guys, I really don't think I . . ."

The black guy grabbed me by my arms, pulling them loosely but firmly behind my waist as he leaned into my back and began kissing my neck and ears. He pressed himself against me tightly, and I was vaguely aware that he was pulling my pants down.

"No, really, I can't . . ."

The Latino guy still had his hand wrapped around my cock, and he pulled me closer to him as the black guy kept kissing me from behind. I was sandwiched between the two men for several seconds, and then the Latino moved his hands to my shoulders and began gently pushing me down onto my knees in front of him. I noticed that as I dropped clumsily to my knees, both men began kissing one another.

When I was completely kneeled in front of him, the Latino moved closer and waved his massive dick in my face. He was very gentle and playful as he slapped the heavy piece of meat against my cheeks. I heard the black guy pushing his own pants down to the floor.

"Suck it, papi," the Latino whispered to me.

It had to be the Midori Melonball, there is simply no other explanation for it. But I did as I was told. Slowly I stuck my tongue out and licked the salty head of the fat cock. My tongue danced around the head and under the silky foreskin for several seconds, and then I sucked three or four inches of his thick dick into my mouth.

"That's it, baby," he said as he wrapped his hands behind my neck and forced another inch of himself into me.

After a couple of minutes of this, I felt a heavy thud on my shoulder. It was warm, hard skin, and I realized the black guy behind me had started humping the back of my neck and shoulders. I slowly pulled my mouth from the sweet Latino cock and turned around to face an equally impressive darker hard-on. I moaned with lust as I stared at the huge black dick and reached out with my tongue to lick the dripping precum that was slowly sliding out of his cock head.

"It's my turn now," the black guy said, and slid half of his dick inside my hungry mouth in one swift thrust.

I opened the back of my throat as wide as I could and

amazed even myself as every last inch of the huge cock slid deeper into my mouth and down my throat. A couple of tears slid down my cheeks as I breathed heavily through my nose. The fat dick was leaking even more precum now, and I could taste it as it slid across the back of my throat.

Had I been in control of my senses I never would have reached over and grabbed hold of the porcelain trough to steady myself, and believe me, I cringe when I recall having done it even now. But at the time, it was the only thing I could do to keep from falling flat on my ass. The Latino dude (now behind me) reached down and wrapped his arms around my waist as he kissed my back and forced me deeper onto his friend's fat black cock. Somehow he managed to pull my legs behind me so that my ass was sticking up in the air only inches from him.

"You want me to fuck you?" he asked with the sexiest voice I have to this day ever heard.

"Mmm-hmm," I moaned. I still maintain that in my deepest consciousness, I meant to say "no," but even I can't lie and say that the animal moan that escaped my lips came even close to resembling a "no."

Certainly my new Latino friend didn't hear it like that either, because a couple of seconds after asking my permission, he spit noisily onto my ass and began sliding his cock against my butt cheeks. It was hot and thick and throbbing with a life of its own, and bright tiny lights floated in front of my eyes as I realized what was about to happen.

"Yeah, dude, suck my cock while my buddy fucks you," the black guy moaned and began pumping himself deeper and faster into my throat.

I swallowed him until his pubic hairs tickled my nose as his "buddy" slid his fat pole into my twitching ass. The bright pins of light got brighter and bigger as the heat of his cock began to spear me, and I tried to pull myself off of him. I think he once again mistook my gesture as trying to wiggle deeper onto him. His arms wrapped tightly around my waist as he slid inch after inch into my butt, and he didn't stop until he was lying against my back, fully buried.

"Oh, papi, you've got a sweet ass, man."

I was delirious with pleasure as both men fucked me with wild abandon. I squeezed my ass muscles around the Latino cock and deepthroated the fat black dick, sucking on it hungrily. Both guys began pumping their cocks into me faster and deeper and harder. All three of us were moaning loudly.

The Latino guy shoved his cock deep into my ass at the exact moment the black guy pulled almost all the way out of my mouth, leaving only his fat, sweet head inside my mouth. My two new friends leaned forward and kissed each other as they plowed me. I looked up with the corner of my eyes and watched as their tongues slid into each other's mouths and danced around there, and tightened my ass and throat muscles even more so they would know I was watching and enjoying their kiss almost as much as the fucking they were giving me.

"Oh, shit, man, I'm gonna shoot," the black guy said as he broke the kiss with his friend.

I reached up with one hand and took his small hairless balls in my palm and massaged them as I swallowed his huge cock again. His big head barely pushed its way past my tonsils before he began shooting. Spurt after spurt of warm, thick cum splashed against my throat and I swallowed it hungrily. I'd never really thought of doing that before, but the big black cock was so thick and hard and buried so deeply in my throat that I didn't really have a choice. I was amazed to find that I actually liked it.

"I'm getting close," the Latino grunted behind me as his cock pounded my twitching ass.

"Wait a second," the black guy said as he pulled his still thick but slowly deflating dick from my mouth. "Turn him around onto his back."

The Latino dude buried himself inside my ass and kept it there as he quickly turned me over onto my back. Even before I was completely situated on the floor, the black guy leaned over and swallowed my own throbbing cock into his hot mouth with one quick move. His big dick now dangled in front of my face, still dripping small drops of cum, and I reached up with my tongue to lick him clean as he sucked me with a powerfully warm and wet mouth.

"Here I come, man," the Latino shouted and quickly pulled his massive cock from my ass. It just barely plopped out of my hungry hole before the first jet of cum flew from the dark red head. It shot way over the black guy sucking me and landed on the floor several inches behind my head. Three or four more spurts landed on the black guy's back and then several shot onto my own balls.

"I'm coming!" I yelled much too loudly as the heat and wetness of the Latino's cum dripped down my balls and into the crack of my ass.

The black guy pulled his mouth off of my cock and wrapped his hand around it as I let go with an amazing load. His face was soon covered with my cum, and the Latino man leaned down and began kissing his friend and licking my load from his face.

"Oh my God," I panted as the last few drops of cum squirted from my cock.

"Did you like that?" the black guy asked me. He was

already starting to stand up and stuff his still half-hard cock into his jeans.

"Un-huh," I moaned.

"Good," the Latino said, already buttoning his shorts. They didn't even begin to conceal the thick piece of meat that created a noticeable line all the way down to the ripped leg hole. "Here's our number. Give us a call. Let's do it again sometime." He tossed a business card onto my stomach, and wrapped his arms around the black guy. They smiled at me and walked out the rest room door together.

I picked up the card and read it. "Jorge & Geoff. Partners in life and in pleasure. $200/hr for one or both for $300." The phone number was the only other ink on the card.

My head reeled as I realized what I had just done. I was still lying on the bathroom floor, covered in sweat and cum, when the door opened and a very cute guy walked in.

"Oh, shit man, I'm sorry," he stammered. "I didn't realize . . ."

"It's okay," I said as I jumped to my feet and pulled my pants up.

I couldn't take my eyes off the new kid who had just walked in. The skin on his face was a few shades darker than mine. A very sexy black stubble grew across his chin. He had short black hair and deep blue eyes. About my height and same build, he was easily the most striking guy I'd ever seen.

"I didn't mean to . . . umm . . . interrupt anything," he said with a very strong Middle Eastern accent.

"Don't worry about it," I said. "It's my fault. I really shouldn't have been doing anything in here. I don't usually . . ."

"Shhh," he said and leaned in to kiss my mouth. "Were you finished, or would you like to go back to my place for some . . . dessert?"

"Well, I guess we can go back to your place," I stammered as he kissed me again and reached down to give my ass a gentle squeeze. "But didn't you have to use the rest room?"

"Not really." He smiled. "I noticed you walk in a few minutes ago. I wanted to talk to you outside, but when I didn't see you come out, I thought I should come in and make sure you were all right."

"I'm fine."

"I can see that."

"That's very nice of you," I said as I felt my face blush. "Are you sure you're not turned off by seeing me like this and knowing what just happened?"

"Are you kidding?" he asked, and moved my hand to his own bulging crotch. It throbbed noticeably under his khaki pants. "In fact, it fucking turns me on."

"Really?"

"As long as you can take some more."

My ass was a little sore from the fucking the Latino had just given me, but it also began to tingle again. My dick was already well on its way to sporting another full hard-on, and my heart was beating erratically.

"I don't think that's a problem," I said.

"I'm Ahmad," the guy said as he draped his arm around my shoulder.

"I'm Sean."

"Let's go to my place, Sean. I only live two blocks from here."

I thought about tossing the business card into the wastebasket before I left, but decided against it. I shoved it into my front pocket as Ahmad and I walked out the bathroom door. As we walked through the bar, I saw Jorge and Geoff ordering a drink at the bar. They looked at me, winked, and held their hands up to their mouths in a "call me" gesture. I winked back and walked out the door with Ahmad.

"I really don't think you'll need to be calling those guys again," he said as we walked up the sidewalk away from the bar.

I laughed to myself and wondered just how my mother would take to the idea of learning Arabic.

Of Boyfriends
and Brothers

"I know it's a lot to ask, but come on, Adam, I don't know what else to do. Chris can't afford to fly all the way out here and back. You know the entire family is gonna be here, and Mom is so excited to see him. It's been almost two years since he's been home."

"But I've never even met him, Brendon. You know how awkward I am around new people. Especially straight in-laws."

Adam held his breath for a moment, the phone pressed against his ear so hard it hurt a little and his knuckles were white.

"You are not awkward around new people, baby. You're a social butterfly, and you know it. And my family loves you, you know that too. It's true you've never met my baby brother, but he knows all about you and us, and he's fine with it. He just wants a ride home so he can be here for the family reunion, and since you're driving out here for it anyway, it wouldn't be that much more trouble for you to drive down to L.A. and pick him up."

"It's *way* out of my way," Adam sulked, already feeling the resolve settling in. "I wasn't planning on taking the southern route."

"I'll make it worth your while when you get here," Brendon whispered, "I promise."

"But . . ."

"Hold on, Mom is right here and wants to say hi."

"No! Brendon, wait, I'll do it. Just don't put your mom on the phone. You know I can't . . ."

"Hello, Adam, this is Mrs. Peterson," came the sweet woman's voice over the receiver. As if she needed an introduction.

It was classic Brendon manipulation, and Adam cursed his boyfriend as he spoke for nearly fifteen minutes with his mother-in-law. By the end of the conversation, he had assured her he would be bringing her youngest son out to Atlanta with him for the family reunion, and she was most appreciative. She put Brendon back on the phone.

"Hi, baby."

"That is *so* not fair. You know I can't say no to your mother."

"Yes, I do. So, we'll see you in a few days then?"

"Yeah, sometime Thursday afternoon probably."

"Good. I miss you."

"Me too," Adam said, and hung up the phone. "Damn it!"

He walked over to the television and popped in his favorite porn video, then dropped sullenly back into bed. In the bottom drawer of his nightstand was the dildo he and Brendon sometimes used to spice up their sex life, and he pulled it out and laid it next to him on the bed. His cock got hard instantly as his hand wrapped around the thick rubber dick, and Adam sighed as he watched a scene in the video and lubed up his own fat cock.

He hadn't come in three days, and his body tingled as he slid his hand slowly up and down his throbbing cock. Sometimes he liked to beat off for quite a while before shooting his load, but he knew he wouldn't be able to now, so he grabbed the dildo next to him and lubed it up. On the video, a cop handcuffed a young man and was in the middle of frisking him; pulling his hard cock out and sucking on it as he did. The boy was helpless, and Adam sighed deeply as he watched his favorite scene and moved the dildo to his ass. The cop in the video plowed the young man, and Adam slowly slid the thick rubber cock up his ass as he imagined himself being bound and fucked by the older, sexy policeman.

He shoved all nine inches of the dick up his ass, and shuddered as the rubber balls reached his ass cheeks. He had to remove his hand from his own dick, because his balls tightened and he felt his load start to build already, with just the pleasure of his ass being speared and spread wide open. The volume on the video was a little low, so Adam grabbed the remote and turned it up a little, allowing him to hear the moans and groans of the cop and the kid who had been stopped for speeding.

Already at the end of the scene, the cop pulled his big dick out of the boy's ass and shot a huge load all across the back of the blonde young man's back, whose hands were still handcuffed behind him. Adam wrapped his hand around his own cock and squeezed the fat dick as he watched the bound speeder shoot his load all over the cop's car door. The dildo in Adam's ass worked its magic, and it only took a few strokes of his hand on his own cock before he came all over himself.

Once he came, the pleasure of the big dildo inside him quickly began to turn to pain, and he pulled it out of his ass slowly. He caught his breath for a moment, letting the cum dry on his chest and stomach, and then got up and headed for the shower.

As he soaped himself up, Adam sulked about his misfortune.

He'd been looking forward to the road trip from San Francisco to Atlanta for the last two months. It wasn't that he didn't love Brendon, he did. But it had been almost two years since they'd spent any time apart at all, and Adam was ready for some alone time. He'd also been looking forward to the one night he'd planned on spending in Phoenix, not quite alone.

He and Brendon had been together for a little over three years, since they were both seniors at San Francisco State University. In that time he had never once cheated on his boyfriend. But lately he'd been fantasizing quite a bit about having wild, uninhibited sex with other guys . . . strangers, friends, famous actors, you name it.

When Brendon first suggested they attend his family reunion in Atlanta, Adam was at first very reluctant. But when he said he wanted to fly out a week earlier and that maybe Adam could drive out and spend just a couple of days with the family, and then the two of them could drive back together . . . well, Adam became more receptive.

The prospect of a few days on the road without his boyfriend actually excited Adam. Especially when his best friend, Rick, insisted that he stay at a bed-and-breakfast in Phoenix. Promising "an experience like nothing you could ever imagine," Rick staunchly refused to tell him anything else. His best friend was a nice guy, but the most sexually mischievous person Adam knew, and he could definitely be counted on to recommend fun places and good times. He made Adam promise to stay at Fantasy House Bed-and-Breakfast. According to Rick, they guaranteed a good time, and never had a single complaint in ten years of operation. That was good enough for Adam, and he booked a room immediately.

Now he was going to have to skip hitting the cruisy bars in Phoenix and baby-sit his lover's baby brother, and it was too late to change his reservations at Fantasy House. He was a little worried about Chris's reaction to staying in a gay bed-and-breakfast, especially one called Fantasy House and shrouded in mystery, but decided it was just too bad. If Chris was coming along and ruining Adam's first time away from Brendon in two years, he would just have to get over whatever homophobia he might have.

He got out of the shower, dried off, and called the number Brendon had given him an hour ago. Chris answered on the first ring, and they agreed to meet the next day around noon, outside the dorm where Chris was a junior at Azusa Pacific College.

The drive along the Pacific Coast Highway the next morning was beautiful, and the closer Adam got to Los Angeles, the less he worried about Chris and the trip to Atlanta together. There was certainly something to be said for the calming effect the ocean had on a person . . . and seeing hundreds of cute, young college boys as he drove around the small campus didn't hurt either.

Chris was easy to spot as Adam pulled up to the dorm. Of course, he'd seen several pictures of Chris over the last three years, but even if he hadn't, he'd have been able to pick him out in a crowd. Only three years younger than Brendon, he carried the same physical characteristics as the rest of the Peterson clan. The short, black wavy hair, crystal blue eyes with lashes that went on for days, irresistible dimples and strong jawbone and clefted chin were dead giveaways. Besides that, he was the only person sitting on the curb in front of the dorm, with a duffel bag at his side.

He was not an exact duplicate of his older brother, however. Though Brendon had a great body, which seemed inherent with his family, he never really worked out. He was not into sports, choosing instead to excel in music and the fine arts.

Chris, on the other hand, was a star athlete all through high school and continued his enthusiasm into college with a full athletic scholarship. He was a couple of inches taller than Brendon, and the muscles that stretched his tank top and jeans were obviously well exercised.

He looked up and smiled when he saw Adam's blue Honda pull up to the curb, and threw his duffel bag in the backseat as he sat up front and introduced himself to his brother-in-law. Chris was extremely outgoing and friendly, and Adam found himself more comfortable with him as each mile passed. They talked equally about Adam and Brendon and Chris and his girlfriend. Adam was pleased to find out that he had a lot in common with his boyfriend's little brother, and there was hardly ever more than a minute's lull in the conversation between L.A. and Phoenix. Chris was cool with staying with Adam in a gay bed-and-breakfast, but decided to stay in the car as Adam went inside and checked in.

"I know I only made reservations for one," Adam told the guy at the front desk, noticing that he was looking out at Chris in the car, "but I unexpectedly got stuck bringing along my boyfriend's brother. I can pay extra if it's necessary, but he knows this is a gay place and is cool with staying with me, if that's all right."

"Oh, it's okay with us," said the clerk. "We're not sticklers about stuff like that here. As long as you're both comfortable, we're happy."

"Thanks."

"We do need to let you know that this is not just any hotel, though. Your stay here will be very unique. Hopefully your friend who recommended us didn't tell you too much about us."

"No. He was very secretive, actually. Just said I'd never

forget it, and that I had to promise not to give away anything when I recommend it to someone else."

"Good. That's exactly what we ask of all of our guests. That, and to have an open mind and have fun while you're here. Oh, and we need you to sign this acknowledgment form."

The clerk turned around to get a room key, and Adam read the form in front of him.

By signing below, I acknowledge that any and all activities entered into while on the premises of Fantasy House are done so voluntarily. I also understand that sometimes we are not aware of our innermost desires, and am open to exploring my subconscious. I release Fantasy House of any liability or fault of any harm that may, in the very unlikely event, result from my stay here, by stating that nothing will happen to me that I do not desire to happen and agree to. In exchange, I understand that if I am not one hundred percent satisfied with my stay at Fantasy House, I will be refunded completely.

The clerk returned with a key and smiled at Adam.

"Is this really necessary?" Adam asked.

"Oh, yes, sir. On that issue, we *are* sticklers."

"Fine." Adam sighed and signed the form. "There's no chance of anything happening with me tonight anyway, now that I have Chris with me."

"Yes, sir," the clerk said. "Your room is number five, around the back and on the corner. Enjoy your stay, and please let me know if there is anything I can assist you with."

The room was large, but simply decorated. A king-size bed filled most of it; a nightstand on either side held a lamp and local interest reading material. Against one wall were a large dresser, a color television with VCR, and a couple of plush chairs. Each room had its own bathroom, and Adam was glad to see it had a tub with hydrojets. From what he could see in the dark, there was no pool or hot tub outside, and he wondered why Rick had so adamantly insisted he stay here. He did see, from the magazines on the nightstands, that there were a couple of gay bars nearby; but now that he had Chris with him, he wasn't even able to go out and play around.

Adam decided to enjoy the hydrojets in the tub, and Chris threw himself on the bed and began channel surfing. The long drive from San Francisco to L.A. and then on to Phoenix had worn him out more than Adam had been aware of, and as he sank into the hot bubbly water he realized just how tired he was. He laid his head back on the edge of the tub, and sulked just a little. Even though he was getting along great with Chris, he'd really been looking forward to hitting the bars and hooking up with a local hunk for a good fuck while he was here.

He reached down and stroked his cock for a few minutes, hoping to get a response, but when it just lay limp in the soapy water, he sighed heavily and decided to call it a night and head to bed. He usually slept in the nude, but with Chris in the same bed, he reluctantly put on his boxer shorts and slipped into the soft, thick cotton robe that hung on the bathroom door.

"Jeez, I thought you'd fallen asleep in there," Chris said when Adam stepped back into the bedroom. He was lying on the bed, hands behind his head, watching television. He was stripped down to only a pair of bright white cotton briefs, and Adam swallowed hard as he took in the beauty of his boyfriend's younger brother.

Chris's tall, muscular body seemed to contain not an ounce of fat, and each muscle was perfectly defined as he stretched across the bed. His huge biceps were cut and bulged impressively as they held his hands behind his head. His massive chest was completely smooth with the exception of a small triangle of short, curly black hair that separated two muscled pecs that were capped with impossibly tiny brown nipples. A defined eight-pack of hard abs graced his stomach.

The snowy white briefs were a stark contrast to his tanned body, and clung tightly to the bulge that pulled the elastic waist of the shorts down just far enough to reveal a glimpse of black curly pubic hair. The cock hiding inside looked long and thick, and Adam found it a little difficult to breathe.

"I almost did," he finally answered, and walked over to his side of the bed. "I'm beat."

On his way around the bed, he couldn't help but steal a glance at the long, muscular legs that stretched out to fill half the king-size bed. Tanned and covered with a light dusting of silky black hair, they looked very strong and perfect, except for a small scar just below one of the knees.

"You *must* be," Chris said as Adam took his robe off, laid it on the chair next to the door, and laid down on his side of the bed. "I know I am, and I've only been on the road half as long as you have."

"Yeah, it's been a long drive all right," Adam admitted, "but not as bad as I expected."

"Well, let's get some sleep," the young Adonis next to him said as he reached up and turned off the lamp on the nightstand next to him and clicked the remote to the television off. "I'll help you drive tomorrow and see how many miles we can put behind us."

"Sounds good," Adam said. *Easy for you to say*, he thought to himself as he rolled onto his side to hide the hard-on that was quickly filling out his boxers.

"G'night Adam. And thanks for letting me tag along."

"No problem," Adam lied as he cursed the pulsing cock inside his shorts. "Good night."

Surprisingly, he fell asleep easily. He dreamed of skiing at his favorite resort in Colorado, trying desperately and in vain to catch up with Brendon, who was skiing half a football field's length in front of him. He was naked in the dream, and using his grossly oversized protruding hard-on to balance himself, rather than the conventional ski poles everyone else was using.

He smiled to himself in his sleep, knowing that he was dreaming, and telling himself how silly it was to be skiing naked in the freezing snow. Adam loved to dream, especially when he knew he was doing it and could go along with it. He stuck his tongue out and licked at the falling snowflakes, reveling in how cold each flake was as he swooshed down the hill and felt the biting cold wind against his naked skin.

In his dream he twisted an ankle, and fell forward into a large snow mogul. He was surprised to feel that the snow was warm and wet. He was even more surprised as he felt the mogul's warmth tighten and massage his hard cock. Something wasn't right here, he thought, and began to count backward from twenty-five, his usual means of bringing himself out of a dream.

He blinked his eyes open slowly, and was at first disoriented when he realized he wasn't in his own room back in San Francisco. Then he remembered he was in Phoenix, on his way to Atlanta, and he relaxed. But the warm, wet massaging sensation on his cock was still there, and when Adam looked down the length of the bed, he almost screamed. Tried to scream, actually, but no sound came from his mouth; only large powdery snowflakes that floated in front of his face and slowly faded away.

Beyond the fading snowflakes, Chris was lying between Adam's legs, sucking on his cock. Adam shook his head fervently, thinking he must still be dreaming, yet knowing he was not. When he tried to sit up on his elbows, Chris pulled his mouth from his cock, and pushed him gently back down onto his back with one strong hand.

"Just relax," Chris said, and Adam thought he was going insane.

It was definitely Chris in front of him. He felt the strength and solid skin as he was pushed back down onto the bed. And he saw Chris, too . . . his face and the same beautiful body he'd admired when he stepped out of the bathroom earlier that night. Yet even as he looked *at* his lover's younger brother, he was looking *through* him. He saw the television set and dresser, which should have been hidden by the massive muscular body lying between them and himself. He looked at Chris's face and saw, in perfect detail even in the dark of the room, his dimples and the tiny mole below his left eye. At the same time, he looked straight through Chris's smiling, transparent face and saw his own legs and feet at the end of the bed.

"What the fuck is going on here?" Adam asked the strong young man in front of him.

"I'm sucking your dick," Chris answered. "Don't you like it?"

"Well, yes," Adam answered, and shook his head again, his eyes transfixed on the apparition in front of him. "But . . ."

"No buts, then, at least not yet," Chris whispered, and moved forward on the bed, closer to Adam's face. Adam's heart pounded wildly in his chest as he watched Chris's face get closer to his own and one strong, warm hand wrapped around the throbbing cock that defied Adam's fear.

Chris leaned forward and pressed his soft, full lips on Adam's and kissed him. This could not be happening, Adam thought as he closed his eyes and tried to count his way backward out of what had to be a dream again. The lips pressing against his own remained, however, and Adam felt a warm tongue lick his lips and gently yet persistently part them. He tasted a faint trace of the cinnamon gum Chris had been chewing earlier during the road trip, and wanted to cry.

Adam opened his eyes again, and Chris broke the kiss. He moved backward a few inches, giving Adam a better look at him. The jet-black hair, crystal blue eyes, cleft chin . . . even the irresistible dimples were all there. Adam even smelled the sweet cologne he'd noticed when he first met Chris earlier that afternoon.

"Freaking out, huh?" Chris asked.

"Well, yeah," Adam answered, slowly gaining some composure.

"Understandable. But don't. Just accept it and enjoy it, okay?"

"All right."

Chris leaned forward again, and kissed his brother's lover, and this time Adam didn't fight it. He opened his mouth and sucked gently on the warm, cinnamon-tasting tongue that probed it. His cock pulsed hotly in Chris's hand, and a gentle squeeze brought a moan of delight from his throat. Chris playfully bit Adam's bottom lip lightly, and smiled as he moved his body so that he was sitting on the edge of the bed, staring at his brother-in-law.

Adam's head spun with a million questions, but before he could ask them, Chris stood up and moved to the head of the bed. He looked through the muscular transparent body moving toward him, and noticed the bleached white briefs lying on the floor a few feet directly behind Chris's see-through chest. His eyes were immediately drawn to the semi-hard cock that was moving closer to his face. When he breathed in, he smelled the sweet mix of cologne and manly sweat, and smiled.

He looked at Chris's heavy cock, and noticed it looked very similar to Brendon's. Long, thick and uncut, the fat cock swung temptingly a few inches from Adam's mouth. Half expecting to feel nothing but air, he reached out and touched it. It grew fully hard as his fingers tugged and squeezed it, and Adam licked his lips in anticipation as he slid the soft, silky foreskin up and down the hard, solid, yet transparent rod. He smiled again when he noticed, near the base of Chris's dick, a tiny black mole, identical to the one Brendon had just below his pubic hair.

"Suck my dick," Chris said huskily in a voice uniquely his, yet tinged with a supernatural power filled with lust and desire.

Adam did as he was told, wrapping his lips around the big uncut cock head and savoring the taste and feel of it on his tongue. It grew even harder as his mouth sucked on it lovingly, and he felt the large veins pounding hotly against his tongue and cheeks as they coursed through the foreskin, stretching tightly against the fat, nine-inch cock.

"That's it, man," Chris whispered. He positioned himself over Adam's body so that, without removing his cock from the hungry mouth sucking on it, he lay gently on top of Adam's body and began kissing and licking Adam's dick in a sixty-nine position.

The room spun as Adam looked through Chris's translucent body and saw the top of the television and wall behind it that should have been blocked by Chris's skin and muscles and bone. Somewhere deep in the back of his mind, he was certainly freaking out, but right then the feel and taste of Chris's huge cock was very real as it slid deep into his throat, and Adam was loving every minute of it.

He breathed in slowly, and opened the back of his throat, allowing the hard pole to slide deep inside him. Breathing only through his nose now, he reached up and caressed the smooth skin of Chris's ass and legs as Chris swallowed his cock all the way to the base. A low, deep moan escaped both boys' throats as they began to fuck each other's mouths with mounting intensity.

It didn't take long at all before Adam felt his balls tingle and shrivel, and the inevitable load started working its way up the length of his cock. He tried to warn Chris, and to pull the sucking mouth off of him, but Chris only increased the pressure and sucked harder, while forcing his own cock harder against Adam's mounting lips.

His load shot from his cock in a fiery stream, and Adam's eyes widened with amazement as he looked at the back of Chris's head and saw his own load shoot stream after stream of cum into what seemed thin air and down Chris's throat at the same time. A second later he felt the cock in his mouth pulse madly, and his throat grew warm as Chris emptied his load deep inside him. Swallowing hungrily, Adam was amazed as wave after wave of his lover's younger brother's cum filled his gut.

Chris reluctantly pulled his mouth from Adam's still hard cock, licking the shaft as he did. Adam figured they were done, but was surprised when Chris stood up on his knees and instead of moving away, inched his smooth, tight ass cheeks closer to Adam's now empty mouth.

"Chris . . ."

"Shut up and eat me, Adam."

The silky, hard cheeks were against Adam's lips before he could think of anything else to say, and he reached up and massaged them with his hands as his tongue slid between the crack.

His head was still spinning with the force of his own orgasm, but the musky, sweet taste of Chris's ass kept his cock hard and his heart began to race again.

Chris wiggled his ass in Adam's face for a moment, and when Adam hesitantly slid his tongue inside the twitching hole, Chris moaned loudly and grabbed Adam's legs firmly.

"Oh, fuck yeah," he said, and tightened his hot ass muscles around Adam's probing tongue.

This can't be happening, Adam kept thinking. But he knew it was, and slowly and lovingly slid his tongue in and out of the burning ass.

"Oh, it's happening, all right," Chris said out loud, reading Adam's thoughts.

He slowly stood up and turned around, still on his knees, and straddled Adam's upper body. A beautiful smile spread across his face, showing off his sexy dimples, and his bright eyes sparkled. Amazingly, his huge cock was fully hard again, and throbbing just inches in front of Adam's face. The fat head poked through the sheath of foreskin and a large drop of precum slid down the underside of it. Adam took a deep breath and licked his lips, ready for another taste of Chris's cock and his sweet load.

"Uh-unh," Chris said, and smiled even more mischievously. "Been there, done that. Now it's time to move on."

He reached behind him and gently took hold of Adam's cock and moved it to his ass.

"Chris . . ." Adam started to protest.

"Shhh . . ." Chris whispered, and leaned down to kiss Adam again. His tongue traced its way around his brother's lover's lips, and this time met with no resistance at all as it slid inside.

The two boys kissed for a long moment, gently at first and then with more fervor. Adam's whole body shuddered when his cock head pressed against Chris's hot ass hole, and Chris wrapped his mouth around Adam's tongue and sucked it gently as he slid himself down onto the big dick.

Adam still tasted the cinnamon gum aftertaste in Chris's mouth, and the ass muscles surrounding and massaging his dick seemed even hotter as Chris took him completely inside. A loud buzzing sound echoed in his ears and bright pins of light spun before his closed eyelids, but nothing in Adam's entire life had ever felt better.

He looked up at the ghost-like figure of his lover's younger brother as he fucked him. Everything about his night was magical, but Adam was getting more used to it by the minute. He looked into Chris's deep blue eyes, still seeing completely through them, yet also catching the ray of light that beamed from them.

Forcing himself to look around the room, a million questions flooded Adam's mind as he thrust himself inside the see-through body of his brother-in-law. Everything around him was solid and perfectly normal. Only Chris was magically translucent and at the same time, fully solid and touchable.

"Stop asking so many fucking questions," Chris grunted as he slid his ass down onto Adam's cock. "Just go with it, man."

Adam did, giving in to the fact that none of this made any sense at all, but not caring. He fucked Chris with long, slow strokes, and watched as Chris's heavy uncut dick bobbed in front of his face. It wasn't until then that he glanced just beyond the big dick, right through Chris's rock hard abdomen, and saw his own cock, very clear and not at all translucent, as it slid into and out of Chris's ass.

Seeing both dicks as they moved in perfect sync with one another proved too much for Adam, and he stopped breathing as he felt his fully engorged cock flex, and his cum worked its way up his shaft.

"Oh, shit," he said loudly, and watched in amazement as his cock shot out several large streams of cum inside Chris's see-through body.

"I feel it, man," Chris said, and stopped sliding up and down so that he could focus on squeezing his ass muscles against the spurting cock inside him. "It's so hot. You ready for mine now?"

Beyond the ability to speak, Adam just lay still and watched as Chris's huge uncut dick began shooting its second load of the night. Incredibly, his own cock was still pouring out a large amount of hot, white cum, and he saw the steam rising slightly from the fluid as it spewed out of his cock head and disappear up inside Chris's body. Chris's load shot wildly, landing all over Adam's face, chest, and stomach. It felt like hot lava landing on him, and when he reached out with his tongue to lick at the drops that landed on his lips, he was not surprised at all to find out it tasted like cinnamon.

When both boys finished coming, they relaxed, and Chris slumped on top of Adam's quivering body. Their hearts slowed down at the same time as they kissed again and fell asleep hugging each other lovingly, Adam's cock still buried deep inside Chris's warm body.

The alarm buzzed at eight o'clock the next morning, and Adam jerked awake. It took him a moment to get his bearings, and he was afraid he was going to find himself still entwined around Chris's sweat and cum-drenched body. He was in bed alone, though, and he heard Chris whistling loudly in the shower. He quickly pulled the covers down and saw that he was still wearing the boxer shorts he'd worn to bed the night before. There were no dried cum spots on his face or body, and he breathed a sigh of relief and lay back down on the bed.

So, it was all a dream after all. But if that were true, then why didn't he wake up with a pounding hard-on, like he did every single day of his adult life . . . except the day after having incredible sex.

He didn't have much time to think about it, as the shower stopped running and Chris stepped into the bedroom. He was drying his hair with one towel, another draped casually around his waist. Adam breathed another sigh of relief as he saw Chris was completely solid and nowhere near being transparent. Each bulging biceps and flexed eight-pack muscle on his body dripped shower water, and kept Adam from seeing what lay behind them.

"Hey, bro," Chris said as he walked over to the bed, "you'd better get up and get showered if we wanna get an early start. We've got a lot of miles to put behind us today."

"Right," Adam answered. "Uh, Chris, did you sleep okay last night?"

"Hell yeah, man. Like a baby. I didn't realize I was so tired."

"Right," Adam said again stupidly, and shook his head as he stood up and walked to the bathroom to take his shower.

As the hot water pelted his body he wondered why his muscles were so sore, and decided he'd ask Chris to start the drive that morning. There was so much to think about the rest of the trip . . . first among them being how he was ever going to thank Rick for recommending the Fantasy House. He whistled happily as he soaped up and thought of how badly he missed Brendon and couldn't wait to see him.

In the Flesh

Being the manager of a gay men's bookstore definitely has its ups and downs. I get to read all the new books that come in before anyone else, get an incredible discount on all the hot items, and peruse the current issues of all the skin mags before putting them out on the shelf, just to make sure we're selling quality merchandise. This just happened to be one of the days in which we received a large order of several of the magazines, and so I had to do a little more perusing than usual.

Before I knew it, the alarm on my watch chimed, alerting me that it was a few minutes before closing time. I turned off the music in the store, turned off the heater and walked around straightening up the shelves and generally making a nuisance of myself as I tried very hard not to be subtle to the remaining three customers as I let them know it was time to put down the magazines I knew they were not going to buy, and go home. I've been doing this job for a couple of years now, and so I am good at it.

I locked the door behind the last straggler and was on my way to close out the register when I heard a knock at the door. Normally when this happens, I just ignore the noise and point at the "Closed" sign in the middle of the glass door. But something made me turn around and open the door this time.

"I'm sorry, but we just closed a few minutes ago," I said as I inched the door open just enough to be heard.

"Oh, man, I know I'm late, but I rushed as fast as I could to get over here before you closed. Traffic is a bitch out there. I'm really just looking for one thing. Do you mind if I come in?"

"Well, it's against policy to let anyone in after the doors are locked," I started my regular excuse. Then I looked into the eyes of the guy standing only a few inches from my own face.

It was him. The short, shaggy blonde hair and sparkling blue eyes were a dead giveaway. The square jaw and dimpled chin burned into my mind like a branding iron. He was wearing a light jacket and jeans, but that didn't matter. I knew exactly what lay under them. I'd just stared at the layout of his naked body in one of the magazines I had earlier perused.

"I'm really sorry I'm a little late," he said in a husky voice that defied his youthful look. "I am the centerfold in this month's issue of *Freshmen* magazine, and I just have to get a couple of copies. I'm heading out of town and who knows when I will find another store that carries it. Can't you just let me in to buy them. It won't take long, I promise."

"Well . . ." I said and pointed stupidly toward the counter area, ". . . the computer . . ."

"Please?" he asked sweetly, and smiled. "You could ring up the sale tomorrow if you have to. But I need them tonight before I leave town."

"Come on in," I said, and stood aside so that he could enter. I closed the door quickly behind him and locked it.

He rushed to the back of the store and grabbed three or four copies of the magazine that had just come in earlier that day, and joined me at my desk.

"I don't know how to thank you. I really did try to get here before you closed," he said as he looked down at the magazine that was opened to his own centerfold and spread across my desk.

"Don't worry about it," I said as I felt the blood rush to my face, "it's no big deal, really."

"So what do you think of my spread?"

"Umm, well, it's great."

"Thanks. I know it probably doesn't seem like it to you, but it was actually a lot of hard work."

"Oh, no," I stumbled, "I can tell it was hard."

He laughed, and shuffled his feet awkwardly as he grinned at me.

My own cock was fully hard, despite my embarrassment. I tried to cover it up with my shirttail, but it was too late. His eyes lingered at the hard line that snaked along the upper leg of my jeans.

"Wanna see it in the flesh?" he asked boldly as he noticed me staring at his crotch.

"Right here?" I asked.

"Sure. Let's just lower the blinds, and I can give you a little solo performance of my photo shoot."

I rushed over to the window and lowered the blinds. My heart was beating extremely fast and I was having trouble breathing. When I turned around to face him, he had already shucked his jacket, and was leaning against my desk next to the counter.

"Come over here," he said, and rubbed the growing bulge in the front of his jeans.

I walked over to him and stood stupidly in front of him. He planted a heavy hand on both of my shoulders and pushed me to my knees on the ground, inches from his now obviously aroused dick.

"Take it out, man."

I unzipped his jeans and pulled them down his muscular legs. His thick uncut cock sprang up and bounced against my cheek even before his pants reached his knees.

"You can suck it if you want to."

I leaned in and licked the salty head of his fat cock for a moment, and then sucked a few inches of the long shaft into my mouth. It was even thicker than it looked in the centerfold, and I had to stretch my jaw muscles to get most of it inside my mouth.

He moaned as I sucked on it hungrily. Then he started pumping it in and out of my drooling lips slowly. "Damn, you can really suck a good dick, dude," he said as I opened my throat and allowed the thick rod to slide deeper inside me.

He fucked my throat for several minutes, then pulled his dick out of my mouth slowly. He reached under my arms and pulled me to my feet.

"What's wrong?" I asked, dazed. "Was I scraping it with my teeth? Didn't it feel good?"

"Hell, yeah. It felt incredible. But I was getting a little close. I was kinda hoping you'd let me fuck your ass."

"Really?" I gasped. I tried not to sound too excited or desperate as I shoved my jeans down around my ankles.

"I'll go slow, I promise."

"We can start out slow and then just take it from there. How does that sound?" I asked as I bent over my desk and spread my ass cheeks.

"Sounds good to me," he said, and I heard him rip the condom package open. He licked my ass as he rolled the rubber onto his cock. Then he stood back up and a moment later I felt the hot, fat head of his big uncut dick press against my twitching hole. "Here I go, man. Just take a deep breath and . . ."

I did take a deep breath, and slid my hungry ass down the entire length of his thick pole in one move. I moaned with lust as I felt it spread my groping muscles to accommodate each throbbing inch as it went deeper inside me. When I felt his pubic hairs tickle the top of my ass and his balls bounce against the bottom of my cheeks, I squeezed.

"Damn, man. No one's ever been able to do that. It's so fucking hot in there."

"I can't believe I was just gawking at the pictures of your cock a couple of hours ago, and now I have it inside me," I groaned like an animal.

He laughed, and I felt his cock thicken inside me with each chuckle. Then he began sliding his cock in and out of my ass. As he promised, he started out slowly and then when I began bucking harder onto him, he picked up the pace. In minutes, his dick was sliding in and out of my eager ass like a well-oiled piston.

I'd been horny all day, mainly due to the fact that I'd stared at the pictures of this guy's huge cock and popped a boner from the time I opened the page to his layout. So it didn't take me very long to get ready once I actually had the real thing deep inside me. I felt the electric tingle begin deep in my balls and course through my belly and all around my body.

"I'm gonna shoot," I moaned as I reached down and grabbed my cock. It only took a couple of tugs before I sprayed my load all over the side of my desk. It seemed to go on forever, and large pools of it dripped down the desk and onto the carpet.

"Shit, man," he grunted as he continued to slide in and out of my twitching hole as I came.

Then he quickly pulled his big dick from my ass and ripped the condom off, throwing it to the floor. The first few shots of his load flew over my back and head, landing all over the computer on the opposite corner of my desk. Several more warm geysers settled onto my back and my quivering ass. It didn't take long before my entire backside was completely covered with his spunk.

"Fuck," he said softly as he tried to catch his breath. "That was too much."

"Thanks," I said, as I straightened up and wiped as much of the cum off my back as I could reach with a paper towel.

"Listen, I'm heading out of town for a couple of days. But maybe we can hook up again when I get back?"

"Yeah, I'd like that."

"Can I get your number?"

I wrote my phone number down on a sticky note as he dressed. Then I ran to the back room and grabbed another copy of the magazine he was in. "I hate to sound like an adoring fan or anything," I said shyly, "but do you think you can sign a copy of the magazine for me?"

He opened it up to the centerfold and scribbled something across the pages. A few seconds later, he was out the door. I remembered he hadn't paid for the few copies of the magazine he'd taken with him. Oh, well, it wouldn't break the store.

When I got back to my desk I read the short note he'd scrawled across the glossy pictures of his hard naked torso.

"Thanks for everything. Next time I see you, I'll pay for the favor . . . In the Flesh."

I smiled and rolled up the magazine and stuck it in my jacket pocket. Then I cleaned up the desk and floor before I walked slowly out the back door and headed home.

Chat Room Lover

I rolled over onto my back and stared at the ceiling through the dark. The king-size bed which seemed so perfect when Kevin and I bought it together three years ago now seemed overwhelmingly large and uncomfortable. I looked across the huge expanse of blankets and pillows to look at the clock on the nightstand on the other side of the bed. Three-forty A.M.

I wasn't surprised. I hadn't slept all the way through a single night in the last two years. I could usually count on about three hours of uninterrupted sleep a night, and would drift off for a few minutes at a time three or four times a night. The lack of eight straight hours of sleep a night had worn me down the first month, but I have slowly been adjusting to it, and now feel I function normally despite the deprivation.

I looked over to the left side of the bed, the side which used to be Kevin's. That familiar tingle surged through my body and I felt the tears well up in my eyes. I blinked hard and threw the comforter aside, allowing the cold air in the room to envelop my body. Kevin always liked to keep the bedroom cold at night so that we would be forced to snuggle, and he liked getting out of the warm bed in the mornings and be chilled as he worked his way through his morning routine. I hated getting out of the warm bed and running across the cold hardwood floor to the bathroom. But I couldn't bring myself to change the personality of the bedroom after Kevin left to "find himself" almost two years ago.

I got out of bed and cursed as I crossed the bedroom to grab my terry cloth bathrobe. Instantly warmed, I slipped on my fleece slippers and walked to the kitchen to fix myself a cup of coffee. It would be useless to try to get any more sleep this morning. Might as well get an early start on the day.

Armed with a cup of extra-strong coffee, I went to the second bedroom, which served as my home office. I flipped on the computer and watched the screen as it came to life with a swirl of colors and sounds. I could hear crickets and a couple of birds outside, and went to open the window. Though a little chilly outside, the cool breeze always felt good, and helped my body get going once it was warmed with coffee.

I sat down at the computer and stared at the screen. It offered so many options. I could work on some spreadsheets that I'd need later in the week for work. I could crank out a letter or two to my mom and sister, whom I hadn't written to in weeks. I could update the mailing list for the theater I volunteered for. So many icons on the screen to choose from. And yet I knew exactly where I'd go from the moment I sat down.

I double-clicked on the little blue triangle in the bottom right-hand corner. AOL. The magical, limitless world inside my little computer. I could pretend I was going to check on my stocks, or research some important project, but I knew from the time my ass hit the chair where I'd be going, and since I was there alone, I might as well not even bother trying to lie about.

Chat rooms. Wonderful inventions, really. Even at this ungodly hour in the morning, one is sure to find hundreds of people up and chatting up a storm about myriad topics. There are rooms devoted specifically to talking about President Bush's (I still cringe at the thought) latest foible. Rooms where you could talk about your spiritual beliefs, get gossip on your favorite entertainers, share your favorite recipes, and everything else you could think of.

And then there are the M4M rooms. Men for Men. I just recently got an AOL account. I don't know why really, it just seemed everyone else had one, and I didn't want to miss out on anything. Chuck, a friend from work, came over and showed me how to get around and do lots of things online. It was he who introduced me to the torrid world of chat rooms; he who led me down the road to temptation in the M4M rooms.

I was addicted, really. I found myself going online at work when it was a little slow and entering a chat room. At home after work I immediately got online and hit the EastBayM4M room. And when I found myself awake at three-forty A.M., I always seemed to wake up a little easier by getting online and starting a chat with other insomniacs. That was the case this morning, and I smiled as I double-clicked myself into the East-BayM4M room and saw there were six guys there.

<<Hi, guys>> I typed as I entered the room.

A few seconds went by, and then <<Welcome>>. It was from StarChild, a screen name I had seen many times before in the room. We had chatted a few times, but didn't have much in common other than our insomnia. I double-clicked on each of the screen names that appeared in the window at the top of my screen. Doing this would bring up a profile of each person in the room, giving me some insight to who I was chatting with. Sometimes the names and profiles were very creative and fun.

This morning all my co-inhabitants seemed a little older and more conservative. George007, Jsimpson, VllyPlayer, John-Boy, Bobby231, and Happy3.

Even when the rooms are filled to the maximum of twenty-three people, they are not always busy with chat. A lot of guys like to get on there and just sit and wait for someone to begin a private chat by sending them an IM, "Instant Message." Today, with only six guys in the room, my screen was almost completely blank.

<<Kinda quiet tonite>> I typed, and waited for a response.

None came, and after about five minutes, I decided to move to another room. As I was scrolling through a list of available rooms, I noticed a new participant enter the EastBay room, and double-clicked on his profile to check him out.

His screen name was ArchGabriel, which I assumed represented the Archangel Gabriel. I smiled as I recalled Kevin's obsession with angels. Reading on I found out that Gabriel lived in Hayward, only a few minutes from my home. He was evasive on his age, as ninety percent of those online are. He enjoyed working out (again as ninety percent online do); slurping pasta noisily, a good back rub, bubble baths by candlelight and alternative music. He was versatile and loved oral, especially 69. He preferred fucking, but if the guy was right, would also bottom every now and then. He described his occupation as "under construction" and quoted an extremely overused line from *Titanic* for his personal quote.

It was not an extremely clever profile, and didn't interest me enough to send him a message. I was still looking through the list of other available rooms when my computer chimed, indicating I had received an IM. A window appeared at the top left corner of my screen. It was from Gabriel.

<<I want you>>

I chuckled at the words. I had little patience with guys who started a conversation with such foolishness. How often had I received IMs starting with "How big are you?" or "I need to suck your dick" or "Will you fuck me now?" It was ridiculous, and I was usually very rude in letting the senders know I thought it so.

<<Sure you do. And just what is it you want from me?>>
<<I want to roll you over on your stomach and—>>
<<I do not get fucked, sorry>> I interrupted, deciding to end the conversation shortly.
<<Let me finish. And I believe you do, btw (by the way)>>

I was astounded at the boldness of this man, claiming he believed I did get fucked even though I had just told him I didn't.

<<What?>>
<<Let me finish. I want to lie you on your stomach, completely naked. The lights would be off and candles burning all around the bed. I take in the beautiful sight of your naked body and smile to myself as I lean over you.>>

Okay, Gabriel had me with him at this point. My cock was already starting to stir under my robe. He typed with such a confident, yet gentle manner, and the vision he'd described was one right out of one of my fantasies.

<<I lean down and lightly kiss the back of your neck. You moan lightly as my lips caress your neck, and I notice chill bumps creep down your neck and back. I slowly move my lips

down your back, kissing and licking your hard smooth body, lightly biting once or twice. This makes you moan again, and I see you lift your ass a little and wiggle in delight in the bed.>>

My heart is racing as I picture this unknown man kissing my naked backside. My neck is extremely sensitive anyway, and I love having my naked body kissed and licked. He is definitely hitting the right spots, and my cock is completely hard and throbbing now. I pull the belt from my robe and wrap my hand around my thick dick and gently squeeze it. A small drop of precum spills from the head and slowly slides down my rod.

<<Do you like this, GeminiBoy?>>
<<Yes>>

I am barely able to type my response.

<<Go on>>
<<Your back is tightly muscled and tan, and as my tongue works its way across your smooth hard skin, I taste the lightly salted taste of your sweat. It tastes good on my tongue and I swallow it, savoring the taste, as I move slowly down your back to your ass.>>

I wonder how he knows my body is muscular and tanned, and then realize I proudly announce it in my profile online. Gabriel is good, and I find myself sliding my hand up and down my thick cock as I read his messages, getting more excited by the minute. I have never done this before. Usually I read the ridiculous smut coming across the screen and just play along, never touching myself, in fact never getting undressed. But this is different, and I cannot hold back the arousal pulsing through my hot cock.

<<My mouth is at the base of your spine now, and your round, smooth bubble butt is only an inch away. You are moving your hips from side to side, and lifting your beautiful ass slightly into the air. You love the way my tongue feels on your body, and are sweating a little heavier down here. I lick and kiss your ass cheeks for a few minutes. Your moans and gyrations tell me you approve.>>

My mouth is dry at this point and my hand is squeezing and pulling on my dick so slowly and steadily that, incredibly, I realize I am close to coming. I want to pull my hand away from my cock, but can't.

<<I slide my tongue from your cheeks and slowly move it to the center, inching it closer to your hole. At first you tighten your cheeks, unsure whether you want me to go there or not. But my lips and tongue are patient, and continue kissing, licking, and lightly biting your ass until, eventually, you relax and my tongue slides between your cheeks and lightly licks your sweet, smooth, asshole. >>

My cock is red and throbbing, the veins looking like they will explode any moment. My heart is racing and I find it hard to swallow.

<<Are you still with me Gemini?>>
<<Oh yes>>
<<Do you like what I'm doing to you?>>
<<Indescribably>>

<<Good. I love the feel of your ass hole against my tongue. It's hot and sweet and a little sweaty as it moves around, asking me for more. You have just taken a shower and the smell of the Dial soap you use smells fresh and clean on your ass. I kiss your hole for a few seconds, and then dart my tongue around the sphincter. You moan deeply and push your ass up higher, asking me to go farther. I oblige and slowly slide my tongue just inside your tight smooth hole.>>

I am extremely close now and know I will shoot in just a few seconds.

<<I'm close man . . . finish me off>> I tell my new friend.

<<Slowly at first I slide my tongue in and out of your twitching ass. I feel it tightening and know you're close to shooting your load, and just when you're about to cum, I slide the entire length of my hot tongue inside your ass, and tickle the inside of your ass as you shoot your big load all over your sheets. Your ass muscles grip my tongue and hold it captive until you are completely drained, and then slowly relax and release me.>>

As I read the words on my screen, I feel the load start deep in my balls and work its way up my shaft. I pull the chair a little ways from the computer and watch with amazement as stream after stream of cum shoot out of my cock and land hot on my chest. I can't believe the amount of cum I shoot. I hear another chime and look back at my screen.

<<I kiss my way slowly back up your back and when I reach your neck, I slowly turn your head around and kiss you

lightly on the lips. Then I take one last look at your beautiful naked body and leave your room. I can't wait for our next meeting. Will you meet me again Gemini? I want you.>>

<<I want you too. When can we meet?>>

<<I will look for you soon.>>

<<No, I mean in person. I want to meet you.>>

<<We will meet soon. I have to go now. Goodnite.>>

<<No! Wait, please>> I type quickly, but when I hit the "send" button, I am told ArchGabriel is no longer logged on.

"Damn," I said quietly, and got up to shower and get ready for work.

I got three hard-ons over the course of the day at work because of Gabriel. I could think of nothing else. I pictured in my mind what he looked like. Tall, muscular, smooth-bodied, black hair, blue eyes and a smile that melted you at once. My ideal man, of course, but since this was all fantasy . . . my fantasy, it was my right to conjure up whomever I wanted. It was all I could do to get through the day. I rushed home right after work and jumped online immediately.

There was no e-mail from my new fantasy man, and when I searched to locate him, the mighty AOL told me he was not currently logged on. I entered the EastBayM4M room and tried chatting with some of the occupants, but found myself bored with them and only stayed online a few minutes.

I didn't hear from Gabriel for the next four days. I figured he was just another of the typical AOL game players who got off on a quickie cybersex session and who had no intention of meeting up with me, either in person or online, again. Oh, well, I could deal with that. Lord knew, I had before.

On the fifth day after I first chatted with Gabriel I was in a SeattleM4M room. I'd gotten bored with the San Francisco and EastBay rooms, and decided I'd go into a Seattle room and pretend I was there. At least the players in that room were new to me, and I to them, and I didn't get as bored with the same old people. I was chatting with a guy named GiveMeBig1. He was quite a character, telling me how he liked to be fucked by ten inches or more, even fists. I was playing right along with him, telling him I was almost eleven inches and wrist-thick, when I heard a new message chime.

<<Hi, Gemini. RU in Seattle tonite?>> It was from Arch-Gabriel.

<<No. Just got bored with the same old guys in East Bay.>>

<<Did you miss me?>>

<<Do I know you?>> I'd decided to act nonchalantly, though my heart was pounding extremely fast.

<<You're upset with me.>>

<<I was just really looking forward to chatting with you again, maybe meet in person.>>

<<Me too.>>

<<Then why didn't you e-mail me or something?>>

<<I'm here now.>>

<<Well, now I don't want to meet you.>> I was pouting, and knew it, but couldn't help myself.

<<Yes, you do.>>

How indignant! <<No, I don't.>>

<<You want me GeminiBoy.>>

<<Yes.>>

<<I want you, too.>>

<<So let's meet. How about dinner tomorrow?>>

<<No.>>

<<We could meet for a drink tonite.>>

<<No>>

<<Well, I've exhausted my suggestions. You have something else in mind?>>

<<I'll come to your place.>>

<<Sorry. I only meet guys from online in a neutral place. Too many psychos out there.>>

<<I'm not a psycho.>>

<<How do I know that?>>

<<You just do. I'll meet you at your place soon.>>

<<Sorry, Gabe. I'm not giving you my address until I meet you first. Thems the rules.>>

<<Don't need your address. Just don't lock your back door for the next couple of weeks. I'll come visit you.>>

<<Are you crazy??>>

<<No. Listen, I gotta run.>>

<<Absolutely NOT. U wait a minute.>>

Too late, he was already logged off. Damn! I signed off AOL without even saying good-bye to my size queen friend in Seattle. I paced my home office for several minutes. What did he mean he didn't need my address? And how did he know I had a back door? I could live in an apartment for all he knew. Or was he talking about my ass . . . did he want me to not have sex for a couple weeks, to save myself for him? Was that what he meant by my back door? Jesus, I was freaking out.

It was now a little after midnight, and I thought I should probably try to get a little sleep. I walked the house, making sure all the doors and windows were locked, especially the back door, and headed off to bed.

The next week passed uneventfully. I went to work like

normal, saw a couple of movies, made dinner and stayed at home. For the first couple of days when I got online, I was nervous about hearing from Gabriel, but after five days, I let go of my paranoia and actually almost forgot about him. I tried to locate him whenever I was on, but he was never signed on. I was a little relieved. He'd freaked me out big time, and if I never heard from him again, that'd be fine with me. I made extra sure all my doors and windows were locked before going to bed every night, and after a couple of nights, felt everything was safe.

Then one night, it must have been almost two weeks after my last chat with Gabriel, I was awakened by a noise in the kitchen. Sometimes older houses creak a lot, and when Kevin and I first moved into this house, I was constantly spooked by the noises it made. But that was five years ago, and I had long since grown accustomed to those creaks and moans. The noise that startled me from my light sleep was not the house. It sounded like someone stubbing their foot on the kitchen table. A moment later I heard it again, and this time, heard a distinct whispered curse.

"Shit," I said and sat up in bed. Someone was in my house. Ever since my family came home from vacation when I was six years old to find our house robbed, I have been scared to death of burglars. I had always had sexual fantasies about it also, but right now I was scared stiff. I could think of nothing except being killed by an over-adrenalined masked burglar. I looked around the room quickly to see if there was anything I could use as a weapon, but couldn't see anything.

I heard a noise right outside my bedroom door, and quickly lay back down, pulling the covers over my shoulder as I did. Maybe if I pretended to be asleep, he would not hurt me. I didn't care if he took everything I owned, as long as he didn't hurt me. I heard the bedroom door open slowly and closed my eyes tightly, barely able to breathe.

The intruder worked his way slowly across the room until he was standing directly next to my side of the bed. My heart was racing and I thought I was going to piss myself as he leaned down to see if I was really asleep. I tried to pattern my breathing to what I thought was a normal sleep pattern as his face got within inches of mine. My eyes were too tightly closed, but I couldn't loosen them any, and hoped it was too dark for him to see how tightly shut they were.

He seemed to be satisfied, because he stood up and moved over to the dresser, where I heard him shuffling through drawers and putting some of my things into a bag. He was being very careful, but I could hear him putting my watch and some other things into what was most likely a canvas bag. Then I heard shuffling of clothes. I spend a lot of money on my clothes, and tried hard not to grind my teeth as I imagined him shoving my Tommy Hilfigers and Calvin Kleins into his stash of my belongings. I just prayed that meant he was almost finished.

I heard a soft thud and realized he had dropped the heavy bag onto the carpeted floor. Why would he drop his stash, I wondered as my heartbeat raced toward the ceiling. Surely he wasn't leaving it behind. I felt, more than heard, him approach my side of the bed again. He pulled something out of his pocket and once again leaned down close to my face. I was lying on my side and I felt a tear roll down my cheek. He leaned to within an inch of my left ear and whispered huskily, "Keep your eyes closed until I'm finished and I won't hurt you."

I sobbed openly but quietly, and kept my eyes closed as he tied first a blindfold across my eyes, and then my hands to the headboard posts. I heard him undressing himself, and then felt the covers jerked from my body and thrown to the floor. I shivered as the cold air in the bedroom hit my naked body. Being tied and blindfolded was bad enough, but naked and shivering in the cold was worse, especially when I couldn't see anything.

I felt the intruder get onto the bed with me and take my chin in his hand. It was strong and forceful, but not painful.

"I won't hurt you, as long as you do as I say," he was disguising his voice. "Is that clear?"

"Yes," I sobbed, and nodded my head.

He leaned down, and with my chin still in his hand, lightly kissed me on the mouth. He licked the tears that were falling onto my lips, and then kissed me fully and tenderly on the lips. His tongue darted slowly in and out of my mouth, his lips pressed tightly against mine.

His hands moved from my face down my chest and directly to my nipples. He pinched them softly and I felt my cock stir despite my fear and the cold air in the room. He moved his mouth from mine and I felt an emptiness on my lips as his kisses trailed down to take the place of his hands on my nipples. His lips encircled my hard nipples and his tongue skated across them, making them cold and warm at the same time. I moaned softly and felt betrayed as I felt more blood surge into my rapidly engorging dick.

"You want more?" the husky voiced asked.

"Mmm-hmm," I moaned again, and before I could even finish my response, I felt the intruder move his body around until his hips were a few inches above my blindfolded face. I could smell the clean musky scent of his crotch, and knew it was close, but couldn't see it because of my blindfold. My heart was racing still, but from anticipation rather than fear now.

"I told you I wanted you. Do you want me too?"

"Yes," I whispered and strained to raise my head to meet his unseen cock. I felt his body raise, to keep my mouth from reaching his dick.

"What do you want?" that husky, deeply exciting voice asked.

"I want you."

"You want this?" he asked and lowered his hip to my face. I felt his thick cock, still slightly soft but getting harder by the second, on my lips.

"Yes," I said, and licked the head with my outstretched tongue.

I opened my mouth and my intruder slid his dick slowly inside. I closed my lips around it and sucked slowly as it got fully hard. It was long, about nine inches (according to my mental ruler), and very thick with throbbing veins running the length of it. The skin felt soft and silky as it slid along my tongue. He began to thrust it deeper into my mouth, and before long had all nine inches buried deep down my throat. I gagged slightly when it was first buried, but quickly adjusted to the girth, and swallowed it all. I could feel the thick meat throbbing against my throat muscles as my burglar moaned in delight when my tonsils danced around his big dick.

I felt him thrusting a little hard and tasted a few big drops of his precum slide down my throat and knew he was getting close to shooting. I was looking forward to a huge load of his cum shooting hot down my throat when he began to slowly pull his huge dick from my mouth. I tightened my grip on his cock with my lips, not wanting to let go, but he pulled all the way out and left the heavy weight of his mammoth cock lying on my mouth and nose.

"Don't stop," I pleaded. "I want to taste you."

"I know you do. I told you you would want to, didn't I?"

"Yes," I said, realizing now that this was Gabriel. From the moment he leaned down to see if I was asleep, something seemed very familiar about my intruder. Now I knew what it was. But I was so delirious with delight from sucking his cock, I couldn't think much about it. "So, let me have it."

"No, I don't think so," he whispered as he leaned over and kissed me again.

"Please. I want you."

"And I want you. But not like this."

"What do you mean?"

"Remember the first time we chatted, you told me you didn't get fucked?"

My heart raced. "Yes."

"Did you mean that?"

I was dizzy. I hadn't been fucked since Kevin over two years ago. He had only fucked me a few times in the five years we were together, and I never really liked it a lot. He was so big and I was so uptight, I could never relax enough to enjoy it much.

"Yes," I said somewhat reluctantly.

"I think that's gonna change tonight." His husky masculine voice and his sweet musky scent, along with the lingering taste and feel of his huge cock in my mouth were working their magic on me, and I found myself unable to argue with my burglar.

"Okay," I said and swallowed. I tried to reach out and touch him, but my hands were tied to the headboard.

"Untie me," I pleaded, "I want to see you."

"I don't think so."

"Please."

Instead of answering he pulled my legs into the air and moved his body between them. Before I knew it, his mouth wrapped around my cock, and I felt his tongue teasing my head as his lips slid farther down my cock. Sucking his dick had gotten me extremely hard and I was very close to shooting already. As his mouth swallowed more of my dick his fingers moved to my ass and tickled around my hole.

"Jesus, man," I moaned, "you gotta stop or I'm gonna shoot."

He moaned loudly, the vibrations from his mouth massaging my throbbing cock, and sucked harder.

"Stop!" I cried out.

He shoved one long finger all the way inside my ass, and swallowed my thick hard cock to the balls in response. I felt my cock head slip past his throat and grabbed the ties that bound my wrists as I felt my dick explode. I've always been a heavy shooter, but I was amazed at the force my load shot out of my cock. Gabriel kept my dick buried deep in his throat as the first three shots poured out of my dick. Then he started to gag with the force of it, and pulled his mouth off of my dick. I felt another five large spurts shoot out of my cock, and since I didn't feel them hit my own torso, I figured they'd landed on Gabriel's face.

I shuddered as the last stream of cum oozed out of my cock head and slid down my shaft. A moment later I felt Gabriel's lips on mine, and could feel my own cum cooling on his lips and chin. When his tongue slid slowly into my mouth I could taste my cum, and my cock started filling with blood again as he kissed me deeply and started working his finger in and out of my twitching ass.

Gabriel moved his mouth from mine slowly down my chest, past my stomach and wrapped it around my thick cock once more. He sucked it until it was fully hard and throbbing, then slid his tongue down to my balls, and on farther down to my ass. He pulled his finger from my asshole and began teasing my ass with little darting tickles around my sphincter. I moaned with delight and raised my ass slightly. Gabriel took his cue and slid his wet tongue all the way inside my ass until his chin rested on my ass cheeks.

"Oh, fuck," I said and my ass twitched around his long smooth tongue as it slid hotly in and out of my ass.

"You want more of me?" he asked in that fake husky voice.

"I want all of you."

He moved his mouth from my ass and a second later I felt the hot head of his thick cock against my ass. My ass automatically tensed up.

"Relax, Anthony," Gabriel said, and I panicked for a moment.

"How do you know—" I started to say, and just then I felt half of Gabriel's fat cock slide very slowly up my ass.

"Oh, fuck, that hurts," I cried out, "pull it out."

"Shhhh," he said, and kept pushing slowly in until it was buried to the balls inside my ass.

"Gabriel, I can't take it. Pull out."

Instead of pulling out, he leaned over and kissed me on the lips again, keeping his cock buried still and deep inside my hot ass. His tongue was warm and still tasted of my cum, and despite the pain I felt in my ass, I started to moan as we kissed. We stayed like that for about a minute, and I was surprised to find the pain subsiding.

Gabriel seemed to have some sixth sense about that, because just as the pain was going away, he began to slowly move his long thick cock in and out of my ass. I could feel each of his throbbing veins as they slid along my ass walls, and my muscles clutched at them as they passed, unwilling to let them go. Gabriel pulled his big dick all the way out of my ass, and then slowly slid it back in to the hilt several times. His dick head pushed slowly inside and made way for the thickness of his shaft. Once it was buried deep inside me, he stopped and flexed his dick, causing first the head to swell, and then inch by inch his shaft swelled until my ass muscles were stretched tightly around his huge tool.

"Oh, God, fuck me, Gabriel," I tried to say around his probing tongue.

Gabriel pulled his mouth from mine and began fucking me hard. He pulled his cock out until only the head remained inside me, then jammed it back in forcefully. It seemed his cock grew an inch with every hard thrust into me, and I was eating it up. I'd never been fucked like this, and couldn't believe how good it felt. Gabriel grabbed my hard dick in his hand and started pumping my own cock in time with his dick sliding into my clutching ass. I could hear him breathing heavily, and felt his cock get even harder and fatter.

"Fuck, Anthony, I'm gonna cum," Gabriel said, but this time his voice wasn't husky at all. I recognized it immediately, and my ass grabbed onto the dick inside me like a vise grip once I did.

"Fuuuuccccckk!" my burglar growled, and pulled his giant cock out of my ass with an audible plop. I heard one huge splash go right over my blindfolded eyes, and then two big hot shots landed on my face. I licked my lips, where one shot landed, and felt several more hot spurts of his load land on my chest and stomach.

He collapsed onto my body and wrapped his arms around my chest and waist, waiting for his heartbeat to slow down. I said nothing, just relishing the feel of his body entwined with mine. After a moment he reached up and untied my hands and pulled the blindfold from my eyes. Little spots of light danced in front of me for a moment as my eyes adjusted to the semi-light coming in from the window.

When they focused, I smiled as Kevin moved his body so we were face to face. Flushed from the intense sex we'd just

had and a little droopy-eyed, he was every bit the picture of angelic beauty I'd remembered but not seen in almost two years.

"Hey, baby," I said softly.

"I've missed you so much."

"I've missed you, too."

"Really?"

"Oh, yeah. I want you back, baby."

"So what does this mean? Have you found yourself?"

"Yeah. Actually I've been here all along, with you. I was
just too blind to see it."

"So, you're not blindfolded anymore?" I asked with a smile.

"No, I can see perfectly now."

"Hmm," I said. I sat on his tummy and waved the blindfold
in front of him as I slowly began to massage his limp cock.
"Maybe we can change that."

CURRENT ESTIMATED JACKPOTS
POWERBALL $195 MIL. ANNUITY
MATCH 6 $2.95 MIL. CASH
CASH 5 $100,000 CASH

POWERBALL   30618095037307070 $2.00

** APR 8/06 SAT **

02 10 20 52 54 POWERBALL 33 06

POWER PLAY: YES
73514/0701

0984 5414 1355 02

PENNSYLVANIA LOTTERY

visit our website at www.palottery.com

NAME _____

ADDRESS _____ PHONE _____

CITY _____ STATE _____ ZIP _____

SIGNATURE _____

IMPORTANT: This ticket is valid only for drawing date(s) shown. Determinations of winners are subject to the rules and regulations of the Pennsylvania Lottery. Department of Revenue, 2850 Turnpike Industrial Drive, Middletown PA, 17057. Void if torn, altered, illegible or incomplete. Not responsible for lost or stolen tickets.

♻ recyclable

PLJ 31524916

Lottery Proceeds Benefit Older Pennsylvanians Every Day

RETAILER NUMBER	DATE PAID

9

Donkey Kong

Moving to San Francisco from Wichita is probably the most important decision I have ever made in my life. Looking back on it now, I can't imagine what my life would be like if I hadn't been brave enough to do it. I've always been somewhat spontaneous; but waking up one morning, getting upset at the fact that it was snowing in December, going to work and turning in my two-weeks notice, and then packing up my car with everything I owned and heading to San Francisco without knowing a soul there was stellar even for me.

But that's what I did. I'd been good about saving up some money (although it was originally planned to be used to finish school at the Christian university I was attending), so finding a place to live until I got a decent job was not really a concern. I found a cute, but somewhat run-down apartment in the Portrero Hill district, right off Army Street, and started looking for a job even before I was completely unpacked and settled in. Luckily, I was able to land the assistant manager position at a Gap store not too far from my apartment. The people there were very nice, but they were so clean-cut and pretentious that they reminded me a little too much of the university I'd just fled so vehemently.

It took me a couple of months to work up the nerve to actually "come out," even though that was the main reason for my leaving Kansas to begin with. Two weeks after my twenty-first birthday, I finally talked myself into giving the "gay lifestyle" a try. I walked into a bookstore on Castro, bought a local gay guide, and headed out to my very first bar.

This might not sound like such a big deal to some people, but believe me, it was a huge step for me. I've been told I could be a poster child for clean-cut, churchgoing young Americans everywhere. I am somewhat short (about five feet nine inches on my tiptoes), with fashionably short brown hair that is bleached at the tips. My blue eyes sparkle constantly and when I smile, twin dimples frame pearly white teeth. Though I never really worked out in a gym, my body is toned and well-built, the result of working on the farms of a couple of families from my church. Somehow I'd managed to stay away from the usual teenage temptations of drugs or alcohol, and I couldn't tolerate even the thought of a cigarette, let alone actually trying one.

But I was determined to change all that, and quickly scanned the bar guide to find one that sounded tolerable. Naively, I chose a bar called the End Up. I was clueless about the name, and so there was no reason for me to doubt the book when it said, "*The odd name was chosen because it is only a couple of blocks from the busy entrance of Highway 101, and inevitably where everyone Ends Up on their way home from work.*" All I cared about was that it described the bar as "filled with a young, preppy, diverse crowd that could teach the ultimate class on having a good time." So I put on a new pair of jeans and button-down polo shirt (perfectly pressed, of course), and headed to 6th and Harrison Streets.

It was very dark inside the bar, even though it was just a little past three in the afternoon on a particularly warm and bright Sunday in San Francisco. The music was loud, and the chatter of seemingly thousands of men was even louder. The air reeked of smoke and alcohol and sweat.

When I walked through the front door, every man in the bar stopped what they were doing and stared at me. The music skidded to a sudden halt, and drinks ceased flowing from the spouts from which big burly men behind the bar were pouring them.

Certainly it didn't help matters much that a heavily muscled man clad in nothing but a pair of very tight shorts stopped me before I was even completely inside, and asked to see my ID. Granted, I had just turned twenty-one a couple of weeks before, and even so, I looked more like fifteen or sixteen. But still, you would think that I would have been given a small break by the cosmic powers that be. I mean, really, was the culture shock of moving from Wichita, Kansas, to San Francisco not enough? Did that mean men have to stop me and ask for my ID so loudly that every guy in the bar turned to stare at me?

I coughed as the smoke filled my lungs, and tried not to stare too hard at the gyrating, more-than-half-naked glistening men as they danced around me. Walking around the small bar, I worked up the courage to order my very first alcoholic beverage. I listened to what the guys around me ordered, and quickly decided that my first impulse of asking for a frozen piña colada was completely out of the question.

"I'll take a Seven and Seven, please," I said confidently to the bartender who was staring at me impatiently. I had no idea what that particular drink was, but I'd heard a couple of other guys ask for it, and it was the best I could do with my limited knowledge of alcohol. I was at least smart enough not to try the drink before I was out on the patio and as far away from anyone else as I could get. Only a few people noticed when I violently choked and spit the drink from my mouth. When I was certain no one was looking I poured the rest of it into the bushes and sat alone chewing on the ice cubes.

I sulked in the same plastic chair on the patio for a little more than an hour, doing nothing but watch in fascination the scene around me. Several guys came up and tried to start a conversation with me, but I think my wide, horrified eyes, stuttering attempts at conversation and the nervous twitch that kept attacking the left side of my face helped them decide that there were better choices elsewhere.

I finally worked up the nerve to try another drink, but decided this time to stick with something that was safer, and a little easier to order. Budweiser seemed like an easy enough choice, and so I boldly walked up to the bar, ordered my beer, and forced myself to walk through the dark building.

It was then that I noticed, stuck in a corner way in the back of the bar, a couple of video games. I made a beeline for them, and was glad to see my favorite, Donkey Kong. I rushed back to the bar, asked for five dollars in quarters, then returned to the game. Finally I was able to relax and enjoy myself in this strange place.

Halfway through my third game, I was lost in my own world. So much so, that I did not notice that I was no longer alone until it was too late. I was pushing the joystick around the game like a madman, helping Kong climb a series of ladders to avoid the ever-menacing barrels, when suddenly I felt a pair of arms wrap around my waist.

"Mind if I play with you?" I heard someone whisper into my right ear. His breath smelled slightly of sweet alcohol and his soft voice caused my heart to stop beating.

The little barrel rolled over Kong, and I stared at the screen in disbelief.

"Umm, I usually just play by myself," I mumbled. I started to turn around to address the guy behind me, but just at that moment he squeezed me tighter and pressed himself against my back and butt.

"Come on," he said in the sexiest voice I had ever heard, "it's funner when you play with someone else."

Since my credit had already been wasted, I allowed myself to turn away from the game and face the guy behind me. I'm sure I must have looked extremely stupid, what with my bulging eyes and my red face and the fact that I was hyperventilating. Correcting his English probably wasn't the sexiest thing I could have done either, but I was unable to stop myself.

"More fun," I said stupidly.

He smiled, and that was all it took for me to be hooked. When I first moved to California I had visions of falling head over heels in love with the typical all-American surfer dude; blonde hair, blue eyes, bulging muscles, the whole thing. This guy was completely opposite of that in every way, but it didn't matter. He was obviously Latino. His jet-black hair, dark brown eyes, copper-colored skin and slight accent gave him away immediately. He was a couple of inches taller than me (but then again, who isn't?) and thin, though not skinny. On his upper lip a few strands of baby-fine hair tried unsuccessfully to form a mustache, and were unable to mask the fact that he was not quite old enough to legally be in the bar.

"That's cute," he said.

"What is?"

"You corrected my English."

"Sorry. I have a degree in English."

"Don't be. It's cute. So is the fact that you're playing Donkey Kong in the middle of a very busy and very cruisy gay bar."

I blushed. "It's my first time here," I tried to explain, but succeeded only in adding to the overall picture of my naiveté.

"Really?" he said sarcastically. "I never would have guessed."

"I mean my first time in a gay bar. Ever."

"A little overwhelming, huh?"

"Yes."

"And are you having a good time?"

This sounded like a loaded question to me, and I wasn't sure quite how to answer it. Did I answer no, and send the message to the first cute gay guy that I had met and was actually a little interested in that I was a bad gay guy and didn't enjoy gay bars? Or did I answer yes, and send the even worse message that I was in fact enjoying myself playing Donkey Kong in a gay bar packed with what most gay guys would surely find very attractive gay men? There was no way I could win.

"Yes?" I said hesitantly.

"Wanna have even more fun?"

"Yes?" I said just as stupidly.

"Come on," he laughed, and leaned in to kiss me as he took my hand in his. "We can go to my place."

His name was Ruben, and my instinct was correct. He wasn't old enough to be inside the bar legally. He was only nineteen years old. "His place" was actually his parents' place; and they lived in Mountain View, a town almost an hour south of San Francisco. He was a freshman in college. He hadn't decided on a major yet, of course, but was leaning toward computer programming.

All of this I learned on the long drive down to "his place," and before I learned that we would have to sneak into his bedroom through a window that opened into the backyard. His mom and dad were home, he informed me as I slid belly first through the narrow window, but they were not expecting him home until much later, and would probably be so engrossed in whatever video they were undoubtedly watching that they would not hear us or know we were there.

I suppose it was not the best time to choose to question our little adventure, but then again, I was not known for my great timing anyway.

"Are you sure this is such a good idea?" I asked as I fell into his bedroom, ripping my jeans along the way.

"It beats playing Donkey Kong back at the End Up, doesn't it?"

"But your parents . . ."

"They're on the other side of the house," Ruben said as he helped me up from his floor. "Besides, they're both a little hard of hearing. They'll never know we're here." He pulled me close to himself, and wrapped his arms tightly around my waist.

Before I could prepare myself for it, he kissed me. His lips were soft and full. He'd been chewing cinnamon gum for the last half hour, and I tasted it as his tongue slid slowly between my lips and snaked sensuously inside my mouth. My heart raced and I felt like I stopped breathing altogether. Ruben sucked gently on my tongue, drawing it into his mouth, and then teasingly wrestled his own tongue in and out of my hungry mouth. My knees buckled.

"You okay?" he asked as he broke the kiss and looked at me directly in my eyes.

"Yeah, I'm just a little new at this, that's all," I whispered, still very much aware that his parents were just on the other side of the thin walls.

"How new?"

I felt myself blush.

"You're kidding? This is your first time?"

"Yeah."

His gorgeous lips parted into the most beautiful smile I had ever seen, revealing pearly white teeth. He pulled me tighter against his body, and I felt his cock harden against my thigh. My own dick was throbbing painfully hard, and Ruben reached down and squeezed it gently, letting me know that he felt it as well.

"Let's take care of this," Ruben said, and let go of my shaking body so that he could undress. He shed his clothes quickly, and then began to unbutton my jeans as he stood in front of me in nothing but a skimpy pair of bleach-white briefs. "I'll get you out of these," he said and kissed me lightly on the lips again. "You can take off your shirt."

I did as he told me, fumbling clumsily with the buttons, but managed to rip the shirt off my torso at the same moment that Ruben popped the last button on my 501s and slid them down my legs. My cock had never been so hard, and the purple head was poking through the underwear against my leg.

"You okay with all this?" Ruben asked as he pushed me backward toward his bed.

The high-pitched croak that escaped my throat could hardly be construed as an acceptable answer, so I nodded my head, which was spinning wildly. I closed my eyes as I fell onto the bed.

Ruben's hot wet mouth enveloped my cock head, and he sucked on it playfully as he slid my underwear down my quivering legs and completely freed me of all my clothes. His tongue snaked around the sensitive head as he swallowed another couple of inches of my shaft into his incredibly hot mouth. He hummed softly as his mouth slid farther down my cock.

And then it happened. My entire body convulsed uncontrollably as shot after shot of cum poured from my dick. The only orgasms I'd had up to that point were chalked up to the talents of my own hand, and this new sensation was much more than I had ever imagined. I expected Ruben to stop sucking me, and to quickly move his face as far from my shooting cock as he could. But instead, he locked his mouth even tighter around the spurting shaft and sucked harder.

Bright pins of light danced around my head, and had I not been lying on the bed, I surely would have blacked out from the pleasure Ruben's mouth was giving me. I have always shot huge loads of cum, but never in my wildest dreams had I imagined shooting one like this.

Ruben's response to my powerful load was to moan loudly and swallow every last drop. After the sixth or seventh huge spurt, he engorged himself on the last few inches of my dick, until I felt myself pushing past his tonsils. Once I was buried deep in his throat, his wet muscles only pumped my cock even more hungrily, and milked the last couple of drops of cum from my dick.

He continued sucking my entire cock deep in his throat for at least a full minute after I stopped shooting, making sure not a single drop of jizz was wasted. Then he slowly pulled his head off of my dick, and let it plop heavily against my stomach. Moving up so that he lay directly on top of me, he kissed me again on the lips.

"You okay?"

I was still trying to catch my breath, and my only response was to nod weakly.

"Good," he said, and leaned down to kiss me again.

His lips were so warm and wet and soft, and his tongue so strong. It slipped past my lips and tickled my own tongue playfully. I tasted my own cum on his mouth, and tried to pull away, but he was too persistent. He refused to take his tongue out of my mouth, sliding it deeper inside me instead. Finally I gave in and sucked on it until I was soon moaning and wanting even more.

As we kissed, Ruben pulled his own underwear off of his body and threw them to the floor. Then he lifted his prone body from mine and moved so that he was straddling my chest.

There it was, only an inch from my face. I gasped and felt my eyes bulge.

"Don't worry," Ruben said softly, "you don't have to take it all at once."

That was reassuring, because I knew there would be no way I would be able to swallow even half of it.

"R-R-Ruben," I stammered, "I've never . . . I don't think I can . . . I don't know how . . ."

"Shhh," he whispered, and leaned down to kiss me again. "You don't have to deepthroat me like I did to you. Just take it slow. Only a couple of inches at first."

I looked up into his eyes with uncertainty. Taking even a couple of inches of his cock still would not be easy. My minimal exposure to seeing other guys' dicks in the school locker rooms had never prepared me for the monster that was staring back at me. It was easily nine or ten inches long, and seemed as thick around as my wrist. A thin, silky layer of foreskin sheathed the long, heavily veined shaft, but was pulled back tightly behind the fat head.

I stuck my tongue out and licked the hot head tentatively. A sticky stream of warm clear fluid slid onto my tongue. I swallowed it uncertainly. It tasted great, and I decided to get a little bolder. Wrapping my lips around the huge head of Ruben's cock, I began to suck.

"That's it, baby," he moaned as he leaned back and closed his eyes. "Just take it slow and easy."

I've never been really good at taking directions, and this time was no exception. Hungry with desire, I pushed my head forward and tried to swallow his massive cock in one swift move, like he had done with mine. When my jaw was stretched almost to the point of pain, his fat cock head slid against the back of my throat and I choked.

"Careful, baby" he said, and tried to pull out of my mouth.

It was no use, though. By now I was intoxicated with the taste and feel of his cock, and I wanted more. I've always been a little stubborn, and I was determined to swallow Ruben, just like he had done with me. My mouth opened as wide as it could, and another quarter of an inch slid deeper into my throat.

"Okay, man," Ruben half laughed and half growled. "If you're sure you wanna try to do this."

I nodded my head.

"Open the back of your throat, like you're gonna yawn, and then swallow at the same time."

I did, and Ruben pushed forward slowly. My eyes bulged even wider as I felt inch after inch of his fat cock slide past my tonsils and deep into my throat. I started to choke, but learned quickly that I needed to breathe through my nose, and stubbornly held his massive dick inside my mouth as I got used to it. When it was buried all the way inside me and I felt his pubic hairs tickling my nose, I relaxed and began sucking on him gently.

Ruben let his big dick just rest inside my throat for a moment, allowing me to get used to the length and thickness. Then he began sliding it in and out of my throat slowly. I loved the feeling of it moving in and out of me, but was also reluctant to let it slide all the way out. I tightened my throat muscles greedily around his rod and sucked with more force.

"Shit, man," Ruben groaned deeply, "I'm gonna shoot."

And he did. The first two shots blasted down my throat and into my stomach. Then he pulled himself out of my mouth quickly and aimed his big dick at my face. Several more jets of hot cum splashed across my lips and cheeks, and I licked at them hungrily. It took what felt like a full minute for Ruben to stop shooting his load on my face. When he was finally done, he fell heavily on top of me.

We held each other, and kissed again. Then we both fell asleep.

I don't know how long we slept. When I did open my eyes again, it was dark inside the bedroom. I was lying on my stomach, and felt the wet warmth of Ruben's tongue licking around my ass hole.

"Ruben . . . ?"

"Shhh," he whispered, and then the electric jolts filled my body again as he went back to licking my ass.

It was really a strange feeling, having my ass licked like that. Some guys would probably say the first time they experience it they are uncomfortable. I could say that too, but I'd be lying. My breath came out in short, staccato bursts. My cock hardened instantly, and a stream of precum trickled out of my cock head. I lifted my ass into the air, giving Ruben a better position, and moaned like an animal when he took his cue and slid his hot, wet tongue deep inside my ass.

"Fuck, that feels good," I moaned. Hearing the word "fuck" come out of my own mouth sounded very strange to me, but I was beyond trying to justify anything I said or felt at this point.

"Do you like this?" Ruben asked as he removed his mouth

from my ass and began kissing my back and working his way up to my neck.

"Oh, yes."

"Good."

He kissed his way back down to my ass again, and picked up where he'd left off. His tongue plowed my ass until it was buried deep inside, and then he pulled out and licked and kissed around the hole. As his tongue worked over my ass, I heard the soft rustling of paper and plastic wrap.

"Relax, okay?" Ruben said as he stopped his tongue worship.

"Okay," I said dreamily. A couple of seconds later, my body tensed and I bit hard into the pillow as I forced myself to muffle a scream.

"It's just my fingers," Ruben whispered, then wiggled them around inside me to prove his point. "Do you want me to stop?"

I shook my head no as wave after wave of electric pleasure swept through my entire body. This was all happening so fast, I thought to myself, and much easier than I would have liked to admit. I was now bucking my ass up to meet the thrusts of Ruben's fingers as they slid into and out of my ass with more speed and intensity.

"I want you to fuck me," I moaned as I thrust myself deeper against his fingers.

"You sure?"

"Yes."

"Okay, then," he said.

He moved himself so that he was lying on top of my back and ass. He kissed my neck and ears as I felt his huge cock move in between my ass cheeks. It was very hot, and throbbing, and seemed even bigger now that it was positioned at my ass hole than it did when it was buried down my throat. He positioned the head at my hole, and began to push gently forward. Needless to say, I tensed, and moaned loudly as I bit into the pillow again.

"You've got to relax your muscles," he whispered into my ear.

I did, a little easier than I thought was possible, and before I really had a chance to protest, Ruben slid himself into my clutching ass. Not a couple of inches or just the head, but all nine or ten inches of fat, hard cock, all at once. The electric bolts of pleasure that I had just moments ago longed for were suddenly replaced by stabbing white pinlights of pain, and I was unable to stop the loud cry of shock and surprise from deep inside my body.

"Shhh," Ruben said, and lovingly but firmly covered my mouth with his hand. His huge dick was buried deep inside me, and throbbing wildly, making it thicker and harder. "My parents will hear us."

I tried to be quiet, really I did, but before I knew it, another loud moan escaped my throat.

"Ruben?" It was a female voice on the other side of the door, undoubtedly his mother. "Are you okay in there?"

"I'm fine, Mom," he said between gritted teeth, and started laughing. This, of course, caused his cock to throb even more wildly and stab me deeper and harder.

I moaned again, but by now the pain was already turning to pleasure. I squeezed my ass muscles against Ruben's hard cock.

"Oh, fuck!" he said just a little too loudly.

"Are you sure?" his mom asked, and tried to open the door.

Both Ruben and I turned and stared at the jiggling door handle with wide, guilty eyes. Had he thought to lock the door earlier? When we saw that the door was indeed locked, and his mother was not going to barge in on us, we started laughing. I squeezed his cock with my ass again, and began thrusting myself on the length of his pole.

"Yes, Mom, I'm sure!" Ruben growled. He was now sliding his dick in and out of my ass with slow, long, and deep thrusts.

"Are you hungry, sweetie? Do you want a sandwich?"

I reached behind me, pulled his mouth to mine, and kissed him on the mouth as he fucked me with long and slow strokes.

"No, I'm fine," he managed to spit out as he broke our kiss.

I was getting close to coming again, and slid my ass up and down the length of his cock with an intensity I didn't even know I had. I reached under myself and pulled on my own cock, which caused my ass muscles to spasm around Ruben's fat cock even more.

"Oh, fuck, man, I'm gonna shoot."

"What?" his mother asked.

Both of us moaned and almost screamed as we bucked and thrust onto and into one another.

"What's going on in there?" she asked suspiciously.

"Nothing!"

I felt his cock grow fatter inside my ass, and bit lightly on his hand as I released my load onto his sheets.

"I'm gonna make you a sandwich, sweetie. It's getting late. Come out here and eat."

"I'm coming!" he said a little too loudly. He pulled his cock out of my ass in one swift move, and ripped the condom from it.

"You don't have to yell," his mother said, and we heard her retreating down the hall. "I was only trying to be nice."

The first shot spewed way over my head and landed on the wall. The next seven or eight landed on my back and ass, though, and I squirmed with delight as the warm sticky load hit me.

"You hungry?" He laughed as he collapsed on top of me.

"Starving," I said as I tried to control the spasms that were still shaking my entire body.

"Me too. Let's go eat. My mom makes a really good sandwich."

He grabbed a T-shirt from the floor next to his bed, wiped both of us clean, and then we got dressed and walked into the kitchen.

His mom did indeed make a great sandwich. She didn't seem the least bit surprised to see a stranger in her house, and in fact went out of her way to make me feel comfortable and invite me back. I took her up on the offer, and actually moved in with Ruben and his family slowly over the next two weeks.

Ruben and I stayed together for two years, and I learned a lot about myself during that time. I came out with a vengeance, and have never regretted it for a moment. Ruben couldn't have been a better first boyfriend, and his family loved me like one of their own.

Ruben and I eventually broke up. But to this day, whenever I make chicken mole, Spanish rice or shredded pork enchiladas, I remember his mother and the great times we spent together in her kitchen. I still cannot, however, make a ham and cheese sandwich without cracking up laughing.

Lessons in Lifeguarding:
Lesson I

"You *will* get a job this summer, young man, or you can just forget about getting that car out of the garage. I'm tired of handing you money like it's candy or grows on trees. It's about time you started carrying your own weight."

I rolled my eyes as Dad carried on at the breakfast table. He got in these moods every now and then, and there was nothing I could do but nod my head and grunt an agreed reply as he went on and on about how when he was a kid things were different. Blah, blah, blah.

"I spoke with Mr. Richards last week. We're still looking for some help in the mailroom. He's willing to talk to you about it. I know it's not glamorous or anything, but it's a good, steady job. It would mean a regular paycheck every two weeks. And we could even ride in to work together."

The spoonful of cereal almost flew from my mouth and sprayed across the table at my dad, who had his head buried in the morning newspaper. I coughed for a moment and then swallowed the donut-shaped oat rings and washed them down with a mouthful of milk.

"Thanks, Dad. I appreciate it, really I do. But I have a job interview this afternoon, as a matter of fact."

"You do?" he asked as he lowered the newspaper and looked at me hopefully.

"Yes," I said a little too quickly. My eyes glanced at the picture of the gymnast on the box of cereal that Dad preferred. "It's at the rec center."

"The rec center? What kind of job is that?"

My mind raced to the bulletin board I'd glanced at every day in the locker room. It was mostly used by people looking for workout partners or roommates, or guys trying to sell their pieces of shit cars to some unsuspecting nerd who didn't have the sense to know that used cars sold by private citizens through bulletin boards only meant trouble.

But last Friday, in the middle of all the hand-scrawled notes on the board, I'd noticed a typed ad. The rec center itself was looking for a few lifeguards for the summer. It didn't pay very much, but they did offer free membership to the entire network of recreation centers throughout the city for a full year. Plus it would get me out of the house on the weekends, so I wouldn't have to put up with listening to Dad's bitching and moaning. And it'd be a great way to work on my tan.

"Lifeguard," I said through a mouthful of cereal. "They're looking for lifeguards."

"That's not a real job," Dad grumbled as he returned to the newspaper. But already I could tell I'd weakened his tirade. He took another drink of his coffee and mumbled something about not making much money at a job like that. I didn't say anything in response, and finally he admitted that at least I'd be doing something honorable. I think I even heard the words "saving someone's life" strewn carelessly among his half-hearted complaint.

"It's a great opportunity," I said. "Not only will it help me keep in shape for the summer, but it will look great on my résumé."

"I suppose," he said, and stood up to leave. He kissed me on the head and walked out the back door to the garage.

"Shit," I said as I looked at the box of cereal in front of me. I knew Dad wouldn't just forget about the conversation, and would ask me about my interview when he got home from work this evening.

I could make a perfect lifeguard, I thought to myself. A little under six feet tall, my body was smooth, tanned and muscular from the couple of years I'd been working out. I did forty-five minutes of cardio every day, so I knew I had the stamina to do the job. And most importantly, I had seven percent body fat and piercing brown bedroom eyes. I'd watched enough *Baywatch* episodes to know that I had exactly what it took to be a successful lifeguard.

I picked up the phone and called the rec center. Luckily, the manager was in that day, and I was able to set up an interview with him for later that afternoon. By four-thirty I was signed up for my first of ten lifeguard lessons that were required before receiving my certificate and being placed at one of the city's rec center pools.

"This is not a job to be taken lightly," the instructor barked at his group of new students. There were four guys and two girls taking the training. It was his experience, he said sadly, only a third of the original group would actually make it through the course and be hired as lifeguards. Pathetic, really, and if we couldn't handle the pressure and the physical demands of the training, then now would be the time to leave.

One girl stood up, in tears, and did just that. The rest of us stayed. The instructor's gruff tone of voice echoed in my waterlogged ears and began to give me a headache. His superior attitude and harsh words reminded me of my dad, and I was determined to not only make it through the training, but become the best damned lifeguard the City Recreational System had ever seen.

Finally, after twenty laps in the pool and the well-practiced speech, we were dismissed. "Hit the showers," the coach yelled abruptly. "And I will see you back here at seven A.M. tomorrow."

A loud groan rumbled through the remaining small group of students, but we straggled to the showers anyway.

I'd been a member of this gym for a couple of years, since my senior year in high school. I'd chosen this particular gym specifically because of its showers. Most of the other gyms I'd checked out had individual shower stalls with solid walls separating their occupants. No fun there at all. But this gym boasted a large shower room with one large pole in the middle that sprouted six showerheads, all out in the open.

As I soaped up, I glanced at the other three guys standing naked and wet next to me. Two of them were already friends. I'd seen them working out together a few times and leaving with their girlfriends in tow. They joked around and kept their conversation pretty much to themselves, and left quickly.

The other guy, though, was taking his time under the hot spray of the shower, as I was. I'd never seen him before, but I certainly liked watching him showering next to me. He was about my age, twenty, maybe twenty-one years old. Short and thin, but well-muscled. His skin was silky smooth and a few shades lighter than my own. He probably took the job so that he could work out for free and deepen his tan, just like me.

"So, what do you think of the instructor?" I asked as I lathered my hair.

"Just what I expected," he replied, as he shook the excess water from his own short, black hair. "Typical jock wannabe who couldn't make it in the big time, and now takes out his frustrations on us poor grunts." He winked at me, and I noticed he had deep blue eyes that were framed by long, dark eyelashes.

I laughed and watched as he soaped up his chest and stomach for the third time. My heart began to race as his hand reached down and cupped his balls so that he could wash between his legs. I tried to keep my eyes on his face, but I couldn't. They followed his hand, and lingered at his crotch, where he lifted the long, fat shaft to one side and rolled his balls in one palm.

Where had he stuffed that thing in those skimpy swim trunks? I wondered as I fought to catch my breath and continued watching him.

"But still, he's kinda hot, don't you think?"

"I . . . well . . . umm . . ." I said and forced myself to look away from his cock and scrubbed my arms and chest vigorously.

"I'd fuck him," the guy said calmly and grinned as he noticed my nervousness. "Except that he'd probably like it a lot more than he's willing to accept, and then he'd kick me off the squad."

My cock began to get hard with the beating of my heart. *Shit!* I thought to myself as I tried to cover the growing hard-on with my hands. It was useless, though. Fully hard, my cock is a little over seven inches long. I was able to conceal most of it, but it pounded harder against my belly and betrayed me.

"But you wouldn't, would you?" he said as he soaped up his fattening cock and began walking slowly closer to me.

"I wouldn't what?"

"Kick me off the squad if I fucked you," he whispered and reached down to wrap my cock in his soapy hand. "I know you'd like it, there's no question about that."

He squeezed my throbbing cock in his hand, and slid the foreskin up and down the shaft. I moaned loudly and leaned against the cold tile wall of the shower as he continued stroking my cock in the warmth of his soapy hand. He leaned in and kissed me as his tight muscular body pressed against my own.

Though my own cock is not small by any means, and was impossible to cover with even both of my hands, his was even bigger. It felt like a live, warm snake as it pushed against my thigh and throbbed wildly across my hip.

"We really shouldn't—" I started to say, but his mouth clamped down on my own and sucked my tongue deep inside. The inside of his mouth was warm and tasted of fresh mint. Who was I kidding? I wanted this more than I'd wanted anything in a really long time. Any pretense of protest would just be stupid. I kissed him long and deep, and reached down between our hard stomachs and rubbed the head of his cock with my thumb and index finger.

"Let's keep the water running," he whispered. "Maybe no one else will come in here if they think there's already someone in here taking a shower."

"All right," I answered.

His strong hands touched my shoulders and gently pushed me to my knees.

"Come on, man. Don't just look at it. Suck it."

I reached out with my tongue and licked at the fat head, lapping at the large drop of precum that dribbled from the slit.

The salty-sweet taste was all it took for me, and I sucked four or five inches of his thick cock into my mouth.

"Oh, yeah," he moaned, "that's it dude. Take some more."

I did. I opened the back of my throat and swallowed his entire cock deep into my gullet. When my jaw was stretched to its limit and my mouth filled with his cock, I swallowed, causing the muscles in my throat to grip his dick and squeeze it.

"Jeez, man, you've got the best fucking mouth I've ever had on my cock."

I tightened my lips around his shaft and slid my mouth up and down the length of his cock. It was at least eight or nine inches long, and I could feel the throbbing veins along the hard meat as my tongue and lips trailed across it. When I had just the head inside my mouth, I sucked harder on it for a moment, then swallowed the entire length deep into my throat again.

"Fuck, man, much more of that, and I'm gonna spray my load into your gut," my new friend said as he pulled his cock out of my slurping mouth.

"Isn't that the point?" I asked hungrily, and reached for his dick again.

He pushed my hand away and lifted me to my feet. "Sometimes," he said, and turned me around so that I faced the wall. "But not now. I wanna fuck that sweet ass, man. I popped a boner just watching you during practice. The way your trunks hugged and kissed your cheeks drove me crazy."

"But what if someone comes in?" I said as I tried to keep the smile from taking over my face.

"Then they can join us, or run away screaming. I don't care."

I took a deep breath as I leaned against the cold tile wall and wiggled my ass against my buddy's smooth front side. His cock throbbed hotly against the skin of my ass, and he playfully rubbed it up and down the crack of my ass cheeks.

"Fuck me," I whimpered, and wiggled backward against him even harder.

"You better believe it," he said. He reached over and squeezed a generous amount of shower soap onto his hand, then let it fall between my groping cheeks.

As the slimy soap trailed down the back of my ass and between my legs, I squeezed my hole, causing it to twitch against the heat of his cock.

"That's it, man. Just take a deep breath," my shower buddy whispered into my ear as he pushed the fat hot head against my hungry hole. "We'll go slow . . ."

"Like hell we will," I said, and shoved myself backward until the head of his cock speared my ass. I gasped when it entered, then lifted one leg up and slid my ass deeper onto his dick until the entire fat pole was buried deep inside me.

"Fuck, man! How'd you do that?"

I squeezed his cock with my ass muscles and moaned as I slid up and down the length of it. I could actually feel the veins as they slid against the smooth skin of my ass cheeks, and his dick grew hotter and thicker inside my clutching butt muscles.

He leaned forward and nibbled on my ear and kissed my neck as he fucked me harder and faster. His huge balls bounced between my ass and the back of my legs as he thrust into me.

I reached down between my legs and pulled on his balls as I stroked my cock. He must have liked that a lot, because he began moaning even louder and twisting his cock deep inside my guts.

"That's it, man," I shouted, with my face pressed against the cold tile wall, "I'm gonna shoot!"

He pulled out of my ass in one swift move that made an audible plop as it left my ass tingling and empty at the same time. Then he swung me around so that I was facing him, and dropped to his knees.

The first squirt of my load flew past his face and onto the floor behind him. But he scooted back a few inches, and the next several shots of my cum landed across his nose and mouth. He moaned and licked at my load as it streamed down his face. My knees began to shake and buckle after about six sprays.

"This is it, man," he said, and stood up quickly. At the same time, he pushed me to my knees.

A second later I felt his load as it splashed across my eyes and nose. I grabbed the back of his legs to steady myself, and this brought his cock even closer to my mouth. I reached out with my tongue and licked at the head, sucking it into my mouth.

"I can't take any more, dude," he said as I felt his knees buckle just as mine had done a few moments earlier.

I sucked even harder on his cock head, milking every last drop of his sweet milky load. When it finally stopped shooting into my mouth, I licked at the head tenderly, and then kissed it as I stood up and hugged my new friend.

"That was incredible, man," he panted. "I think we're gonna have a lot of fun together this summer."

"Me too," I said as I licked my lips. "By the way, my name is Christian."

"I'm Bradon."

"You always take this long a shower, Bradon?"

"I do now."

"Right on."

Lessons in Lifeguarding: Lesson II

As the weeks went on, I found I actually enjoyed the lifeguard training a lot more than I thought I would. Sure, it was a lot of hard work. But even after just a couple of sessions I noticed that I was getting stronger and my endurance was improving. I could now swim fifty laps of the pool without cramping up and feeling like I was going to die. Swimming was the perfect sport for me, and I was a natural. I glided through the water like an eel, and was easily the fastest swimmer on the team. Don't think that the prolonged glances from all the girls and even many of the other guys in the rec center went unnoticed, either.

"You're good, Christian," Coach Patterson said as he wrapped his arm around my neck. "Maybe one of the best swimmers I've had the pleasure of coaching."

I beamed, and glanced around to make sure the others in the class had heard the compliment. Bradon winked at me and blew me a discreet kiss. Tasha, now the only girl left in the group, adjusted her bikini top to show off even more cleavage than she had earlier, and puckered her lips. Even Lance and Glen, the two straight guys who'd always showered so quickly and left to join their girlfriends without saying a word to me, gave me the thumbs-up.

"But you need to build up your strength a little," Coach said. "Swimming alone is one thing, but if you have to drag another limp body to safety, then you've gotta be strong enough to carry not only your own weight, but theirs as well. You need to work on lifting some weights a little, son."

I glanced over at Bradon, with pleading eyes, hoping he'd be able to stay around and work out with me. But he shrugged his shoulders and pointed at his wrist, where his watch would normally be. "Sorry," he mouthed silently.

"I guess I could stay a little late this afternoon and lift a little." I sighed as the rest of the group got up and headed toward the showers.

"No need to overdo it all at once," Coach said. "You've just had a good workout in the pool. We wouldn't want you to exhaust yourself or hurt your muscles too much."

"I'll take it easy," I promised. Dad was home this afternoon, and I really wasn't in the mood to listen to him moan and groan about the horrible week he'd had at work and how I should maybe mow the lawn or something. "If it's okay, I'll just hang around and lift a little before heading home."

"That's my boy!" Coach beamed as he patted my shoulders. "Lock up when you're done, all right?" he said as he tossed me a spare set of keys to the gym and turned to leave.

I'd lifted weights a lot over the past few years, and had prided myself on my strength. So I was surprised as I went through my routine and felt my muscles twitching and giving out on me with much less weight than I had been used to lifting. I guess swimming took a greater toll on my body than I had imagined.

I worked my legs first, and then my arms. Halfway through my biceps curls, Bradon walked up to me and gave me a quick peck on the lips.

"Sorry I can't stay and help you out today," he said as he hunched his gym bag across his shoulders, "but I promised my mom I'd pick her up from her hair appointment. She'll be really pissed if I don't show up."

"That's all right," I said, and walked with him to the door. "I'm just gonna do a few more reps and then take off myself."

"Okay. But don't wear yourself out," Bradon said as he pulled me against his torso and kissed me again. "I want you to be in great shape next week, so I can fuck that sweet ass of yours again."

I felt myself blush and looked around to make sure we were alone before returning his kiss. "I'll be fine," I said, "and I'm gonna hold you to that promise."

I locked the door behind him and returned to the weight benches. Boosted by Coach Patterson's compliment and Bradon's unabashed kiss, I was more determined than ever to bulk up, and kept adding more weights to the bars despite the agonizing pain that my muscles were going through. I kept repeating the phrases, "No Pain, No Gain" and "Feel the Burn" to myself as I bench-pressed much more than I should have.

As I lay flat on my back on the bench, my arms raised high above my chest, I felt my quivering muscles give way. Two hundred pounds of solid iron hovered above my face and chest, and I struggled to bring the pole down steadily.

"What the fuck?" someone yelled, and I heard footsteps

running in my direction just as the bar started to fall toward my chest and throat.

A couple of seconds later, Lance and Glen were on either side of me. Each of them grabbed an end of the bar and lifted it to the safety catch. My arms fell limply to my sides and I gasped for breath as I looked up from the bench at my rescuers. Both of them were wearing thin gray sweat shorts. Glen wore a tank top, and Lance was shirtless. They were both powerfully built, and their muscles glistened and bulged as they set the bar on its rest. The strong scent of Irish Spring soap permeated from their direction, and I could tell they had just left the showers.

"What are you doing?" Lance asked as he and Glen moved closer together.

They were standing directly over my face, and I couldn't help but glance up their legs through the bottom of their shorts.

"I . . . was . . . trying . . ." I gasped as I tried to catch my breath. From this vantage point I could see that Glen was wearing a jockstrap under his shorts. Lance was not, and his cock hung to the left and halfway down the loose leggings of his shorts. I could make out the silky sheath of foreskin that covered the entire shaft and half of the fat head.

"Don't you know you should never lift this much weight without having a spotter?" Lance asked.

"I didn't think . . ."

"Yeah, you can say that again," Glen chimed in. "You can get hurt that way."

"Thanks for helping me out." I panted. "I don't know what I would've done if you hadn't been there."

Lance noticed that I was still staring at his cock through the leg opening of his shorts. He nudged Glen and smiled as he reached down and groped his fat cock. "Don't worry about it. But maybe you can help us out a little, if you know what I mean?"

"What are you talking about?" Glen asked him, and then noticed that I was looking back and forth between their loose short legs.

I smiled, and reached up above my head. My hands slid up between Lance's legs and his shorts and wrapped around his long fat dick.

"Fuck yeah," Lance moaned as I stroked his cock. The head and a couple of inches of hardening shaft now peeked through the leg of his shorts.

"I don't know if this is such a good idea," Glen said. But he couldn't take his eyes off my hand as it tugged and pulled at his buddy's big dick. "Somebody might walk in . . ."

With my free hand I reached inside my sweats pocket and pulled out the keys to the gym. I dangled them in front of him for a moment, and then dropped them to the floor. Then I reached up inside his shorts and gently squeezed his balls and cock still tucked inside his jock.

"Lance?" Glen asked uncertainly.

"Fuck it, dude," Lance replied as he lowered his now fully hard cock to my mouth. "Lori hasn't been giving me any lately. I'm about ready to pop at this point. A mouth is a mouth."

I stuck out my tongue and licked at the hard head of his cock as he pulled his legs wider apart. I tugged the rest of his cock out of the leg opening and pulled him down closer to me. As he lowered himself into my hot mouth, I yanked Glen's shorts down to his ankles and kneaded his cock through his jockstrap.

"But . . . he's . . . a . . ."

"Who fuckin' cares, man?" Lance asked as the last inch of

his long cock disappeared deep into my throat. "Look at this. He swallowed my whole cock."

I sucked greedily on Lance's cock as I pulled Glen's dick free from his jock. It was already starting to get hard as well. A couple of seconds later, he was kicking his shorts and jock off his legs and onto the floor.

"Don't be so fucking greedy, man," Glen said to his friend, and pushed Lance to one side, so that his cock slid from my mouth. He replaced it with his own quickly fattening dick. As I licked the head and sucked on his cock, he moaned and slid the entire length all the way down my throat.

Lance laughed, and then walked to the foot of my workout bench. "Look, dude. He's really getting into sucking our big fat cocks. He's got a boner himself," he said as he tugged at the waistband of my sweats.

"This doesn't mean . . ." Glen started to say.

"Oh, shut up," Lance said as he pulled my sweats all the way off my legs. "It doesn't mean anything. You want his ass or his mouth?"

I helped Lance with my sweats by kicking them off my legs and pulling myself into a doggie position on the bench. All the while, I never let go of Glen's cock inside my mouth.

"I think I'll stay up here. He's got a fuckin' incredible mouth."

I awarded this acknowledgment by swallowing the last inch of his cock and squeezing it with my throat muscles. Glen's knees buckled, and he grabbed the support rods of the weight bench to steady himself. I would've laughed if my face hadn't been stuffed with his thick cock.

"No complaints here, dude," Lance said, and spread my legs a little wider with his strong hands. "His ass looks like it's pretty hot, too." He dropped to his knees and began licking my ass hole as his best friend fucked my mouth. "Damn, man. His ass is as smooth as a fucking baby's bottom. And pretty tight, too, from the looks of it."

I clenched my ass muscles as his hands kneaded my round globes and his tongue darted in and out of my hole. When I was nice and wet from his tongue bath, he shoved first one finger and then a second deep inside my ass. My moans of pleasure spurred him on and let him know I was more than happy with the progression of events.

"Fuck him, man," Glen said huskily. "I wanna see your cock slide up his ass and fuck his brains out."

"Me too," I said as I pulled my mouth off Glen's dick for just a moment so that I could catch my breath.

"You don't have to ask me twice," Lance said, and stood up so that the fat hot head of his cock rubbed against my ass hole.

I took a deep breath and started sucking on Glen's cock again as Lance pressed himself against my ass. His head popped inside in one slick move, and I gasped as my mouth tightened around Glen's fat pole. I leaned backward and impaled myself on Lance's dick in one steady move.

"Fuck, man!" Lance yelled, and grabbed the sides of my waist and pulled my ass harder onto his long thick cock.

My own dick grew fully hard and swung heavily between my spread legs as the two friends fucked me from both ends. I could taste the salty-sweet drops of precum from Glen's cock on my tongue, and swallowed it hungrily as Lance speared my ass and twisted his cock so that it rubbed against the walls of my clutching ass. I was filled with more cock than I'd ever had inside me at one time, and couldn't have been happier.

The weight bench creaked and moaned underneath me as the two friends found their groove and fucked me harder and deeper. Just as Glen slid his cock deep down my throat, Lance pulled his fat cock out of my ass so that only the head tickled the inside of my ass. Then Lance leaned forward and shoved himself deep inside me as Glen pulled his cock all the way out of my mouth and teased my lips with the gooey sweet precum that dribbled from its head.

"Give me more," I panted, taking the opportunity of having my mouth free for a short moment. "Fuck me harder."

They did. Glen grabbed my head and pulled it back onto his cock. Lance tightened his grip on my waist and pulled me backward onto his thick dick. Though there is no doubt in my mind that this was the first time the two friends had double-fucked another guy, they instinctively knew when to push and when to pull so that neither of them was fighting over which would slide into or out of my quivering body.

"I can't take it anymore," Glen said loudly. "I'm gonna shoot." He pulled his cock out of my mouth and sprayed a huge load of warm thick cum over my head and across my back.

"Shit, man," Lance said, shocked, "you shot all the way onto my chest!" That must have been all it took to set him off as well, because he quickly pulled his dick out of my ass and splattered his heavy load all over my back and ass.

"I'm coming!!" I yelled as the last few drops of the two friends' loads landed on my naked body.

"But you're not even touching yourself," Glen gasped when he saw my cock grow thicker and then shoot a huge load across the vinyl bench below me.

It took several seconds, but when my cock was drained of its load, I fell limply to the bench and straddled it on my stomach.

"That was too fucking hot, man," Lance said as he reached down and pulled his shorts back on.

"Hell, yeah," Glen agreed and began to get dressed again.

"You guys were great," I said breathlessly, and rolled over onto my back on the bench.

"Not a word of this to anyone," Lance said uncertainly.

"My lips are sealed," I said, and smiled as I licked Glen's dripping cum from across my lips. "It's just between the three of us."

"Promise?"

"Cross my heart," I said, and did.

"Cool." Glen smiled and winked at me. "And whatever you do, don't forget . . . never try to lift this much weight alone again."

"Next time I feel like Hercules, I'll be sure to ask for a spotter. I promise."

"You know where to find us," Lance called back over his shoulder as he and Glen walked back toward the showers.

I smiled as I watched the two friends push and shove one another jokingly as they left the gym floor. I'd been upset that Bradon hadn't stayed behind to help me workout. But as it turned out, I had gotten all the help I could ever have wanted or imagined.

This job as a lifeguard was shaping up to be more than just a job. It was a dream come true.

Lessons in Lifeguarding: Lesson III

I completed the mandatory lifeguard training at the top of the class. Coach Patterson gushed about how I had become the best student he'd ever had, and how the rest of the group could learn a little something from the dedication and pride I exhibited in my quest to become the best damned lifeguard out there.

I kinda felt sorry for Tasha, the only girl in the group. She'd tried so hard, but being a lifeguard was just not in her blood. Though she passed all the required trainings, she struggled through them. It was obvious the only reason she was putting herself through the tough training was because she didn't want to be slinging burgers all summer.

Bradon, Lance, and Glen did much better, but they were still nowhere near as naturally good as I was. They ruffed my hair, and punched me on the arm teasingly as Coach ranted on and on about me.

Bradon and I had sucked and fucked each other at least twice a week since we'd met in the training class three weeks ago. I still lived at home, and was always afraid Dad would surprise us by coming home early, and so hooking up at my place was out of the question. Bradon lived on campus and shared a dorm room with two straight roommates, which made finding private time there impossible as well. But I had told Coach that I wanted to get some extra training time in, and he'd given me a spare set of keys to the pool and gym. Bradon and I always dallied around, making sure we were the last people left in the building, then we'd suck and fuck in the shower or out on the gym floor.

Glen and Lance quickly caught on, and once they were sure that neither Bradon nor I would blow the whistle on them, they joined us a couple of times. They were still way too closeted to admit that they might like taking it up the ass, but they were more than happy to bend Bradon and I over and fuck our brains out. I saw them looking at each other as they slid their big dicks in our asses, and I knew it wouldn't be long before the two best friends decided to "give it the good old college try." My bet was that Glen wanted to know just how good his buddy's cock would feel up his ass, and that before the summer was over they would both find out.

The training course had proved so much fun that I actually dreaded the day we all "graduated." Receiving the certificate was great, but at the end of the last class we were all given our individual assignments. Tasha was to remain at the rec center and keep watch over the preschoolers while their mothers worked out. Glen and Lance were assigned to public pools close to their homes. But the worst part was when Coach revealed that since Bradon and I were the two best students, we were being assigned the most coveted placements. Bradon was going to Sloan's Lake, and I was to become the assistant head lifeguard at Cherry Creek Reservoir. Though the pay and prestige were inarguably the best, the two bodies of water were on opposite ends of the city. Since we both would be working the same hours, and Bradon was taking a couple of night classes during the summer, finding time to hook up would be almost impossible.

Lisa was the head lifeguard at Cherry Creek Reservoir, and from the moment I met her, I knew she was a total bitch. She'd been working with her best friend, Kathy, for several months, and made no secret of the fact that she'd expected Kathy to have been named her second-in-command. She was pissed at Coach Patterson, the department director, for giving the position to me. And she took it all out on me every chance she got.

I stayed away from Lisa as much as possible. It wasn't that difficult. She spent most of her time in the guardhouse, either on the phone to her boyfriend or playing cards with Kathy. I, on the other hand, spent all my time in the water and soaking up the sun on the beach. There were more than enough gorgeous, hunky, muscular men to watch and to daydream about. My backside got much more tanned than did my front side, because I had to lie on my stomach on the sand to hide all the hard-ons I kept getting every time a hot guy came anywhere near me.

I discovered the public restroom after only a couple of days. I made sure Lisa was watching the beach, and decided to scope it out. The men's room consisted of two stalls, two urinals and an old rusted sink that looked like it would fall off the wall if anyone tried to use it.

Both stalls were empty, and so I walked into the farthest one. My eyes lit up as I saw that both walls of the stall had holes about the size of my fist crudely sawed out at just below my eye level. I dropped my shorts and began to tug on my cock. It began to get hard immediately, like it usually did in public places. After just a couple of minutes, I was sliding my fist up and down the length of my throbbing dick, and waiting for someone to walk in.

It didn't take long. I heard the door to the stall next to me open and then latch shut. My heart began to race as I leaned back against the toilet tank and continued stroking my hard cock. When the guy in the stall next to me dropped his shorts, I leaned forward and peeked inside the hole in the wall.

I recognized the guy immediately. I'd been staring at him all day. He was a few years older than me, maybe twenty-three or twenty-four. He was well over six feet tall, with black wavy hair and deep brown eyes. His muscles were well defined, and smooth as marble. A large tattoo dominated his shoulder, and I thought I remembered the symbol from some Greek mythology class I'd taken in school. As he spread a blanket across the sand, I decided to walk over and start a conversation with him. But before I could, his frumpy wife and young kid showed up. The wife was bitching about the spot he'd chosen, and the kid was crying at the top of his lungs. I'd noticed the look of defeat in his eyes as he pulled on a pair of earphones and lay down, drowning out the reality that was his life.

Now he was sitting in the stall next to me, with his shorts wrapped around his ankles, and I couldn't take my eyes off him. Water dripped from his shoulder-length hair and onto his muscular chest. His nipples hardened as the cold drops cascaded across them. I followed the water as it slid down his ripped torso, and became entangled in the coarse black pubic hair. Then I gasped as I saw his thick cock dangling between his legs. He must have heard me, because he leaned back against the toilet, and lifted his hips a little, so that I could get an even better view. His hands tugged at his hairy balls and stroked the huge cock until it throbbed between his fingers.

I dropped to my knees and licked my lips as I leaned in closer and peered through the hole in the wall separating us.

"You wanna suck my dick?" he asked. His voice was low and had a slight accent, though I couldn't tell if it was indeed Greek, or Italian, or Latino . . . or something altogether else. Truth be known, I didn't really care.

"Sure," I answered, and licked my lips again.

"You think it's safe in here?"

"Yeah, nobody ever comes in here," I lied. Since that was my first time in the public restroom, I had no idea how many people passed through those doors. Truth be known, I didn't really care.

He leaned against the wall and slid his entire cock through the hole. The foreskin was pulled back tightly against the base of his dick, and the cock head was pink and moist.

I thought about licking the head for a while, teasing him before I showed him what I could really do. But by the time my mouth reached his swollen head, I was dizzy with lust. I opened my mouth and throat and swallowed as much of his big cock as I could in one swift move. There were still a couple of inches left when the head of his massive cock hit the back of my throat, but I couldn't take any more of him inside my mouth without gagging, so I stopped. I tightened my lips around his shaft and licked at his hot cock with my tongue as I slid up and down the length of it.

My own cock was hard and throbbing inside my shorts, and strained to be released. I shoved the shorts around my ankles and let some of my own spit fall from the huge cock in my mouth down onto my dick. I licked and sucked at his fat pole as I stroked my own cock. My legs touched his from under the partition, and chill bumps swept across my body as I felt his thick hairy legs brushing against my smooth kneecaps.

He moaned and started thrusting himself in and out of my hungry mouth, slowly at first and then faster and deeper. His cock was hot and I tasted the salty sweet precum as it oozed from his head and onto my tongue.

Before I could stop it, I sprayed my load. It felt like a geyser, and went on and on. I knew my spunk must have splashed against his legs, and a moment later it was confirmed.

"Damn, man. You shot all over my fuckin' leg!" he moaned.

Despite the startle in his voice, I could tell that feeling my cum drip down his leg was turning him on. His cock grew fatter and hotter inside my mouth, and he started to pull it out. But I was to have none of that. Instead, I clamped my lips around his cock even tighter and sucked harder.

"You gotta let go, man. I'm gonna shoot!"

Like hell I did. I swallowed the last couple of inches of his big dick deeper into my throat and massaged it with my throat muscles. A couple of seconds later, he moaned louder, and leaned his quivering body tight against the partition as he unloaded himself down my throat and into my stomach. If my load seemed like a geyser, then his was Old Faithful. It poured down my gullet in warm thick spurts, and I swallowed it hungrily.

"Fuck, dude, that was great," he whispered as he pulled his still dribbling cock from my sore and tired mouth. He pulled up his shorts in one swift move.

"Thanks," I said. I licked the remaining cum from my lips as I listened to him leave the restroom.

The rest of the summer was over almost before I knew it. Though I'd gotten to spend quite a bit of time in the sun and even in the water, I'd actually only had to rescue two people over the three-month period I was there. More of my time was spent on swimming out and retrieving escaped inner tubes, running errands for Lisa, and working on my tan and watching cute guys than actually lifeguarding. And a lot of the time was spent in the public restroom.

Lisa took advantage of her seniority and took the last week of summer vacation off for a little R and R herself. Now that I was in charge of the other three lifeguards, we began to have some fun. We joked around and partied together and generally agreed that Lisa and Kathy were both snobby bitches, and that Cherry Creek Reservoir was a more fun place without them.

The day after the park closed to the public, I decided to throw a party for all of the lifeguards and their friends. We had a beach dance and a barbecue and played games and had lots to drink. The party lasted long into the night. There were about twenty of us all together. I'd noticed that several of the guys had gone into the restroom. None of them stayed very long, but I knew that they must have been aware of the glory holes, and I was looking forward to later in the evening, when they'd had a few more drinks and might be a little less inhibited.

It must have around eleven o'clock in the evening that I spotted it. Out on the water, about fifty yards from shore, the moonlight reflected off a couple of flailing arms. I had just gone to the guardhouse to call Dad and let him know I'd be a little later than I thought, so I was away from the rest of the crowd. I yelled as loudly as I could, so that I could get some help, but the music and the laughter from the party drowned me out way before anyone could hear me.

I ripped off my tank top and sneakers, and dove into the cool water as quickly as I could. I'd had way too much to drink and eat, and there is no way to justify jumping in the water and trying to swim like I did, but I couldn't help it. Instinct took over, and I knew that I needed to save that person from drowning. Taking deep breaths as my head bobbed out of the water, I forced myself to sober up quickly.

"Don't panic," I shouted to the swimmer as I got within earshot. "I'll help you, just remain calm."

Just then the swimmer's flailing arms and head disappeared beneath the black surface of the lake.

"Shit!" I said to myself, and swam faster toward where the body had been.

As I reached the spot I'd last seen the swimmer, I stopped and floated, trying to catch my bearings and to see if I could see any sign of the person who so desperately needed my help.

Suddenly I felt a pair of hands grab the legs of my shorts and pull them down. At first I thought the victim was panicking and just reaching for anything to grab onto. Then, a second later, I felt a warm mouth wrap around my cock and a tongue lick at it under the water. The mouth sucked on my dick for a moment, just long enough to get it to respond. As my cock thickened, and my head spun with the excitement and liquor, the body from below me surfaced and bobbed in front of me.

"Bradon!" I panted, unable to believe my eyes. "What the fuck are you doing here? I thought you said you couldn't make it."

"I lied," he said as he smiled and gasped to catch his breath. "Thought I'd surprise you."

"Well, you did."

"Good. Here, put this around your neck," he said, and tossed me a life jacket.

"What . . ."

"Just do it," he said, and slid a finger all the way inside my ass in one move. It was then that I noticed he was also wearing a life jacket.

"What if it hadn't been me who rushed out here to save your fucking life?" I panted even as I slid the orange jacket around my neck.

"Then I guess someone else would've gotten this," he said, and rubbed his already hard cock against my leg.

"What do you think you're doing?" I asked.

"I think I'm gonna fuck you out here in the middle of the lake."

"But we can't . . ."

"Like hell we can't," he said, and turned me around so that my back pressed against the front of his body.

As I snapped the belt lock into place, I spread my legs. Bradon pushed his hips forward and his cock slid inside my ass in one swift move. The mossy water helped make it easier. Our bodies bobbed in the water with the gentle current, and I relaxed my ass muscles as I slid up and down the length of his long thick cock.

I couldn't believe how easy it was for us to be fucking out in the middle of the lake. It was like nothing I'd ever experienced. The weightlessness I felt, the cool water lapping at my warm body, the way I could feel every inch of Bradon's big cock as it slid into and out of my clutching ass.

Bradon wrapped his arms around my neck and kissed me on the ear as he fucked me. I thrust my ass backward to take as much of him inside me as possible, and leaned back and kissed him on the lips.

"I've missed you," I said as I tightened my ass muscles around his fat cock.

"Me too," he said, and squeezed me tighter. "Fuck man, I'm gonna shoot."

"Not yet," I whined and stroked his face.

"Too late," he groaned, and pulled his cock out of my ass.

Then he reached down in front of me and wrapped his hand around my hard cock. He squeezed it a couple of times and I shot my load into his hand and the lake.

"So, can I join the party now?" Bradon asked as the last of my load sprayed into the murky water.

"Hell, yeah," I said, and kissed him again. "But first we'd better get our shorts back on. Somebody might notice . . ."

"Oh, shit," Bradon screeched, and began swimming out to the middle of the lake.

It took me a few seconds to realize that he'd let go of our shorts and we were stranded out in the middle of the lake with no clothes. I laughed, and floated on my back as Bradon fished around the lake for our shorts. My cock was still hard and reflected in the moonlight as I backstroked closer to the shore. Bradon soon gave up and joined me, and we swam as far away from the crowd as possible before we scurried onto the beach and ran to his car.

In the distance we listened to the music and laughter from the rest of the party. There was no doubt this had been the best damn summer of my life.

Balcony Buddy

I should have known better than to book a vacation in Puerto Vallarta in the middle of July. It's not like I haven't been there a hundred times, certainly enough to have known better. All the good gay bed-and-breakfasts were booked up months ago. And July is the absolute worst time to visit Vallarta. Everyone seems to be taking their vacation at the same time, and the quaint Mexican port town is packed with tourists. The heat is almost unbearable, and the rain pours from the sky in torrents every single day, making the already humid air feel like you're walking through a sauna.

But I wasn't thinking clearly, and booked the stupid vacation on the spur of the moment. Steven had just walked out on me after six wonderful months together. There was talk of a layoff coming at my job. And then Judy, my travel agent, called and said she had a wonderful vacation deal available, but only if I booked it immediately. So, I did.

The only gay accommodation Judy was able to find a room for me in was at Hotel Descanso del Sol. Tackling the endless stairs just to get to the lobby was so exhausting that I even toyed with the idea of trying to find another hotel, even if it was a straight one, that was closer to the beach and the boardwalk. But judging from the mass of people I'd encountered at the airport and the busy streets on the taxi ride to the hotel, I knew my chances of finding something more comfortable were pretty slim.

I lugged my overpacked suitcase up the stairs to the lobby. I was completely out of breath by the time I reached the top, and drenched with sweat as I gasped for breath and pulled out my credit card.

"Hello, Mr. Wolfe," the receptionist said cheerily.

I looked up into the dreamiest, most seductive brown bedroom eyes I could have imagined. Long black curly eyelashes batted slowly open and closed, over half-sleepy eyes that reminded me of Marilyn Monroe. The beautiful young man smiled, and twin dimples graced either side of his soft, pink lips that parted slightly to reveal a pearly white smile that was hotter than the humid air outside.

My cock sprung to attention immediately, and I forced myself to swallow the tiny bit of saliva that stuck in my parched throat. Eduardo informed me that my room was on the third floor, and that there was no elevator. I moaned and groaned and whined, but apparently I had the very last available room.

"It's not a bad room," Eduardo said in his heavy, sexy accent. "And I can help you carry your bags up the stairs."

"That's very nice of you," I said, still trying to hide my hard-on. "But it's not necessary. I can make it if I take the stairs slowly."

"It's no problem at all," he said, and smiled even broader at me. "In fact, your room is right around the corner from my own. My shift is over in ten minutes, and if you want to leave your suitcase here, I will bring it up when I get off."

"Okay," I said as I signed my credit card slip, and turned

around to leave before I started drooling all over myself in front of Eduardo.

I took the stairs slowly to the top floor and opened the door to my room. I was amazed at how spacious and bright and clean the room was. I glanced at the king-size bed and contemplated lying down for a few minutes. But I was sticky with sweat and humidity, and the lure of a cool shower was stronger than that of a quick nap. Besides, Eduardo would be bringing my suitcase up in a few moments. If I timed everything just right, he would be knocking on my door as I stepped, wet and fresh and . . . aroused, from the shower. I'd seen enough porn videos to know what would happen next.

I stood under the cascading water and soaped myself up thoroughly. My cock grew instantly hard again as I soaped up and massaged it. I moaned loudly as my fist wrapped around my swollen cock and moved up and down the shaft. The soap was oily and created a foamy blanket around my dick as I stroked myself slowly at first, and then with more vigor. Before long, my knees began to shake, and I found it difficult to breathe. A moment later I leaned against the cold tile wall of the shower as my thick white load shot from my cock and swirled down the drain.

"Shit," I said, as I caught my breath, and quickly dried myself off. What kind of wild rendezvous could I expect with Eduardo now that I'd already wasted my load on the shower drain?

I stepped out of the shower and walked into the main room, with the damp white towel wrapped around my waist. My suitcase was standing right next to the bed.

"No, no, no," I moaned as I realized Eduardo could not have missed my little scene in the shower. I threw myself onto the bed, not even bothering to remove the towel or get dressed, and clicked the television on with the remote.

The sun was just beginning to set, and gray shadows crept into my room from the windows and the open balcony door. My eyes were heavy and I was exhausted after my trip, so I decided to take the nap after all. I could sleep for a couple of hours, then get up, get dressed and go to dinner before heading out to Paco Paco's, the local hot gay nightclub.

When I woke up, I was disoriented. I was in a strange room. The huge bed was much bigger than my own at home, and the blankets were crisp and clean and freshly washed. None of the paintings on the wall looked familiar. And what was that salty-fishy smell?

Then I remembered where I was. I rubbed my eyes and slid out of bed. The towel slipped from around my waist, and revealed a bouncing hard-on that I always had upon waking up from a deep sleep. I let it fall to the floor as I searched the room for a clock. Finally, I spotted it, across the room on the dresser next to the television.

Nine-thirty. Just my luck to have slept through happy hour and wake up just in time to grab a bite to eat before heading out for the evening. I walked over to the large patio doors and started to shut them.

As I neared the double doors, I heard the ocean waves breaking onto the sandy beach a few blocks away. Seagulls cawed overhead, and the sound mixed with the chirping of nearby crickets. I stopped at the open balcony door and took in a deep breath of fresh sea air.

It was then that I saw him. His patio balcony was a few feet from my own, to the left. It was dark outside, but several candles were set on the ledge of the balcony and cast an orange glow onto the surface of the large balcony. He was sitting in a deck chair, leaning back so that his face was hidden in the shadows but his outstretched body was in plain sight. Completely naked, his smooth copper skin reflected beautifully in the candlelight. His long muscular legs stretched out several feet in front of him. The twin mounds of his pecs were capped with tiny brown nipples. His washboard abs were hard and defined. His belly button bordered on being an "outie" and trapped a few drops of sweat that trickled down from his ripped, smooth torso.

A thick trail of short, black curly hair trailed from his belly button and down to his bushy pubic hair. His long, thick uncut cock lay limp over the top of his huge, shaved balls.

Then I realized that if I could see him so clearly, he could probably see me just as well. I stepped backward and hid behind the curtain on the balcony door.

On the balcony next door, the guy reached down and tugged lightly at his heavy cock. A few seconds later the shaft began to get hard, and the shiny head peeked out from under the thin, silky foreskin. With his other hand he cupped his balls, and rolled them lovingly across his palm.

I watched the long dark cock grow harder and fatter as the hand with long thick fingers squeezed it and rolled the foreskin up and down the length of the shaft. Huge veins bulged from the big dick, and a clear drop of precum peeked out of the head and slid slowly down the fat shaft.

I swallowed hard and grabbed my own dick, beating it off slowly as I spied on my neighbor. If I hadn't already blown a load a few hours ago in the shower, then I would surely be in danger of staining the curtains any moment now. But as it was, I knew I would be good to play for another few minutes, anyway.

I craned my neck and tried to get a look at the guy's face, but it was still completely hidden in the shadows of the night. And even the candles were beginning to flicker low. Soon they would be out completely, and I would be denied the beautiful sight before me. I reached over and turned on my balcony light, hoping it wouldn't scare him away.

The glow was dim, but it did light enough of both balconies to see the show even better than before. I could now see that the man on the chair only a few feet from my own balcony was wearing a baseball cap. But he kept his head tilted down so that I couldn't see his face, regardless of how hard I tried.

Then he let go of the hand holding his smooth balls, and motioned for me to move out from behind the curtains.

I stepped out on the patio, and walked over to the short wall that separated our balconies. My hard cock bounced up and down eagerly several inches in front of me. It was nowhere near as big as my new friend's, but still I was proud of how engorged and ready it looked. I reached down and stroked myself as I watched him do the same. After a couple of minutes, I sucked one of my fingers into my mouth, then slid it down between my ass cheeks. Without hesitation I shoved my finger into my ass while I slid my other hand up and down the length of my cock.

The guy next door motioned for me to turn around. At first I was hesitant, because if I did, then I wouldn't be able to continue watching him stroke his own huge cock. Instead, I'd be forced to look out at the black night that was on the other side of my balcony. Then I realized why he wanted me to turn around, and I quickly did as I removed my finger from my ass.

A moment later I felt his warm, soft breath whisping against my twitching hole. He blew on it for a second or two, and then his tongue licked up and down between the smooth globes of my ass. I sighed loudly as he lapped at my butt, and before I'd had a chance to collect my breath, his tongue slid slowly all the way inside my ass. I moaned even louder, and felt the muscles of my butt devour his tongue.

I wanted it to go on like that forever, but knew it would not. If he kept this up, I would shoot my load all over the stucco siding of the balcony before I had a chance to warn him.

"Fuck me," I moaned with animal lust.

He pulled his tongue out of my tight hole, and grabbed one hard cheek in each hand as he kneaded and massaged my ass. A moment later I felt the hot head of his thick cock press against my still twitching hole. I heard him spit, and a second later felt the warm slimy saliva land on my ass and slide between my exposed hole and his fat cock head. Then he pushed forward, and slid all the way into me in one slow but deliberate stroke.

I squealed as I felt inch after inch of his hot thick cock spear my ass, spreading the muscles inside me as it went deeper and deeper. When his pubic hairs tickled my cheeks and his heavy swinging balls bumped my upper leg, I squeezed his cock and moaned loudly as I felt it grow thicker inside me in response.

I really can't remember whether he started shoving himself in and out of my ass or whether I was the one who slid up and down the huge length of his massive pole. But it didn't matter. In seconds, we were fucking wildly, and our moans mingled with the chirping of the crickets and the sound of the waves crashing against the surf below us and a few blocks away.

"Shit, man," I gasped hoarsely, "I'm gonna come."

"Me too," my neighbor said as he pumped faster and deeper inside me.

"Fuuuuuucccckkk," I grunted as I sprayed my load all over the short wall in front of me. Several shots spewed from my cock, and I was surprised at the force of my orgasm, since I'd already come a few hours earlier.

Then, without warning, my neighbor pulled himself out of my ass in one quick motion, leaving my ass tingling and empty. A second later I felt the thick, warm jets of his load land all over my back and ass. His load was incredibly thick and hot, and seemed to last forever. The first few shots were already dripping down my ribs and landing on the floor below as he continued shooting more and more of the sticky spunk onto my quivering body.

And then he was gone. I heard him turn and walk away before my shaky legs permitted me to stand up and look around at him. The last I saw of him was his tanned backside, his wide shoulders winding down to the perfect V of his slim waist. His ass was perfectly smooth and as dark as the rest of him. And then he was inside his room, the curtains pulled close across the door, and the light inside the room turned off.

The rest of my vacation was nice. I met a lot of new friends and had a great time. Who cared if Steven was a jerk and left me? Who cared if I might be facing being laid off sometime soon?

As I was checking out, Eduardo, the receptionist, smiled warmly at me. "I hope you enjoyed your stay with us," he said in a voice I immediately recognized. "I know I certainly did."

I gasped softly as I realized what had happened on my balcony a couple of nights earlier. Eduardo winked at me, and watched as I wheeled my suitcase across the lobby and lugged it down the flight of stairs.

As I got into the taxi, I glanced up at my balcony. I quickly pulled a pen out of my pocket and jotted down my room number. My next trip to Vallarta was only three months away, and I knew exactly where I was going to stay.

Fashionably Laid

I've often heard the statement that the best things come in small packages, and indeed have regularly declared it as my personal motto during various stages of my life. Being five feet seven inches tall has offered up certain advantages on rare occasions, but still, given my druthers, I'd opt to be a few inches taller.

So you can imagine my surprise when I was asked to model in a fashion show fund-raiser for my fraternity and our sister sorority. Because I live in a frat house with several of the varsity team jocks, I just assumed that they would be the first to be asked to model. But we were in critical need of major funding, and the organizers were taking the event seriously. A few of the varsity team members were being included, in order to draw the largest possible crowd, but for the most part, the muscular athletes were too clumsy and awkward and not quite serious enough for the fashion show.

Though stature-challenged, I apparently possess most of the other essentials for being a top fashion model. I work out four times a week and keep my body in great shape. My skin is perfectly smooth, and the copper brown color of a frothy cinnamon mocha at the local coffee shop. My eyes are hazel but have a yellow-orange hue to them, and are accented by thick black eyebrows. My hair is short and black and slightly wavy. And rather than being clumsy or awkward, I carry myself with a sense of grace and dignity that might sometimes be mistaken as aristocratic.

Still, I hesitated about accepting the invitation to strut my stuff in front of hundreds of students and rich alumni. Until Mrs. Robinson, the show coordinator, informed me that Gerard Montez had just agreed to model in the swimsuit portion of the show. Gerard was the six feet tall, bronze-skinned, blue-eyed, tightly muscled Puerto Rican captain of the soccer team. I cannot begin to count the number of times I've beaten off while fantasizing about the way my fingers would rake through his short, wavy black hair as he kissed me with his full, soft lips and then . . .

"Well, if you're sure it'd help the school, I suppose I can agree to participate," I managed to stutter. I silently prayed that Mrs. Robinson did not notice the throbbing erection that had suddenly popped up and pulsed against the crotch of my jeans at the mere mention of Gerard's name.

"I'm quite sure," she said, and smiled sweetly. Or was that a knowing smirk?

"Count me in, then." I pulled the shirttail out of the waistband of my jeans and let it fall over the front of my crotch.

"Thanks so much, Bradley. I knew I could count on you."

"No problem," I muttered as I walked away from her and rushed back to the frat house.

Soccer practice had just begun and I knew I would probably not have any trouble finding a few moments of privacy so that I could take care of the hard-on that was raging in my jeans. I wasn't wrong. As I rushed up the stairs and down the hall to my room, I saw that the house was empty.

I tossed a video into the VCR, and ripped my clothes off as I flung myself onto the bed. I had forty minutes before my roommate returned from soccer practice. That was more than enough time to blow my load, I thought as I reached for the bottle of lube in the desk drawer next to my bed.

Closing my eyes, I wrapped my fist around my cock and slid it up and down the hard skin-stretched shaft. After only a couple of strokes, I could tell that I was already about to pop, and I slowed down as I opened my eyes and watched the video. On screen a white-skinned muscular redhead was pounding himself into a blonde-haired, green-eyed skinny kid who was moaning and groaning and pretending it was his first time getting fucked, even though he thrust his ass up to meet every inch of the redhead's big dick.

Having seen the video a dozen times, I knew it well. But that didn't matter. What I saw this time was Gerard's hard, naked body sliding into my clutching ass as I cried out for even more. I closed my eyes again and thrust my hard cock into my fist as I wiggled around on the bed, trying hard not to shoot my load too soon, but feeling desperately like I was not going to be successful.

I removed my hand from my cock and took a couple of deep breaths. When I opened my eyes, the two guys on the video were going at it really heavy. The skinny blonde kid rolled his eyes back in his head as the redhead slid his long fat cock deeper inside him and grunted like an animal.

"Oh, fuck it," I moaned. I slathered some of the lube from my cock onto my fingers and slowly slid one into my ass. This is a position I had been in many times before, and it didn't take long for me to warm up to it. A moment later, as the two actors on the video were getting ready to shoot all over themselves, I had three fingers inside my ass and was bucking up to meet my own thrusting fist.

"Brad?"

My eyes flew open and I whimpered as I saw my roommate Luis staring at me with a shocked look on his face. He was wearing a ragged T-shirt and a very tight and frayed pair of sweat shorts. His sneakers were laced together and thrown across his shoulder.

"What are you doing here?" I asked dazedly as I pulled my fingers slowly out of my ass. "I thought you were at practice."

"I hurt my ankle, so I left a little early. What's going on?" Luis asked as he looked away from my quickly deflating cock to the video playing on the television across the room.

"I . . . umm . . ."

"Shit, man. I didn't know you were into that."

"Well, it's just that I . . . well . . ."

On the screen, the redhead ripped his fat cock out of the blonde kid's ass and shot a huge load all over his chest and face. The blonde moaned and groaned as his own thick load spilled out of his cock head and slid down his shaft all over his hand.

"Fuck, man, that is hot," Luis said as he stepped all the way inside the room and closed the door behind him.

"Luis, you're not supposed to be here," I said indignantly as I felt the blood rush to my head.

"Yeah, but I am. And it looks like you could use some help with that," he said, and nodded toward my now soft cock.

I stared in disbelief as my roommate threw his sneakers onto his bed, walked across the room and knelt at the side of my bed. My heart raced as I watched his hand reaching for me, but there wasn't much I could do. My own hands were slathered in lube and all sticky.

He took my soft cock in his hands and wiped most of the

lube off it as he wrapped his fingers around it and squeezed softly.

In just a few seconds my dick began to respond, and it started to grow hard again. "Luis, what are you doing? I mean, I know what you're doing, but are you sure you want to . . ."

Instead of answering me, he opened his mouth, dropped his head into my lap and sucked the head of my cock between his warm lips. He licked at the head and sucked softly on my cock as his hands tugged and pulled at my balls and caressed my nipples.

I moaned loudly and grew completely hard inside his hot mouth. The next scene had already started on the video, and I wrapped my hands behind my head and watched the threeway on screen unfold before me as Luis swallowed more and more of my dick. Then I slowly began sliding my hard cock in and out of his sucking mouth, until I felt the back of his throat tickle my head as Luis choked a little.

"Fuck, man," I moaned as my roommate's head bobbed up and down the length of my shaft. "We've lived together for almost two years. How come this is the first time we've done this?"

Luis slid his hot mouth off my cock, and smiled as he licked my precum off his lips. "Dunno. I just didn't know you were into guys, I guess. It's not like I haven't wanted to or anything."

"Too fucking much, man," I gasped. "But we've got to stop for a moment, or I'm gonna shoot my load right now."

"No need to stop." Luis grinned sheepishly. "Let's just switch positions."

Before I could respond, Luis stood up and dropped his shorts to his ankles and roughly ripped the T-shirt off. He was still wearing his jockstrap, but his long, uncut cock pushed its way out of the elastic side band. He moved closer to my head and pulled the jock fabric back enough so that the entire length of his fat dick popped out and throbbed only inches from my mouth.

I grabbed his cock with my fist and guided the thick pole to my mouth. My tongue licked around his warm pulsing head, and I swallowed a mouthful of his sweet precum.

Luis moaned loudly as I deepthroated his dick in one move. His cock throbbed wildly in my mouth and I could tell that he was tightening his ass cheeks as I sucked him. I reached around and squeezed one of his marble-smooth globes in each hand and caressed his silky smooth skin as he fucked my mouth.

With his dick buried deep inside my throat, I looked up his torso. His six-pack abs were as smooth and hard as his ass, and his pecs were perfectly muscled mounds that were capped with tiny brown nipples. Farther up I noticed a tiny scar under his clefted chin and squared jaw that I'd never seen before. His pink tongue snaked out and licked his thin, brown lips as he moaned. I caught just a glimpse of his deep brown eyes for a moment, and then he shook his head, and a patch of his shoulder-length, straight black hair fell over his forehead and covered them.

"Damn, man, you suck cock like . . ."

Just then the bedroom door flew open. "Hey, Brad, Mrs. Robinson told me that you had agreed to help out with the fashion show. I thought we could . . ."

Gerard stopped in mid-sentence as he stared at Luis's cock buried deep inside my throat.

My eyes bulged wildly and I choked on Luis's big dick. I panicked, and tried to pull my mouth off him, but Luis grabbed the back of my head and pushed himself deeper inside my throat and mouth.

"What the fuck?" Gerard asked.

"Get in here, man, and shut the door before anyone else walks by and sees us," Luis told Gerard.

Gerard reached behind him and shut the door, but stayed where he was, just inside the doorway for a few moments. No one moved, and I realized I wasn't breathing as I held Luis's cock tight inside my throat. I felt my face flush with embarrassment at having the object of my every fantasy for the past two years watching me deepthroat his best friend. Then I noticed the bulge at the crotch of Gerard's jeans begin to grow and throb.

"Shit, man, I was going to ask if you wanted to help me pick out a couple of swim trunks that I should model for the show. But I think I've got a better idea now," he said as he tossed a plastic bag full of potential swim wear onto the desk and walked closer to the bed.

I started to pull myself off of Luis's cock again, and sit up on the bed. But Gerard planted a heavy hand on my chest and kept me lying on my back.

"Keep sucking his dick," Gerard said softly. "It'll take me just a sec to get out of these clothes."

A high-pitched ringing began in the back of my ears, and my heart raced as I watched Gerard begin unbuttoning his jacket and kick off his sneakers.

"You heard him," Luis said, and thrust his big dick in and out of my mouth. "Suck my cock."

I licked and lapped at the big dick in my mouth as I watched Gerard quickly strip. His tightly muscled chest and stomach were light-skinned and dusted with a soft coating of short, silky black hair. The patch of hair beneath his belly button grew thicker, and trailed down to the pubic hairs that quickly poked out of his bleached white jockeys. I swallowed a mouthful of sweet precum as Gerard pulled his briefs down thick muscular legs and kicked them off to one side.

Once released from the confines of his shorts, Gerard's long, fat uncut cock throbbed wildly in front of him. He was only inches away, and I could see the blood pulsing through the river of veins that wrapped around his huge dick. The foreskin covered half the head, and was stretching tighter across the thick white shaft with every passing second.

My own cock bounced across my stomach as I sucked Luis's dick and stared at Gerard's fat snake.

"No reason Luis should be having all the fun," Gerard whispered, and reached down to wrap his long, thick fingers around my cock.

A second later I felt his hot mouth suck the head of my cock inside. The wet walls of his cheeks wrapped around my hot cock head and massaged it. He sucked hungrily on the head for a few moments, and then opened the back of his throat and swallowed the entire length of my shaft deep into his throat.

That was all it took for me. Having my mouth fucked with Luis's big Puerto Rican dick and my own cock swallowed by Gerard's hungry mouth sent me over the edge. I grabbed the sheets on the sides of the bed with both hands and moaned as I shot my load deep into Gerard's hot throat.

"Oh, shit, man," Gerard said as he removed his mouth from my still hard cock. He licked some of my remaining cum from his lips, and wiped his mouth with the back of his hand. "I hope that doesn't mean we're through. 'Cuz I'm not even close to finishing."

"Me either," Luis agreed.

"I'm usually good for at least a couple of loads a day," I gasped as Luis's thick cock slipped from my mouth. "And this is my first one today."

"Great," Gerard said, "because I really want you to suck

my cock. From the glassy look in Luis's eyes, you've got quite a talent for it."

Luis took his cue and switched places with his best friend. I hungrily licked at Gerard's thick uncut cock, trying hard not to seem quite as desperate as I actually was to swallow the entire massive pole all at once. Luis was at the foot of the bed, and gently lifted my legs into the air, exposing the pink twitching hole between my brown ass cheeks. At first he just blew short wisps of air onto the hole, and then he reached out with his tongue and tickled it lightly.

"Oh, Christ," I moaned, and swallowed the entire length of Gerard's fat nine-inch cock deep inside my throat as Luis licked my ass.

"Fuck, man, you've got the best damned mouth I've ever felt," Gerard gasped as my throat muscles squeezed and massaged his thick uncut dick.

His massive balls swung heavily and bounced across my nose as I lapped at his pole. They were completely shaved smooth, and a stark contrast to the thick coarse hair that graced his muscular legs and the musky, sweaty area between his ass and balls.

Luis's tongue snaked its way inside my hole inch by inch, until it was buried deep inside me. I arched my back on the bed as I impaled myself as completely as possible onto his wet, warm tongue. My own cock was still fully hard, and dripping a river of precum as it bounced hotly across my stomach.

"Don't get too comfortable down there, buddy," Gerard said to his friend. "I know how you can get carried away."

"But . . ." Luis protested as he slipped his tongue out of my ass and tugged on his cock.

"Forget it, dude. His ass is mine. I've been dreaming about fucking that tight sweet hole for months. Let's trade places again."

I stared back and forth in total disbelief at the two friends as they debated the fate of ass. Could it really be that the guy I'd dreamed about so many times had actually also been dreaming about me the whole time? I'd lost the skill of speech long ago, and was reduced to a series of grunts and moans as Gerard and Luis exchanged the comfortable silent glances of longtime friends. Finally, they pulled away from me, leaving me feeling completely empty for a moment as they traded places.

"That's cool," Luis said as he playfully slapped his hard cock against my face, drizzling it with a sticky trail of warm precum. "I guess I can't complain too much when I get to fuck the hottest mouth on campus."

"Yeah, but slow down a little." Gerard laughed as he lay lightly on top of me and nibbled softly on my lips. "I've got some unfinished business with that mouth first," he whispered, and pressed his soft, full lips against mine in a tender kiss. His tongue licked my lips for a few seconds, and then slowly slid into my hungry mouth.

I sucked on his tongue as if it were my last supper. Gerard wriggled his heavy cock between our sweaty stomachs, and rubbed it against my own dick until both were covered with the sticky wetness of our excitement. All the while, he kissed me gently, and held my jaws in his strong hands as his fingers caressed my face.

I couldn't believe all that was happening. Luis had been my roommate for almost two years, and never once had I imagined having sex with him. I mean, he was fucking sexy as hell, there was no denying that. His dark, lean, smooth body would normally have been enough to set me off immediately. Not to mention the shoulder-length straight black hair and dark eyes that could melt granite. The Puerto Rican accent that he'd worked so hard on losing was a complete turn on for me, and I had secretly hoped he'd never lose it. But he was my roommate, for crying out loud, and was one of the most popular jocks on campus. Who would ever have thought, even for a moment, that he would be into a scene like this? Certainly not me.

But then again, I had been completely preoccupied fantasizing about my roommate's best friend from the moment I laid eyes on him. His tall, creamy white, muscular body that was sexily dusted with thick black curly hair was the object of my every desire and jack off sessions the last two years. I'd seen him in the showers a few times, and had to rush through my rinsing process in order to drape the towel around my waist and conceal my raging hard-on. His Puerto Rican accent was even stronger than his friend's, but Gerard was proud of his heritage and never tried to conceal it in any way. His short, wavy black hair, blue eyes and sexy voice made him an instant hit with everyone on campus, and the fact that he was a star athlete and captain of the soccer team certainly added fuel to my fantasy fires.

"Can I fuck you?" Gerard whispered in my ear, bringing me back to the reality that was all around me.

"Yes," I moaned.

He moved his body farther down my own, and gently spread my legs as he crouched between them. He pulled the foreskin back from his shaft, and with his fingers, scooped up a glob of precum from my navel and rubbed it across his cock head.

"Christ," Luis said, and moved his throbbing cock to my mouth, "I thought you two were never gonna let me back in."

I opened my mouth wide, and swallowed the fat curved cock until his balls rested against my forehead. Farther down the bed, Gerard's sticky fingers slid slowly into my ass and stretched the hole a little at a time. When his third finger was buried deep inside my ass, I began bucking.

"Now you're ready," Gerard said, and he removed his fingers.

For just a moment, my ass was left empty, twitching and exposed. But then a second later I felt the hot skin of Gerard's thick cock head as it rubbed against my hole, and then slid slowly inside.

I moaned loudly, and Gerard stopped pushing into me. I think he mistook my moan for one of pain, and since my mouth was filled with Luis's cock, I couldn't tell him otherwise. At least not with words. So instead, I lifted my ass off the mattress and slid all the way down the length of his massive dick and squeezed it tightly once it was buried deep inside my ass.

"Fuck me!" Gerard almost yelled.

"Man, if I knew you were this good, I would have fucked you a long time ago," Luis said to me as he slid his cock in and out of my mouth with slow, deep jabs.

At the same time, Gerard thrust his fat cock in and out of my ass with long, deliberate and gentle strokes. He leaned forward and licked my nipples as he fucked me, and then kissed his way up my neck and to my mouth. Once there, he joined me in sucking Luis's already slippery wet cock as it fucked my mouth. At the same time, he kissed me on the lips, and bit my bottom lip tenderly.

The feeling of being skewered by these two Latino sex gods was more than I could take for very long. Since Gerard was leaning forward to kiss me and suck Luis at the same time that I was, my cock was rubbing against his belly, lubricated with my own precum. I thrust my ass higher and deeper onto Gerard's hot fat cock, and moaned as I felt my second load of the day quickly approach.

Luis and Gerard must have sensed the impending orgasm,

because they both began thrusting into me faster and harder. The unison moans of all three of us filled the room.

Gerard was the first to pull his cock out of my quivering body. The head barely popped out of my ass before the first hot jet of cum spewed from it. The heavy white spray flew over my head and landed on Luis's chest. Luis moaned and shoved his cock all the way down my throat just as his creamy load emptied into my gut. Tasting Luis's sweet juice and seeing Gerard's thick cum fly from his cock and land on my face and chest and stomach set me over the edge. My own dick erupted and splashed my second load all over my body and onto the bed.

The gushers of cum seemed to go on for minutes, and when it was all over the three of us lay limp and spent tired, trying to catch our breath.

"Shit!" Luis said, startled as he looked at the clock next to the bed. "I'm supposed to meet Barbara and some friends for coffee in just a few minutes." He jumped up and started to get dressed. "You guys don't mind if I take off, do you?"

"I think we'll manage just fine," Gerard said as he wrapped his arms around me, and pulled me closer to him so he could kiss me. "Besides, we've got work to do. Mrs. Robinson wants an answer on which of these swim trunks I'm planning on modeling in a couple of hours. Maybe you can help me choose a couple?" he asked me as he squeezed me tighter to his hot, sweaty body.

"I'd be happy to."

"Right on," Luis said as he grabbed his backpack and headed toward the door. "I'll catch up with you guys later. Maybe we can have a little repeat performance."

"We'll see you later tonight," Gerard said. "But I think I'd prefer keeping Brad for myself. If that's okay with you?" he asked me.

I nodded my head numbly as I snuggled closer to Gerard. "That's definitely all right with me," I said.

"If you say so. Don't forget to get around to picking out some trunks for the show, though. Mrs. Robinson is counting on you both."

"Good-bye, Luis," Gerard said. I noticed his cock was already starting to get hard again as we hugged, and he pulled me closer to kiss me again.

Bathhouse Billy

"*That's it, man. Shove it up my ass. Deeper. Harder. I can take it.*"

Those were the words that pushed me over the edge and to the point of no return.

I'd been inside the tiny, dark closet-size stall for nearly fifteen minutes, and was just about to give up and leave, when I heard the flimsy door of the stall to my left open and swing shut quickly. By the time I leaned into the large oval shaped hole in the middle of the wall, it was too late. I couldn't see what the guy on the other side looked like.

Not like it really mattered. There were only seven or eight other guys in the entire bathhouse, and none of them were complete trolls. After walking aimlessly around the dark mazes and empty hot tubs for almost two hours, I had decided to just slip into one of the glory hole stalls and wait. I was so horny that I would gladly have sucked or been fucked by any of the other patrons in the large almost empty building.

I dropped to my knees and was just about to rub my fingers against the edge of the glory hole, signaling for the guy on the other side to shove his cock through so I could swallow it deep into my throat. It was a routine I'd mastered over my many trips to the bathhouse. Among my friends, I am known as Bathhouse Billy, and it is a widely known fact that I love sucking big, fat, anonymous cocks through the glory holes more than just about anything.

But this time, I was not in charge. This time, the guy on the other end of the wall beat me to the punch and rubbed his fingers along the curved hole of the wall. I tried to move his fingers away, and trace my own circle around the oval opening, but he pushed my hand aside and stuck his tongue through the hole insistently.

"Let me suck your cock, man," he said huskily. "I wanna get it all hard and wet so you can shove it up my ass and fuck my brains out."

I shook my head dazedly, but stood up and leaned into the hole anyway. My cock was barely through the smoothed out hole before his tongue reached out and licked the head of it, then sucked it into his warm mouth. He lapped at my head for a few seconds, and wrapped his lips tighter around the shaft as he sucked the rest of my eight-inch dick into his hungry mouth.

I moaned as my cock got instantly hard and began to pump in and out of the unseen mouth on the other side of the wall. I'd always prided myself on being a great cocksucker, and had been assured on more than one occasion that I was not mistaken in my assessment. But if I was even half as good as the guy swallowing my cock, then I should have won several awards by now.

My knees began to buckle, and I found it difficult to breathe. The shaved, low-hanging sac that held my balls shrank up closer to the base of my throbbing cock. Little red dots started flashing before my eyes in the darkness of the room as the familiar tingle started deep in my belly.

Before I could pull my cock from the demanding mouth, my body went limp as I shot seven or eight thick jets of come down his throat. He swallowed all of them, and continued sucking on my dick, milking every last drop from it.

"Fuck, man, that was great," the husky voice whispered. "Can you keep it up for some more? I really want that fat cock inside my ass."

Normally I am finished after my first load. But hearing this unseen man pleading for me to fuck him was more than I was used to. My cock bounced excitedly, and remained fully hard and ready.

Within seconds, the hot wet mouth on the other side of the wall was replaced with the unmistakable smooth-marble hard muscle that could only be one thing. The stranger pushed his ass against and around my cock, begging for me to take control.

I did. I reached through the hole in the wall and grabbed his ass with both hands. Then I pulled it up against the wall, and held it steady as I knelt in front of the hole. I stuck my tongue out and licked his ass vigorously, making sure I used as much saliva as I could muster. His moans of approval were all I needed. I snaked my tongue inside the hot hole in the center of his muscular ass, and pushed forward until I was all the way inside.

"Oh, yeah, dude, that's it. That feels great. But now I want the real thing. I want your big dick up inside my ass."

I withdrew my tongue and rose to my feet immediately. All of the glory hole stalls were always well equipped with condoms, and I fumbled around in the dark until I found the small tray that held them. I ripped the top off one of the cellophane packets and rolled the pre-lubed rubber down my hard shaft.

"Come on, man. Give it to me."

Damn, this guy was pushy. I grabbed my cock by the base and shoved it back through the hole in the wall. It didn't take long at all for me to find his hot ass hole, and I pushed forward in one quick stab. I expected him to cry out in protest, or whimper and try to pull off my spearing cock. I'd teach him a thing or two.

Instead, his hot ass muscles gripped my throbbing cock and squeezed like they were milking an overstuffed udder. The guy on the other side of the wall squealed in delight, and wiggled his muscular body up and down the length of my dick. I felt his ass as it enveloped my cock and rode it with wild abandon. The thin wall separating us creaked in protest as his body continuously slammed against it.

"Fuck me, dude. Fuck my tight ass harder."

Up to this point, I hadn't really needed to be the aggressor. He'd pretty much done all the work. But now I was determined to give him the fuck of his life. I withdrew my long cock until only the fat head remained inside his ass, then slammed it back in ferociously. I repeated the movement over and over again, thinking I was really showing this guy who was who. To myself, I counted to ten and tried to think of anything gross or disgusting so that I wouldn't shoot too soon.

"More," he cried out loudly. "I want more."

More? My head spun as pinpoints of light flashed before my eyes for the second time that night. Because he was on the other side of the thin wall and I couldn't grab him by the waist, I hooked my hands over the top of the wall and held on tight as I rammed my cock into his ass harder and faster. Once I was buried inside him, I twisted at my waist, so that my cock scraped the inside walls of his clutching butt.

"Oh, yeah, that's it. That's what I want. Fuck me harder."

Sweat was pouring down my face and body as I thrust myself into him with every ounce of strength I had. My own knees were beginning to shake with the force of my fucking. I knew it wouldn't be too long before I was unable to hold back and spew my load deep inside this guy's gut. I tried to slow down a little, but his tight ass only grasped my cock even tighter and swallowed me deep inside him, refusing to let me out. Tiny little fingers of ass muscles massaged my cock and tickled the head as it pushed up against the deepest part of his insides.

"That's it, man. Shove it up my ass. Deeper. Harder. I can take it."

"Oh, fuck, man, I'm gonna come," I almost yelled.

In an instant, he pulled himself off of my rock hard cock and I felt a brush of cool air surround the base of my dick and balls.

"Pull off the rubber," he panted. "I want you to shoot on my face."

"It's too late," I moaned, "I'm com . . ."

His hands reached through the hole, grabbed my cock and ripped the condom off just as the first spurt of come shot up my shaft and out the head.

My body rocked as wave after wave of my load spewed from my cock. My knees gave out after a few seconds, and I leaned against the wall for support. I heard the guy on the other side moaning loudly. I imagined each moan was the result of my hot come splashing against his face.

When I was completely spent, I felt his tongue lap at my cock, licking up whatever drop of come might have been lingering along the shaft of my cock head. Then a couple of seconds later, as I was still trying to catch my breath, I heard the door on his side of the wall squeak open and shut again. His footsteps faded down the hall even before I could open my door and see his face or body.

Mama's Boy

It was a dumpy old motel on the side of the road. The rain was pouring down so hard that I could barely see the front of my car anymore, and I was in the middle of the plains of Kansas. It was almost three o'clock in the morning and I was struggling to keep my eyes open and on the road. So, I pulled into the parking lot and ran inside the office as quickly as I could.

The old lady who eventually hobbled out from behind a tattered curtain behind the counter must have been close to ninety years old. She was not amused with being awakened in the middle of the night.

"You're in room 115. Very last room across the parking lot. Bottom floor."

"Thanks," I said as I took my key and sprinted back to my car.

The entire motel consisted of thirty rooms situated on two floors constructed in a crude U shape. The tiny parking lot covered the empty space between the two wings.

I grabbed my duffel bag from the backseat and got inside as quickly as possible. Then I got undressed and slid into bed.

Half an hour later I still laid wide awake. Even at this time of the morning, the air outside was very warm and the rain had made it even more humid than it normally was in the mid-western plains. Crudely patched rectangular holes under the windows in every room suggested they had once held air-conditioning units, but not for a very long time. Sweat drenched my body and made falling asleep nearly impossible. I'd noticed a soda and juice machine near the middle of the building and decided to get up and buy a can of cranberry juice.

My clothes were strewn carelessly across the floor. Only my boxer shorts were anywhere near the bed. What the hell, I thought, it's completely dark outside and not another soul was anywhere in sight. Surely the old lady was snoring away in her own room.

So I slipped on my shorts, grabbed a handful of coins from next to my keys on the dresser, and sprinted out the door toward the vending machine. The only non-carbonated beverage left in the machine was apple juice, and I sighed as I dropped the quarters into the slot and punched the button for my juice.

As I turned around to walk back to my room, I noticed the light. It was just a thin sliver, but it was coming from the slightly opened door of a room not too far from my own. I walked cautiously toward the room. A strong gust of wind swept across the parking lot and blew the heavy door open a couple more inches as I reached it. Peeking inside, I saw the blankets carelessly tossed to the foot of the bed, just as I had done with mine.

Sprawling across the rumpled sheets was a man a few years older than me. He looked to be in his early to mid thirties. His dark skin and black curly hair were a stark contrast to the overly bleached white sheets on the bed.

I couldn't have pictured a more perfect man regardless of the number of wishes I'd been granted. A little over six feet tall, his sweat-glistened copper skin bulged with perfectly sculpted muscles. His nipples were tiny and hard. The only visible signs of hair on his torso were a small triangular patch of dark curly chest hairs snuggled between his massive pecs and a thick black line of fur that snaked its way from his ripped navel to his pubic hair. His turquoise blue eyes were framed by thick eyebrows and long, curly eyelashes.

When I finally allowed myself to glance away from his face and down to his cock, I gasped. It was at least ten inches long, and so thick that his big hands barely fit around the shaft. It was sheathed with a silky layer of foreskin, and a river of veins popped out across it. A long string of clear, sticky fluid peeked from the fat head, and then slid menacingly slow down the monster cock.

My own dick ached with hardness, and stabbed through the fly of my boxer shorts. I leaned against the door frame as a wisp of rain-cooled wind swirled up the legs of my thin shorts and kissed my cock.

Inside the room, the guy on the bed pounded his own cock harder and faster. Precum slid from the cock head. He soaked his thick middle finger with the sticky stuff.

I watched in amazement as he lifted his ass off the bed and slowly moved his finger toward the pink, twitching hole. I fought to catch my breath as he slid his fat finger deep inside his ass, all the way to the knuckles on his fist.

"Oh, shit," he moaned as he finger-fucked himself.

I dropped my can of juice, and when I reached for it, knocked my head against the door.

"What the fuck?" the man yelled as he quickly pulled his finger from his ass and scrambled to pull the blankets over his naked body.

"I'm sorry," I stammered as I picked up my apple juice. "I was just . . ."

"You were just spying on me," he said angrily.

"No, really, I wasn't. I was only going for some juice. I swear."

"Then why do you have a big old boner sticking out of your shorts?"

I gasped as I realized my cock was still hard and pounding, and sticking through the fly of my boxers.

"Wanna come inside?" he asked, and threw the covers back to the foot of the bed, exposing himself once again. "This time, why don't we make sure the door is closed."

"I'm not sure . . ."

"Close the door and come here."

I stepped inside his room, closed the door and walked slowly toward his bed.

He reached out, grabbed me by the arm and pulled me onto the bed in one swift move. With his other hand, he yanked my shorts down my legs.

"I don't want any . . ." I started to protest, but before I got any further, he wrapped his lips around my throbbing cock and sucked me deep inside his hot mouth.

His hand massaged my ass cheeks as he slammed me farther down his throat. His tongue swirled across first the head and then the shaft of my cock. Before I knew it I was buried inside the warmth of his mouth and his throat muscles tightened around my dick with intense strength.

My head spun with contradicting thoughts. This guy could very easily cause me serious harm. He was older, stronger, more powerful than me. If he wanted to, he could easily beat me senseless. But his hungry mouth on my cock and the gentle way his hands massaged my ass and legs suggested he intended me no harm. Still, I couldn't be too cautious.

"Please don't hurt me," I managed to grunt as I forced myself not to shoot a load down his sucking throat.

He pulled his mouth off my cock. "Why would I hurt you?"

"I really didn't mean to watch you. I was just getting a drink, and I saw your light on, and then I thought some-one . . ."

"It's okay." He laughed, and gently pushed my head down to his fat cock.

When I opened my mouth to make a bigger fool of myself, he slid the salty tip of his dick inside. I swallowed as much of his cock as I could, then wrapped my fist around what was left around the base.

"Oh, man, dude," he moaned, "I'm so close."

"Me too," I said as I pulled his dick out of my mouth and started beating my cock faster.

"No."

"What?" I panted.

He pulled my hand away from my cock, and held it firmly to my side. After a couple of seconds he rolled over onto his stomach and raised his ass high into the air. "Fuck me," he whispered.

"But . . ." I said.

He grabbed my head and gently pushed it down to his ass.

Before I had time to think about it, I stuck my tongue out and licked at his ass hole. I was amazed at how quickly I took to being the aggressor. My tongue darted in and out of his twitching hole like I'd done this particular act a hundred times.

"That feels really great, man," he moaned. "But now I want your cock inside me."

I raised myself onto my knees and grabbed his smooth hard ass cheeks in both hands.

He tightened his ass muscles under my grip, and wiggled his butt high into the air.

"Are you sure?" I asked even as I reached for the condom on the nightstand next to the bed.

His ass pressed against my cock head and he moaned loudly as it popped inside his tight hole. He caught his breath for just a couple of seconds, and then shoved himself all the way onto my cock, not stopping until my balls brushed his cheeks.

"Oh, man, this is incredible," I spit out as I slid my dick in and out of his clutching ass.

He moaned as he thrust himself back and forth across my cock.

Without pulling himself off my cock, he rolled over onto his back. His ass muscles gripped my dick and squeezed lovingly. As I pumped deeper inside him, he pulled my head down to his own and kissed me on the lips. His tongue darted in and out of my mouth and he bit my lips gently.

I shoved my dick deep into his ass, and then pulled slowly out until only the head remained inside. Then I did it again and again. As I fucked and kissed him, he began bucking up to meet my thrusts. He stared up at me with his beautiful blue eyes, and then he winked at me as his ass tightened around my cock.

A second later I felt his warm, thick cum shooting onto my stomach. It seemed to go on forever, covering both of us in a sticky wet blanket. That was all it took for me. I moaned loudly as I shoved my tongue into his mouth and kissed him hungrily. My cock was buried to the balls inside him, and I felt it grow even thicker as it poured its load inside the warm, clutching ass. I pulled out of the guy's ass and rolled over onto my back on the bed in time to see the last few squirts of cum shoot into the condom.

"Damn, that was great," the man said as he stood up and began to gather his clothes.

"What's the hurry?" I asked sleepily. "It's still raining like crazy out there. You're not going to get very far in this weather, anyway. You might as well stay here and sleep with me a couple of hours."

"Oh, I can't." He sighed as he finished tying his shoes. "Mother doesn't like it when I mingle with the guests."

"What?" I asked, not trusting that I'd heard him correctly.

But he was already out the door and running across the parking lot. I watched as he pulled the keys from his pocket, unlocked the office door and stepped inside.

A moment later a faint light flicked on from somewhere deep inside the office. I sat on the edge of the bed, stunned, as the shadow of the frail old woman glided alone behind the closed drapes.

My head spun to the motel sign lighted dimly with a single bulb.

The Cates Motel.

I ran to my room, threw on my clothes as quickly as possible and ran barefoot to the car. As I fumbled to get the keys into the ignition, I glanced over at the office. The shadow from inside was moving quicker than before, and heading toward the door.

My tires squealed as they spun rocks over the parking lot and toward the motel.

I never looked back.

The Right to Remain Silent

Every city of any significant size has a public park that is notorious for the anonymous sex that occurs among the dark shadows, overgrown trees and shrubs, and public toilets. It doesn't take a Sherlock Holmes to find them either, and only took me one trip to the local bookstore and overhearing a couple of conversations to find that out once I moved here. Here in Denver, it is Chessman Park. I would much later find out that the local police were in the middle of a crackdown on the public sex offenders, and were concentrating on arresting multitudes of gay men caught between the bushes. But by then it would be too late.

I was only twenty-five years old myself when Daniel walked out and left me for a younger guy. He was my first boyfriend, and I'd met him about three weeks after I'd moved to San Francisco. It was only a couple of months after my twentieth birthday, and I wasn't really out of the closet. At thirty years old, Daniel was my manager at work, and it didn't take any time at all for him to pick me out, pick me up and ask me to move in with him. I was naïve enough and stupid enough to think it would last forever.

Funny how some people's idea of forever translates as five years. But for Daniel that was apparently the case. He came home from work one day, announced he'd been having an affair with a new employee of his for the past six months, and that they had decided it was time to deepen their commitment. I was immediately on the phone with my best friend Tammy, and within an hour she had convinced me to pack up my things and move to Denver.

"You need to get as far away from that asshole as you can," she told me between my sobs.

"Denver isn't really that far from San Francisco," I cried, but was already hastily throwing clothes into my suitcase.

"It's far enough."

"And Daniel is in Denver a couple of times a year for work." I wiped the tears from my eyes and snapped the suitcase shut.

"It's a big city, Sean. Besides, by the time he decides to come looking for you here, you'll already have found another boyfriend. Fuck him."

And so I moved. A month later I was horny as hell, and not having had quite the good fortune of finding a new boyfriend as quickly as Tammy had promised, I decided to hit the park. If I couldn't find a boyfriend with the bat of my eyes, I could at least get myself laid. And that's exactly what I planned on doing.

I'd driven around the park several times while the sun was still out, and had scoped out the small groups of trees that held the most promise. It was hard for me to believe that the park would actually be as packed with horny men as I'd heard, because in the middle of the day it was almost empty. By eleven at night, however, I was not disappointed. It was indeed crawling with men.

I got out of my car and walked into the heart of the park. Within five minutes, I spotted someone who grabbed my attention. From what I could tell with the help of the moonlight and street lamp, he was around my age, maybe a few years older. Certainly much younger than the majority of the men stalking the place. Wearing a pair of cut-off denim shorts and a tank top, I could see that he was muscular and obviously took great pride in his body.

He watched me for several minutes, and then sauntered into a group of trees a few yards away. When I didn't follow him immediately, he grabbed his crotch, smiled and tilted his head toward the shaded area behind him.

My heart raced, and I hesitated for a moment. But when I noticed several other guys quickly working their way toward him, I stepped forward and moved into the small grove of heavily branched trees.

"Hi," I said as I walked in front of him.

He nodded.

I took a few steps into the shadows and leaned against the thick trunk of one of the trees. A few of the other guys tried to follow me into the clearing, but I noticed that my new friend kept pushing them away, either with his eyes or with his arms a couple of times.

When the stream of men stopped coming near us, he walked over to me, pushed himself gently against my body and began running his hands across my chest and stomach.

"My name's Sean," I stammered as my cock responded to his caresses. "What's yours?"

"Shut up," he said.

I was amazed at how deep and masculine his voice was. I

also was not particularly pleased with his tone of voice with me, and started to tell him so. But just then his strong hands planted themselves on both of my shoulders and forced me to my knees.

"Really, that's not necessary," I said weakly. I was already mesmerized with the growing bulge in the front of his shorts.

"Fuck you, man. I'll tell you what's necessary and what isn't," he growled, and quickly pulled his cock out of his shorts. It was already halfway hard, huge and thick. "Suck it."

"Look, I don't respond well to . . ."

He kicked me in the stomach, hard enough to double me over and take my breath away. Then he grabbed me by the hair and pulled my head back up so that it was eye level with his now raging hard-on.

"Don't even think about screaming," he said between gritted teeth, "or I swear to God, you'll regret it."

I didn't scream, or anything close to it. Instead, I began to cry. Giant tears fell down my cheeks as I tried desperately to catch my breath.

"I said to suck my dick, and I don't like to repeat myself," he said as he pulled my head toward his crotch.

I opened my mouth and licked at the head of his fat cock head as my breath slowly returned to me. His dick throbbed under my tongue, and grew even harder as I sucked on the first few inches of his shaft. Though I couldn't really see it at this close range, I could taste and feel a thick layer of foreskin stretched tightly across the length of his cock and just under the bulbous head. In spite of my fear and the pain in my gut, I felt my own cock begin to harden.

He shoved the entire length of his dick deep into my throat. I started to choke on the first couple of thrusts, then relaxed as

I breathed through my nose. The huge cock slammed past my throat muscles and fucked my mouth relentlessly.

"That's it, faggot, suck my cock."

I tensed at hearing the F word, and began to panic. Though I'd obviously heard of gay bashing, and had even known a couple of guys who had fallen victim to it, I never really thought that it could happen to me. Visions of my being stabbed, or shot or beaten to a pulp flashed before my eyes. More tears fell from my eyes, and the muscles in my throat constricted with fear.

"Fuck yeah, man, I'm gonna shoot," the guy growled.

And then he did. Wave after wave of his hot cum sprayed against the back of my throat and slid into my guts. His hands held my head tight against his cock until the last drop of slimy jizz dripped into my body.

I heard men shouting from several directions all at once. Some of them were nelly screams from what I could only imagine as being drag queens. Others were more masculine, yet still obviously filled with fear. And then there were the gruff, authoritative orders being barked by what were obviously several police officers.

The guy with his cock buried down my throat pulled out of my mouth suddenly, and kicked me again in the ribs, knocking me onto my side.

"Not a single word from you, motherfucker, or I swear to Christ I will kick your brains out."

I couldn't have uttered a word had I wanted to, and lay on my side crying. The guy quickly shoved his cock back into his shorts, and rushed out of the circle of trees. I heard several men yelling and running past me. Some of them were screaming profanities at the police, others were obviously cops yelling for the guys to drop to the ground and remain perfectly still.

"Is there anyone in there, Ray?" I heard an older man ask from only a few feet away from my head.

"No, it's clear, Sarge," came the familiar voice.

My eyes bulged with fear and I tried to sit up. The pain in my ribs throbbed, and my head ached.

"You sure?" the Sergeant asked. "Maybe they're hiding."

"Nah," Ray said. "I caught one guy cruising the fuck out of me, and was trying to lure him in there, but he got away when he heard the screaming."

"All right," Sarge said hesitantly. "Guess we'd better herd these guys into the station and get them booked. I'll meet you there in a couple of minutes."

"Yes, sir," Ray said.

He started to walk away with his boss and I thought I was actually in the clear. Then just barely within earshot, I heard Ray speak again.

"Fuck, I dropped my badge back there in the trees," he said casually, and started walking back toward me.

"You need help?" Sarge asked.

"Nah. You go on, I'll meet you there in a few minutes."

"All right."

I was just catching my breath and getting to my feet when Ray pushed aside a couple of branches and walked back into the clearing.

"Turn the fuck around and put your hands on that tree trunk," he ordered.

I did as he said, turning around slowly, and grabbed the thick trunk of the largest tree. A couple of seconds later Ray's hands were all over my body. It took me a moment to realize he was frisking me.

"I don't have any weapons," I said weakly. "Look, can't you just let me go?"

A strong elbow pushed against my back, and then he pulled my hands behind my back and handcuffed me.

"Lean against the tree, faggot, and keep your mouth shut," he whispered into my ear as he shoved the front of my body against the tree.

He grabbed the top of my pants, pulled them quickly down to my ankles and then ripped my underwear violently from my waist.

"Come on, man," I pleaded, "you don't have to do this. You've already . . ."

"One more word from that fucking mouth of yours, and I'll carry your bloody body to jail," he said.

I stopped in mid-sentence and heard him lower his shorts. A moment later the fat, hard and hot head of his cock was pressing against my ass. Even though I was hand-cuffed and still hurting from his kicks earlier, I tried to fight against him. I kicked back with my legs and struggled to turn around.

His right foot kicked me in the back of the knee and I dropped to the ground. He pushed my head forward, so that I was looking straight ahead, and kneeling on my knees, with my chin against the ground. My ass was sticking straight up in the air, and it was only seconds before I felt his huge dick slide into me.

"One fucking squeal from you and you're dead. You got that?" he asked as he slid his cock all the way inside my ass in one swift move.

"Yes," I cried.

He grabbed onto my hands and began pulling my body backward onto his cock as he fucked me deeper and harder.

As his cock speared my ass, he leaned forward and began kissing my back and neck. Despite my pain and fear, I began to get hard.

"Fuck me," I whispered as he slid his dick slowly in and out of my ass.

"Yeah, man, I'm fucking your sweet ass."

I tightened my ass muscles against his increasingly hot and fat cock, and shoved myself deeper onto him.

"You like getting fucked, don't you, dude?"

"Yeah," I growled huskily.

"Maybe I should stop."

"No," I gasped and impaled myself onto him as hard as I could. "Please don't."

"You sure?"

"Yes."

"Okay then, man. Take my big dick deep inside you."

He slid himself in and out of my ass with deeper and faster strokes for several minutes. Whenever I tried to say anything else, he clasped his hand across my mouth and bit my ears and neck and back lightly.

"You want me to spray my cum inside your ass, man?" he asked.

I shook my head no, and licked his hand. He removed it from my mouth and rested both of his hands on either side of my ass.

"I want you to shoot your load on my face," I panted heavily.

"Yeah?"

"Yeah."

Without pulling his cock out of my ass, Ray turned me roughly around onto my back and laid me on the ground. My hands were still cuffed, and the metal scraped roughly against my skin as did the pine covered flooring. He continued fucking me with increasingly fast and short jabs for another minute or so, then quickly pulled himself out of my clutching ass.

"Fuck man, I'm gonna shoot!" Ray screamed loudly.

"STOP RIGHT THERE!" someone shouted, and rushed into the clearing where Ray and I were fucking.

"Shit," Ray screamed, and his load started splashing all over my body. Six or seven shots of hot sticky cum landed on my face, chest and stomach

"Freeze!" the sergeant yelled, and kicked Ray squarely in the back.

Ray landed on top of me, his face smearing into his own cum lying across my body.

"Ray?"

"It's me, Sarge. Don't shoot," Ray said quickly as he spit out a mouthful of his own cooling cum.

"What the fuck are you doing?"

"I umm . . ."

"Shut up," Sarge said, and shoved Ray head first into the ground. "Are you okay?" he asked me as he laid one booted foot on Ray's back and reached down to uncuff me.

"Yes, I'm fine," I said.

"I can't fucking believe this, Ray. You're in such serious shit."

"Sarge, I can explain . . ."

"Shut the fuck up," Sarge yelled as he helped me to my feet. "You want to press charges, son?"

I looked down at Ray, and noticed his tight, smooth ass. He was beginning to cry.

"Maybe it won't come to that," I said.

"Well, it's your call," Sarge said, and looked from my throbbing cock and down to Ray's ass.

"Please," Ray begged. He was still crying.

Sarge smiled at me and twirled the handcuffs around on his index finger.

"Can I use those?" I asked boldly.

"Be my guest," he said, and handed me the cuffs.

"What?" Ray asked, bewildered.

I reached down and roughly pulled Ray's hands behind his back, clasping the cuffs around them tightly.

"Ow, shit!" Ray cried out.

"Shut the fuck up, punk," I said boldly, and looked up at Sarge just to make sure I wasn't overstepping my bounds. "One more word out of you and I'm gonna beat you to a pulp."

Sarge smiled and began to walk back toward the way he'd just burst into the clearing. "I'll be right outside here in case you need me," he told me.

"Sarge, you can't be serious!" Ray sobbed.

"You gonna let him get away with that?" Sarge asked me as he walked out into the park.

"Not a chance," I said as I lowered myself onto Ray's back.

The hard globes of his tight smooth ass were cold against my hot throbbing cock. I spit a large glob of saliva onto them and slid my dick teasingly along his ass crack.

"Come on, man," Ray said hesitantly. "You're not really gonna do this, are you?"

"Shut up, punk!" I yelled louder than I meant to even in my heightened state of excitement.

Ray tightened his ass cheeks, trying to prevent me from entering him.

It didn't work.

His scream of pain pierced the night, causing several birds to fly frightened from their perches atop the surrounding trees.

As I slammed my cock into his tight hot ass, I heard Sarge chuckling to himself a few feet away.

A Continental Summer

It's been a long summer to say the least. Don't ask me why, but when I made the decision to audition for the U.S. tour of Continental Singers eleven months ago, riding around in a bus with thirty-seven other high school and college kids, performing in a different city every night for three months, seemed like just the thing to lift my spirits after my first year in college.

Getting to know all the other kids my age from all over the U.S., playing pranks on our married "chaperone" directors, and seeing new cities are wonderful experiences. Our sponsors, members of the schools and churches we sing in, always treat us like we walk on water; and what twenty-year old doesn't get off on that?

But it's a lot more work than I'd ever imagined. We're trapped in a cramped bus that is on it's last leg, has no bathroom, and a very temperamental air-conditioning system that halfway works maybe two days a week. That might be all right if we were touring Alaska, but makes it really rough when we've spent the majority of our time in the hot and humid southern states in the middle of summer.

There are nineteen girls on my particular tour, and of course, they can't calibrate their menstrual cycles, so it seems someone is always having a bad case of PMS. The nineteen guys on the tour (including myself) probably use more gel and hair spray than the girls, and just can't be bothered with their petty female problems. Between the bitching and moaning of the girls PMSing and the whining and groaning of lovesick boys who left their girlfriends back home for the summer, our ten-to-fourteen-hour bus rides every day are an unimaginable joy, let me tell you.

When we arrive at our performance site each night, the girls bitch and cry about having to lug all of our suitcases into dressing rooms and the guys bitch and cry about having to set up the bleachers and heavy equipment. Then we put on our "Continental Smiles" as we eat the potluck dinner provided before performances, and have about an hour to dress and get ready to sing and dance our little hearts out.

It was really a lot of fun the first few weeks, but it just got on my nerves after a while. Except the staying with host families part. I like that a lot. It's so interesting to meet people from other parts of the country, and they are always so nice to us. Each family volunteers to take two to four of us into their home after the shows, feed us the next morning and get us back to the bus for ungodly early departures. Once the larger group is broken down into smaller groups of the same sex, we are much more tolerable and usually have fun together.

I was almost one of the lovesick boys who'd left his girlfriend behind for the summer. My preacher's daughter, nonetheless. But we split up six months ago, when I was sure I'd be gone for the whole summer; which disrupted her plans of getting engaged, apparently. It turns out to be a good thing though, because about halfway through the tour I began experiencing those feelings most of us do in our teens and early adulthood, and found myself daydreaming of a couple of the guys on my tour. I could lie and say I tried to suppress those thoughts, but the truth is they are probably the only thing that have kept me sane the last half of the tour.

Justin is twenty-two years old and just graduated from UCLA with a degree in music performance a week before we started the tour. Besides being a musical genius on keyboards (he learned our entire two-hour concert in just a couple of rehearsals), he is every girl's dream and about half the guys' wet dreams. He's the epitome of Mr. All-America: tall, lean, blonde hair and blue eyes, long eye lashes, muscular, with a golden tan and pearl-white perfect smile. Everybody on our tour loves him, and he seemingly loves all of us, too. He's one of those guys who can talk nonstop for hours but never irritate anyone.

Richard is just the opposite, but somehow has managed to consume about as much of my daydreaming time as Justin. Rich is nineteen years old, about five feet seven inches of solid muscle (it's obvious he spends a lot of time at the gym), with jet-black hair and large, beautiful brown, almond-shaped eyes that always seem a little sad. His father is Puerto Rican and his mother is Filippina, which means he has gorgeous, smooth brown skin. He's pretty shy for the most part, but when he opens his mouth to sing, he blows us all away. He has a solo in our show that leaves not a dry eye in the building.

The last time I was host-paired with Justin was three weeks ago in Tulsa, Oklahoma. Our hosts were the Kendalls, a fairly young couple whose only son was also on tour with the Continental Singers, but a different group than ours (there are fifteen different groups touring different parts of the world).

After our show, we all went to the Kendalls' home and talked for about an hour or so before heading to bed shortly after eleven.

I was nervous about stripping down to my underwear for bed in front of Justin that night. I'd been lusting after him since the first night we spent together, and was sure he'd be able to tell and get me kicked off the tour. But he talked softly as he undressed in front of me and climbed into bed still chatting away as if he were none the wiser.

I pulled the covers up to my chin and tried to keep the small talk going for a little while, and then said good night. I noticed Justin was tossing and turning restlessly for quite a while, but figured he was just wound up from the performance and couldn't sleep. About an hour after we laid down, I found my eyelids getting heavy and drifted off to sleep.

I'm not sure how long I'd been asleep when I woke up slowly. I woke up on my side, a little disoriented, not knowing where I was at first. I blinked a few times and remembered we were in Tulsa as I turned over onto my back. Justin was not in bed beside me, and I rubbed my eyes to adjust to the darkness and orient myself a little better.

That's when I noticed the light coming from the doorway to the bathroom that connected to our room. I thought Justin had probably gotten up to pee in the middle of the night, but when I didn't hear the giveaway tinkling from the toilet after a couple of minutes, I got out of bed and walked to the bathroom door. Sometimes the food provided at our potlucks is not the best, and I was just about to knock on the door and ask Justin if he was sick when I heard a low, moaning sound come from inside the bathroom. The door was open just a couple of inches, so I peeked in.

Justin was sitting on the floor, naked, with his back against the bathtub. His long legs were spread wide and one hand was wrapped around his cock, sliding up and down slowly. His head leaned backward and his eyes were closed. His top teeth lightly bit his bottom lip as he gently massaged his hard cock and moaned softly.

I'd dreamed about his dick many times over the past few weeks, and each time his cock looked almost exactly the same. It was always long and thick, with big, bulging veins on it. I guess that's what I expected to see on a guy who was perfect in every way. I was a little surprised to see that in the flesh, it was not quite what I'd expected. It was very average, actually; probably the only part of Justin that was average. Maybe six and a half inches long fully hard, average thickness, cut.

Not that its averageness made it any less appealing to me. On the contrary, just seeing it pulse in his hand and hearing him moan in delight made my heart race wildly. As my own cock grew hard and pressed against my underwear, I felt a large drop of precum ooze out of my piss slit and cover my dick head. I sat on the floor and crossed my legs, making myself more comfortable so I could watch Justin get himself off.

He slid his hand up and down his hard cock very slowly and lovingly, and seemed content to take his time, which was fine with me. A couple of times it looked like he was going to shoot, but then he stopped and moved his hand away from his dick and took a deep breath. I got a clear shot of his full cock when he did that, and found it hard to swallow as I watched it pulse against his belly.

I reached down to touch my own dick a couple of times, but realized I would cream almost instantly if I did, so I just left my dick inside my underwear and returned to watching Justin.

He was in his own little world, oblivious to the fact he was being watched. He repositioned himself a couple of times on the floor to make himself more comfortable, and a couple of times he reached down with his free hand and massaged his balls and the area around his ass as he stroked his cock. I don't know how he kept from shooting several times before he did.

But he obviously had other plans, and what he did next sent me over the edge. He laid flat on his back, lifted his ass off the floor and threw his legs behind his head, so that his dick was only a couple of inches from his mouth. He moaned a little louder, and grabbed his cock in one hand and the back of one of his legs in the other. He pulled down on his leg until the head of his dick just barely touched his lips.

I swear I stopped breathing, and I'm sure the only thing that kept him from hearing me gasp was that his own moaning was even louder.

His tongue licked around the head of his cock a couple of times, and then he slowly sucked the head all the way into his mouth. I'd never imagined this was even possible, and was mesmerized as I watched Justin lick and suck on his own dick head. My heartbeat tripled in my chest and my cock pounded against my underwear as I watched secretly from behind the door.

Justin's face began to turn a little red as he moved both hands to press harder against his legs, and I watched more of his cock slide slowly inside his mouth. He was now quivering a little as he had a couple of inches of his own dick in his mouth, and I could hear him sucking on it pretty strongly.

He opened his eyes and moaned a little louder, and then I saw his entire body convulse for a moment. He stayed in that position for a few seconds, and then let go of his legs, and his cock slowly pulled out of his mouth. With his dick head only an inch away from his mouth, he squeezed his cock with one hand, and a long, final drop of white, silky cum trickled from his cock and onto his tongue.

He swallowed hard and took a deep sigh as his legs un-folded and his body slumped limply onto the floor. I realized I was still sitting there, entranced with Justin's show, and stood up to tiptoe as quietly as possible back to the bed. It wasn't until that moment that I realized the front of my shorts were soaked with hot, sticky cum. I hadn't even touched my own cock and I'd shot a huge load all over myself!

I didn't have time to rummage through my suitcase for a new pair of underwear, since I heard Justin pulling his own on; and so I just ran and jumped into bed, sticky and wet, and pulled the covers over my shoulders, pretending to be asleep.

Justin was in bed and asleep in less than two minutes. I, on the other hand, spent the rest of the night sticky, confused, excited and unable to sleep.

I tried hard not to stare at Justin too much the next few days. I couldn't believe how he kept right on talking and laughing and singing as if nothing out of the ordinary had happened, but I was resolved not to be the one to let it slip. I could be just as good an actor as he. I did, however, make absolutely sure that my roomies were one hundred percent asleep before I found it necessary to slip away quietly into the bathrooms of kind hosts from that point on.

Next week is our last week of tour. We're back in sunny California now, and emotions are at an all-time high. We seem to have forgotten all about the bitching and moaning we've been doing the last half of the tour, and now everyone is crying that we don't want it to end. Addresses are being exchanged, promises never to forget one another, all the same old crap.

Last night's concert was exceptional. Not only have we had three months to perfect it, but it was in Richard's home church, so everyone was that much more hyped. It's always exciting when you perform in one of the member's hometown, and everyone goes out of their way to make it special.

Richard was just as quiet and reserved yesterday as he always is, sitting alone near the back of the bus and writing in his journal. Everyone has a special place in their hearts for him, and was all jittery about performing for his home crowd, but he kept cool the whole time. We unpacked and set up our equipment as usual, and then Roger, our assistant director, gave out our host assignments.

I was a little surprised when I learned I would be staying with Richard at his home. I figured he'd just get to stay by himself. I looked over at him when our names were called out, but he didn't even look up from his journal, so I didn't think anything else about it.

Like I said, the concert went great. Richard's solo drew a rousing standing ovation, and he blushed as he walked back to the bleachers and joined the rest of us. He was so cute. Several of us were teary-eyed as we watched him. We all know he will be famous some day, and are happy for him. But at the moment he was just one of us, and we finished the concert as one of our best.

After the concert, we tore down the equipment and loaded the bus, and then all headed to our host homes. It was a little later than usual, since everyone in Richard's church wanted to chat a little more than most after the concert, and we were exhausted.

Mr. and Mrs. Gomez were the perfect hosts. They could tell Richard and I were tired, and though I'm sure they'd have loved to stay up and talk for hours, they only kept us up for about half an hour before retiring themselves.

Richard showed me his room and we looked through some of his high school yearbooks, laughing and joking around at how cool everyone thought they were. This morning was an early bus board, though, so we decided to hit the sack fairly early.

I offered to sleep on the couch so that Richard could have his bed to himself, but he refused and said it was more than big enough for the both of us. We undressed and laid in bed next to one another, making small talk for a few minutes and then growing quiet.

I was just about to fall asleep when I felt Richard roll over onto his side and face me. I was lying on my side, too, with my back to him, and could feel his soft breath on the back of my neck. I kept my eyes closed, not knowing whether he was awake or asleep, my heart doubling its pounding in my chest. I could still smell the sweet fragrance of his cologne and his minty breath on my neck, and I struggled to keep my breathing normal. I wasn't sure what was happening, but figured feigning sleep was the best course of action.

It seems Richard thought a little differently than me, because a moment later he moved his body even closer to me and draped his arm around my waist, until his front side was spooning my backside. I felt his semi-hard cock press against my ass through my underwear, and couldn't suppress a sigh, hard as I tried.

"Are you awake?" he whispered.

"Yeah." I swallowed hard, and stared straight ahead in the darkness of his room as my heart raced even faster. "I guess winding down from tonight's concert is a little harder than usual. I'm sure it's even worse for you," I whispered back.

"Maybe a little."

"You were great tonight, Richard. I hope you remember all of us when you're big and famous."

My attempt at small talk seemed trivial, but I didn't know what else to do.

He scooted closer to me and hugged me tighter for a moment. His smooth, muscular chest was resting against my shoulder and his face was an inch from my ear. His hand moved slowly under the blanket and caressed my stomach. I tried very hard not to gasp, but don't think I was very successful.

"Look, Chad, I know I can get kicked off the tour for this, but I figure what the hell. There's only a week left, and I'm already home, right?"

His voice sounded a little shaky, but his arms were strong as he turned me onto my back and stared into my eyes from just above me.

"I'm not sure . . ."

"Shhhh," he said and leaned down to kiss me. His lips were soft and sweet with a touch of the Scope he'd used before bed. He cupped my chin in his hands and kissed me harder, letting his tongue trace my lips a couple of times before gently pushing its way into my mouth.

I don't know where the loud ringing in my ears came from, but my head began to spin as Richard's tongue worked its way slowly into and around my mouth. I felt my body go limp (all but one rebellious appendage of it, that is) as I sighed and sucked softly on his probing tongue.

He pulled out from my mouth as he kicked the blankets to the floor and moved his body so that it laid flat on top of mine. His body was hot, and every muscle tight and hard and smooth as it lay gently on me. Even in the dark I could see his eyes never left mine as he stroked my face and down my neck and chest.

"If this isn't cool with you, just let me know," he whispered. "I'm sure we could pretend it never happened and get through this last week."

I wrapped one arm around his thin waist and pulled him down for another kiss.

"This is definitely cool with me."

He smiled and reached down to squeeze my cock gently. I shuddered as I felt his hand caress me. His hand moved from my dick to the top of my underwear, and he pulled them off in one slow move. I was fully hard and my dick throbbed against my stomach. Richard lowered his body back onto mine so that my naked cock was sandwiched between us.

"You feel so good, Chad," he said quietly.

"So do you," I answered, as I reached with both hands into his underwear and let my hands move slowly across his smooth, tight ass for a moment before pulling them off.

He lifted his body so that his underwear could slip down his legs, and his thick, heavy dick flopped onto my stomach, resting right next to my own cock. The skin was soft and silky, and I could feel the heat from it even before it touched my belly.

I tried to show some restraint, I swear I did, but out of nowhere my hand reached down and wrapped around his cock. It was long and thick, and the silky foreskin moved freely across it as I moved my hand slowly up and down the length of his pole.

Richard took a deep breath, and laid flat on his back next to me. He was still smiling, his eyes looking into mine as I kissed him and massaged his cock in my hand.

His mouth was so sweet and his lips so soft, I could have stayed there forever and been happy. But I also wanted to know what the rest of him felt like, so I began moving my kisses down his neck and across his tight, smooth chest. He took another deep breath as my tongue licked his tiny hairless nipples, and I felt his cock twitch wildly in my hand. It was now so thick I could barely wrap my fist around it, and by the time my tongue found its way to Richard's belly button, his cock head and an inch or so of his big shaft was brushing against my chin.

I loved the way his smooth, tight abs felt on my tongue, tightening as I trailed closer and closer to his dick. I kissed his stomach for a few seconds longer, and then stuck my tongue out to reach the tip of his cock. It was hot and wet, with a trail of precum sliding from the slit and across the head and onto my fingers.

I swallowed a little of it nervously. I wasn't quite sure what to expect, having never tasted it before, but I guess I liked it, because before I knew it, I sucked his entire cock head into my mouth and licked hungrily around the head for more of the salty, sticky fluid. I remembered Justin sucking himself off and swallowing his own cum, and wondered if this was what it tasted like as I eagerly licked Richard's cock head until it was dry of his precum.

"Lie down with me," Richard said, and turned me around on the bed so that we were cock-to-mouth.

I was drunk with the taste of his dick, and went right back to the task of licking and sucking on it. I had his entire head and an inch or so of his thick shaft in my mouth when I felt his mouth wrap around my own dick head, and I almost choked. He seemed to enjoy my cock as much as I enjoyed his; and his hot, wet mouth sucked quietly, but with such heat and force that I had to pull out quickly before I shot my load.

Richard pulled me back down to his mouth by my waist, but this time he let my throbbing cock rest across his chin as his tongue licked and kissed its way along the underside of my balls and toward my ass.

I was dizzy with the delight of all that was happening. His tongue licked softly but hungrily across my balls and ass until I thought I'd faint with pleasure. When I stopped to think about it and realized I had half of Richard's thick, uncut dick down my throat, I choked and had to come up for air. I tried to sit up and change positions, but Richard held me tight at the waist, and kept licking around my ass.

"Do you like this?" he asked after a couple of minutes. I could only moan my response.

After a couple more licks, Richard pulled me up and off of him, and kissed me on the mouth again, tenderly. I started to say something, but before I got a chance, he laid me on my stomach on his bed and spread my legs wide. I could no longer see him, but felt his mouth and tongue as they tickled my ass, and heard him open a drawer on the nightstand next to the bed. If I had been thinking clearly, I could probably have figured out what was happening, but at the moment his tongue slid slowly and steadily into my ass, I couldn't even have told you my name.

His tongue felt like wet fire as it slid into and out of my ass. Then he pulled it all the way out and kissed my ass cheeks gently before spreading them and sliding his tongue back inside me. Somewhere along the line Richard added a finger along with his tongue. I couldn't tell you when, because I was delirious with pleasure as I was being opened in ways I'd never imagined. Two probing fingers soon replaced his tongue in my ass, and I felt Richard's kisses moving across the back of my neck.

"Just relax, okay, Chad," I heard him whisper from a million miles away. I heard the ripping of plastic wrap as I wondered to myself how much more relaxed I could possibly get.

He slowly rolled me over onto my back and leaned down to kiss me again. His lips were softer and his tongue sweeter than anything I could remember. I felt the head of his cock press gently on my ass hole, and a second later, realized why I was in the position I was in, and that his kisses were meant to be a distraction.

Richard's cock head slipped inside me with what seemed like

no resistance at all, but once inside, I tightened up and cried out in pain. Richard kept his tongue inside my mouth and held me tightly against him as I tried to wriggle off of his huge pole.

"Shhhh," he whispered and kissed my lips softly, "my parents are right across the hall."

I hadn't realized I'd cried out so loudly the first time, until he started sliding his dick deeper inside, and I groaned out loud again.

"Kiss me, Chad. It won't hurt so bad," he said, and put his lips gently on top of mine.

I certainly didn't see how kissing him would make the pain in my ass hurt less, but he looked so sweet and I trusted him so completely, I did what he told me. I kissed his lips for a second, and when he started moving even more of himself inside me, I slid my tongue into his mouth as I closed my eyes in pain. He wrapped his hot mouth around my tongue and sucked on it softly as he continued moving his hips forward for what seemed like hours. I felt each of his thick, eight inches spread my ass open slowly, and when he was all the way inside me, he rested there for a moment and just kept kissing me.

"You all right?" he whispered in my ear at the same moment I felt myself relax completely and the pain turn to pure pleasure.

I nodded, and a tear trickled down my cheeks. Richard wiped it away and kissed my nose.

"You sure?"

I tightened my ass muscles around his cock and lifted myself deeper onto him in response. He smiled, and even in the dark I saw his brown eyes sparkle as he began to move himself in and out of my ass with a slow, steady rhythm. It wasn't long before I was lifting myself up to meet his deep thrusts with a rhythm of my own, and both of us moaned in pleasure as our bodies seemed to become one.

Richard's eyes never left mine as he fucked me, and he blew me small little kisses every time I raised my ass and squeezed it against his thick cock as it drove deeper inside me. We both struggled not to moan too loudly, extremely aware of his parents sleeping in the room right across the hall.

I had never felt anything like this in my life, and wanted it to go on forever. A couple of times Richard grabbed my cock to stroke it, but I was so close I had to move his hand away. Every nerve in my body was on fire, and just the touch of his hand on my dick would make me shoot.

He was content to just keep fucking me, leaning down for a kiss every couple of minutes, and when he was getting close himself, he stopped thrusting and we both just lay still, his hard cock buried inside me, trying to calm itself down for another few minutes of bliss.

We went on like that for what seemed like hours. I thought I could have gone on forever, but was surprised when my cock shot out a huge jet of cum that flew past my face and landed on Richard's headboard. A couple more followed, landing on my face and chest, even though I hadn't touched my cock since Richard entered me.

With each shot of cum from my cock, I felt my ass tighten even stronger against Richard's thick, uncut cock. He closed his eyes and moaned loudly, oblivious now to his parents' proximity, and shoved himself into me deeply with a couple of thrusts of his hips. Before I knew it, he pulled out, leaving me with an empty feeling I'd never imagined. He quickly ripped the condom from his cock and stood up straight, standing over my quivering body.

The cum flew from his cock like someone had turned on a

faucet at full force. Three shots hit the wall and headboard behind my head. Several more landed on my face and chest and stomach. I was amazed at how much cum was pouring out of Richard's thick brown cock. Instinctively I stuck my tongue out and licked off some that landed on my lips, and was surprised to feel how hot and sweet it was.

When he finished coming, Richard laid down on top of me for a moment, trying to catch his breath. When I felt the heartbeat in his chest return to normal and his breathing slow down, he rolled off me and onto his side next to me.

"I'm so sorry, Chad," he said and began to wipe his dripping cum from my face. "I didn't mean to shoot all over you. I had no idea there'd be that much and it'd get on your face."

"Shhh," I said and licked my lips for any remaining trace of him there. "It's okay. I liked it."

"You did?"

I nodded and smiled. "A lot."

"Me too," he said softly and pulled me down and laid my head against his chest.

We fell asleep with Richard's arms around me almost immediately, and apparently neither of us moved an inch during the night. The next thing I knew, it was morning and Mrs. Gomez was knocking on the bedroom door to wake us up for breakfast.

When he first opened his eyes, Richard had a panicked, guilty look on his face. But when I smiled and leaned over to kiss him on the mouth, he smiled back and hugged me.

Somehow we showered and got through breakfast with what seemed like perfect normality. When we arrived at the church and started loading the bus, no one seemed any different than they had the other ninety-whatever days we'd been on the road, and we were soon off and running to our next city.

Richard sat near the back of the bus where he usually did,

and wrote in his journal, but I noticed several times he looked up and smiled at me when I looked back at him.

About an hour ago, Scott, our director, came over and asked Cynthia if she would trade places with him for a moment. He needed to speak with me. My heart raced, as I just knew he'd found out about last night, and was kicking me off the tour. But I couldn't have been further from the truth.

"Chad, I noticed last week when we sent around the form asking everyone if they were going to tour again next year or not, you put down that you were undecided."

"Yeah. I'm just not sure I can afford to take another summer off," I said hesitantly.

"Would you consider touring if I could make it a little more affordable for you?"

"What do you mean?"

"I've been asked to direct the eastern European tour next year. That tour has been my personal goal for three years now, and I'm very excited about it."

"Congratulations, Scott," I said, and hugged him.

"Thanks. I'd like for you to be my assistant director next year."

"What?" I couldn't believe my ears.

"It's a lot of work, as you know. Coordinating communications with the churches and schools, disciplining other tour members, assigning members with their host families, even directing the group a few times. Well, you know all that Roger has done on this tour."

"Yeah, it's a lot of work."

"Yes, it is. But it's fun and rewarding, too. And it pays really well I might add."

"I don't know, Scott."

"Come on Chad, I'd really like you to. Several members of

this group are already confirmed to go with me next year, because I specifically want them there. Karla, Veronica, Richard, Justin, Beth, and Leo have all said yes. That just leaves you now. What do you say?"

I glanced back at Richard. He had both hands brought to his lips in a pleading pose, and he winked at me and smiled.

"Sure, I'd be happy to," I said as I turned back to Scott.

"Great! We'll iron out the details and sign the contract when we get back to L.A. Thanks, Chad, I really appreciate it. I think we'll have a great time."

I laid my head back in the seat and closed my eyes, already thinking of all the great times that lay ahead for me next summer. Being assistant director was a great responsibility. Richard was gonna tour with me again, and so was Justin. I couldn't wait to start handing out the host family assignments! Oh, and all the other responsibilities too, of course!

Best Man

God damn this rain. Jon clutched the arm of his seat as the plane took another small dip, and he gnashed his back teeth together. God damn the pilot who must have just graduated from junior flight school and could not control the turbulence. God damn the lightning outside the plane, and the fat woman next to him who kept trying to talk to him while she shoved another bag of peanuts in her mouth, and the man in the seat in front of him who leaned back as far as his seat would recline and commented on how incredible the storm was and refused to close his window shade. And while he was at it, God damn his baby sister for having to get married on Sunday and who insisted he fly out to be a groomsman. She knew he was terrified of flying. Surely she had inside information of this hurricane-force storm he was flying through, and had probably gone to great lengths to make sure he was on this particular flight. God damn her.

Jon had no idea what standard the airline industry used when determining when it was safe for flight attendants to be up and about, serving food and beverages and smiling like the Cheshire cat. But he was astonished beyond words when he saw the pretty attendant rolling the beverage cart down the aisle toward him. He was sure the oxygen masks were going to come rushing out of their compartments any time now. Jon was one of those passengers who actually followed along with the safety instruction cards as the attendants explained emergency procedures. He always kept his seat belt fastened while seated; these warnings were given for a reason, after all. And if he were by chance assigned a seat next to an emergency exit, he always asked to be reseated. If the plane were to take a dive or hit water, it was every man for himself, and he certainly could not be expected to help anyone else get out of the plane before he was out.

"Would you care for anything to drink, sir?" the attendant asked, already filling a plastic cup with ice. The fat woman next to Jon was reaching into the cart for a handful of little bags of peanuts, and the flight attendant watched her with amusement.

"Vodka and tonic, please," Jon said. "Three of them."

The stewardess's head jerked around from the peanut lady to Jon. "Sir, we'll be beginning our descent into Denver in about twenty minutes. You won't have time to have three drinks."

"Three, please. Here's the twelve dollars for the drinks and eight for your tip. I'll have time."

The fat peanut lady and the pretty flight attendant both looked at him with the same bewildered look on their faces.

"Sir?"

Jon waved the twenty-dollar bill in front of the attendant, and gave her a look that said, "Don't mess with me . . . I'm in a very damning mood right now and you could be next."

She took the money from his hand and gave him three little bottles of Smirnoff and a can of tonic water. The look of disapproval on her face was unmistakable as she moved on to take the orders of the other less gluttonous passengers. Jon didn't care. Damn her, anyway.

He needed these drinks to get through this flight. And he had no idea what to expect when he landed in Denver. His sister had planned on meeting him at the airport, but called at the last minute and said she was going to be stuck in New York overnight. Jon would have to stay at her place by himself tonight, and she would see him tomorrow morning when she got in. She left the key with Robbie, her next door neighbor, and asked him to pick Jon up at the airport. He'd never met Robbie, knew nothing about him as a matter of fact. He certainly wasn't going to feel like chatting it up with a stranger after this flight through hell, and thought that if he had to do so, he at least deserved to have a few drinks in him first.

The landing was surprisingly smooth. Jon was sure the pilot had improved considerably in the last twenty minutes, and that it had nothing to do with the Smirnoff. He was up and out of his seat before the plane had come to a full and complete stop and the seat belt light had been turned off. On the ground and safe, he felt a little more rebellious. He handed the fat woman next to him his full bag of peanuts, knowing she would stay seated until the bag was empty, and stepped over her into the aisle so that he could get his carry on bag and get off the plane as quickly as possible.

He stepped out of the walk tunnel and into the spacious gate lobby area and took a deep breath. He was safe. In Denver, a strange city for him, far removed from his home in Los Angeles, having no idea where he was going and knowing not a soul in the city. But safe.

He looked around the gate area for any sign of Robbie. Karen hadn't told Jon anything about her neighbor, so he had no idea what to look for. There was a middle-aged, gray-haired man holding a briefcase and watching the gate expectantly. He doubted this gentleman called himself Robbie, and his doubts were confirmed when a young brunette ran into his arms, full of kisses. A couple of teenage punk rock boys played longingly with cigarettes clipped above their ears, but it didn't look like they were waiting for anyone on this flight.

"Jon?" the deep male voice came from behind his ears.

Jon turned around and looked at the young man who'd spoken his name. He tried to swallow but was unable to. Standing in front of him was the most beautiful man he'd ever seen. About six feet tall, with slightly wet, wavy blonde hair and sparkling blue eyes accented with long curly eyelashes, he looked directly into Jon's eyes and smiled. His face wore a two-day stubble that seemed almost groomed, and a pair of dimples peeked shyly out from the shadow. His smile revealed perfect white teeth.

"You're Jon, right? Karen's brother from L.A?"

"Uhh, yes. I'm sorry. You must be Robbie."

"Yeah." Robbie laughed softly. "But please call me Rob. Your sister insists on treating me like a little kid. Hopefully it doesn't run in the family."

"Okay, Rob it is," Jon said, and held out his hand. "Nice to meet you."

"Ditto. Is this all you have?" he asked, nodding toward Jon's carry-on which was slung over his shoulder.

"Yeah, I travel light."

"Cool, let's get outta here. Did you eat on the plane?"

"No," Jon answered, realizing he'd given his only source of nourishment to the woman sitting next to him.

"Good. I rushed over here straight from the gym and didn't have time to eat myself. Let's grab a bite before we head home, what do you say?"

"Perfect. I'm starved."

The drive from Denver International Airport into Denver was almost as agonizing as the flight. Not because of turbulence or fat women who spoke with chunks of peanuts hanging on her teeth, but because Jon could not keep his eyes away from Robbie. He was still dressed in his workout shorts and a skimpy tank top. His muscular legs, covered with a soft layer of curly blonde hair, flexed every time he moved his feet to the clutch to switch gears. His pecs, smooth as silk, stretched the tank top across them, and his nipples peeked out the side of it, small but hard. His hand laid lazily across the steering wheel and his arm muscles tightened slightly with each turn. Jon noticed Robbie wasn't wearing a wedding ring, and swallowed hard as he looked out his window to avoid slobbering all over himself as he stared at his sister's neighbor.

They pulled into the parking lot of a quaint little Chinese restaurant, and Robbie pulled his gym bag from the backseat of his Acura.

"I was running late from the gym and didn't have a chance to change into my decent clothes. This isn't exactly a black tie kinda restaurant, but I think they'd frown on my wearing sweaty gym clothes in there. You don't mind if I change real quick, do you?"

He was already pulling a pair of jeans and a long sleeve denim shirt from his gym bag. Jon forced himself to blink and take a deep breath before he said, "No, that's fine."

He pretended to look for something in his own bag as Robbie stripped his tank top from his shoulders. Jon couldn't help but look out of the corners of his eyes and peek at the magnificent body next to him. Robbie's torso was completely hairless, smooth and rock hard. His firm pecs rounded down to perfect tiny nipples that stood at attention. His stomach boasted a perfect six-pack, hard and defined and defied several laws of nature, Jon was sure.

He made quite a production of moving some clothes around in his bag, grunting as if he were upset he couldn't find anything, just as Robbie kicked off his tennis shoes and moved his hands to his gym shorts. He hadn't bothered to put on the shirt he'd pulled from his gym bag. Jon looked out of the corner of his eyes again in time to see him loop his thumbs into the waistband of his white gym shorts and pull them slowly down his thick muscular legs. It took all he had not to moan out loud as Robbie threw the shorts and tank top into the backseat. Robbie leaned up and twisted a little to reach the backseat, and when he did, his hips tilted up and moved a few inches closer to Jon.

Jon couldn't help it. He had to look. Robbie was wearing only a jockstrap and a pair of white socks now; and as he moved to toss the clothes in the backseat, his hips thrust his crotch in Jon's direction. Jon looked at the jockstrap and his mouth felt like the Mojave desert. He could clearly see the outline of Robbie's dick as it stretched the fabric of the jockstrap. It was long and thick and curved down to cup the balls. It looked like it was barely able to be constrained by the material.

Jon forced himself to look away while Robbie finished dressing, and was grateful when they were finally ready to go inside.

Dinner was almost impossible. He had no idea what he ordered, nor if he enjoyed it or not. Throughout dinner, he was mesmerized with Robbie. As they spoke (about what, Jon would never be able to recall) he was transfixed on the beautiful face in front of him. Robbie ate three helpings of his food, and seemed to enjoy it very much. When he spoke between bites, Jon couldn't move his eyes from the full, pink lips as they moved together and then parted to show those pearly white teeth. And when he licked some of the sauce from his mouth, his tongue seemed to dance across his lips. Robbie spoke very excitedly about the work he was doing with a group of runaway kids and about his workouts, and he laughed heartily, seemingly oblivious to the effect he was having on Jon.

The effect was that Jon had a raging hard-on from the time Robbie began changing clothes in the car and all throughout dinner. Thank God they were seated at a booth and no one could see. Jon was confused about this hard-on. He shouldn't have it, but it felt so good. The past three months had been a rough time for him. He broke up with his girlfriend of four years, seemingly for no apparent reason. It hurt her deeply, he knew that. But probably not as much as it would have hurt her had she known he was not turned on by her anymore. Whenever they were together he could only think about his new assistant at work. Matthew.

He had no idea where the thoughts came from, and he certainly hadn't acted on them. But every waking minute seemed to pass with him daydreaming about sucking Matthew's dick or having Matthew kiss him while jacking him off. Two weeks after he hired Matthew, he broke up with Melissa; stating simply that he needed to sort through some important issues in his life and he needed to be alone to do it. With Melissa no longer in his bed or his house, it was easier for Jon to "sort through" those issues. He spent every night beating off while dreaming about Matthew, remembering the smell of his cologne on that day and the way his ass muscles flexed when he walked. He'd come more in the last three months without Melissa than he had in the four years they were together.

But he was confused about these feelings. Surely he wasn't gay, that couldn't be possible. He'd had steady girlfriends all his life, and until Matthew, had never given any thought whatsoever to another guy. Until now.

He put his hand discreetly in his lap and gently massaged the hard-on pressed against his jeans as he watched Robbie ramble on about who knew what. His cock tingled as his hand rubbed the head and moved slowly up and down the length of the shaft. It didn't take a full minute of this before Jon felt the familiar tightening of his balls and thickening of his cock. He moved his hand away from his crotch and put it back on the table just in time. He'd almost blown his load right there in the restaurant and in his jeans.

God damn Robbie, anyway.

They paid their check and drove the short distance to the duplex Karen shared with Robbie. Robbie talked the entire trip, barely stopping long enough to breathe. When they got to Karen's place, Robbie came in and showed Jon around. When he had made sure Jon was comfortable and settled in, he said good night and told Jon he'd be right next door if he needed anything.

It was a little after ten, and Jon was exhausted and decided to go straight to bed. He still hadn't lost the hard-on he'd gotten in the car watching Robbie change clothes, and knew he'd have to take care of that before he'd get a wink of sleep. He lay on top of his sister's bed and took his cock in his hand. His body shuttered as his fist closed around the shaft and moved slowly up and down. He closed his eyes and thought of Robbie undressing in the car, and moaned softly as he felt a drop of precum squeeze out of the head of his cock. He played with the slippery liquid for a little bit, rubbing it around his head, and then more down the shaft. It only took a couple of minutes before he felt like he would explode. He was dripping more precum now, and it flowed easily down the length of his cock, lubricating it and causing Jon to thrust his cock hard and fast into his hand.

It happened before he could even prepare himself for it. Stream after stream of cum shot out of his cock. Two jets raced past his head and landed on the headboard, another landed on his cheeks, and several more on his chest and stomach. His eyes bulged as he watched shot after shot of hot cum fly from his dick. He'd never shot this much in his life, and was fascinated with the force of his own orgasm.

When he finished shooting his load, he simply laid limp on the bed, and drifted off to sleep, his cum left to dry on his body.

Jon was a sound sleeper, and didn't hear the front door to Karen's apartment open and close quietly. His dreams were intriguing, and kept his full attention. They were of Matthew and of Robbie. He'd walked in on them while they were making love in his office on his desk. Oh, how angry he was; infuriated that his trusted assistant and this new beautiful boy had desecrated his desk with their animal lust. They were embarrassed and nervous and pleaded with him not to report them to the police. He thought there might be a way around that; and before he had a chance to strip his clothes off, the two boys were on their knees in front of him, pulling his dick out of his pants and licking it.

Jon's dick was throbbing, and the hot mouths on his cock felt so real. He'd never had a dream this hot before, and wanted it to last forever. He felt his legs being pushed slightly apart, and stirred himself awake. He opened his eyes slowly and as they adjusted to the dark room and focused, he saw he was not alone in the bed. He started to jump up, but a strong hand gently pushed him back down onto the bed.

"Just lie back and relax," the deep voice said.

Jon was fully awake now, and knew the mouth wrapped around his dick was Robbie's. His heart pounded hard and he didn't know whether he should get up and make Robbie leave, or just lie back and relax, as he was told.

Robbie's mouth was warm and soft, and his tongue darted lightly around Jon's cock head. He maneuvered himself between Jon's legs and took hold of his balls and rolled them gently in his strong hands. His mouth slowly began to slide down more and more of Jon's big dick, and before long, he had the full eight inches buried deep in his hot mouth.

Jon moaned loudly and moved his hands to Robbie's head. His hair was so soft and silky. Robbie must have liked it, because he moaned when Jon ran his fingers through his hair, and the soft moan caused a little vibration around Jon's cock. Robbie deepthroated Jon's dick for a couple of minutes and then pulled his mouth slowly from the big dick, licking the shaft as he came off it.

"Do you like that?" he asked as he moved his mouth to Jon's ear.

"Yes," Jon whispered.

Robbie slipped his tongue into Jon's ear and lightly traced his way around and inside until Jon was wriggling in delight. His cock was throbbing harder than ever.

"I taste cum on your face, Jon. Did you shoot already?" Robbie whispered.

Jon's heartbeat rushed erratically. He forgot he'd already shot a huge load just a few hours . . . minutes . . . ago.

"I'm sorry. I should've washed up."

"No. I like it."

Robbie kissed around Jon's ear, nibbling softly, and traced Jon's entire face with his soft kisses. Jon had never been kissed by another man before, and he felt the blood flow madly through his body with excitement and nervousness.

When Robbie's mouth reached Jon's, Jon drew in a deep breath, and without realizing it, closed his mouth.

Robbie reached down and wrapped his hand around Jon's thick cock, and squeezed it. When Jon moaned loudly, Robbie knew he was ready, and he moved his mouth back to Jon's. He reached out with his tongue and traced lightly around Jon's lips, licking and tickling them softly. Then he put his lips on Jon's and kissed him. He could feel Jon's mouth tighten a little at first, but when he moved his tongue back to Jon's lips, it slipped easily into Jon's mouth.

The two men kissed passionately for several minutes, and it was Robbie who broke it.

"I want you to suck my dick, Jon. Will you do that for me?"

Jon looked up into Robbie's angelic face, and before he knew what he was doing, he nodded his head yes.

Robbie smiled and moved his body slowly up the length of Jon's, until his dick was in front of Jon's face. Jon swallowed hard and stared at the dick for a moment. It was about seven inches long, thick and veiny. The short blonde hairs were clipped short around the base, and the big balls were smooth and hung low and heavy. It was throbbing excitedly, and Jon wondered how he was ever going to suck it.

"You okay?" Robbie asked.

Jon nodded yes, and decided the only thing to do was to jump right in. He leaned forward a little and stuck his tongue out until it touched the head of Robbie's dick. It was hot and hard, and Jon was surprised to find how good it felt on his tongue. He circled the head a couple of times, and then wrapped his lips around the head and sucked softly on it.

Robbie moaned his delight, and pushed a little more of his dick inside Jon's mouth. He rubbed his fingers through Jon's hair and gently pulled his head farther down his cock. Jon choked on the dick as it slid back into his throat, and Robbie pulled out of his mouth.

"Here, let me show you how," he said, and maneuvered himself into a sixty-nine position.

He took Jon's thick cock, and sucked gently on the head. Jon followed his cue and sucked on just the head of Robbie's cock. He could feel the precum sliding out of his own cock head and wondered why Robbie didn't have any. Robbie didn't seem to mind though; and in fact, licked it up and swallowed it with what seemed to Jon like pleasure.

Jon decided he liked sucking dick after all, and once that decision was out of the way, he swallowed Robbie's cock deep into his throat. He gagged only once, and then learned how to open his throat so the thick, veiny cock could easily slide down his warm, wet tunnel.

Robbie was sucking Jon's fat cock so expertly, and taking it deep into his throat where he tightened his throat muscles around the throbbing dick. Jon thrust his hips forward, fucking Robbie's face with his dick, and felt his balls tighten at the base of his cock.

"I'm gonna come, Robbie," he gasped.

"Call me Rob," Rob said as he pulled his mouth from Jon's pulsing dick, "and no you're not. Not yet."

"What?"

"I don't want you to come this way."

"Why not?" Jon asked, stunned. He was so close and it felt so good.

"I want you to fuck me."

Jon just stared at Rob with a dazed look on his face. He watched as Rob opened a condom and slid it down his hard dick. Rob spit some saliva in his hand and rubbed it onto his ass. He leaned over and kissed Jon soft on the lips again, and in the same move, lowered his ass onto Jon's cock.

He moaned loudly and bit softly on Jon's tongue as his hot, tight ass slid all the way down the big pole in one move. When every inch of Jon's dick was buried deep inside Rob's ass, Rob stopped moving and just sat still for a moment, kissing Jon and breathing heavily. Jon's dick was throbbing inside Rob's ass, and he was seriously concerned he would shoot then and there. Rob must have sensed he was close, because he didn't move at all, and when Jon tried to move, he held him still and said, "Wait."

When he was sure Jon wouldn't shoot immediately, Rob began tightening his ass muscles around Jon's big, thick dick, squeezing it and slowly sliding up and down its length. Jon reached up and began playing with Rob's nipples as he slowly thrust his dick in and out of Rob's tight ass. He could only thrust his cock a few strokes before he felt the impending orgasm creeping up, and would have to stop and just rest inside the hot ass.

Rob was practicing his own restraint exercises, because Jon's cock felt better than any he could remember having up his ass. Karen's brother was so damn cute, and nice, and that huge dick was almost more than he could take all at once. He'd been fucked a few times, but never like this. Everything about this man seemed perfect, and now, with his big dick up his ass, Rob was on the verge of losing control.

He reached behind him and found the sensitive spot between Jon's cock and ass. He licked his finger and massaged around Jon's ass for a few moments. Jon moaned lustfully as he felt Rob's finger probing his butt, and grabbed Rob's cock while he thrust his dick deeper and harder into Rob's ass.

Jon's big dick was hitting all the right spots, and Rob knew he wouldn't be able to take much more of it before he came.

He thrust his finger deep into Jon's ass in one swift move, and slid his ass down hard on the big cock, squeezing it with his ass muscles as it slid down the thick pole.

"Oh, fuck, Rob, I'm gonna come," Jon said, and buried his dick into his friend's ass and held it still.

Rob felt Jon's dick thicken as it shot several jets of cum inside him. At the same time, Jon's ass twitched hotly around his finger. That was all it took for Rob, and with only a soft moan of ecstasy, he shot all over Jon's body. Hot cum shot out of his dick and landed on Jon's face, chest and stomach. There was so much of it that Jon had to close his eyes to keep it from blinding him. Rob's hot, throbbing ass milked the last drop of cum from his dick, and when Rob finished showering him with cum, he opened his eyes.

Rob was looking directly into his eyes, a smile on his face. He slid off Jon's dick and lay next to him on the bed.

"Fuck me," Jon said, not able to express the elation he felt.

"You liked it?"

"My God, yes. I hope it won't be the last time."

"Oh, I'm sure it won't."

"I take it you're coming to Karen's wedding?" Jon asked.

"Uh, yeah. I kinda have to."

"Have to?"

"I'm the best man. Karen is marrying my brother."

"What?" Jon laughed. "Oh, my God. Does she know you're gay?"

Rob laughed, too. "Of course. And she knows you are, too."

"What?"

Rob reached over and pounded on the wall a couple of times. Jon just looked at him like he was crazy, and in about twenty seconds the phone rang.

"My bedroom is on the other side of this wall," Rob said. "That's for you." He nodded toward the phone.

Jon picked up the phone "Hello."

"Hi, big brother. Welcome to Denver."

"Karen? Where are you?"

He heard three soft knocks on the bedroom wall.

"Oh, my God!" Jon cried, and dropped the phone to the floor as he buried himself in Rob's arms.

Rodeo Romance

The Marlboro Man is a god in this town. Tall, dark and handsome, and more than just a little mysterious with that black cowboy hat shadowing most of his face. I am the farthest thing from a cowboy myself, but I must admit that looking at the billboards and magazine ads of this strong, virile icon of butchness has raised more than just my attention on occasion.

Gary and Tim, my two best friends, have been harping on me for a couple of months to come to Charlie's, Denver's gay country and western bar. It is their haunt and they have been tirelessly trying to get me to check it out. The guys are not all cowboys, they assured me, and those that are, are cute cowboys.

I finally agreed to meet them and check it out. It was traumatic for me just getting ready for my first night in Hicksville. I put on my most ragged pair of jeans, discarding the urge to go outside and roll around in the dirt after putting them on. I have my limits. I do not own a cowboy hat, boots or a flannel shirt, and almost cried as I found myself at a loss for something cowboyish to wear. After trying almost everything in my closet and checking it out in the mirror, I decided on a sweatshirt and my oldest pair of Doc Martin's.

Fuck 'em if they can't take a joke. And if Gary or Tim said one goddamned word about my clothes, I'd slap them both and walk out the door. I hadn't wanted to come here anyway. But the almighty annual Colorado Gay Rodeo starts tomorrow, and my two best friends promised me that Charlie's would be wall-to-wall gorgeous men, most of them from out of town, and I wouldn't believe the cruising that would be going on. So I agreed to come.

I walked into the bar and decided I was quickly dying from secondhand smoke inhalation. Mr. Marlboro was not only rugged, handsome and mysterious. He was also rich, from the looks of the amount of smoke in this crowd. The cloud of smoke in the room was almost thick enough to hold my drink in midair. I could see about half the tiny dance floor through the haze . . . if I squinted. I kept running out to the patio every five minutes to breathe, and I cursed my friends each time I caught my breath.

They were late, of course. Undoubtedly Gary's fag hag Ginger called him just as he was walking out the door and Tim got sidetracked with one of his semi-famous porn star acquaintances at the Wrangler. They were always the same excuses. I, of course was on time, as always, and getting more pissed off by the minute at having to wait for them alone in a strange place.

"Is it always this crowded?" The voice was deep and twinged with a slight southern accent. And it scared the hell out of me. I turned around to see who'd sneaked up behind me.

Someone had ripped the picture from the billboard, shrunk him down to size and plopped him right in front of me. It was the Marlboro Man, right down to the tilted cowboy hat and five o'clock shadow. He was easily six-four, with deep black hair and beautiful gray eyes. I pushed my chest out and straightened my posture, to make myself as tall and butch as possible.

"Uhh, I don't know," I answered, "this is my first time here."

"Really? Are you from out of town, too?"

"No. Just not much into the country scene. I'm supposed to be meeting some friends here."

"I see. That's too bad."

"Oh, they're just friends, really."

"No." he laughed. "That you're not into the country scene."

"Oh, well, some of it isn't so bad," I stumbled, realizing I may have given him the idea I wasn't interested.

He smiled and took a big swallow of his beer, finishing it in one gulp.

"Can I buy you a beer?" he asked.

"Sure," I answered, resisting the temptation to ask for a Long Island Iced Tea instead. As he walked to the patio bar to get our beers, I noticed his tight round ass and long muscular legs. A hot flash rushed through my body and I ran my hand quickly through my hair.

I'd never really been attracted to a real cowboy before. They seemed dumb and smelly and clumsy when I saw them on TV. But my Marlboro Man was nothing like that. He was quiet, yet confident; he walked with the grace of a lion and he smelled wonderfully of Tommy.

Gary and Tim came ambling onto the patio while my cowboy was still at the bar. As usual, they looked like they hadn't a care in the world and that being almost an hour late was perfectly normal.

"Nice of you to drop by," I greeted them.

"Sorry," Gary started, "Ginger . . ."

"Yeah, I know the routine."

"Why are you out here?" Tim asked, "It's freezing."

"I can't breathe inside. Besides, I'm being courted."

"Oh, the duchess has found herself a duke," Gary quipped. "Where is he?"

"At the bar."

Gary and Tim both turned to look at the bar. There were several people crowded around the small window.

"The tall one with the hat."

"The cowboy with the nice ass?" Tim asked and raised his eyebrow.

"I know, he isn't my type at all. But wait until you see him up close. He's gorgeous."

"I can see he's gorgeous from here," Gary said. "A little old for you, isn't he? I mean, he must already have pubic hair."

"Shut up, bitch," I answered, "here he comes."

He returned with our beers and I introduced my two friends. We found out his name was Bronson and he was in town for the rodeo from Phoenix. He was staying with his ex and would be here two weeks altogether. The four of us talked for about half an hour before Tim started flirting with Bronson and I shooed him and Gary away so I could be alone with my cowboy.

Bronson and I talked for another ten minutes or so and then he told me he had to head home and get some rest. He had to get up early for the rodeo's opening exercise. I wanted desperately to take him home, but he just smiled and said he appreciated the offer but had to be at the rodeo site at five o'clock in the morning and had a friend coming by to pick him up.

"But I'll be really disappointed if you don't show up tomorrow to watch me."

"Oh, I'm not the rodeo kinda guy. Never been to one as a matter of fact."

"Then how do you know you're not the rodeo kinda guy?"

"Well, I've never slept with a woman either, and I know I'm not straight," I said, then blushed when I realized how stupid it sounded.

"You've got a point." He laughed. "But will you make an exception?"

My knees almost buckled as I saw him leaning toward me. He tilted his head to the side and kissed me softly on the lips. His lips tasted lightly of Corona and spearmint gum, and I breathed deeply as his tongue slipped just inside my mouth.

"For me?"

"Okay," I said.

"I'll see you tomorrow, then," he said and squeezed my hand before he walked away.

I sat down on one of the patio chairs and shook my head to get the blood flowing up there again. Less than ten seconds later Tim and Gary came stumbling through the door, clucking like a couple of old hens.

"Sooo?" Gary inquired.

"What's the story?" Tim asked.

"No story."

"Come on, duchess," Gary said, "don't make us drag it out of you."

"Looks like I'm going to the rodeo tomorrow," I said, and smiled.

My two best friends looked at each other and broke into uncontrollable laughter at the same time. Tim started to choke on his beer, and the three of us walked back inside to the smokehouse.

The rodeo started at noon, but I decided to be fashionably late. I arrived at twelve-oh-five, just in time to see most of the parade of participants. Phoenix had the largest contingent, other than Denver of course, but I had no trouble finding Bronson. He would be riding a bull (of course) later in the competition.

The parade was long, and once the Phoenix guys and gals passed, became quite boring. I left the stands and went in search of some food. There were about eight food stands a little ways from the bleachers and rodeo arena. I was hungry and feeling quite manly in the cow shit atmosphere, and so I decided on a hot dog, a cheeseburger, a barbecue beef sandwich with chips and a large Pepsi. I ate about half of each of them, but my plate looked impressive to those passersby who chose to look.

After eating I decided to go shopping. There was a huge tent behind the stands that housed about thirty vendor tables. Vendors from Denver and visiting cities sold jewelry, clothing, toys, stuffed animals, and everything else you can think of. I bought a rainbow ring, a T-shirt and a belt.

As I walked out of the shopping tent I felt two strong arms grab me from behind. One wrapped around my head with a large hand clasped over my mouth, the other wrapped around my chest, pinning my arms to my chest. My eyes bulged in terror as I felt myself being dragged, effortlessly despite my attempted struggle, past the porta potties and into the area where they kept the animal trailers. I could hear the announcer saying the calf-roping event was just about to start, and thought to myself I'd be killed while some poor little calf was having his legs tied up in the air. Oh, how I'd switch places with that baby cow in a heartbeat!

My abductor led me to a large trailer that I assume had carried a few horses and forced me up the ramp and inside, where several bales of hay were stacked up against the far wall. He released his strong grip on me and turned me around to face him.

It was Bronson, and I dropped my shopping bag and began to tremble as I looked at him.

He was even more handsome than I remembered from last night. He was wearing a southwestern-designed western shirt that highlighted his beautiful gray eyes, and a crisp pair of Wrangler jeans. The same cowboy hat as last night, but now it was pulled back high on his forehead, allowing more of his deep black hair to fall across his face. He hadn't shaved since last night, and his stubble had grown just long enough to make him sexier than ever. He smiled impishly and leaned in to me and kissed me softly on the lips.

"Sorry about being so rough," he said shyly.

"That's okay," I said, trying to catch my breath. "I kinda liked it."

"I thought you would." He smiled again.

I took his hands and placed them on my hips as I leaned into him and kissed him hard on the lips. I tasted the spearmint gum he likes to chew, and sucked softly on his tongue to taste even more. His strong hands pulled my hips closer to him, and as we kissed I felt him get hard against my stomach.

"Oh, man," Bronson gasped as we broke our kiss, "I really need you."

"Yeah?"

"Oh, yeah."

"Well, I'm all yours," I said and gave him a light peck on the lips. "What time are you finished here?"

"No, I mean now."

"What?" I stepped back and looked at him with my best Scarlett O'Hara look. "Right now? Here?"

"Yes. Bull riding is next and I'm second up. I have about twenty minutes before I'm up."

"Well, can't we wait until you're finished? We could go back to my place."

"I can't. I'm announcing a couple of events starting at three o'clock. I can't leave. Besides"—he moved my hand to his crotch—"I have this little problem. I won't ride worth shit if we don't take care of it now."

"Bronson, we're in a *horse trailer*!"

He smiled and began to unbutton my shirt.

"A horse trailer, Bronson," I repeated weakly.

He leaned down and began kissing my neck softly as he continued to take off my shirt. He let the shirt drop carelessly to the floor and caressed my bare chest with his hands. His left hand moved down and gently squeezed my groin.

"Horse trailers are nice," I whispered, and gave in to my cowboy.

I quickly and gracelessly tore the shirt from his body. I gasped as I saw his strongly muscled and slightly hairy chest. The hair got thicker and heavier right under his navel, and disappeared into his jeans. My mouth was dry as I began to unbuckle his belt and slide his jeans down his long muscular legs.

He pulled me close to his body and kissed me as he slipped his boots and jeans off in one smooth movement. When he was completely naked he pulled the jeans from my legs and grasped my ass with his strong hands. He moaned and pressed our bodies together. I felt his hard cock throbbing against my stomach and took a deep breath as his tongue slipped slowly in and out of my mouth.

He broke our kiss and led me by my hand over to the bed of hay. There was a blanket lying beside the hay, and he quickly spread it out across the makeshift bed and laid me gently on it. Then he laid down beside me and wrapped me in his strong arms. I was spooned against him, my back against his chest. His cock was hard and hot against my ass cheeks, and I couldn't wait any longer to have it.

I turned around and moved down to his crotch. I was surprised when I saw it. Inside his jeans and against my ass it felt much bigger than it really was. Not that it was small by any means; about seven inches long but very fat with thick throbbing veins. It radiated enough heat to fuel a small apartment, and throbbed with an almost musical beat.

I wrapped my lips around the thick head and slid my tongue around it a couple of times. Bronson moaned softly and ran his hands through my hair. I looked up and saw his gray eyes were sparkling. He smiled and I moved my mouth from his cock head and slid my tongue slowly up and down the length of his dick. I loved the way his thick, throbbing veins tickled my tongue as it worked its way down and around his hot thick cock.

"Oh, baby, that feels good," Bronson moaned.

"You like that?"

"Oh, yeah."

"Well, maybe you'll like this, too," I said, and very slowly swallowed the entire length and girth of his hot dick. I felt the head slip into my throat and kept it there for a moment, squeezing it with my throat muscles. Bronson moaned louder and lifted his hips from the blanket, trying to get even more of his dick deeper into my throat. He was already buried inside though, with his balls pressing against my chin.

I pulled my mouth back a little, sliding my lips up and down his shaft. About every fifth time down I swallowed him completely. I loved the feel of his thick dick sliding all the way down my throat and feeling the veins pound wildly against my muscles there. Apparently Bronson loved it too. After about five minutes of this sucking action he began to breathe heavily, and held my head down against his groin.

I tightened my mouth even harder around his cock and sucked like a baby with a bottle. I felt his body tighten and his dick expand even thicker inside my mouth. He quickly pulled me off his cock, but not quite in time. The first shot of hot cum landed on my tongue just as he pulled out of my mouth. It was hot and sweet as I swallowed it, just as the rest of his load landed hotly on my face and chest.

My own dick was throbbing wildly also, despite the fact that neither of us had even touched it. I was not close to coming though, and was a little disappointed that we were finished already.

"I'm not close yet," I whispered in Bronson's ear. "Can you suck me a little?"

"No," he said, and I looked surprised. "I really want to, but I don't have time to suck you and still fuck you, too."

"What?" I asked and looked down at his cock. It was not only still fully hard, but still pulsing excitedly.

"Can I fuck you? Please?"

I wanted nothing more badly, and let him know. He was still lying on his back, so I moved myself up to his chest. He pulled his jeans to his side and removed a condom from the pocket. While he opened the packet and slid the rubber down his cock, I moved my cock closer to his mouth. He sucked softly on the head and first inch or so while he was preparing his dick to enter my ass.

His mouth felt really good on my dick, but I knew we only had a few minutes before he'd be called for his bull riding, so I did away with most of the preliminaries. I held his dick in my right hand and moved my ass down to it. Taking a deep breath, I lowered myself onto his dick until I felt the head slip in. The thickness of it sent bolts of sharp pain up my spine, and I tried to pull it out, but Bronson held me still on it. He didn't try to push any more of his cock inside me until he felt me relax.

It didn't take long. My Marlboro Man had gotten me so excited and I wanted him inside me more than I'd wanted anyone in a long time. I relaxed all at once, and slid down Bronson's thick cock in one smooth movement. He moaned loudly as his cock pushed its way deep inside my ass. When his balls reached my ass cheeks he rested there for a moment, and then began moving his hips up and around in circles. It sent shockwaves through my body, and I gasped for breath as my ass muscles tightened around his hot cock.

Someone pounded on the side of the trailer and I nearly screamed.

"Bronson, you in there?" the stranger called.

"Yeah, out in a minute," Bronson answered, never missing a stroke of his cock into my ass.

"Calvin is mounting now. You've got about three minutes buddy."

"Got it!" Bronson said loudly. "Thank you."

His cock was pounding in and out of my ass with lightning-like speed. I could tell he was getting close because his breathing sped up and I felt his cock getting thicker inside my ass, like it had the first time he'd shot a few minutes ago.

I was close, too. His cock was hitting me in all the right places, and my own dick was getting fat and red with the blood rushing through it. I reached down and grabbed it in my hand, and the sensation immediately sent waves of pleasure through my body. I felt my ass tighten even more, and Bronson moaned again.

It happened even quicker than I thought it would. Three strokes of my hand was all it took. The first jet of cum shot right past Bronson's face and landed on the hay behind him. The next two shots landed on his face, and a couple more on his chest and stomach. It was the largest load I'd shot in a very long time. Each shot made my ass contract around Bronson's fat cock, and sent him over the edge.

He pulled his dick out and quickly ripped the condom off. He shot three or four thick hot spurts of cum onto my back. When the last of his cum was on my back and ass, he pulled me to his chest and hugged me tightly.

I kissed him for a moment, and then stood up.

"You'd better get going," I said.

"I know. But I don't want to go. I don't want you to go, either. Will you stick around?"

"Sure." I smiled.

"And tonight?"

"Hey, you're here for two weeks, right? I'm yours. Now get out there and ride that bull. Think of me."

He smiled and rushed out of the trailer, leaving me trying desperately to find something to clean up with.

Long Road Home

I stepped onto the bus with less than my usual enthusiasm. In fact, the long string of four-letter words that rambled through my head surprised even me. A couple of them must have slipped through my tight lips, because the driver gave me a stern look of disapproval as I handed him my ticket. Oh, well, fuck him, I thought as I readjusted my backpack across my shoulders and fought my way down the narrow aisle. It wasn't his car that had broken down two days ago. Nor was it his stubborn sister who insisted on having him sing at her wedding; his Algebra test he'd flunked because he had to make last minute travel arrangements and couldn't study, or his hundred-fifty dollars that he'd been saving for a new stereo that had been sacrificed for the bus ticket. So fuck him, I said to myself as I looked back timidly to make sure he hadn't heard my tirade of profanity.

The bus was less than a third of the way filled, and there were only two stops between Wichita and Amarillo. As the bus pulled away from the stop and maneuvered its way back onto the highway I scanned the empty seats to find which would be the best. I stumbled past a group of eight elderly women occupying the front seats and cackling like a bunch of hens. I obviously wanted to be as far away from them as possible, but not so far away that I was sitting next to the stinky bathroom in the back. So I hiked my backpack into the overhead bin about two thirds of the way back and sat in a relatively empty section of the bus.

Despite a crying baby and a few excited young kids in the very back of the bus, I was able to stretch out and fall asleep relatively easily. The low humming of the diesel engine and swaying motion of the big bus helped me stay asleep until it ground noisily to a stop a few hours later.

I woke up and rubbed my sleepy eyes just as the Brady Bunch in the back of the bus shuffled noisily past my seat and off the bus. I was thankful to have them off. I realized that I now had the entire back of the bus to myself and breathed a sigh of relief as I stretched and looked out the window. The sun was just setting on the horizon, and I figured I had a good chance of sleeping the rest of the way to Amarillo . . . just as soon as I emptied my bladder.

Walking to the bathroom in the back of the bus, I wasn't surprised that I had a semi-hard–on. Pervert, I thought to myself as I realized that I was aroused by the not-so-small amount of pain due to the pressure in my gut. I walked into the bathroom, shut and locked the door and pulled my swollen cock out of my jeans and aimed it at the toilet. Just as the steady stream of piss began to pour into the basin, the bus jerked into reverse and began backing up. I wrapped my left fist loosely around my dick and tried to keep the flow somewhere near the bulls-eye, and reached out with my right hand to steady myself against the wall.

A small mirror mounted on the wall was positioned just right so that I saw my own cock in the reflection. Though almost finished peeing, my dick was still fat and tingled in my hand, and I toyed with the idea of staying in the bathroom and beating off.

Then I heard a faint male voice yell from outside and suddenly the bus halted to a stop, knocking me off balance and ridding my mind of anything other than getting back to the safety of my seat and back to sleep.

I stuffed my cock back into my jeans and buttoned them up, then washed my hands and rinsed my mouth in the tiny sink in the bus's bathroom. Walking back to my seat, I was glad to see that the entire back of the bus was still empty. Besides the eight old ladies up front, there were only three other people on the bus, all seated near the front. Maybe I'd move a few seats farther back away from the cackling hens up front, I thought as I got closer to my seat.

Or maybe not. As I sat down and leaned my head against the pillow propped against the window, I noticed a young guy stretched across the two seats directly opposite the aisle from mine, in exactly the same position I was in. Obviously it was his voice I'd heard yelling for the bus to stop while I contemplated beating off in the bathroom just a moment ago.

He was about my age, maybe a couple of years older. His long, muscular legs hung over the side of the seat into the aisle. He was wearing an Oklahoma Sooners sweatshirt, and it looked comfortable on his obviously massive chest. A matching Sooners baseball cap was perched atop his short, blond hair; and even in the semi-dark of the bus, I could make out the faint stubble on his chin and upper lip. I was envious. Even though I was a sophomore at Wichita State University, I still could not grow much facial hair. This guy was probably a senior at Oklahoma, I reasoned, and continued admiring him.

His eyes were already closed, but I imagined them as bright blue. The arms criss-crossed against his chest were hairy and thickly muscled, a fact I could confirm because the sleeves of his sweatshirt were pushed up almost to the elbow. He had broad shoulders and a thick chest, and as my eyes wandered lustfully down his torso, I saw that his waist was fairly small; a stark contrast to the rest of him.

The bus pulled back onto the highway and accelerated to its cruising speed as I arranged my pillow and leaned my head against the window so that I had full view of my new friend. My eyes found their way to his crotch, and I took a deep breath as the massive bulge there commanded my attention. One of his legs was leaning against the back of the seats in front of him while the other stretched across the empty seat next to him and into the aisle between us. I had a perfect view of his crotch, and it didn't take long at all before I felt my own dick stir in my jeans as I stared.

The road was a little bumpy and jerked the bus around clumsily as we left the city limits of Liberal, Kansas. The motion caused my dick to stiffen even harder in my jeans, and I watched the guy across from me with barely confinable lust as he slept. As we crossed the Oklahoma panhandle border, I noticed the bulge in the guy's jeans growing even bigger. I swallowed hard as he tilted his head more comfortably on his pillow. With his eyes still closed, he reached down and shifted the dick in his jeans so that the round bulge quickly became a long, thick line stretching down the inside of his thigh.

I forced my eyes shut and tried to rid myself of all thoughts of this hunk so that I could sleep, but it was useless. My own dick was throbbing so hard it hurt, so I dipped my hand into the waist of my jeans to rearrange myself. Just then the bus hit a pothole in the road, and the bus jerked heavily. My eyes opened sleepily and I looked across the aisle at the new guy. The corners of his mouth were turned up just slightly into a grin.

I was horrified as I realized my hand was buried deep inside my jeans, groping my cock, and that he was watching me. My heart dropped into my stomach as I fumbled to pull my hand out of the front of my Levi's.

Mr. Oklahoma Sooner leaned forward, reached up and turned on the little overhead light that was used for reading when the bus was dark, as it was now, and leaned back onto his pillow against the window. I could see his smile better now, and twin dimples graced his cheeks in the almost completely dark bus. He licked his lips sexily and raised one eyebrow at me as I freed my hand from its confines. I was right . . . his eyes were bright blue, and they sparkled at me tauntingly.

If I hadn't already been lying down, I would have fallen from shaky knees just looking into his beautiful face. I felt myself blushing, but Sooner was completely cool and collected as he moved his gaze from my eyes to his own crotch. It was obvious he meant for me to follow, and I did so almost involuntarily.

When my eyes reached his midsection, I saw his hands squeezing and tracing his hard-on teasingly. A lump formed in my throat as I stared at the fat mound lying against his leg. He moved one hand from his bulge to the top of his jeans and unbuttoned them slowly. In one quick move he unzipped the blue jeans and reached inside to pull his fat cock out into plain view.

The overhead light was positioned perfectly so that I saw it in all its beauty. The skin was very light and stretched tight around one of the fattest cocks I'd ever seen . . . or even imagined. His hand, even though large, barely fit around it. A huge, throbbing vein pulsed along its underside, and several smaller, but still significant, blue veins branched off from the main one and wrapped around the dick.

I looked away quickly to make sure none of the remaining passengers were watching us. We were safe; the old women were engaged in a card game, the remaining three passengers were all sleeping several rows in front of us, and the driver had closed the tinted glass door separating his sanctuary from that of the main coach.

So I quickly looked back. In the few seconds that I had looked away, Sooner had pulled his jeans halfway down his thighs. I gasped as I saw his huge dick completely free. Now I could see that not only was his cock rock hard and mammoth in size, but his balls were also enormous and hung low between his spread legs.

My eyes darted back and forth from Sooner's face to his cock, unsure which sight was more beautiful. His eyes never left mine, however, even as he gripped his big dick in one hand and stroked it slowly. He jerked himself for several minutes, then moved his hand away from his cock as he closed his eyes and leaned farther back into his pillow. I could tell he had gotten himself close, and my thought was confirmed as I stole another quick look down at his dick. A large, clear drop of precum oozed out of the slit in the big head, wiggled there for a moment, then slid slowly down all nine or ten fat inches of throbbing muscle until it disappeared under his balls.

He gestured with a little jerk of his head for me to come over and join him. Looking at the front of the bus once more, and sure I was not being watched, I crawled quickly across the aisle. Sooner spread his legs as wide as he could to give me room, and I squeezed myself between his massive legs, completely out of the aisle and view of anyone who might look back. My face was inches from his cock at this point, and I smelled his clean, musky scent wafting into my nostrils.

"Lick it," Sooner whispered huskily.

I did. Starting at his heavy balls, I stuck out my tongue and lapped at whatever remained of his trail of precum. His balls twitched as I licked them, and I was only able to pull one at a time into my hungry mouth. I could taste the mixture of soap, sweat and precum that glistened his skin, and a shiver worked its way through my body.

Reluctantly I moved from his balls, and began licking my way up his rod. His veins pulsed lightly against my tongue as I slowly worked my way up the fat pole. When I reached the top, my mouth opened wide and I wrapped my lips around his thick head. A low moan escaped his throat, and I felt one large strong hand grip the back of my head and push me deeper onto him. His cock filled my mouth easily, and my tongue licked as much as it could of the big pole inside my closed mouth as I continued swallowing.

"Yeah, man," he said when I had half of his dick stuffed in my hungry mouth.

It was at that point that I realized I couldn't breath and panicked. I stifled a gag as quietly as possible and breathed deeply through my nose, which automatically caused the back of my throat to open wider. Sooner seized the moment, and thrust my head harder into his crotch. His large cock head pushed its way past where my tonsils had been about ten years ago, and my eyes widened as I felt the fat length of his entire pole spreading my throat muscles apart. He didn't stop pushing the back of my head until my lips touched the base of his cock, where it met his ball sac.

I never knew I was such a gifted cocksucker until I felt him fucking my mouth with greater and greater intensity. If anyone had told me I'd be able to deepthroat such a big dick I would have laughed at them; but here I was, swallowing it whole and even trying to get more. I don't know how long I sucked his huge dick, but I could have gone on like that for hours. Sooner had other ideas, though. As I licked and lapped and swallowed his cock, he reached down and unbuttoned my jeans, sliding them carefully down my legs until they were around my ankles.

"You want it, don't you kid?" he sneered sexily.

"Mmm-hmm," I answered through a mouthful of cock.

"Stand up and turn around."

I was reluctant to let go of his cock from my mouth, but he lifted me with strong arms and turned me around so that my chin rested on the head of the seat in front of us and my exposed ass was inches from his face.

Sooner put a gentle hand on each of my ass cheeks and played with them lovingly as his mouth worked my hole. I felt his soft lips kiss my ass cheeks gently, and slowly work their way closer to my quivering hole. I cursed myself for not being able to control myself, but when his hot lips surrounded the tiny circle and sucked on it gently as his tongue slid all around it and then slowly and strongly snaked its way inside, I moaned deeply and forgot everything else.

As he kissed my twitching hole, I lost my breath and shot a load of cum all over the back of the seat in front of me. This made my ass spasm even more around Sooner's tongue, and he laughed quietly even as he slid the last inch of his hot tongue inside me and tenderly bit my ass.

I thought we were finished, and was about to pull up my pants and head back to my seat, but Sooner pushed my hands away and shifted in his seat so that one strong leg was planted on either side of me.

"Come here, man, sit on me," he said.

There was really no choice on my part; he held me by the waist and steadily moved my body so that I was sitting in his lap. I felt his huge cock head press against my ass and took a deep breath as he pulled me down onto him. I know his cock was only about nine or ten inches long, but the hot throbbing pole felt like it was three feet long as it forced my ass muscles to spread and twitch around it. He didn't let go of my waist until I was completely impaled on his fat cock.

Then he moved his hands away from me completely and began fucking me slowly and deeply. I moaned a little too loudly as his hot fat cock speared my ass and made bright, sparkly lights float in front of my eyes. I felt his breath and his lips hot on the back of my neck and ears, and squeezed my ass even tighter to let him know how much I liked it. He moaned deeply, then bit my ear softly and whispered, "Turn around. I want to kiss you."

It was not the easiest request in the world, but I was determined to do it. I lifted my knees up to my chest, which forced every fat inch of his dick deeper into me, and slowly turned around on the hard rod until I was facing him. When I looked at his beautiful face, his eyes were closed and he was biting his bottom lip. His low moan confirmed he was enjoying it as much as I was.

He opened his eyes and smiled at me, and I thought I would melt then and there. "Kiss me," he instructed, and I did. His lips were soft and full and sweet. His hot tongue slid sensually into my mouth at the exact moment his huge dick slid out of my ass, making sure my body was never empty at any one time. Then as the big cock slid slowly back into my hole, he withdrew his tongue from my mouth and nibbled my lips lovingly.

We fucked like this for fifteen or twenty minutes. I could tell he was getting close, so when he reached down to stroke my cock, I didn't stop him. Just the feel of his strong, warm fist wrapped around my dick was all it took. I blasted a load even larger than the first one a few minutes before. Hot, steamy cum shot out of my dick and landed all over my T-shirt, and all over the front of Sooner, too.

When the first spurt of my load hit his chin, he leaned his head back and smiled. At the same time I felt his cock in my ass grow incredibly thicker and pulse in long throbbing bursts. The tip of his cock head was deep inside me, but I still felt the warmth of the latex as it filled with his cum and pressed against my prostate.

When both of us were exhausted, we slumped against one another for a minute or two. Suddenly the driver announced we were approaching Dalhart, Texas, our last stop before Amarillo.

"This is my stop, man," Sooner said, and gave me a quick kiss as he lifted me off his shrinking dick.

A couple of people up front began moving as well, and that got me up and moving. I quickly pulled up my pants and shuffled clumsily back over to my seat. Sooner carefully removed the condom from his deflated cock, twisted the end of it into a knot, and tossed it across the aisle to me with a wink. The long rubber chute was half filled, and the cum inside was still warm. I smiled as he finished fastening his Levi's and pulled the gym bag from the overhead bin. He walked to the front of the bus without a glance back, and was on the street almost before it had come to a full and complete stop.

I carefully packed the used condom in my backpack, not sure why or what I would ever use it for, but wanting to keep it anyway. The trip from Dalhart to Amarillo was only about an hour, and I slumped back into my pillow and prepared to grab a well-deserved nap before reaching the Big A and facing my family. My ass tingled the last leg of the trip, and my throat and jaw were very sore, but it didn't take long at all before I'd chalked this trip as one of my all-time favorites.

Birthday Blues Cruise

Normally I despise birthdays. I used to like them when I was a teenager and in my early twenties, when all my friends bought me gifts and threw me parties. But once I hit twenty-five, the parties tapered off and the gifts turned to just cards and "Congratulations!", and I lost my enthusiasm for growing older.

This year was different, though. Last month I turned thirty. For two weeks before my birthday I cried. I moped. I drank. I stayed home and read poetry and didn't answer my phone. I cried some more. I truly worked the drama thing.

Three days before my birthday, my best friend Pamela knocked on my door at three in the afternoon. I answered it still in my pajamas, shoving a whole white fudge–covered Oreo in my mouth and swallowing it with a mouthful of milk.

"My God, child," Pamela said with disgust as she pushed past me and walked into my apartment. "I've gotten here just in time."

"Just in time for what?" I asked as I tried not to choke on the cookie.

"To save you. You look like shit."

"Really?" I looked in the mirror. "I don't feel like shit. I think I look fine," I said and straightened my ruffled hair.

"You look like you've been run over by an eighteen-wheeler. But I'm here to change all that."

"What if I don't want to change all that?" I said, and popped another cookie into my mouth defiantly.

"Well, I guess I could take them back then and get a refund."

I stopped in mid-chew and stared at her with my eyes wide open and my mouth half open. She always knew how to get my attention.

"Did you get me a gift?" I asked, spitting a few cookie crumbs onto the floor as I spoke.

"Well, kinda."

I swallowed my cookie carefully and jumped onto the couch, crossing my legs like a little kid.

"What did you get me?"

"I don't know if I should tell you now," she said coyly. "I mean after all, you don't want to end this misery you're enjoying so much. I think this might actually cause you to be happy and get you all excited."

"I changed my mind. I want happy. I want excited. Tell me, please."

"Well, you know Mark works for Palace Cruises, right?"

My heartbeat sped up.

"Yeah."

"And you know he gets free passes and some really good discounts, right?"

I swallowed hard, and tried desperately to retain my composure.

"Well, he's asked me to join him on a cruise, and I'm gonna

bring you back a T-shirt from Mexico!" she said excitedly and began jumping up and down.

I looked at her with a numb look on my face and bit another Oreo in half.

"Just kidding," she said and sat next to me. "You and me and Mark are going to Mexico for five days and six nights. We leave Thursday at noon."

"Shut up!" I screamed.

"I swear. He got a free ticket for me and we both chipped in and got a discounted ticket for you. Puerto Vallarta, baby."

"Oh, my God," I screamed and threw my arms around Pamela's neck and kissed her on the mouth. "But that's in like two days. I have to work."

"Call in dead," she said as she stood up and got ready to leave. "It's not far from the truth anyway."

The ship was huge. I'd never been on a cruise ship before, and was a little nervous. I'd seen *Titanic* three times and walked on board with shaky knees. I paid close attention to the emergency drills and silently counted the seating capacity of the lifeboats.

Once my jitters went away I relaxed and set about having the time of my life. It would take a day and a half to get to Puerto Vallarta. We'd spend two days there and then take another day and a half to return to Los Angeles.

The first night on the ship was torture. After the novelty of actually being on a cruise ship wore off and I'd walked the entire ship getting acquainted with it, I realized there weren't a whole lot of things to keep a gay man excited. There were four bars and dance clubs on the boat, all straight. The gym was filled with macho straight guys trying desperately to pick up on scantily clad Cindy Crawford wannabes. Even shopping was no fun; the boutiques catered to women and sports-minded men.

But it was so sweet of Pamela and Mark to get me the ticket, and I was determined to make them believe I was having a great time. The three of us had dinner with an elderly couple and a high price call girl who was meeting her "sweetie" in Puerto Vallarta. Then we saw a Las Vegas style show which was actually quite nice. It had lots of beautiful young men in skimpy shirts and tight pants. They were right off the pages of an International Male catalog, and I was in heaven. I was determined to find out where they hung out and spend as much time as possible with them the rest of the trip. Oh, yeah, and I think there were a few women in the show too, kicking their legs in the air and such.

I went to bed around two in the morning, exhausted. I'd been so down for the last couple of weeks, that it exhausted me to start a little vacation. I fell asleep that night dreaming about being in the middle of an orgy with those eight adorable dancers from the show earlier in the evening.

I woke around nine the next morning and joined Pamela and Mark for breakfast in the dining room. They were almost finished, but stayed and humored me as I consumed mass quantities of fuel for the day ahead.

We pulled into port in Puerto Vallarta a little after noon. I'd been to PV twice before, when Brad and I were together, and was more than a little giddy to play tour guide to Pamela and Mark. We walked the Malecon, Puerto Vallarta's famous boardwalk, and shopped like idiots. Then we had dinner at a quaint little restaurant and watched the sun set grandly over the Pacific Ocean.

After dinner we went back to the ship and changed clothes

for a night on the town. I'd had my share of the straight nightlife, and drew the line once we were in Puerto Vallarta . . . Mexico's new gay Mecca. Pamela and Mark went to the Hard Rock Café, and I headed straight for Paco Paco's, PV's largest gay nightclub.

It was only eleven in the evening, still early for the night scene in Mexico, and there were only a few patrons milling around. I knew from experience that in half an hour it would start to get more crowded and that by midnight the place would be packed. I ordered a drink and walked around the bar, noticing I was getting more than a few stares from the locals who'd arrived early to get prime picking of the touristas.

In the back area of the bar a stripper was dancing, still fully clothed, on top of a bar. In Mexico the strippers are allowed to take it all off, and even get hard. I moved briskly to the bar and watched in fascination as the young dancer stripped sexily down to his skimpy underwear and teased his small audience. He said hi to a few of the men standing around. Apparently they were all regulars and knew him. Then he danced his way over to me and stopped in front of me, still elevated above me on the bar.

"*Hola*," he said, smiling and gyrating his hips only inches from my face.

"*Hola*," I answered, and felt my face flush with nervousness.

"Where you from?" he asked with a thick, sexy accent.

"Los Angeles."

"Ooooh. My little Angel," he said and leaned down, resting his arms on my shoulders. "Can I have a drink of your beer, Angel?"

"Sure," I said, my voice easily an octave higher than normal. He took a small drink of my beer and then stood up, my beer still in his hand. He began gyrating his hips in small circles in front of me. He was wearing a white thong that was barely able to conceal his cock, and I noticed as he danced the thin material of his thong began to stretch outward a little, outlining his dick even more.

He pretended to hand me my beer back, but when I reached for it, he smiled and pulled it back from me. He lifted it high above his head and poured the remaining beer onto his chest very slowly. I watched as the beer poured over his smooth muscular chest and trailed down his stomach. He had a washboard stomach, and my mouth went dry as I watched the beer disappear into the ridges along his abs and then slide slowly back out and continue down to the next set of rock hard muscles.

He continued pouring the beer onto his body until the last drop was working its way down his chest. His torso was covered and shining with my beer. His underwear was completely soaked by now, and I could easily see his cock getting harder and pushing the cotton fabric to its limits.

"You like?" the young boy asked.

"Yes," I whispered, and cleared my throat. "Very nice."

He slipped his thumbs under the elastic waistband and slowly pulled the thong down his long, hairless legs and threw them onto my face. I pulled them off and laid them on the bar in front of me, blushing like a virgin on her first date.

The stripper danced in front of me, his eyes never leaving mine and a big smile covering his face. His cock, now free of its restraint, swung long and heavy in front of me, getting bigger and harder by the second. It wasn't long before he was fully hard, the foreskin pulled back loosely to show the red, swollen head of his dick.

He knelt down in front of me again, and again rested his arms on my neck. This close I could see how beautiful he really was. He couldn't have been more than nineteen or twenty, with short jet-black hair, dark brown eyes with long curly eyelashes, smooth copper skin, and twin dimples that immediately made me want to kiss them.

"*Te gusto, Papi?*" he asked.

"Oh, yes. I like you very much," I answered.

He looked nervously around for a moment to see if any of the club's management was watching. Satisfied they were not, he took my hand and moved it to his cock, wrapping my fingers around it. He had a very big dick for such a young kid. Hell, he had a really big dick for any age. It was about eight inches long and really thick, with veins running beautifully along the shaft. The foreskin covering his dick was silky smooth and moved gracefully across the rod when I moved my fingers up and down the cock. My hand barely fit around the fat dick, and I could feel the veins throbbing under the skin.

"Oh, Angel, that feels so good," he whispered.

I kept pumping his dick in my hand as he thrust his hips back and forth. Then he looked around again to make sure we weren't being watched, and once again satisfied we weren't, he gently pulled my head into his crotch.

I noticed he smelled sweetly of baby oil as he moved me closer to his dick. I reached out with my tongue when I was within range, and gently licked his hot dick head. He allowed me to continue licking just the head for a moment, and then pushed my head closer. I opened my mouth and closed my lips around his thick pole as he slowly pushed me farther down on his cock. I felt each inch of his big dick slide into my mouth, and before long, felt his cock head slide past my tonsils and down into my throat. I relaxed and let his dick keep sliding inside me until his balls rested against my chin.

"Ay, Papi," he whispered, and I tightened my throat muscles as my tongue swirled around the thick base of his dick. He moaned softly as I moved up and down his dick, sucking him like I hadn't eaten just an hour ago.

I sucked his dick for about two minutes before we heard the voice behind us.

"Javier!" the male voice said loudly.

Javier pulled his dick from my mouth and stood up on the bar in front of me. His dick was pounding visibly, and still dripping with my saliva. He looked me directly in the eyes and blew a kiss at me while he stroked his dick. It only took a couple of strokes before he closed his eyes and leaned back a little. He moaned loudly, drawing the attention of the rest of the small audience. Then he shot one of the largest loads I've ever seen.

The first jet of cum shot way over my head. The next couple landed hotly on my face, and the last six or seven fell to the bar between us. I licked at my face, trying to get a taste of this handsome boy, but most of it had landed on my forehead and around my eyes, and I couldn't reach much of it, so I quickly wiped it off.

The manager pulled Javier aside and was speaking quite heatedly with him. I could make out enough of the conversation to hear Javier swear I hadn't touched him, and that he'd merely beat off for me, which was not against the rules. The manager didn't look too convinced, but dropped it after a while. He told Javier to go get dressed.

I wiped my face more thoroughly and collected myself as I walked out into the main dance floor. It was getting crowded on this side of the wall now. I got another beer and stood against one of the walls, watching the crowd around me. Before too long, Javier walked over to me and asked me to dance. He was a very nice guy and at the end of the evening, asked me to go back to his place.

I spent the night with him, and all the next day. When I had to head back to the ship he went with me, and as we said good-bye I could tell he was sad. He looked like he was going to cry as we hugged good-bye, and we promised to keep in touch.

Back on the boat I went straight to my cabin. Pamela was there, sitting in my chair and reading a book.

"Where have you been?" she almost screamed at me as I walked in the door.

"I met a friend last night. Stayed at his place."

"Oh, my God!" she screamed, and ran up and threw her arms around me. "Tell me all about it."

I told her all about it and she was thoroughly jealous. Seems Mark had a little too much to drink that night and passed out on her.

Mark and Pamela and I spent the rest of the day together. We had dinner with a middle-aged couple who were going on a nudist cruise next month, and who kept fondling each other under the table. It was disgusting. After dinner we wreaked havoc on the swimming pool, then saw another show; this time it was a female impersonator doing a very bad Bette Davis. Mark and Pam were going dancing afterward, but I was tired and said I was going to bed early. Javier had worn me out.

I'd been asleep a little over an hour when I heard my door open. I do not wake up easily, and I tried to adjust my eyes as I turned over and looked toward the door.

"Who's there?" I asked, cursing myself for forgetting to lock the door.

"Shhh," was all I heard.

It was still dark, and I couldn't see very well, but I felt the covers being pulled back on the other side of the bed, and saw a shadow slide into bed with me. I was scared now, not knowing who was in bed with me. I couldn't get my eyes to adjust to the dark, and started to sit up in the bed. Strong arms pushed me back down onto the bed and held me there.

"What do you want?" I asked shakily.

"This," the familiar voice said, and I felt the man lean over me and press his lips firmly against mine.

I panicked as I realized it was Mark in bed with me. I tried to struggle against him and sit up, but he was much stronger than me, and kept me pinned down. He kissed me for a long moment and then stopped and loosened his grip on me.

"Mark, what are you doing?"

"Isn't that obvious?" he asked, and rubbed his cock against my leg. It felt hot and hard as he moved it up and down my thigh.

"What about Pamela?" I asked, sure I must be dreaming. I'd fantasized about fucking Mark from the moment I met him six months ago. He was about six feet four, with light brown hair and beautiful green eyes. He always had a sexy stubble on his face, and his pearl-white teeth sparkled when he smiled. He worked out every day and had a fantastic body. I'd beat off thinking about him many times.

"Shhh," he repeated. "Just lie back and enjoy this, all right?"

He moved his body so that he was lying on top of me now, and held my hands above my head with one of his own strong, large hands.

"Okay," I said, barely a whisper escaping my lips.

He rubbed his cock against my belly for about a minute

and then straddled my chest, pointing his dick right at my face. My eyes had adjusted to the dark by then and I swallowed hard as I saw his cock. It was probably the longest dick I'd ever seen, maybe ten or even eleven inches long, but surprisingly not very thick at all. It was one of those dicks that arched up and then curved downward the last couple of inches. It bobbed up and down a couple of times, hitting me on the chin once or twice.

"Suck it," Mark said, and moved it closer to my mouth.

I opened my mouth and licked the head. He moaned softly and moved even closer, forcing an inch or two of his hard cock inside my mouth. I reached up and wrapped both hands, one over the other, around the base of his cock. I swallowed a little more of his dick, until my mouth reached my hands. Now his entire cock was wrapped by me; my hands enveloping about seven inches, and my mouth swallowing the last three or four.

Mark moaned again, louder this time, and began humping my hands and mouth. I moved my hands away and slowly sucked a little more of his cock inside my mouth. Mark was getting a little impatient and began sliding more and more of his dick into me. I finally gave up on the slow and sensual approach, and opened my mouth wider as he slid the entire length of his throbbing cock into my mouth. Because it was curved quite a bit, it slid easily deep inside my throat. When his balls touched my chin I tightened my throat muscles around his cock. He collapsed against the wall behind me and sat still for a few moments, enjoying the feel of my throat muscles massaging his dick.

"Oh, shit, that feels great, man," he said.

I took hold of his hips and forced him to pull his cock out

of my mouth. I needed to breathe a little, and inhaled deeply as he rolled over onto his back and lay beside me.

"Why did you stop?" he asked. "I was almost ready to blow my load."

"I know. But I want something else."

"What?"

"I want you to fuck me."

"You mean you want my dick up your ass?"

"Yeah." I laughed. "That's what I mean."

"Oh, man, I've never done that before."

"You ever done *this* much with another guy before?"

"No," he said and turned onto his side, facing me.

"So . . ."

"Well, I guess it's cool."

"Good," I said, and reached down and took his cock in my hand. It was still hard and throbbing.

I rolled Mark over onto his back and sucked his cock for a few seconds, getting it wet and as hard as it could. I loved swallowing his long cock deep into my throat and watching him squirm with delight. Without taking his big dick out of my mouth, I reached over and removed a condom from the nightstand next to my bed. I ripped the package open and removed the rubber.

I sucked harder on Mark's dick for another couple minutes, and then reluctantly let the long cock slip out of my mouth. His dick had started to pulse crazily and I knew he was getting close. His eyes were closed and he had a dazed look on his face as I rolled the condom down his long, hard cock.

I spat some saliva on my fingers and rubbed it around my ass hole, then sat on Mark's chest, positioning his cock head at the entrance of my ass. His dick was throbbing like mad and it took a couple of tries to get it to stay in place at my hole. I squeezed it hard and lowered my ass onto his cock so that just the head slipped in. I heard Mark groan loudly as sharp bolts of pain shot through my ass and up my spine. Mark tried to shove more of his dick up into my ass, but I held him still, pinching his nipples lightly as I got used to the hot dick head inside me.

It didn't take long before the pain turned to pleasure, and I lowered myself onto his dick. I went slowly, savoring each inch as it slid slowly up inside me. His cock got a little thicker near the base and I felt my ass muscles stretching to accommodate the entire length and thickness of his dick. When I reached his balls, I took a deep breath and squeezed his cock inside me.

Mark opened his eyes and I noticed they were sparkling.

"Fuck, man. That is so hot."

I smiled and leaned forward to kiss him. As I did, my ass tightened around Mark's dick, and he lifted his hips to shove his cock deeper inside my ass. This sent shudders through my body as I wrapped my lips around his tongue. Mark kissed me deeply, and began fucking me. I was surprised that he was so passionate. He was a great kisser and his cock found a steady rhythm that was driving me crazy. His long cock reached places I never knew existed, and pushed me closer to ecstasy than I would have thought possible.

"Oh, baby, this is great. Do you like my cock up your ass?" he asked.

I moaned my response and maneuvered us so that I was lying on my back with Mark's cock buried deep in my ass. He began breathing faster and thrusting his cock in my ass with short, stabbing moves. I knew he was close a few times, but I forced him to slow down and take it nice and slow. But even I had my limits, and his long, hard dick was pushing them. I needed to shoot my load.

"I'm gonna come, man!" Mark almost screamed.

I tightened my ass around his cock and shoved it harder onto his dick in response. He tilted his head back and let out an animal-like growl, shoving his cock deep into my ass and holding it there. I felt his cock contract as he convulsed on top of me. That was all it took to push me over the edge myself.

The first of the cum began dripping out of the head of my cock slowly. Then a couple of long jets of hot cum shot out of my cock with incredible force. Both shots landed on Mark's chin, and I saw him flinch as they hit him. He closed his eyes and tried to move his head out of the way. I could tell he was uncomfortable with my cum on him, so I directed the rest of my load so that it landed on my own chest and belly.

Mark collapsed on top of me after I finished shooting my load.

"Sorry," I said as I tried to wipe my cum from his face. His cock was still inside my ass.

"No problem. Just took me by surprise, that's all."

"Hey, Mark," I said apprehensively, "what about Pamela?"

"What about her? She told me you had a crush on me after the first time I met you."

"What?" I asked indignantly. Mark laughed.

"Don't worry, it's cool. She's been worried about you lately, and wanted to do something fun for your birthday. The cruise was my idea. This," he said, and flexed his dick still inside my ass, "was hers."

"She wanted you to fuck me?" I asked incredulously.

"Yep."

"Oh, my God!" I said and covered my head with a pillow.

"Happy Birthday, Randy," he said as he pulled out of my

ass and discarded the cum-filled condom. "You'd better get some rest. I noticed one of those dancers with the tight pants giving you the eye yesterday."

"Oh, my God."

Mark laughed and left my room. I curled up under the covers. A moment later I heard the door to Pamela and Mark's room, which was next door to mine, open and close. A few minutes later I heard their bedsprings squeak and Pamela moaning loudly. I laughed and wondered if she had heard Mark and I as well. I fell asleep with a smile on my face, wondering what conversation would be like at breakfast in a couple hours.

Just Another
Walk in the Park

I love my puppy Spanky very much. He's a nine-month-old pug and looks exactly like the chubby, wrinkled kid from the old *Little Rascals* television series. Even better, though, he does all the things I'd hoped he would when I got him almost a year ago . . . brings joy and laughter into my life again; makes me responsible and caring toward another living being; keeps me company on cold (and not-so-cold), lonely nights when all my human friends are busy and forget how needy I am once I break up with my "boyfriend of the month."

Walking Spanky is usually a lot of fun. I live in an apartment complex right on Cheesman Park. No more need be said for anyone who lives in Denver, but for the sake of non-Denverites, Cheesman is The Park. Infamous for its police raids in years past, and the cracking down on all the outdoors sex that used to go on there (long before I moved there, and not at all why I chose to live here!), it's quieted down over the last few years. A little.

Unofficially recognized as the "gay" park in Denver, it is

always bustling with people, especially when the weather is nice. It's a festive place for volleyball and Frisbee enthusiasts, roller-bladers, dog-walkers and other active-minded persons. Especially since the city of Denver overturned an ordinance a couple years back banning nudity in public parks. The Park is once again gaining somewhat of a "reputation." Not one to gossip, suffice to say Cheesman is still a very fun place to go to see and be seen, with or without clothes. (Nude volleyball, by the way . . . two very enthusiastic thumbs up!)

Spanky is a particular puppy when it comes to relieving himself. Never satisfied to just lift his leg and let it fly on any tree or post, he makes a big production of strutting the entire park, looking for just the right spot. Sometimes it's really cute. At two or three in the morning, however, it can be very frustrating.

I was very frustrated last week. Spanky's newest favorite time to take his human out for a walk is three in the morning, and last Thursday was no exception. Right in the middle of a really great dream, I was awakened with his slobbery mouth nibbling my ear. He snorted and huffed until I finally got out of bed, threw on a pair of sweats and harnessed him. Extremely upset at having to pull my raging cock out of Brad Pitt's mouth right as I was ready to shoot, I slammed the door shut behind us and started walking through The Park with my puppy.

I'd been having dreams of all the heartthrobs over the last few months . . . Leonardo, Tom, Denzel, Matt and Ben (together and separately), even Harrison and Mel. But that night's dream with Brad, well, it was special. And I really resented Spanky for pulling me out of it, dammit! My hard dick refused to soften, but I figured it was three in the morning, and even if it did push my sweats a few inches out in front of me, no one would be in the park to notice, and I'd be okay.

We were about halfway around the park, walking in front of an apartment complex, not unlike my own, with a row of balconies, when I heard a "pssst" from just above. Spanky stopped in his tracks and his ears perked up, then he kept sniffing the ground for the right place to do his business. I looked around me to find the source of the noise. It didn't take long.

It was completely dark outside, of course, but the bright moon cast a little bit of light, some of which crept between the trees and partly illuminated the balcony immediately above me. A man stood there, totally naked and sporting a beautiful hard-on. His balcony had an overhang that hid his face almost completely in its shadow. All I could make out was a squared jawline and a pair of full, pouty, lips. The rest of his body was in plain sight, though, and I drew in a deep breath as I took it all in. He had a broad, defined chest and chiseled stomach that was covered with a light layer of black, curly hair. His waistline was much lighter in tone than the rest of him, obviously due to a tanning bed. The cock being caressed by his big hand was fairly average in length, from what I could see, but very thick. His legs were long and muscular as well, and covered in the same layer of black curly hair as his chest.

Spanky had obviously finished his business and was pulling at the harness to continue our little walk, but I was just as stubborn to stay where I was. The man took a couple of steps forward and thrust his cock through the iron bars on his balcony, dangling it like a carrot in front of a horse. He was careful to keep his face in the shadows, but I was given a glorious view of the rest of his torso. His fat cock bobbed up and down a few feet from my face, and I felt my own dick spring back to full hardness in my sweats in no time at all.

The guy on the balcony reached down and tugged gently on his cock and I noticed his hand, even though pretty large, barely fit around his throbbing cock. I licked my lips as I watched the guy squeeze his tool and caress it slowly and lovingly. I looked around me to make sure no one else was near us. Satisfied we were alone, I scolded Spanky until he laid down on the cool grass, and rubbed my hand across the bulge that was stretching my sweats.

"Pull it out," the stranger whispered in a deep voice that sent chills through my entire body.

I looked around me again, nervous about being out in the open like that, but not a person, light, or sound was in sight, so I took a deep breath and pulled my cock out of my sweats, letting my balls rest on the top of the elastic waistband. I wrapped my fist around it and squeezed it for a couple of seconds, savoring the tingle I felt course through my cock and down my legs. I could have continued beating off like that for hours, it seemed, but my stranger in the dark had other plans.

"Move your hand away," he instructed in his sexy voice. "I want to see it."

I did as I was told, and moved my hand to my sides, my dick hanging over the top of my sweats and throbbing like it wanted to take off or something. Mr. Balcony let out a deep moan, and moved his fist steadily up, down and around his thick rod.

"Pull your foreskin out so I can see it."

Since I was fully hard, I barely had enough foreskin to pull over the head; but I was eager to please my new friend, and stretched as much of the silky skin as I could over my cock head and inserted what I could of my finger inside the cave it created.

Another groan from the guy above me, and I saw him move his free hand to his chest and gently squeeze his nipple as he stroked his cock. The muscles on his stomach tightened and flexed as one hand played with his hairy chest and the other squeezed and pulled on his cock. It was more than I could take, after a while, and I decided to be bolder than I have in a long time.

"Can I come up?" I asked quietly. Spanky snorted at this, but when I gave him my stern look, he laid back down and was quiet.

"No."

Gulp. It takes a lot of work for me to muster up the nerve and be that bold, and I could barely catch my breath when he rejected me.

"Why not?" I asked, hoping it didn't sound like I was whining.

"Because I'm finished," he said huskily. The words were not even completely out of his mouth before he arched his body forward, pushing his hips against the iron railing and his cock a few inches closer to where I was standing below.

Before I could even register what was happening, he let go with a load like none I'd ever seen. Huge, streaming jets shot out of his cock head. One landed on my cheek, very warm and thick; another on my arm, and several more fell to the ground directly in front of me. It seemed to go on for at least a minute, and he moaned the entire time.

I quickly reached down and grabbed my own dick and started sliding my hand across the shaft. I figured the guy at least wanted to see me shoot as well, and I was so close it took only a few strokes before I let go with my own load. I was still letting fly with a large load myself, when the guy on the balcony turned around and started walking back into his apartment. Just before he slid the glass door shut, I caught a quick glimpse of the beautiful tattoo that graced his tightly muscled ass. It was a large tattoo, covering almost an entire cheek, of Donald and Daisy Duck kissing. I'll never forget it, because it seemed so cute and out of place on such a big, brawny and obviously masculine man.

I was completely stunned, my knees still shaking with the force of my orgasm as he walked away. *What just happened,* I asked myself as the last couple of drops of cum dripped from my aching cock. Surely he at least wanted to see me shoot my own load, I mean, why else would he be out there and telling me to show it to him? I shook my head to clear the buzzing sound I was hearing, and hastily stuffed my shrinking dick back into my sweats.

Spanky and I trotted back to my apartment and got back into bed. He fell asleep almost immediately, snoring like he hadn't a care in the world. I, on the other hand, could not stop thinking about the guy, the cute tattoo, or what had just happened. I believe the last time I looked at the clock was at a quarter to five.

They say those born under the astrological sign of Gemini tend to dwell on things and have addictive personalities. I wish I could say I broke the mold, but I'd be lying. I became obsessed with the man on the balcony and the fantasy of repeating our little rendezvous, possibly even going farther. Every night for the next four, I made sure Spanky drank plenty of water really late at night. Then around two in the morning, I walked him around the park.

Of course, he pissed and was ready for bed about fifteen minutes into the walk and became impatient with my loitering around my stranger's apartment. I am the master, however, and if I want to obsess, I will obsess. So I took Spanky back home, put him to bed, and then went back out and stood among a clump of trees just a few feet from the now familiar balcony. Hope for any sign of life proved to no avail however, and I ended up heading back home and to bed after four every morning, lonely and frustrated.

Last night my frustration got the best of me. Four early mornings with no Donald Duck Tattoo Man was all I could take. Strike three and I was out. But my cock had barely been limp at all since that first meeting, and I needed some release. Tuesday nights are very popular with the gay crowd in Denver, because the Midtowne Spa, one of Denver's three bathhouses, offers rooms at half price all day. I'd never been there myself before—I was always afraid I'd run into someone I know and be embarrassed. But a couple of guys I went out with had gone, and said it was always a lot of fun on Tuesdays, and it was all the talk online, so I decided to give it a try.

I had to drive by the place a couple of times before I worked up the nerve to stop. The very conspicuous, triangular-shaped brick building took up half a block. There was a brass sign above the front door that stated its name, and even a large, colorful neon sign lighting up the street corner in an area of town not particularly known for being one of the safest. But that didn't seem to matter to a lot of people, because even at ten-thirty at night, the parking lot was full, and I had to drive a couple of blocks away to find a place to park on the street.

My heart was pounding like crazy as I walked closer to the place. I almost chickened out a couple of times, even stood across the street in front of an apartment complex and watched three or four other guys go in first. When they opened the front door, loud but muffled house music spilled out into the night. Once the door swung shut behind them, however, I couldn't hear a thing. Soundproofed, seemingly secure (since none of the other six guys I watched go in hesitated even a little before entering), I finally worked up the nerve to walk across the street and go in.

Just inside the front door was a small hallway where all six guys I'd watched go in were standing around, waiting to pay and get through the door that led to the main rooms. No one said a word to anyone else. We didn't even look at each other in the eyes out there in the well-lighted hallway. We ignored one another by reading the sign stating the spa was a gay establishment, and if that was a problem, or if any activity associated with that was a problem, that you should leave through the same door you'd just walked in through. Bold. There were also advertisements for several special events that were being hosted in the next few weeks, lots of pictures of naked men in various states of arousal, and safe sex admonishments all over the walls.

There was a small glass window along the wall facing the door. One young man stood behind the glass partition asking for membership cards, whether the men in line wanted rooms (which were all full and on a long waiting list at this point) or lockers, and taking money. I briefly saw three other employees, trying very hard to look like they were accomplishing something, but actually just hanging around doing nothing.

Apparently the computer was "screwed up again" and none of the employees could figure out what the hell they were doing. Meanwhile, we on the other side of the glass window began shuffling our feet, looking around nervously and moaning and groaning under our breath about the incompetence of the staff.

Twenty minutes later, after purchasing a membership card and paying for a locker, I was buzzed into the main room and hastily given a towel and general directions to the locker room. My heart pounded crazily in my chest as I undressed and wrapped the skimpy white towel around my waist, and safely locked my clothes and my sanity in the dingy gray locker.

I watched the guy who'd entered before me slip his locker key (which was attached to an elastic band) around his ankle and tuck his key under the elastic, and so I did the same. I sat on a bench in the locker room for a good ten minutes, until my heartbeat returned to a normal rate, and then started walking around, exploring this new place that reeked of sweat and sex and blasted dance music loudly from hidden speakers.

I will be the first to admit that I am directionally challenged to begin with. But the maze of hallways that held the doors to rooms on the first floor of this building had me dizzy in no time at all, and I had no idea where I was going. Some of the doors were closed, but most were left wide open. The only light coming from inside the rooms seemed to come from the images of porn flicks playing on television sets mounted in the corner of the ceilings of each room. I was mesmerized, and looked in each room as I walked through the hallway maze. Inside was exactly the same scene, regardless of the room number . . . one man, lying naked on a narrow bed, stroking his hard cock and staring at the video playing in the top corner of his room.

Most of the men I saw were middle-aged, and more than just a little overweight. Many of them glanced down from the videos to see the guys walking the hallways. I was shocked at how many times I saw or heard the men openly gesturing me to come into their rooms. Even though I am considerably younger and in much better shape than ninety percent of them, I was astounded at the directness of their invitations.

I kept walking, exploring the layout of the place and becoming less nervous and more intrigued by the minute. I somehow found my way to the "Wet Area," and was glad to see a large, seemingly clean, if not overly chlorinated hot tub with only one other guy in it. I made a mental note to come back and enjoy it after I finished exploring the place. Just a few feet down the hall from the hot tub was an empty dry sauna room that was so hot I burned my feet when I walked in. Across the hall from the sauna was the steam room. I watched a steady flow of men walk in and out of there, and was amazed at the amount of steam that poured out of the door every time it was opened. Already too hot from the sauna, I decided to skip the steam room for now, and re-traced my steps through the maze of rooms.

I heard the moans and groans of a few guys behind the closed doors of rooms, and felt my cock begin to stiffen with each step. Somehow I found myself at the top of a staircase that led to the basement. The entire wall was lined with television screens, and as I walked down the stairs, I watched videos of guys sucking and fucking and in various forms of orgies and deviant acts. By the time I reached the bottom of the stairs, my dick was throbbing and pushing my towel a ways out in front of me. I felt the blood rushing through my body, and was both stunned and ashamed at how turned on I was being around so much blatant sex.

Downstairs was even darker and more mysterious than the first level, and I found myself touching the walls as I worked my way through yet another maze. The only light down here was dim blue fluorescent, and it took a while for my eyes to adjust. I felt a couple of hands grope my cock as I walked blindly along, but I was too confused and afraid to stop.

Finally my eyes adjusted to the dim lighting, and I found myself in a large room with winding walls. It was another maze, and I wondered to myself why the owners were so intent on losing their customers in such confusion. There were glory holes placed strategically every couple of feet, and a few narrow doors broke the monotony.

Some of the guys down here were older and out of shape also, but many more were younger, with hard, muscular bodies. I began to feel more at home here, and was glad to see that several of the younger guys followed me with their eyes as I walked slowly around the rooms, acquainting myself with the layout.

I was almost at the end of the room and ready to turn around and head back, when I noticed a beautiful guy leaning against one of the narrow doors. Tall and muscular, with light hair and what seemed like light eyes, he smiled at me when I walked past him. I smiled back and he boldly nodded at me to go into the door right next to his as he disappeared inside the door he was leaning against. My heart was pounding like crazy, and I was a little stunned. But I saw that someone else was already hastily trying to make their way to the door he'd nodded for me to go into, so I quickly opened the door and stepped inside.

It was even darker inside the tiny closet-size stall. It took a moment for my eyes to adjust again. When they did, I noticed a large glory hole strategically placed in each of the three walls that surrounded me. It took no more than a couple of seconds before two hard cocks poked through two of the glory holes. But the one that was lining the wall of the guy who'd gestured at me remained dark and empty.

I wiped a bead of sweat from my forehead and tried to take a deep breath as I thought about what to do next. One of the cocks bobbing through the glory holes was really small and a little wrinkled and didn't interest me at all. The other one looked pretty good though; fairly long, dark, uncut, and thick . . . just like I like them. I reached down and stroked it gently with my hand, but continued to look at the hole where I knew the cute, muscular guy was behind.

Who knows what the guy attached to the long, uncut dick looked like, but it throbbed hotly in my hand, and I decided what the hell. I dropped to my knees and licked at the head of the dick, then slowly began to suck more of it into my mouth. The skin felt soft and tasted slightly of soap. It felt great as I took more of the hard shaft into my mouth. I sucked lightly at first, then more eagerly for a minute or so.

It didn't take long at all before I felt the rod in my mouth begin to swell even thicker and I tasted the first drop of precum on my tongue. The guy on the other side of the wall pushed himself all the way against it, until I felt the weak pressed wood structure begin to shake. I pulled my mouth slowly from his cock just as his first shot of cum squirted from the head and splashed across my nose and lips. I jerked backward, more from surprise than anything, as he showered me with his cum, and landed on my ass on the floor.

As the man squeezed out the last reluctant drops of cum from his cock, I unwrapped the towel from my waist and wiped my face. The cock disappeared and I heard the squeaking of a door as he opened it and left his cubicle. My own dick was rock hard and already leaking a little precum of its own, and I sighed as I looked over at the dark hole of the stall where the cute guy had gone. There was no cock sticking through it, but I thought I could make out a pair of eyes a few inches from inside.

I stood up and started to wrap the towel back around my

waist and throbbing cock, when I saw two fingers poke through the hole, and heard the voice that stopped me in my tracks.

"We're not done yet," came the deep whisper from just on the other side of the wall. "Drop the towel and move over here."

I recognized the voice immediately. It was the guy from the balcony on Cheesman Park a few days ago. Instantly my cock sprang back to full throb, and I did as I was told. I dropped the towel to the floor and moved over to stand directly in front of the glory hole separating us.

His big, strong hand reached through the large hole and wrapped around my cock, sending a wave of pleasure through my body that I thought I'd faint from. His grip was strong, but not rough as he pulled me up against the wall, forcing my dick through the glory hole.

I felt the tip of his tongue lick around the hole in my cock head and then slip inside as his lips wrapped around the rest of my head. His mouth was hot and very wet, and I had to count to ten to prevent myself from shooting right there. He sucked me gently at first, then with more vigor, until I was pressing my body against the wall and preparing to let go with a load equal to the one he'd missed the other night.

But he once again had another plan in mind, and when I felt the cum churning in my balls, he pulled his mouth from my aching cock. I groaned in disappointment, and kept it where it was, throbbing and anxious. Instead of feeling the welcoming warmth of his mouth again, however, I felt his hand reach through the hole and push at my stomach, moving me away from the wall. Reluctantly, I stepped back and pulled my cock from the glory hole.

"On your knees," he instructed, and I was there almost before he finished the command.

I licked my lips and gathered a mouthful of saliva, preparing to suck the fat, beautiful cock I remembered. Instead, he pressed his ass against the hole. Two perfectly round and smooth, hard globes filled the glory hole, and flexed tauntingly in front of my eyes.

"Eat me," he said.

He was obviously a man of very few words, but very commanding with those he used, and I obeyed happily. I bit each of his cheeks softly, just to let him know how upset I was about the other night, then allowed my tongue to find its way to his ass crack. I lightly licked up and down the crevice, and closed my eyes with the pleasure of feeling his smooth ass muscles squeeze my tongue.

He tasted better than anything I could remember in a long time. A mix of recently showered cleanliness and hot, sweaty and musky man filled my mouth, and I nearly lost my load again, right on the floor. His smooth, tight ass cheeks danced around my eager tongue, and pulled it deeper inside him. I usually don't like being on the giving end of ass play, but I was intoxicated by this man and his butt. I slowly opened my eyes and saw the faint tattoo of Donald and Daisy Duck peeking just an inch or so around the corner in the dark of his stall.

I grabbed one of his ass cheeks in each hand and gently massaged them as I ate like I was at my last supper. It really was the guy from the balcony, and I finally had him here, all to myself. My tongue licked and probed his ass hole, and my lips kissed his cheeks until I heard him moan with delight.

"Fuck me," he said in a breathy whisper.

My dick jumped to attention at that, and I swear my heart stopped beating. This man was more than I could ever hope to dream of . . . better even than Brad Pitt and Tom Cruise in the best of my dreams. Easily six foot two, with solid, hard muscles and the face of an Adonis; he was the epitome of Manliness to me. I remembered the way his chest and stomach muscles tightened and flexed magnificently for me as he shot his load over the balcony a few days ago. His arms were large and defined as he held his fat cock as it shot its load in the moonlight just for me. Did he really want *me* to fuck *him*?

"Don't make me tell you again."

I didn't. I stood up and pressed my cock against the smooth skin of his ass cheeks as they pressed through the glory hole. His butt felt cool and slightly sweaty against my hot, hard cock. I pressed harder against the wall, sliding my dick between his ass and up and down his chiseled lower back. He moaned with pleasure, and I smiled privately.

We moved at the same time, he an inch to the left, and me an inch backward, to position the head of my cock right at his eager hole. My head was still spinning as I felt the tight sphincter relax just a little and the first inch of my cock slid effortlessly inside him. His ass muscles tightened, surrounding my cock head with a burning wet heat, and once again I counted to ten. Picturing the Donald Duck tattoo just a few inches away helped calm me down a little, and I was able to refrain from blasting off a load up his ass then and there.

It became very obvious really quickly that he wanted my cock up his ass as badly as I did. Once I was buried inside him, I was no longer in control . . . if I ever was. His tight ass grabbed my cock and slid up and down the length of it mercilessly. He started out with slow, gentle pushes against my cock, but before long was thrusting himself on me with incredible speed and control. Though not nearly as thick as his own, my dick is pretty fat, and I marveled at how his ass muscles stretched just far enough to keep themselves tight around my cock. I stood still there, not daring to move a muscle, and allowed him to slide up and down the length of my dick.

He began to breath heavily after a few minutes, and I felt the grip on my pole tighten even more. I knew he was close, and Donald Duck or no Donald Duck, I was not about to hold back this time. My knees began to shake uncontrollably, and I pulled my cock out of his ass a second before the first spray of cum shot out. It flew up in the air and back down onto my own cock, hot and sticky.

"Hit me with it," he said, not as quietly this time.

I pointed my cock back at his ass and watched as six or seven heavy spurts of cum landed on his ass. Barely able to breathe, and definitely not able to stand on my own two feet, I slumped to the floor and sat on my own legs. A couple of seconds later, his thick cock shoved itself through the hole, as glorious as I remembered it. I sat Indian-style and watched as it shot one jet after another of hot cum onto my face and chest. It all seemed to be in slow motion, and I smiled as he showered me with his load.

He kept his cock in the glory hole for at least a minute after he'd finished shooting. I could hear him breathing heavily, trying to slow it down as his dick slowly, yet magnificently, began to shrink. Even completely soft it was thick and beautiful, and I leaned forward and kissed it softly just before he pulled it out of the hole. A second later I heard his door open and squeak shut, and I listened to his heavy footsteps as they retreated down the hall.

I continued sitting on the floor of the stall, cum drying all over my body, but too weak to get up. A couple more guys came into adjoining stalls and shoved their dicks through the glory holes, but I couldn't have cared less. About five minutes later I halfheartedly dried myself off with my towel, and walked, weak-kneed back upstairs and to the locker room.

My heart stopped beating and I stopped in my tracks as I

was halfway across the room. I saw a piece of paper taped to my locker. After taking a deep breath I walked over and removed the tape and opened the note.

"Leaving town tomorrow morning for business trip. Be back on Friday. Will meet you at eight in front of my place. Bring Spanky . . . I have a Cocker Spaniel. Think they'll get along great!"

Cab Fare

I'd been looking forward to this vacation for six weeks; could think of almost nothing else, as a matter of fact. Richard and I split up two months ago, and the first thing I did after the breakup was book this vacation to Puerto Vallarta. I've never been on a vacation by myself; there was always family or a lover with me. Seven days at a tropical beach resort would be just what I needed to put things in perspective.

I'd been to Puerto Vallarta with Richard a couple of times before, but was still overwhelmed with the heat and humidity as I stepped from the plane and walked to the big shuttle bus that drove us the entire fifty feet from the plane to the terminal. I was sweating before I had taken the last step down from the plane, and wiped my forehead as I entered the crowded shuttle. *I'd better get used to it,* I thought as I sat in the last available seat.

In Mexico the taxis do not use meters. You tell the driver where you want to go and ask him how much he would charge for the ride. They can pretty much charge whatever they like. I was lucky, and got a very cute, young driver who apparently liked short blonde Americans. My hotel was way on the other side of town, as far from the airport as you can be and still be inside the city limits.

"*Cuanto para Hotel Paco Paco?*" I asked in my rusty Spanish.

The cabbie smiled, displaying perfect white teeth and his eyes sparkled.

"You speak very good Spanish," he said in perfect English with a sexy accent.

"Thank you." I breathed a sigh of relief.

He looked me directly in the eyes, and then looked over my body. The smile never left his face.

"Ten pesos."

I thought I'd either heard him wrong or that the economy had done a quick upswing while I was en route there. Normally it would cost anywhere from sixty to eighty pesos for the ride. I stood outside the cab, a little dazed and not saying a word.

"It's a good price," the cabbie said, thinking I was deliberating.

"No, no, I know it's a good price. A very good price, as a matter of fact. Are you sure?"

"Sure," he said and got out of the cab to open the trunk and help me put my two overpacked suitcases in it. When I started to get in the backseat, he insisted I sit up front with him.

The ride was hot, but pleasant. I'm sure the driver was taking a very long route to get there, but I didn't mind. He was beautiful with his copper skin, black hair and light brown eyes with long, curly eyelashes. He was wearing a tank top that displayed his smooth muscular chest, and a pair of shorts that hugged his strong, hairy legs and seemed barely able to contain his huge bulge. I kept sneaking a peek at his crotch, and I think he noticed, because it seemed to grow even bigger and I swear a couple of times I saw it swell and shrink again as if he were flexing it for me.

Rodrigo spoke great English. He told me he'd studied English for six years and that his sister-in-law was American and helped him a lot with his vocabulary and accent. His soft, whispery voice was mesmerizing and listening to him made my own groin swell a little.

I was a little disappointed when we finally pulled into the driveway of the hotel. I didn't want to let Rodrigo go. But I was a little eager to get unpacked and relax after my long trip. Rodrigo unloaded my luggage, and lingered around as long as possible. He insisted on carrying my bags upstairs to the lobby. When I tried to pay him his ten pesos, he smiled and told me to keep it.

"No, Rodrigo, I can't. Please, take it."

"No. You keep it. You can buy me a drink when we see each other again. I'm sure we will."

I wondered why he thought we'd see each other again, and looked a little perplexed.

"I'll see you later, papacito," he said and got in the car and drove away. I saw him look back at me through the rearview mirror, and he waved.

I went back into the lobby and checked in. Enrique, the receptionist, was a cute young man with enough charm for three. He couldn't have been more than nineteen or twenty, a little skinny, dressed in jeans and a polo shirt. He wore braces and had a twin set of dimples on either side of his smile that I could dive into and get lost in. He laid his hands on mine while explaining the amenities and layout of the hotel, and when I started to leave, he squeezed my hand gently. Boy, was I glad I'd chosen to stay in a gay hotel this time around. Already I felt so comfortable.

I decided to take a nap and asked Enrique to give me a

wake-up call at seven o'clock. He said sure, and wrote the note down on a Post-It and placed it on the computer screen as he winked at me. I smiled and walked down the hall to my room. When I looked back right before I entered my room, Enrique was still looking at me and smiling.

My room was very large, with a king-size bed dominating one wall. French doors opened onto a quaint patio and an outside breeze and ceiling fan kept the room very comfortable. I got undressed, leaving on only my boxers, and lay down. I found myself watching the ceiling fan swirl above me and drifted off to sleep thinking of Rodrigo.

We were in the cab still, and he was pointing out the popular tourist spots along the winding road. His bare arms flexed slightly with each turn of the wheel, and the thin layer of sweat on his triceps made them glisten. I swallowed hard and tried to turn my gaze away from him, but couldn't. Instead my eyes moved down his chest and chiseled stomach that was perfectly outlined through his tank top. The bottom of his shirt tucked neatly into the waist of his shorts. I tried to stop looking again when my eyes reached his belt, but it was even more useless than before.

Somewhere in the back of my mind I must have realized Rodrigo had stopped talking, but it didn't register with me. All of my attention was focused on the huge round bulge beneath his belt. It was pulsing under the weight of the denim, seeming alive and trying to escape.

"See what you do to me, Papi," Rodrigo said, breaking the silence.

I forced myself to look away, and cleared my throat.

"It's okay to look. I don't mind."

"I'm sorry," I stammered. "I didn't mean to . . ."

"Come here," he said, and with a big strong hand he pulled my head closer to his crotch.

"Rodrigo, you're driving."

"It's okay, I'll be careful. Just taste it."

His hand pressed harder against the back of my head until my mouth was touching the fabric barely covering his cock. I could hardly catch my breath as my lips softly massaged his crotch. I felt the heat of his dick all the way through his shorts as it pulsed and grew with the heat and wetness of my mouth.

Rodrigo quickly undid his belt with his free hand and unbuttoned his shorts. I moved his hand away and slowly pulled the zipper down. He was wearing no underwear, and as the zipper lowered, his black pubic hair came into view. I almost creamed myself right there, but the prospect of what lay ahead kept me going. I reached inside his shorts and wrapped my hand around his throbbing cock. I was surprised at how soft and silky the skin on his cock felt in my hand.

I pulled it out of his shorts and looked at it for the first time. With all my fantasizing about it, it was better even than I'd imagined. A little longer than my own, not very thick, and lighter in color than I'd expected. It was covered with a maze of thick, throbbing veins. He was cut, and the head of his cock was covered in a layer of precum.

I stuck out my tongue and felt the sticky fluid on the tip and was just about ready to swallow his entire cock when he stopped me.

"Wait a second Papi. There's a light about a block ahead. Take down my pants when we get there. It's easier."

My heart pounded heavily. My face was only inches away from his beautiful dick, and it took all I had not to devour it then and there. A moment later we stopped at the light, and Rodrigo hastily pulled his shorts down to his ankles.

I moved in immediately, licking all the precum from his cock head, then lowering my mouth slowly down the length of his dick. He moaned and thrust his hips upward, sliding his dick in and out of my eager mouth. I loved feeling the bumps of his big veins as they slid along my lips, and after about a minute I was able to swallow the entire length of his cock. The head slipped past my tonsils and down my throat, and rested there for a moment. His entire dick expanded with his every heartbeat, filling my mouth and throat and sending waves of pleasure through my body.

I kept his cock deep inside my throat and began sucking just as the light turned green and Rodrigo moved the car forward with traffic. His moans began to intensify and I felt his dick was getting harder.

"*Ya vengo*," he said, warning me he was about to shoot, but it was too late. With his cock still in my mouth, I looked up into his face, and saw Richard. The first blast flew past my tonsils and down my throat. My eyes widened with surprise as I saw my ex and pulled my mouth from his exploding cock. Four more large shots of hot cum landed on my cheeks and mouth. The car screeched to a sudden halt, and I blinked twice, trying to figure out what was happening. Why was my ex boyfriend driving this cab in Mexico and what had he done with Rodrigo?

The shock of seeing Richard's face brought me slowly out of my sleep, and I opened my eyes and looked around me. It was a dream, of course. Why in the world had I seen Richard's face when I looked up? I should have recognized it was his dick I'd pulled out of Rodrigo's denim shorts and forced myself awake right then. I guess I wasn't as over that asshole as I'd thought I was. A light knock on my door startled me, and I stood up to answer it.

I opened the door about halfway and tried to focus my eyes against the bright light out in the hallway.

"Hi." It was Enrique. "It's seven o'clock."

"Oh," I said and rubbed my eyes. "Nice wake-up call."

"Well, you asked to be woke up at seven and I get off at seven, so I thought a knock at your door would be better than the loud telephone."

I'd forgotten that I was only wearing my boxers, and when I noticed Enrique's eyes looking down past my waist I looked down to see my cock was pushing against the front of the shorts. I had a full hard-on, obviously still from my dream, and the tent my cock was creating caused the fly front to spread wide open. Enrique saw my pubic hair and the base of my hard dick, and swallowed hard.

"I'm sorry," I said, and tried to rearrange myself and hide behind the door a little. "I was dreaming. Guess I didn't realize it got to me so bad."

"I'm not sorry," he said. "It's nice."

I blushed and started to close the door. Enrique put this foot against the bottom of the door, preventing it from closing. I looked at him and he was also blushing and staring at his foot keeping the door open. My cock hadn't gone done even a little, and now the thought of this cute kid flirting with me got it throbbing even more.

"I'm off work now," he said softly.

I looked into the hallway and saw it was clear. Smiling, I opened the door and moved to one side so Enrique could enter my room.

He took a deep breath and walked into the room slowly. I pulled him to me and gently kissed him on the neck. His body shuddered and went almost limp and a soft moan escaped his throat. I moved my mouth slowly up his neck and then kissed his soft pink lips. At first he just stood there and allowed me to kiss him, then he slowly opened his mouth and gently sucked my tongue into it. My cock became so hard it hurt as Enrique sucked softly on my tongue and returned my kisses. His mouth was warm and sweet, tasting like peppermint candies.

As we kissed he reached down and wrapped his fist around my dick. The front of my shorts was wet with my own precum, and as he caressed my cock it became wetter. Enrique dropped to his knees and licked the outline of my dick through my shorts, sucking on the spots my precum had made. He moaned with delight, and pulled my hard-on through the fly.

It was wet and sticky, which seemed to excite him even more. He blew a soft stream of air onto it and looked up at my face. I was waking up quickly, but still thought he looked like an angel with his face so close to my cock, his pink lips parting slightly with anticipation.

I closed my eyes and a second later felt his mouth envelop my throbbing cock. It wasn't just warm, it was hot! He just held my cock inside his mouth for a moment, lying on his tongue. Then his tongue began moving softly across the underside of my shaft, and circling it. If he'd stopped right there I could say it was one of the best blow jobs I'd ever had. But he didn't stop. Instead he began sucking gently on my cock as his tongue continued to tickle it. I felt the blood pump faster into my dick, making it grow thicker and harder. It wasn't long before I felt the cum churning in my balls, and began to moan as I pictured me emptying my load in this boy's mouth.

But Enrique had other plans. He stopped sucking on my dick and stood up. He kissed me softly on the lips again as he quickly shed himself of his clothes. When he was completely naked he moved us both to the bed and laid me gently on my back as he laid next to me.

He was beautiful. A couple inches taller than me and a little thin, but with well-defined muscles. The only hair on his torso was a thick patch that began at his belly button and trailed down to the base of his cock. I followed it lustfully and let my eyes rest on his crotch. He had a gorgeous dick. It was uncut and lying halfway hard against his left leg. Half of the head was sticking out of the foreskin, and I leaned over to suck on it. Enrique allowed me to suck his cock for a couple of minutes, and then let me know what he really wanted.

He rolled over onto his stomach and raised his ass slightly in the air. It was, without a doubt, the most magnificent ass I'd ever laid eyes upon. Perfectly round and full, riding high on his waist, and smooth as marble. It was lighter than the rest of him, obviously from his skimpy bathing suit, but still coppery brown.

I caressed his butt slowly for a moment, then could hold myself back no longer, and leaned down to kiss it. I spread the cheeks apart and saw his hole. It was so small and smooth and pink. I imitated Enrique's own move on my cock earlier and blew a stream of air on the ass hole, and he squirmed with pleasure.

"*Besame*," he whispered, asking me to kiss him down there.

I laid flat on my stomach behind him and leaned in closer to his butt. His entire body smelled clean and a little like baby powder. I leaned over and began kissing his ass cheeks, biting them softly from time to time. His moans and squirms told me he liked it, and so I moved on. I stuck out my tongue and traced the small of his back down into the crack of his ass cheeks. When I found his hole, I rested there for a moment, teasing him.

"Yes," he groaned. "Don't stop."

I pulled my tongue back into my mouth, and began kissing his hole with my lips. I felt his ass twitch, grasping for more, and slowly slid my tongue from my mouth so that it barely touched his quivering hole. Then I circled the hole with my tongue and slowly slid it inside him.

Enrique grabbed the comforter and moaned his delight. My tongue was deep inside him, his ass grasping it and massaging it gently. His ass was as hot as his mouth had been earlier, and my cock once again hurt with the intensity of my erection. I knew I had to fuck this boy soon or I'd cum all over my bed.

Apparently Enrique had the same idea because he pulled himself up from the bed and maneuvered me onto my back. He licked and sucked on my dick some more and reached down to retrieve a condom from his pocket. He rolled it down the length of my shaft and sucked on it a little more, making sure it was plenty wet.

"Do you want me?" he asked as he squatted only inches from my hard cock.

"Yes," I gasped out weakly.

"I want you, too," he said and lowered himself onto me.

I felt his ass spread slowly, allowing my cock head to slip in. He took a short breath and held just my head inside him for a moment. Then I felt him relax as he slowly slid his hot ass down my entire shaft. The deeper I went inside him the hotter he was, and his ass gripped my cock like a vise grip. When he had all of my dick inside him he sat still for a moment, his ass twitching and dancing around my thickness.

I began moving in and out of him in short strokes. He leaned down and kissed me, causing his ass to tighten around me even more. I was getting so close to coming, and he could tell, so he slowed things down a little. He pulled himself off my cock and rolled onto his back. I put my dick between his cheeks and rubbed it against his soft skin for a moment as I kissed him. Then, with his mouth sucking sweetly on my tongue, I slid my dick back into his welcoming hole.

He thrust his ass up to meet my strokes, and let me know we did not have to be gentle anymore. I pulled my cock out of his ass completely and then shoved it back in in one swift stroke. Enrique let out a cry but also grabbed my ass and pulled me back into him equally as hard. At that point it was useless for me to stop. I spread his long legs wide apart and lifted his ass higher into the air. My cock slid into his ass harder and deeper with each thrust. He smiled at me and squeezed his ass against my throbbing cock.

"I'm gonna come, Enrique!" I almost shouted.

"On my chest," he instructed.

I quickly pulled myself from his twitching ass and yanked the condom from my dick. The rubber was barely on the floor when the first jet of cum shot from my dick. I was aiming for his chest as he'd said, but the cum flew past his chest and onto his face. Three large shots landed on his nose and cheeks and lips, and Enrique licked at them hungrily. As the last couple of shots of my load landed on his chest, I heard him moan and a second later felt several squirts of hot liquid hit my ass and back. Enrique emptied what seemed like a quart of hot cum onto both of us, and then lay back, spent.

We laid on the bed, neither saying a word for a couple of minutes. Then Enrique got up and dressed quietly. I thought maybe he was angry or feeling guilty or something, but after he was dressed he walked over and kissed me softly on the lips again.

"Let's do this again before you leave."

I kissed him back and said sure.

Dinner was at a quaint little restaurant on the Malecon, the famous boardwalk along Puerto Vallarta's beautiful beach. It wasn't a gay restaurant, but almost half the patrons and an even larger number of the staff were obviously gay. I began feeling very happy. Well, okay, maybe the correct word would be buzzed. The mixture of the three margaritas and the ambience of Puerto Vallarta were working their magic on me.

I went dancing at a little club called Los Balcones. It was situated upstairs above a clothing store and had several balconies for patrons to sit and visit as they watched the tourists and locals mingle below on the street. Inside, the bar was a little too dark and the music a little too loud, but out on the balconies was very pleasant and I decided to stay out there. The bartenders and waiters were all extremely accommodating and equally as beautiful. I realized that so far every employee I'd seen in a gay establishment had been very pretty. It must be some kind of requirement here that you look like a supermodel. Not that I was complaining by any means.

I decided to make an early night of it, since it was only Thursday, and headed back to the hotel. Enrique greeted me with a smile and said good night. As I turned the corner I heard him whistle at me.

The next morning I woke around ten. I grabbed a danish and a cup of coffee from the complimentary continental breakfast at the hotel and then headed straight for the beach. I'm sure I looked like the typical American tourist, carrying my folding chair, towel, backpack (which held my sunglasses, lotion, water and a book) and wearing the sandals I'd picked up at the airport.

My *Fodor's Gay Guide to Mexico* informed me of the "gay beach" which was located only a block or so from my hotel. The beaches in Puerto Vallarta have little kiosk restaurants and bars running all along them. Each of the kiosks has a different color of chair they provide to their beach customers. The gay beach is called Blue Chairs, because the outside restaurant there, which is gay, has blue chairs. As I walked along the beach, it would not have been difficult to locate the gay beach. Not only because the blue chairs are so bright, but because you could see about fifty giddy gay boys in scanty bikinis dancing around the beach, jumping into the water and basically making a lot of noise, from a mile down the beach.

I laughed to myself as I found a chair there and settled in. Lotion applied, sunglasses on, book in hand, I was ready to bake until I was as dark as the locals. Within a couple of minutes a waiter appeared and two minutes later I had a mai-tai in hand. Life was good.

I tanned lying on my stomach for about forty minutes before deciding I needed to hit the ocean for a while. The water was surprisingly warm. A group of guys were practicing their volleyball maneuvers in the water, and so I swam a little ways out and just floated for a few minutes.

Making my way back to my chair, I stopped along the way and picked up a couple of seashells. Just as I reached my chair, I noticed Rodrigo, my cabbie from yesterday. He was lying on a towel on the sand a couple of chairs down from mine. He was lying on his back, looking right at me. He smiled and waved. My heart skipped a beat as I saw him in nothing but a skimpy bikini. It was yellow and made the most beautiful contrast against his oiled copper skin. Once again, his bulge was barely contained . . . in fact, the elastic band below his navel was stretching from his waist.

I smiled and started to walk over to him, when I noticed the guy next to him. Right next to him. He was lying on his stomach with his face looking away from us. He was Mexican, tall and muscular, not quite as dark as Rodrigo. As I looked at the both of them, he reached over and laid his hand on Rodrigo's chest.

I lost my smile. I lost my hard-on. I lost my will to live. Okay, that might be a little exaggerated, but I was very disappointed as I sat down and oiled the front of my body. I put on my sunglasses, ordered another mai-tai, and pretended to read my book. I looked over at Rodrigo a few times, and every time I did, he was looking at me. A couple of times he smiled at me, and once he even tilted his glass at me. Damn it, he knew I was watching him.

I took off my glasses and stopped pretending to read. Rodrigo's boyfriend was still turned with his back against us, so I felt okay looking right at Rodrigo. He kept smiling that beautiful smile at me and winked a couple of times. Then he reached down and squeezed his cock, right in front of me and everyone else on the beach. I choked on my mai-tai and sat up to stop from coughing. I watched as Rodrigo leaned over to tell his friend something, then get up and walk toward the kiosk. His eyes never left mine as he walked past the kiosk and toward the parking lot. I stood up and started following him. I stopped and leaned against the kiosk wall where I could see Rodrigo reach into a jeep and pull out a blanket. He looked over to see that I was watching, then began walking the other way down the beach.

I followed him again, a few feet down the beach and noticed the crowds were growing thinner. Rodrigo rounded a corner of the beach, curving around a huge rock and disappeared. I sped up, not wanting to lose him, and as I rounded the jutting rock, was grabbed by the arm and pulled to the ground. Startled, I tried to fight to get back to my feet. Instead I was pinned to the ground, and I saw Rodrigo sitting on top of my chest.

"Hi," he said, and leaned down to kiss me.

"Hi," I said, not really wanting to break the kiss.

"I told you I'd see you again."

"Yeah, but I can't buy you a drink here."

"This is all I want to drink," Rodrigo said, and reached down and gently cupped my cock in his hands.

I moaned, but struggled against him.

"Isn't that your boyfriend?"

"Yes."

"Doesn't he . . ."

"He's probably asleep. Don't worry."

"I can't, Rodrigo."

"Yes, you can. You want to, don't you?"

"Yes." I'd decided if it didn't bother Rodrigo that he had a boyfriend, it didn't bother me, either. After all, I was only here a week. "But I can't do it here. Someone might come by."

"Over here," he said, and pulled me behind a couple of large bushes that were up against the rock wall.

We slipped behind the bushes and spread the blanket out on the ground. Rodrigo laid me on my back and began kissing my nipples. His tongue was hot and wet and sent chills up my entire body. He bit them lightly and began working his way down my chest and stomach. By the time he reached my swim trunks, my cock was pounding hotly against the fabric, doing its own little dance.

"*Ay papacito, quieres más?*" Rodrigo asked in such a husky, strongly accented voice that I almost creamed right there.

"Yes. I want more."

He took the waist of my shorts and pulled them down with his teeth until they were lying on the sand beside us. My dick was lying across my stomach, dripping precum like crazy, and still throbbing even though it'd been released from the confines of my shorts.

Rodrigo leaned over and licked the precum from the head of my cock and then began licking and sucking on the head. My head is extremely sensitive, and I squirmed in delight as he sucked gently on it.

"*¿Te gusta?*" he asked and immediately resumed his sucking.

"Oh, yes, I like it very much."

He began swallowing more and more of my cock slowly, savoring every inch. My dick is only about six and a half inches long, but fairly thick, and Rodrigo seemed to enjoy taking his time with it. When it was buried deep in his throat, he tightened his throat muscles and began humming, creating a fantastic vibration around my shaft. It only took about five minutes of this before I felt the cum churning in my balls.

"I'm close, Rodrigo," I warned him, and he pulled off my cock immediately.

"I don't want you to come yet. Will you suck me also?"

"Sure," I answered, already tasting his precum in my mind.

He sat down and pulled off his trunks and laid them next to mine on the sand. Then he maneuvered himself so that he was sitting on my chest. My eyes bulged with disbelief and I lost a breath as I saw his cock. He obviously had enjoyed sucking my dick, because his own cock was fully hard and throbbing excitedly in front of my face. I've never seen a dick that big, and doubt I ever will again. Easily eleven or twelve inches long, and almost as thick as my wrist, it was covered with a silky sheath of foreskin that pulsed with thick veins and covered the entire shaft and half the large head. It was the same copper color as the rest of him.

"Jesus, Rodrigo. What the hell is that?" I asked in amazement.

"Do you like?"

"Hell, yes, I like."

"You'll suck it, then?"

I didn't even bother answering with words. I just leaned my head forward and licked all the precum off his cock head, and pulled the skin back to expose the entire head and shaft of his huge cock. I'd never sucked a dick this big, but I was determined to take Rodrigo's, even if I choked to death on it. I licked around the head for a moment, and then began taking more and more of his mammoth cock deeper into my mouth. I had about half of the huge pole in my mouth before I had to stop. It was so thick I couldn't take any more in my mouth without choking.

"Come on Papi," Rodrigo encouraged, "you can take more. Just relax."

I did as I was told and relaxed my muscles. It worked, and I felt Rodrigo slowly push more and more of his dick inside my mouth. I felt the big head slide past my tonsils and keep going, and my eyes bulged as I saw he was still pushing into me and I wasn't choking, even though I had to have at least nine inches of his manmeat inside my throat.

Rodrigo moaned loudly as he slowly let the last couple of inches slide inside my mouth. When his large shaved balls were resting on my chin he stopped and just let the large dick rest inside my mouth and down my throat. I gagged a couple of times and then realized I needed to breathe through my nose. Once I got used to that I was able to use my mouth for other things. I started swallowing and humming around Rodrigo's cock like he had with mine. He was so thick and hard his dick was stretching my throat muscles, and the sensation of my throat action sent Rodrigo over the edge. He moaned again and I felt his cock contracting and knew he was about to shoot.

At the last second he yanked his huge dick from my mouth, and shot a huge load of hot cum all over my face. I would never have thought one person could shoot such a large load, but when he was finished, my entire face and chest were covered with his hot, sticky cum.

My own cock was still hard and throbbing, but I was not close to coming since I hadn't even touched my dick while I was swallowing Rodrigo. I started to jerk it a little, and Rodrigo pulled my hand away.

"Let me," he said, and started sucking it again.

He teased the head and stuck his tongue in my piss slit, licking the inside membranes. He was a great cocksucker and didn't take long at all before I felt my jizz building inside my balls again.

Once again Rodrigo pulled his mouth from my cock when I was close. He stood up and pulled a condom from the small backpack he'd brought with the towel. He ripped the package open and slipped the condom on with expert speed. I couldn't believe that after spewing such a huge load just a couple of minutes ago that he was still fully hard. His fat cock was still bobbing with excitement and the veins popped out of his shaft like speed bumps on a busy street.

"Rodrigo, there is no way I can take that up my ass," I said and started to sit up on the towel.

"Shhh, Papi. You can take it," he whispered with that Ricardo Montalban accent that melted me to the core. He looked right into my eyes and his own sparkled as he winked at me. "I won't hurt you, I promise."

He laid me back down on the towel and lay on top of me, kissing me and caressing my body. His heavy cock rubbed against mine and worked its way between my legs, massaging my balls as it did. It felt so good, all hot and throbbing, and I sighed.

"¿*Te gusta*, baby?"

"Fuck, yeah."

"Good," he said and lifted my legs into the air. He pressed the head of his fat cock against my ass hole and I tensed up.

"Just relax, chico. I'll go slow."

He eased the big head inside my ass hole and stopped with just the head inside. My ass burned like hell and I tried to pull off of his cock, but he held me firm against it.

"Take it out, Rodrigo. It hurts."

"No, I won't. It will stop hurting in a minute."

He lay still with only his cock head inside me for a moment, and then when he felt my ass muscles relax a little, started pushing slowly more and more of his cock deeper in my ass. It was big and so fucking thick that it took about five minutes before it was buried deep in my ass until his balls were resting heavily on my ass cheeks. He kept it there, lying still for a couple of minutes.

"Is that better, babycito?"

The only response I could produce was a cross between a grunt and a moan. I'm sure I sounded like an animal in heat, but an intelligible response was just plain impossible. His huge cock filled my ass and more. My hot ass muscles stretched and squeezed his massive dick until I could feel the veins in his rod pulsing against them even through the condom.

He started to slip his dick out of my ass, and I moaned again with pleasure as I felt it moving inside me. He leaned down and kissed me on the lips as his cock began to pump slowly in and out of my tight ass, and a minute later I felt that familiar feeling of my cum building up again. I was determined not to let anything stop me this time. I had never felt anything so fantastic in all my life, and I was going to blow the largest load known to man all over this hot Mexican stud.

"Rodrigo?" It was an unfamiliar voice to me. "¿Rodrigo, donde estás?"

Rodrigo stopped in mid swing, his cock pulled almost all the way out of my ass, with only the head and a couple of inches remaining inside.

"Oh, shit," he said, "it's Ramón."

It didn't take a genius to know who Ramón was, and my eyes bulged with terror. Rodrigo's boyfriend was several inches taller than me, and about thirty pounds of pure muscle heavier.

"What..."

"Shhhh," Rodrigo whispered and slid his thick hard dick slowly back into my ass until he was lying flat on top of me. It took all I had not to moan loudly, but I managed to just expel my breath in a whisper.

We were still behind the bushes, and looked like we were completely covered, but I wasn't entirely sure. We heard Ramón getting closer to the bushes and both of us held our breath as he stopped within a foot of where his boyfriend's cock was still hard inside me.

"Rodrigo!" Ramón yelled down the beach, and when he did, Rodrigo's cock swelled to unimaginable thickness inside my ass. I started to gasp, and Rodrigo put his hand over my mouth to keep it quiet. He was getting turned on by the fact his boyfriend was inches away from us, and as Ramón took yet another step closer, Rodrigo began slowly pumping his fat cock in and out of my ass. He was still holding his hand over my mouth as I looked up in astonishment while he fucked me slow and deep. I kissed his hand to let him know it was okay, he could move it from my mouth. I could hear Ramón's breathing less than a foot from us, and I have to admit it was turning me on, too.

Rodrigo started fucking me a little harder, pulling his dick all the way out of my ass and then sliding it back in slowly, then pumping faster and harder. He could tell I was struggling not to scream or moan or grunt like an animal again, and I think it was getting him off.

Ramón started to walk away, and I guess Rodrigo decided he needed to finish up with me and get back to his boyfriend before something serious happened. A few sharp jabs inside my ass was all it took for both of us. I shot my load all over my stomach and onto Rodrigo's chest and stomach as I felt his cock throb uncontrollably inside me. When the last drop of my own cum was sliding down my shaft, Rodrigo pulled his cock out of my ass and ripped the condom off violently. He pointed his cock up and in the direction of the bushes. Four huge jets of cum shot out of his cock, and completely over the bushes. The first two landed in the footprints Ramón left in the sand in front of us, and several others landed in the bushes. I've never seen anyone shoot such huge loads, and just stared as he emptied his cock and balls of their load.

He quickly pulled on his swim trunks over his shrinking cock, and leaned down to kiss me.

"Ramón goes to work at ten tonight. He's a bouncer. I'll come to your hotel room after he leaves, okay?"

"I don't know . . ."

"Leave your door unlocked and be naked on your bed."

I just stared at him, stunned, as he ran to catch up to his boyfriend. I couldn't imagine the explanation he would find for his absence.

But I knew I would be lying naked on my bed with my door unlocked at around ten-thirty.

Truth or Dare

I was set up, plain and simple. Had I known the diabolical plan my cousin had contrived, I would never have agreed to go to his stupid birthday party. But I didn't know, and I was still a little naïve, and it was his twenty-first birthday. And he was my favorite cousin and best friend. So I really had no choice but to go.

It was a small affair, especially by Gregg's standards. Only six of us, for dinner at Gregg's apartment, a few adult beverages, and maybe a board game or two after. I thought it sounded a little mellow, but I was proud of Gregg. In high school he'd been a real hell raiser, drinking excessively, drugging a little more than could be justified as "experimenting," and hanging out with thugs. I was really worried about him for a while. But then he met his girlfriend, Veronica, and all of a sudden he straightened his act up, stopped drugging altogether, drank only socially, got a job, and became this really nice and thoughtful guy that everyone wanted to be around.

Gregg wasn't my biological cousin. He was my stepmom's second cousin. But he was only three months older than me, and we hung around and did everything together. We were much closer than any real cousins I know. When we enrolled at Stanford, everyone thought we were brothers. I shared everything with him, and he with me. And so, when I started struggling with my sexuality, I didn't think twice about talking with Gregg about it. He and Veronica were very supportive and even tried going to a couple of gay bars with me. But they felt more comfortable there than I did, and on the few attempts at "coming out" at those bars, I left feeling more frustrated and confused than I had when I walked in.

At the night of Gregg's birthday party, I should have known something was up, but I didn't. I should have paid attention to the fact that I knew Gregg and Veronica, and another friend Jerome and his girlfriend, Claire, and that the only person I didn't know was a really cute blond named Jason. But I didn't.

All through dinner, Gregg and Veronica made every attempt to engage Jason and me in conversation, while Jerome and Claire giggled and held hands and kissed, even as they chewed and swallowed their food. Getting us to talk wasn't hard, because Jason and I had a lot in common. We were both sophomores at Stanford. We both loved music and theater and tennis and football and our favorite TV show was *The Simpsons.* But at the same time, it *was* hard, because he was so fucking beautiful that I couldn't take my eyes off him, and I sported a boner every time he smiled at me. And it didn't help that he kept tilting his head just slightly as he looked up at me with those beautiful baby blue eyes.

When dinner was over, we moved into the living room and shared a couple of pitchers of margaritas while we played cards. And then Gregg played his ace card.

"What do you say we play a little Truth or Dare?" he asked with a sly grin on his face.

I spat a mouthful of mango margarita across the room. "I don't think . . ."

"What a great idea!" Claire shouted a little too loudly and began clapping her hands together.

"Really, Gregg," I said shakily as I grabbed his arm and squeezed hard.

"Oww," he whined, and shrugged my hand from his arm. "Don't be such a pussy."

"I'm in," Jerome said as he swallowed the last of his drink.

"Me too," Claire said, excitedly, and began to unbutton her blouse.

"Wait 'til we get started," Jerome said and stood up to get another pitcher of margarita.

Claire pouted and looked over at Veronica.

"I'm up for it," Veronica said, and leaned in to kiss Gregg on the lips.

I looked over at Jason with what I hoped to be a grown-up look of pleading for support, but what I fear was more of a childish look of desperation, fear and "where's my pacifier, because I really need to go find a nice little corner and pout for a while."

"I'm game," Jason said, and smiled at me. "You okay with this, Tyson?"

The dimples on either side of his full pink lips drove me crazy, and when he smiled at me and licked those lips, I thought I'd spray my load all over the living room.

"Really, guys, I don't think this is a good idea," I pleaded, and then downed more than half a glass of mango margarita in one swallow. "We're all good friends, and this could really . . ." I cringed as the "brain freeze" gripped my heart and squeezed it until I thought I'd pass out.

"Well, too bad. You're outvoted, so sit back and enjoy, okay," Gregg said, and winked at Veronica.

We drew cards to determine the order of play. High card got to ask a Truth question or come up with a Dare for the low card draw. The first couple of rounds were typically slow. Veronica was a little shy and stuck with Truth questions. Jerome was a little more bold, and ventured into a Dare or two, but kept them pretty clean. Claire was a big exhibitionist, and when she drew the high card, she dared Gregg to allow her to play the rest of the game with her top off.

And then the inevitable happened. I drew the low card and Gregg drew the high card. I looked at him like a deer caught in headlights, and begged him with my eyes to be kind.

"I dare you to kiss Jason on the lips for one minute."

Jerome and Claire stopped feeling one another up and just looked at Gregg as if he were insane. Their mouths were dropped and open.

"Gregg, I can't do that," I said through gritted teeth. "It's not fair to . . ."

"I don't mind," Jason said softly.

Jerome and Claire turned their gawking stare to Jason, and Gregg and Veronica smiled and snuggled up against one another.

"But . . ." I started to protest some more.

"Tyson, I dare you to kiss Jason . . ."

"Yes, I heard you!" I said, and glared at him.

"Then do it."

I looked over at Jason and was amazed when I saw him scoot closer to me. Jerome and Claire sucked in a mouthful of air and watched with wide eyes as I leaned in toward Jason. Jerome's hand had stopped mid-squeeze on his girlfriend's bare breast, and Claire's legs closed as she sat up straight to get a better look.

I took a deep breath and then leaned in to kiss Jason. As my lips touched his, I was painfully aware of the fact that I was shaking uncontrollably and my heart was racing. I'd never been with another guy before, never kissed another guy's lips. Hell, I'd never even looked at another guy's cock. When in the locker room at school, I took every measure to look away when the opportunity presented itself to sneak a peek at my classmates' dicks. The last thing I wanted or needed was to have my own cock betray me while I was naked and in a room full of other naked men.

And so I didn't know what to expect. But I needn't have worried. Jason's lips were soft and warm and every bit as delicious as I'd imagined them to be when I first saw him earlier that night. I let my own lips just barely brush his and wondered how we would maintain that hold for a full minute. But that concern was brushed aside quickly as Jason parted his lips and licked my own lightly with his tongue. At first I thought I'd have a heart attack, and then, when he sucked on my lips and gently forced his tongue between my lips, I thought I'd die.

I sucked on his tongue for what seemed like eternity, and marveled at how warm and sweet it was. My cock had gotten hard from the moment he began to scoot closer to me, but now it was so hard it ached. I wanted Jason so badly, I couldn't think straight. Thoughts spun through my head too fast for me to register them. I was confused. I'd never felt like this before. I'd never allowed myself, for more than a couple of minutes . . . the amount of time it took me to beat off as quickly as possible, to entertain the thought of what this moment would feel like. And now, here I was, in the flesh, sucking on the tongue of one of the hottest guys I'd ever seen.

"Time's up," Veronica said, excitedly. "Wow! That was so hot. It got me all worked up."

"Okay, now it's my turn to draw," Claire said a little

nervously as she swallowed a mouthful of her drink and reached for the cards.

"Fuck that shit," Jerome said, and pulled the cards away from Claire.

"But it's my turn to . . ."

"Jason, I dare you to pull Tyson's cock out of his jeans and suck it."

"Hey," Claire cried, "that's not fair. It's my turn . . ."

"Shut up!" Gregg said. "Suck his cock, Jason."

Jason looked tentatively at me, and raised his eyebrows as he licked his lips.

What the fuck, I thought to myself, and leaned back against the couch and spread my legs. I would normally never have agreed to this, but the margaritas were working their magic on me.

Jason moved between my legs and unbuttoned my jeans. My cock was fully hard, and throbbing, and so when he pulled my underwear down below the waist of my jeans, my cock sprung up against my belly.

"Ooooh," Veronica squealed as she snuggled against Gregg's chest. "You didn't tell me he had such a big dick."

"I didn't know," Gregg said. "I've never seen it before now. At least not hard."

My cock isn't huge by any stretch of the imagination. It's a little long, I guess, maybe eight inches or so and reaches just past my bellybutton when it's fully hard. It's only average in girth, but it gets really red and hard, and the veins pop impressively, so it looks a little bigger than it actually is.

Jason smiled at me, and then leaned down and swallowed the entire shaft in one swallow.

"Oh, Christ," I said as I sucked air into my mouth and

leaned further back against the sofa as I raised my hips slightly to push my cock deeper into Jason's throat.

His mouth was incredibly hot and wet, and his tongue was soft and strong at the same time as it swirled around the head of my cock and then snaked down the shaft. Jason's cheeks wrapped tightly around my cock and massaged it as it slid deeper and deeper down his throat.

I looked over and noticed that the others were rearranging themselves around the room so they could get a better view. Gregg and Jerome were both sporting their own boners and rubbing them through their jeans. Veronica watched wide-eyed as Jason sucked my cock hungrily. Claire was still sulking a little bit but was working her way to a better view of the action on the floor below her.

I'd never been sucked off before by a guy or a girl, and so it didn't take long before I was ready to shoot. Jason swallowed my cock all the way to the balls, and then wrapped his mouth tighter around it as it was buried deep inside his throat. I'd never felt anything so good.

"You better stop, dude," I said hoarsely as I forced the words through my parched throat. "I'm gonna come."

I thought Jason would stop, and allow my cock to slip from his mouth. But he had something else in mind. Though I didn't think it possible, his lips and mouth wrapped tighter around my cock, and he sucked on it even more frantically. The heat and wetness and the feel of his throat muscles squeezing around my shaft was more than I could take.

"Fuck, man, I'm coming," I almost yelled.

Again, I thought Jason would release my dick and watch as I sprayed my load all over myself. But instead, he continued sucking on it, and reached down between my balls and ass and massaged the sensitive area there. I moaned loudly and tightened every muscle in my body as I let go with the most intense load I'd ever experienced.

The first spew flew from my cock with what felt like warp force. Jason gagged just a little after that first spew, but kept his lips wrapped around my cock and continued sucking. Five or six more spasms racked through my body, and I felt Jason's throat tighten as he swallowed each of them.

It seemed to go on for an hour, and when I was completely spent, Jason let most of my cock slide from his throat, but he kept the head inside his mouth and sucked on it gently. I remained fully hard, and struggled to regain my breath.

"Damn, that was hot," Jerome said as he rubbed his crotch.

"Jason, I dare you to take off your clothes so we can see your dick," Veronica said, and giggled as she took another drink of her margarita and moved away from Gregg a few inches.

Jason didn't hesitate, and kicked his pants off in one move and threw his shirt across the room.

I gasped as I looked at him completely naked. His was the most magnificent body I'd ever seen. His smooth, tanned chest was muscular and sculpted to perfection. Tiny, perky nipples barely poked up above the rest of his skin. His torso was perfectly shiny and hairless except for the thick trail of dark hair that snaked from just below his belly button to his pubes. My eyes bulged as I stared at his cock. I'd never imagined, let alone seen, a cock so big. It was easily ten inches long, and as big around as my wrist. It was fully hard and throbbing, but I noticed a thin layer of foreskin covering about a third of the head. Thick veins ran from the base to the bottom of the head and pulsed wildly as his cock lay against his belly.

Veronica and Claire both gasped and moved closer to get a better look at the monster cock.

"Fuck, dude," Jerome said. "What the fuck is that?"

Jason laughed nervously, and looked at me and smiled.

"Suck me," he said, and pulled me closer to him.

"I don't think I can," I said. "I've never sucked a dick before. It's really big."

"Just relax and go slow. You don't have to deepthroat me. Just take what you can."

I took a deep breath and lowered my head to his crotch. I thought I might hesitate about sucking it, afraid of it for some reason. But I wasn't. I stuck out my tongue and licked the fat head for a moment, and then opened my mouth and sucked the head into my mouth. It felt good and it didn't take long before I lowered my head and took a couple more inches into my mouth.

Jason moaned and lifted his hips a little so that another inch slipped into my throat. When I gagged a little he stopped. I'd never felt anything so good in my life. His cock felt and tasted better than I could ever have imagined. I sucked on it as hungrily as I could, trying hard not to scrape it with my teeth.

"Okay, I can't take this anymore," Veronica said, and pushed Gregg onto the floor. "Get naked and join them."

"What?" Gregg squeaked.

"You heard me."

"Do it, dude," Jason said as he slid another inch of his cock into my throat.

Gregg shook his head a couple times, to clear the cobwebs, I think, and then he shrugged and shucked his clothes.

I'd never paid attention to my cousin or thought about him sexually. But as I glanced up at his naked body while I sucked Jason's cock, I realized how beautiful he was. He was a track star at Stanford, and so his body was finely defined and well-toned. He had a dusting of black hair on his muscular chest. His legs were thick and brawny, and shaved hairless. Large veins popped out on them and snaked their way to his big feet.

His cock was fully hard and jutted out in front of him about seven inches or so. It was a little smaller than mine, but looked beautiful and perfectly proportioned on his handsome body.

"Jerome, get down there and join them," Veronica ordered.

"No way," Jerome said, and looked around himself uncomfortably.

"Way," Veronica said. "Don't tell me you're not into this. Your rock-hard dick is giving you away."

Jerome and Claire both looked down at his crotch. A long line worked its way halfway down his thigh. They looked at each other as if they were unsure what to do with that information.

"Do it," Veronica ordered.

Jerome stood up and stripped off his clothes. He was an extremely handsome guy. His mother was French and his father was Cherokee, and so he had dark and beautiful features. He was tall and thin, but well muscled. There wasn't a strand of hair on his body. His cock was a little longer and a little thicker than mine, but a little shorter and a little thinner than Jason's. A large drop of precum dripped out of his cock head and slid down his shaft.

I'd stopped sucking Jason's cock by this time, and the four of us guys just kind of sat around naked on the floor, uncertain where to go from there. Veronica and Claire sat next to one another on the sofa and glanced back and forth between us guys.

"Okay, it's my turn," Claire finally said. "Jerome, I dare you to lick Tyson's ass, and Gregg, I dare you to suck Jason's cock."

"Hey, that's not fair," Gregg said. "You can't have two turns at once."

"Shut up and suck his dick," Veronica said.

Jerome pulled me onto all fours and positioned me so that my ass was face level to him. Then he grabbed Gregg by the head and shoved it down into Jason's crotch. Apparently the alcohol had gotten to him, and he was now fully into the action at hand.

Thinking back on it now, I cannot believe that that was the first time Jerome had ever eaten ass. His tongue was like magic on my butt. He licked my cheeks for a few minutes, and then snaked his tongue inside my ass and licked around the walls for a while. Then he shoved it deeper inside and fucked my ass with it. At first it was a little uncomfortable, but after a couple of minutes, I was shoving my ass against him and begging for more.

I watched as Gregg made a decent attempt at sucking Jason's cock. I'm sure it was the first time he'd ever had a dick in his mouth, and the look on his face told me he was still a little unsure about whether or not he liked it. But I have to give him kudos, because he didn't give up, and he had about three inches or so inside his mouth.

"It's big enough for two," Veronica said. "Tyson, go help Gregg suck Jason's dick."

I crawled over to where Jason and Gregg were sitting. I figured Jerome would stop eating my ass, but I was wrong. He crawled over with me, never taking his tongue out of my twitching ass. I leaned down and licked one side of Jason's giant cock while Gregg licked and sucked on the other side. We licked and sucked up and down the shaft, and when our mouths reached the bulbous head, we both licked off the slick precum and then kissed one another with Jason's big head between our mouths. Jerome continued licking and sucking and kissing my ass, and I found it impossible not to rock back and forth against his tongue and mouth.

I was on sensory overload. I'd never allowed myself to think too much about another guy's body or to daydream about being with another guy. I made extra attempts at avoiding naked guys at school. Sure, I fantasized a little about having sex with a guy when I beat off, but I always made quick work of it and then felt guilty about it when I finished. But this was so much more than I'd ever imagined it could be. With all the hard cocks all around me, and with Jerome's mouth and tongue sending me over the edge with the work he was doing on my ass, I thought I would shoot a gallon of cum and then die of exhaustion. I didn't think it could get any better than that moment. But I was wrong.

"Okay, let's get down to business," Veronica said. "Jason, I want you to fuck Tyson."

"I can't take that . . ." I started to protest.

"Yes, you can," Jason whispered eagerly. "I'll go easy, I promise."

"It's too big. I can't do it."

"You've never been fucked, right?"

"No."

"Well, then, the size of your first dick doesn't matter. It's gonna hurt for a minute or two, regardless of the size. Even a small cock would feel uncomfortable for a few minutes your first time. A bigger one isn't gonna hurt any more."

"Then why would I want to do this?"

"It'll only hurt for a moment. Then it will feel really good."

"You sure?"

"Absolutely."

Jerome and Gregg were looking back and forth from Jason and me to one another, as if they couldn't believe the conversation or that they were gonna witness this.

"I'm still not sure," I said, hesitantly.

Jerome pushed me onto my knees again, and turned me around so that my ass was facing Jason.

I felt Jason moving behind me, and then I felt his hot cock slide against my ass cheek. I gasped, and tightened up my body. When I felt the giant cock move across my ass cheek and then rest in the crevice of my ass, I tightened up even more and moaned as I lowered my head to the floor.

"Relax, dude," Jason said, and began sliding his cock up and down the length of my ass crack.

It took me a couple moments to relax, but I finally did, and a second later I felt a stab of pain as Jason's cock head pierced my ass hole and slipped inside. I cried out and felt my whole body tighten up as a ball of fire ripped through my bowels and traveled to every nerve ending in my body. I tried to pull my ass off of his thick hard cock, but his big hands on my shoulders kept me anchored.

"Just relax, baby," he whispered as he leaned in to kiss my ear. "I promise it will feel much better really soon."

I bit my lip and felt a tear fall down my cheek. This was impossible. It was never going to feel good. It hurt like hell. How could anyone ever think this was . . . ? And then it happened. In an instant the pain turned into a tingle, and that tingle spread through my entire body. My cock throbbed with excitement and leaked a little more precum. My ass relaxed and I felt all ten inches of Jason's cock slide deep inside my ass and rest only when his balls rested against my ass cheeks.

"Oh, God, man," Jason moaned. "That's fucking incredible."

I'd heard that demonic possession was possible, but until that moment I wasn't sure that I believed it. But that is the only logical explanation for what happened next. I moaned like an animal in heat and thrust my entire body backward onto Jason's fat, hard cock. A lightning bolt of pain speared me deep inside my belly, but that only spurred me on to deeper pleasure. Before I could stop myself, I was bucking my body against Jason's and begging for more and more of his cock inside me.

Jerome and Gregg stared at me with wide eyes, not sure what to do next. Thank goodness for Veronica and Claire.

"Gregg, get underneath him," Veronica ordered. "Suck his dick while Jason fucks him."

Gregg bolted into action as if he'd been poked with an electrical prod, and slid underneath me, between my knees and my hands. He stuck out his tongue and licked at the head of my cock for a moment, and then swallowed the entire length deep into his throat. For just a second, I thought coherently that my cousin must have been holding out while pretending sucking Jason's cock had been his first time. But then the sensation of his hot mouth wrapped around my cock and the feeling of my head slipping past his tonsils drowned out all rational thought.

"And you," Claire directed Jerome, "get over in front of Tyson and fuck his mouth."

Jerome didn't hesitate to move in front of my face. He slapped his hard cock against my cheeks and chin a couple of times, and then rested the fat head of his dick against my lips. I kissed it and stuck my tongue out to lick it for a few seconds. And then I opened my mouth wide, wrapped my lips around his head, and slid my entire head down the length of his hard cock. I gagged just a little as his fat cock slid against the back of my throat, and then I opened my throat wider and savored the feel of his hot cock as it rested deep in my throat.

I was delirious at this point. Every inch of my body was on fire. Jason's huge cock was buried deep inside my ass, just resting there and waiting for my cue to fuck the hell out of me. Jerome's hot cock tasted delicious in my mouth, and pulsed wildly deep inside my throat. And Gregg's warm, wet mouth sucked hungrily on my own cock, feeling much better than anything I'd ever dreamed possible.

For a moment, everyone was still and quiet. No one moved

a muscle or said a word. Then I moaned, and that was all it took for all hell to break loose.

Jason slid his gigantic cock all the way outside of my ass, making an audible "plop" and causing me to feel more empty than I had ever felt before. Then he slammed the huge pole back inside me, deep inside my bowels, until his balls bounced off my ass. He began sliding in and out of me faster and faster, each time sending shockwaves of pleasure through my entire body.

Jerome followed Jason's lead and began pumping his thick cock in and out of my mouth, faster and faster. Every time his fat head slipped out of my throat and across my tongue, I prayed he would not pull all the way out. He obliged, and pulled back just enough to keep his cock head in my hungry mouth, and then he'd slide all the way back inside me again. A couple of times, he began to breathe heavily and threatened to come. So I pulled my mouth off of his cock and forced him to calm down before putting his dick back inside me and continuing.

Gregg sucked on my cock like a baby with a bottle. I couldn't believe how warm and wet his mouth was. And what a hungry little cocksucker he was! When all eight inches of my cock was buried in his throat, he wrapped his lips tighter around me and sucked on it until I thought he'd milk me dry.

Jason and Jerome quickly got into a synched rhythm. Every time Jason pulled his big cock out of my ass, Jerome would thrust his cock deeper into my throat. And when Jerome would withdraw his cock from my throat, Jason slid his cock back inside my ass. Both boys had really large dicks, and I swore I could feel each and every vein on both big dicks as they slid deep inside me. My ass and throat were both stretched beyond what I ever thought possible.

Gregg lapped and swallowed my cock with reckless abandon, and moaned loudly every time Jason's thrust inside my ass would drive my cock deeper into his throat. When I glanced down while sucking Jerome's cock, I saw that Gregg was beating his own cock like a madman.

It was all just too much for me to take for too long a time. Though I'd have loved for that moment to go on for hours, after only ten or fifteen minutes, I felt my balls tighten and the beginning of my orgasm building deep inside my guts. I tried to warn the others, but with Jerome's cock deep inside my mouth, the only thing that eeked out was a deep moan that only made the other guys increase their frenzied pace. Jason and Jerome's cocks thrust deeper and harder into me, and Gregg swallowed my cock and sucked on it gently and frantically at the same time.

Bright fireworks exploded in my head as my body tensed and shot stream after stream of cum deep into Gregg's mouth. He choked a little on the first couple of jets, and then swallowed all eight inches of my cock into his throat as he milked the last few spurts of cum down his gullet.

My body twitched and quivered a few seconds while Gregg finished sucking me dry. And then I collapsed onto the floor just as Gregg moved out from under me. The big cocks on either end of me ripped from my body in the most emptying feeling I have ever experienced.

Jason grabbed me by the legs and flipped me over onto my back. He spread my legs and crawled between them. He towered over me, stroking his big cock as he aimed it at my chest. Jerome straddled my head, and Gregg scrambled to his knees at my side. They all beat their cocks furiously, and moaned in unison.

As if on cue, all three guys sprayed their loads across my body at the same time. Jason blasted a load that splashed across my body with the force of a water hydrant. The first couple of shots flew past my head and landed on Jerome's flat tummy.

That was enough to send Jerome over the edge, and he showered his load across my face and chest. Some of it landed in my mouth and on my lips, and I lapped at it hungrily. Jason was still unloading the last few shots of his orgasm onto my cock and balls when Gregg grunted like a caveman and released his load onto my chest and stomach.

When they were finished, I was covered from cock to eyes in warm, sticky cum. We were all moaning and panting, and the three of them collapsed on top of me. We stayed that way for several minutes, and then unraveled from one another.

"Wow!" Gregg said. "What the fuck was that all about?"

We looked over to see what the girls thought about everything that had just happened. They were both crashed out, leaning against one another with their mouths open and snoring loudly. An empty margarita blender laid upturned on the sofa beside them.

"Hey," Jerome said as he stood up and walked over to the girls. "This was all their idea. What do you think we should do about this?"

"Forget them." Jason smiled. "Truth or Dare?"

We all laughed, grabbed a cock in each hand and waded through the mess of clothes and empty margarita glasses to find our way to the bedroom.

Traveling Tailor

"God damn it!"

Gerald slammed his fist down onto his desk and kicked the heavy wooden leg. Of all the times for his shitty luck to show its face. He should have paid attention to his horoscope and just stayed home today.

He hadn't split the seam in his pants since he was a fat awkward kid. It was a common occurrence back then, some twenty years ago, and the other kids had been merciless in their teasing. To this day he could remember running home; or rolling home, to be more precise, crying and slamming the door behind him to close out their laughter.

But that was twenty years ago, and now as he approached thirty, he finally was going to have the last laugh. Later this afternoon, Gerald Gomez was going to pitch the ad campaign that everyone knew would make him the youngest partner in Dallas's largest advertising agency. Not to mention the only Latino partner. Smith, Davidson & Young would soon become Smith, Davidson, Young & Gomez.

Only one obstacle stood in his way before making it official. This afternoon's presentation that would surely clench the

Bruce Callahan account that had eluded the agency for more than ten years. They'd all tried tiredly and shamelessly to snatch the account from Barnes, Kemp & Johnson. And they had all failed.

But Gerald hadn't failed. For the last six months he'd wined and dined the oil tycoon, and it was finally paying off. Bruce Callahan had taken a liking to Gerald, and last week Callahan had all but handed the account to Gerald. All that was left was the final presentation this afternoon, and even that was just formality. At Callahan's insistence, the other three partners had cleared their calendars to attend the presentation. Barnes, Kemp & Johnson were also going to be present, according to Bruce's demands. The buzz was around town and it was common knowledge what was going to go down at three o'clock.

But that was still two hours away. Gerald was dressed in his finest suit, and as he sat at his desk just a few moments ago he heard the undeniable rip of his inseam. When he moved his leg to look down at it in disgust, the tear spread even farther. It now stretched from mid thigh to just below his knee.

He cursed himself for all the hours he'd spent at the gym over the last three or four years. No longer the fat kid in town, he was now just over six feet of solid, lean but bulging muscle. Muscle that ripped his pant leg. He'd grown out of the awkward fat kid and into a striking young man. His black hair, deep brown eyes, smooth copper skin and bright white smile were now his weapon. He got whatever he wanted because there was absolutely nothing working against him anymore.

Except for the goddammed tear in his pant leg.

"Karen," he shouted into his intercom to his secretary, "get in here now."

"I'm sorry, Mr. Gomez," he heard a tiny scared voice from

far away, "Karen isn't here. She took some papers across the street for Mr. Davidson."

Gerald pushed the intercom button off and swore under his breath. Davidson had his own girl, why the hell was he always pulling Karen away to run his errands. Sweat began to trickle down his neck as he panicked.

It was then that he remembered the tailor shop that occupied the small space on the first floor of his office building, right before the elevators. He'd passed it thousands of times, smiling politely at the elderly woman who was always busy behind the counter. Traveling Tailor, the shop was called, because it catered to downtown offices and traveled to its customers who didn't have time to come to them.

He rummaged through his desk drawer for the building directory and frantically flipped the pages until he spotted the simple black and white ad. He dialed the number so quickly that his first two attempts were wrong numbers. Then he took a deep breath and dialed more slowly.

"Traveling Tailor," came the sweet elderly woman's voice. It was thick with an accent Gerald struggled to place. Russian maybe, or German. He wasn't sure.

"Hi. This is Gerald Gomez, with Smith, Davidson & Young. We're in your same building, up on the fifty-eighth floor."

"Yes, Mr. Gomez, how can I help you?"

"Well, I have somewhat of an emergency," Gerald said. "Actually, it's a really big emergency. I just ripped my pant leg, and I have a very important meeting in a couple of hours. I really need your help."

"Yes, sir. I am in the middle of another emergency right now. Ms. Cartwright on the seventy-second floor has pulled her hem." Gerald thought he heard a tone of sarcasm in her voice.

"But this is *really* important." he bit his bottom lip. "My meeting is in an hour," he lied and sat forward in his chair.

"Ms. Cartwright's meeting is in twenty minutes."

Gerald swatted at the air around the phone and gave the old woman the middle finger.

"But I'm almost finished here. I can maybe come up there in about half an hour."

"That would be fine," Gerald said between clenched teeth. He knew this was his only chance at fixing the huge rip in his pants. "Thank you."

"My pleasure sir," the old woman said. "I'll be up as soon as I can."

Gerald hung up the phone and counted to ten. It wouldn't do any good to brood or get angry. He had to keep his cool. He had to be ready for the most important pitch of his career.

So he pulled the only file on his desk in front of him and scanned its contents, practicing his inflection and hand gestures that would close the biggest upset in recent Dallas business history. The Callahan account was worth more than sixty million dollars, and Gerald practiced his theatrics until he felt they were perfect.

He was shocked when Karen buzzed him only fifteen minutes later.

"Gerald, Mr. Callahan is on line two for you. And the 'traveling tailor' is here for you," she said with a puzzled tone.

"Great!" Gerald said as he picked up the cordless phone and hit the button for line two. "Send her in."

"Bruce, how are you," he asked as the door to his office opened, and he stood up to walk around the front of his desk.

A young blonde boy carrying a small case walked in and closed the door. He was wearing a letter jacket from Texas A&M University, and looked like he had just finished basketball practice for the college team. His hair was slightly ruffled and his cheeks had a blush to them that hinted of a recent intense workout.

Gerald leaned against the front of his desk and spread his legs so that the young man could see the huge tear. The boy leaned down in front of Gerald and pulled on the torn pant leg to see what he had to work with.

"I spoke with a woman," he whispered as he covered the mouthpiece of the phone. Obviously Bruce Callahan was in the middle of a long one-sided conversation.

"Yeah," the boy replied quietly, "Gramma said it was an emergency, so she sent me up. Don't worry, I know what I'm doing."

Gerald nodded and went back to his conversation.

"I know Bruce, but don't worry about a thing. I'm all set here," he said and looked down at the kid again.

The boy's face was inches from his crotch, and Gerald felt his cock stir inside his pants as he felt the kid's hot breath hit his bare leg through the ripped seam. The tailor's hands brushed his thigh a couple of times, and Gerald panicked as he noticed the long line of his hardening cock spread across the front of his slacks. Damn, he should've worn briefs instead of boxers today, he thought.

"Yes, we're fully expecting they *will* be upset."

The blonde kid reached inside the gaping hole in the leg of Gerald's pants and caressed Gerald's smooth muscular thigh.

Was that an intentional squeeze? Gerald blushed as his cock throbbed even harder.

The kid looked up and smiled, and his bright blue eyes sparkled as he licked his lips.

Gerald swallowed hard and tried to keep his calm, cursing

his inability to control the burning heat he felt as the blush spread across his cheeks.

"You know how much we appreciate this, Bruce," he managed out as the kid's hands found their way to his belt and began to unbuckle it. "Don't worry about a thing."

The front of Gerald's pants unbuttoned quickly, and he felt the young tailor press his face against the bulging crotch as his arms wrapped around Gerald's legs. Precum was already leaking out of the head of his cock and staining the front of his slacks when the blonde boy slid the waist of the pants down Gerald's long legs.

"Me too." He breathed heavily, and closed his eyes. The college student had reached inside Gerald's boxers and pulled out his throbbing uncut cock.

"Bruce, I've gotta run," Gerald said quickly. "I'll see you in a couple hours."

One fist wrapped around Gerald's long, fat pole and slowly slid the foreskin back and forth along the length.

"Good-bye."

Gerald reached around him to hang up the phone just as the hot, wet mouth covered his cock head. The kid's tongue tickled his head for a moment, while he sucked greedily on the thick shaft.

"Shit, kid, that feels good."

The tailor swallowed half of Gerald's dick and looked up and winked. Gerald slid his long cock all the way inside the boy's throat a couple of times, stopping only when the kid choked.

"Sorry," Gerald said as he pulled completely out of the hot mouth.

"Don't be," the college student/tailor said, and stood up to face Gerald. "I'm Rick," he said and leaned in to kiss Gerald on the lips.

"Gerald," Gerald said between deep kisses. He tasted himself on Rick's tongue.

"So, Gerald," Rick said as he pulled away and began to undress himself, "I hear you have an emergency."

"Yeah." Gerald was used to being in control of just about every situation, so he was dumbfounded as the kid boldly stripped right there in his office.

"Well, so do I," Rick said breathlessly as he quickly unbuttoned his jeans and pushed them to his ankles. He'd already opened his jacket and unbuttoned his shirt, and Gerald stared at his well-muscled chest and hard, flat stomach. The thick trail of blonde hair that started at his navel and ended at his pubic hair took Gerald's breath away.

"Really? And what is your emergency?"

"I work out in the gym downstairs, and had a really good workout earlier this morning. You know about the showers in the gym, Gerald?"

"No," Gerald panted out his lie. His cock pounded and was still leaking precum, and he found it difficult to talk.

"Well, the showers can be pretty fun sometimes. Today the guy in the shower next to me was giving me quite a show, and I got a little horny."

"Uh-huh."

"But it turns out he was just teasing me. I kinda wanted a little more than just teasing, you know? He left right as I was ready to go down on him. You can imagine how frustrated I was, right?"

"Right."

"I figured I would get dressed and then head over to my

buddy Mark's. He's always up for a good time. But as I was dressing, Gramma paged me. She insisted that I rush up here."

"You should always listen to your gramma," Gerald said, and reached forward to caress Rick's hard and sweaty chest.

"You talk too much," Rick replied, making fun of the first complete sentence Gerald had been able to make since his cock got hard. "If we're gonna get these slacks of yours fixed before your meeting, you'd better stop talking and start fucking me."

He clumsily pulled Gerald's shirt from his torso, then kissed him on the lips again. Gerald sucked on the warm probing tongue and fought to regain some amount of control of the situation. It was useless, though. Rick was obviously hungry for his dick, and the cocky college kid was used to getting what he wanted.

Rick turned around with his back to Gerald and leaned forward. His ass was extremely well-muscled and had a light coating of baby-fine blonde hair on it. Gerald squeezed the cheeks in both hands, then pressed his cock against the crack between them.

"That's it, Gerald." Rick moaned, and spread his cheeks wider. "Fuck me."

Normally Gerald would start by licking the ass, getting it relaxed and wet, but Rick was obviously in control here, and was in no mood for foreplay. That suited Gerald just fine, since he was pressed for time anyway. His dick head leaked a steady stream of precum, and helped lube up Rick's hungry ass. He spread some of it around the tiny puckered hole and moaned loudly as he felt the hot skin of his giant cock slide up and down the length of Rick's ass crack.

Rick reached behind him with one hand and moved Gerald's throbbing dick right to his twitching hole. Then he took a deep breath and slowly slid backward onto the fat cock, until it was buried deep inside him.

"Damn, you're huge," he whispered, short of breath.

"You talk too much," Gerald grunted, and began sliding in and out of the hottest and tightest ass he'd fucked in years.

Rick's ass muscles squeezed the big dick, and Gerald felt the foreskin moving across his long, thick shaft as he fucked the kid. He reached around and pinched Rick's nipples and ran his hand along the washboard stomach of the college kid. They found a rhythm very quickly, and fucked as if they'd been partners for years.

Normally Gerald could go for quite a while. But when Rick pulled Gerald's hand to his mouth and began sucking on his fingers, Gerald knew today was going to be different. The kid was damned talented, he thought as his fingers slid down Rick's hot throat just as Gerald's dick buried itself inside his ass.

When Rick reached down and stroked his own cock, his ass tightened even stronger around Gerald's fiery cock, and Gerald felt the cum churn in his balls as it prepared to shoot out his shaft.

"Fuck, Gerald, I'm gonna shoot," Rick almost yelled, and before he even finished the sentence, Gerald saw the kid's load spew across the floor. Several jets flew out and with each one, the ass muscles enveloping Gerald's cock grew tighter and hotter.

"Me too." Gerald breathed heavily and pumped faster and deeper.

Rick pulled himself off of Gerald's cock and fell to the floor, facing the huge brown dick. He stuck out his tongue just as the first shot poured onto his face, and kept his mouth open as Gerald's load sprayed across his face. Three or four of the hot jets actually landed in Rick's mouth, and he swallowed them hungrily. But most of the load landed on his forehead, in his eyes and on his cheeks.

"Man, you have a great cock," Rick said and leaned backward onto his elbows.

"And you have a great ass."

Just then the intercom buzzed and Karen's voice broke through.

"Gerald, there's a Mrs. Schneider on line one for you. Something about a traveling tailor?"

"Can you tell her I'll be just one minute, please."

"Yes, sir."

Rick was already getting up and starting to dress.

Gerald picked his pants up from the floor and handed them to the tailor. He would definitely have to give this kid a big tip, he thought to himself as he stood naked in the middle of the office trying to catch his breath.

"I'll have these fixed for you in no time," Rick said. He kissed Gerald on the lips and pushed him down into his leather executive chair.

"Gramma's on line one." He smiled. "She doesn't like to be kept waiting."

"This is Gerald Gomez," Gerald said calmly into the phone as his heavy uncut dick lay limp between his legs. "Yes, he's here and getting me all fixed up right now. Thanks for being so helpful."

Stepbrothers

My dad and I have never been very close. My parents were divorced when I was eight years old and I don't think I really ever got over it. My father moved out of the house and across town. I spent a few weekends with him for a few years, and I have to say he tried hard to make us both feel comfortable. Then he started dating more regularly and seemed to take less interest in making me feel at home with him. I spent less and less time with him, and by the time I entered high school I almost never saw him at all.

Dad moved to New York City my senior year in high school to take a senior position with an advertising firm there. It was a big move for him; twice the salary he was making in Denver, and all the high society shit he always knew he was born for. To his credit though, he did show up for my graduation, baring the keys to a new car and the news that he was engaged to a wonderful woman named Janice. It was the last time I'd seen him or talked with him, though we exchange cards at Christmas and birthdays.

So you can imagine my shock when I got his call last week. I'm a junior in college now, so it had been almost three years since I'd heard his voice. I almost didn't recognize it; he sounded more like an old friend of the family's than my dad. I almost shot off my mouth and asked how he got my number, but didn't. After all, he was paying for my education, and I was driving a nice Lexus because of him. The least I could do was entertain him with a phone call every three years or so.

How was I doing? Did I enjoy my classes? Am I dating anyone? Blah, blah, blah. I continued writing my essay that was due next week as he talked, only half hearing what he was saying.

"Well, son, the reason I called was to invite you out to New York for a few days."

"What?" I asked, believing I'd heard him wrong.

"Next week, actually. It's my birthday, you know . . ."

I'd forgotten, actually.

". . . the big five-oh. Janice insists on throwing a big party for me, and you know how she is when she sets her mind to something."

I didn't, actually. I'd never met the woman or even spoken with her.

"There will be about a hundred and fifty people here. All snobs with tight lips and even tighter, surgery-enhanced asses." He tried to sound irritated but I could actually detect a smile and sense of satisfaction in his voice. "I know it's not exactly the sort of thing you like all that much, but it'd mean the world to me if you could make it."

"I'm sorry, Dad. I can't. I'm really swamped at school and . . ."

"Nonsense. It's only for four days. You can bring any work you have with you and work on it here if you have to."

"Really, Dad . . ."

"Son, please. I haven't asked much from you, have I? Janice

is dying to meet you and she really wants you here to celebrate with us. Her son Tyson is flying all the way out from Los Angeles to be here. How can I tell her my own son won't come out from Denver?"

Typical dad. He wasn't asking because *he* wanted me there, but because his little Janice did. Anything to make the little missus happy.

"Really, Dad, I can't afford . . ."

"It's already taken care of. Your flight leaves Thursday afternoon at three. The ticket will be waiting for you at the United counter. I will pick you up at JFK when you get here. You head back to Denver Sunday afternoon. Please Chris, don't say no."

Well, how could I? So now I was sitting in first class, finishing a glass of wine and preparing to land at JFK airport. I was a little nervous about seeing him after three years. Had he changed much? Would we get along?

I took a deep breath as I walked along the tunnel from the plane to the gate. Dad said he'd meet me at the gate, which I was grateful for. The prospect of finding my way around one of the busiest airports in the world by myself was not one I was particularly amused with. I looked around the group of people waiting at the gate for their loved ones. Dad wasn't there, and I sat down on one of the vinyl chairs as I remembered he was always late.

About five minutes passed, and all the other passengers on my flight were long gone, when I saw a woman trying very hard not to break into a run and still look elegant while she tried to balance a large purse on her bouncing shoulders and keep her six-inch heels from twisting under her.

It was almost comical, until a look of recognition hit her

face, lighting it up like the Las Vegas strip, and I realized this was my stepmother.

"Oh, it is so nice to see you," she said as she dropped the purse to the ground and hugged me tightly. She smelled strongly of sweet expensive perfume, and when she planted a big loud kiss on my cheek I was sure she'd left a permanent pink lip mark there.

"Janice?" I asked stupidly.

"Well, of course I am," she said brightly as she held me at arm's length to look me over. "My goodness, you've grown so much since the last picture I've seen of you!"

That was not true, I'd sent Dad a new picture just a couple of months ago. But I wasn't about to argue with this woman. I smiled lamely instead, and probably blushed.

"Did you bring luggage?" she asked.

"Nah, just this," I pulled my backpack over my shoulders.

"Oh, good. I like a man who travels lightly," she said, and grabbed me by the arm, escorting me out of the airport.

It seems Dad had to work late and had sent Janice to pick me up instead. The drive from JFK to Dad's house just across the river in New Jersey was nothing short of torturous. Janice had a knack for the spoken word, and had apparently come well-stocked with topics to discuss. Traffic was light, according to Janice, and so we should count our blessings that it only took a little less than an hour to get home.

"Well, it looks like your father beat us home," she said as we pulled into a long curved driveway.

Dad came out and met us as we unloaded the car. Seems Janice had gone shopping before picking me up. Dad kissed her lovingly on the lips and then greeted me with a hug.

"Nice to see you, son. Man, you have grown a bit, haven't you?"

"I guess so," I agreed again.

"Well, let's get inside. Jan, Tyson just called and said he was running a little late. He said since he got it from you, you'd understand. He'll be here in about an hour."

We went inside and watched with wonder as Janice proudly showed off her new purchases. A mink coat, a couple of silk blouses, four new pairs of shoes and a Gucci handbag for herself. "And this," she said as she made a big production of hiding the last bag from my father, "is for you. No peeking."

Dad smiled fondly at her and showed no hint whatsoever of being upset at her spending all that money. He seemed proud, actually. From the looks of their home, he certainly could afford what she'd spent with no problem. And he looked genuinely happy with Janice and his new life. Some of my resentment and bitterness began to melt away a little.

We sat in the family room talking and enjoying a glass of wine while waiting for Janice's son Tyson to arrive. I could smell a pork loin roast cooking and a couple of voices coming from the kitchen. Dad and Janice obviously had household help.

About forty-five minutes after I arrived I heard the door open and a male voice yelled out hello.

"Tyson!" Janice yelled with delight. "We're in the sitting room, darling."

I don't know exactly what I expected in Tyson, but I was completely taken by surprise when he walked in. He was short, about five feet six inches, but from the way he filled out his jeans and polo shirt, very well built. His hair was jet-black, and brushed carelessly back from his face, with a couple of long wisps hanging over his forehead. His eyes were deep blue, almost turquoise, with long thin eyebrows and a James Dean intensity to them. His skin was creamy pale, with just a hint of a five o'clock shadow. I was overwhelmed with the beauty of this kid.

Janice ran to the door to meet him and threw her arms around him lovingly. I thought for a moment she was going to cry, and Tyson smiled at me and rolled his eyes with that *What are you gonna do?* look. He let his mother hug him for a long moment, and then broke the embrace and walked over to my dad. They hugged for a decent amount of time, and squeezed each other lovingly when they let go. It looked like they were good friends.

"Ty, this is my son Christian," Dad said, leading Tyson to me.

"Chris," I corrected as I shook his hand. He had a firm handshake, and held my hand for longer than I was accustomed to, but I didn't mind at all. His skin was soft and warm and felt good in mine.

"Nice to meet you, Chris. I've heard a lot about you." His crystal blue eyes literally sparkled and his smile displayed perfectly aligned, pearl-white teeth.

"Well, only believe the good things," I said nervously, and everyone laughed.

We sat down to dinner and talked for about two hours. Janice and Tyson were anxious to learn more about me, and as the evening wore on, I warmed up to them very much. Janice was a sweetheart, if a little dizzy at times. But she was funny and I liked her a lot.

Tyson was a sophomore at UCLA, majoring in computer programming. He had a 4.0 GPA and was on the tennis and wrestling teams. He had an apartment off campus and loved to entertain friends. Four months ago he had an offer to do some modeling, and had done six jobs so far. His agency thought he could really go far in the business, despite his size, and was pushing him to do more, but he wasn't sure he enjoyed it that much. No, he was not dating anyone, thank you, and please stop with the pressure.

The evening was very enjoyable, but I began to get a little tired. Janice explained that the guest room was still being remodeled and that if it was all right with me, I'd be sharing Tyson's room. My heartbeat tripled, and I said that would be fine. I was a pretty low-maintenance type of guy.

I said good night, hugs and kisses to Janice and Dad, and Tyson took me upstairs and showed me the room. He apologized for only having the one bed available, but it was a king-size bed and he was a quiet sleeper, he assured me, so we should be okay. I seriously doubted I would be "okay" lying in the same bed with this beautiful man for three nights, but I was more than willing not to be okay!

He went back downstairs to have another after-dinner drink and visit with his mom and my dad for a little longer, and said he'd try to be as quiet as possible when he came to bed.

I stripped down to my underwear and crawled into bed, pulling the covers up to my chin. The bed was very soft and comfortable and the sheets were recently washed and smelled clean and fresh. A little moonlight shone through the window to lightly illuminate the large bedroom. It seemed very serene and comfortable, and before long I felt myself giving in to the comfortable bed and falling asleep.

I'm not sure how long I'd been asleep when I felt Tyson crawl into bed. It was a huge bed and he was way over on the other side, but I'm a light sleeper and felt him slide under the covers anyway. My heart sped up just knowing I was in the same bed with him, but I stayed lying on my side and pretended to be asleep. Tyson was lying on his side as well, with his back to me.

"Chris, are you awake?" he whispered, his back still to me.

I struggled with whether I should answer or not, and decided not to. Better to pretend I'm asleep.

Tyson rolled over onto his other side to face me, but didn't say anything at first. I could hear him breathing, and soon felt him moving his body closer to mine under the covers. I could actually hear my heartbeat in my chest and struggled not to begin breathing faster and give myself away.

Tyson slowly moved his arm around my shoulder and rested his hand against my chest. I'm sure he felt my heart pounding wildly there, but he didn't let on. He moved his body closer to mine, until I could feel the heat from his skin only an inch or so away from mine. His hand moved very slowly down my chest and to my stomach. He traced a line around my belly button and my abs automatically tightened, outlining my six-pack I've been working so hard to get.

I heard him sigh deeply, and he moved his entire body to press up against mine. His lightly hairy chest felt so good against my smooth back, his legs wrapped around mine and his hard cock pressed gently against my underwear. I stopped breathing, I'm sure, but a moan escaped my throat anyway.

"I know you're awake, Chris," he whispered into my ear from behind me. He rubbed my knotted stomach and pressed his cock a little firmer against my ass. "You okay with this?"

I turned over onto my back and looked at his beautiful face. It looked almost magical in the moonlight.

"Yeah, I think so," I answered.

"Good."

He leaned down and kissed me softly on the lips. His mouth tasted sweet, a mixture of brandy and Scope. He lightly outlined my lips with his tongue for a moment and then slid it into my mouth slowly and tenderly. I sucked slowly on it, savoring the flavor of the alcohol-tinged mouthwash. He probed deeper into my mouth and tickled the roof of my mouth. His lips were so soft and I could smell the lingering scent of his cologne.

Tyson moved his body to lie on top of mine, and I felt how strong and tight his muscles were. His hands cupped my face as he kissed me harder and deeper, and I felt his hard dick grind gently against my own underwear-clad cock. It was throbbing crazily in my shorts, straining to get out. Tyson must have sensed that, because he reached down with one hand and slowly pulled them off and dropped them to the floor.

"God, you feel good, Tyson," I gasped between his kisses.

"Do you like this?"

"Oh, yes."

"Good. And what about this?" he asked as his tongue began licking my nipples and moving down my torso.

"Oh, yes."

My dick was fully hard now and the head rested just above my navel. Tyson's stubbly chin brushed it a couple of times as he licked my stomach, and I felt his hot breath on it a couple of times. I moaned and pushed my hips forward, trying to touch his mouth with my cock head. He made a point of licking farther up my abs to get away from it, and lightly bit my tummy.

"Jesus, Tyson, that is incredible."

"Yeah?"

"Yeah."

He kissed my nipples, then left a trail of light kisses back down my abs and this time he kept going and before I realized it, he had the head of my dick wrapped warmly in his mouth. I shuddered with pleasure as his tongue darted inside my slit and around the entire head. I must have leaked a little precum, because I felt his mouth suck on the head and he moaned loudly.

I raised my hips again, and this time instead of moving away, he opened his mouth wider and allowed my shaft to slip deeper into the heat of his mouth. I have a fairly large dick, about eight inches when fully hard, and Tyson swallowed about half of it before slowly pulling back and sucking his way back up to the head. He lingered there for a few seconds, and then slid slowly back down my shaft, this time not stopping until his chin was resting against my balls. I felt my cock head slide past his tonsils and his throat muscles massaged the first couple of inches of my cock.

"Damn, Tyson, that feels so good," I whispered.

"Mmmm-hmmm," he responded as well as he could with a mouthful of dick.

He sucked my dick with passion for a few minutes, massaging my balls and tickling my ass hole as he did. I was getting very close, and didn't want it to end yet, so I pulled his mouth from my cock and up to my face. I kissed him gently on the mouth and hugged his body to mine.

Tyson broke the kiss and moved his body up so that he was sitting on my chest. My eyes widened when I saw his cock. It had felt big when it was pressing against my underwear, but it was phenomenal now. At least a couple of inches longer than mine, uncut and thick with a lot of veins. It bobbed in front of my face expectantly, and I looked up at Tyson's face. He was looking at me, smiling a shy little smile and looking a little apprehensive.

"Is it okay?" he asked softly.

"Okay?" I asked, astonished. "It's beautiful."

"A lot of guys don't like it because it's so big."

"Well, it is big, but it's so nice."

He smiled and I reached out with my tongue to lick the head. It was partially covered with foreskin, and I pulled on the silky skin with my lips, stretching it until it covered the head completely. I sneaked a peek up at Tyson's face and saw him smile. His bright blue eyes sparkled and his skin had a light blue tint to it from the moonlight. I felt like I'd died and gone to heaven and was in bed with an angel.

I wrapped my fist around Tyson's thick cock and gently pulled the skin back, looking at his head for the first time. It was not large, smaller than what I'd expect on a dick that large and fat. But it was perfect. A small drop of precum slid down the underside of his dick as I pulled the skin back, and I reached to lick it off. It was sweet and silky, and I was drunk with the taste of it immediately. Wrapping my lips around the head, I sucked softly on it, making Tyson moan with delight.

He let me play with the head for a minute or so, and then slowly began sliding the thick uncut cock farther into my mouth. I wasn't nearly as talented at sucking cock as Tyson, and was only able to take about half of his big dick into my mouth without choking on it. That seemed to be okay with Tyson, and he pumped his dick in and out of my mouth gently instinctively just to the point I was able to take it.

He slowly fucked my mouth for about five minutes, and then replaced his cock with his mouth. We kissed for a long time, each savoring the taste and feel of the other's tongue. Then he moved back down to my cock and sucked it softly as he lifted my legs into the air.

His fingers probed my crack as his tongue tickled my cock. When his fingers reached my ass hole, I tightened up a little. I'd been fucked a few times since I began having sex with guys a year and a half ago, but not many. And never by a dick as huge as Tyson's. Tyson seemed to sense this, and kept sucking my dick as his fingers massaged around my ass hole for a couple of minutes. I relaxed a little, and Tyson took that as his cue. He licked his middle finger and slid about an inch into my hot hole. I tightened a little again, and tried to pull myself off his finger, but he held me steady with his finger just barely inside me, sucking me softly the whole time.

It actually began to feel good after a few seconds, and I moaned softly and relaxed more. In one move Tyson slid his finger all the way inside my ass and swallowed my dick to the balls. I expected it to hurt more than it did. Instead, I almost came then and there with the pleasure.

"I'm gonna come, man," I moaned.

Tyson quickly pulled his finger out of my ass and his mouth from my cock.

"Not yet, Chris. Don't come."

I grabbed the sheets with my hands and squeezed hard, trying to make the orgasm I felt building go away. A couple of small drops of precum slid out of my dick head, but I was successful in stopping the full onslaught. Tyson laid on top of me and we kissed for a few minutes so I could calm down a little.

"You ready now?" Tyson asked when he could tell I was.

"I don't know if I can, Tyson. I'm not used . . ."

"Shhhh. Just relax. I won't hurt you, okay?"

I nodded, and closed my eyes as I felt Tyson move down to my ass. His tongue darted around my ass hole and I moaned as he slid it deeper inside. It was wet and warm and felt great in my ass.

When I began moving my ass around his tongue, Tyson knew I was ready. He stood up, slid a condom as far down as it would reach on his cock, and let a small amount of spit drop onto his hard cock. I gasped as I saw again how big his cock was, and closed my eyes to keep from thinking about it.

Tyson pressed his dick head against my hole and gently pushed forward. The small head slipped in easily, and Tyson let it rest just inside my ass for a moment, allowing me to get used to it. I took a deep breath and relaxed my ass muscles as much as I could. Then he started sliding his cock slowly inside me. I felt the big dick get thicker and thicker as it slid deeper inside me, but to my surprise, instead of hurting, it was actually feeling very good. Each inch of his huge cock got thicker inside me, and my ass was eating it up.

I opened my eyes and found them staring into Tyson's beautiful blue ones. I can't describe the look in his eyes or on his face as his dick slid the last inch inside my hot, tight ass. He smiled and leaned down to kiss me tenderly on the lips. He kept his big dick still inside my ass for what seemed like an eternity. I could actually feel the blood pumping through his cock as it pulsated against the walls of my ass.

It was I, not Tyson, who began moving. His cock felt so good inside me, I had to feel it moving, so I started sliding my ass up and down the length of his pole. He looked stunned as I tightened my ass muscles as they moved along his long, thick cock. I licked my lips and when Tyson saw my tongue he leaned down and kissed me hard on the lips, never missing a stroke of his dick inside my ass.

"Fuck me, Tyson." I moaned around his probing tongue.

"Oh, baby, you feel so good."

"Your dick feels incredible inside me, man," I said.

He lifted my legs higher into the air, making my ass tighten even more, and I felt his cock get thicker inside me as my muscles squeezed him. He began pumping my ass harder and faster, and I could tell he was getting close. My own load started churning in my balls, and I knew I was going to shoot any minute now.

"I'm gonna come, Tyson," I said breathlessly.

"Go ahead, man, shoot. I'm close, too."

He pulled his cock all the way out of my ass and shoved it back in all the way to the balls, and that was all it took for me. With Tyson's long thick shaft buried in my ass, I shot the largest load of my life. Three shots went way over my head and landed on the wall behind me, while the last four or five landed on my chest and stomach. I felt my ass grasping Tyson's dick and squeezing with each contraction. I looked up into Tyson's face, and saw he was about to shoot his own load. His eyes were closed tightly and he pulled his dick out of me in one swift motion, throwing the condom to the floor.

I've never seen so much cum in all my life. Three or four shots spewed straight into the air, high above even Tyson's head and landed on my face. I closed my eyes to keep the hot cum from landing in them, so I don't know how many more jets shot from his dick, but when I opened my eyes, my body was covered with cum. It was impossible to tell my own cum from Tyson's, but there was barely an inch of my body that wasn't warm with the stuff.

Tyson collapsed onto my body and we fell asleep hugging one another and covered in cum. We woke up a couple of hours later and repeated our lovemaking, only this time I fucked him. The next three days were some of the most fun of my life.

Tyson and I visit each other a couple times a month. Dad and Janice couldn't be happier that we're such good friends. If they only knew we've given new meaning to the term "Brotherly Love."

Make a Wish . . .
and Blow

Some fucking birthday, David thought to himself as he swallowed the last drop of his Long Island Iced Tea. How in hell could it happen that all of his friends were out of town? It's true, he had always said he never wanted to make a big deal of turning twenty-five, and didn't want a party or anything. But you'd think a couple of them would have made sure they were here to buy him a drink and keep him from spending the evening alone. What kind of best friends were Brad and Tom anyway?

At least the bartender had been sympathetic and bought him a drink, he thought as he set the empty glass down on the ledge overlooking the dance floor below him. The speakers to the massive music system were only inches away, and he watched the ice in his glass jump with the pounding beat as hundreds of young, cute guys gyrated and hip-hopped their way around the crowded bar.

He looked at his watch and was surprised to see it was only eleven-thirty. He'd been at Tracks 2000 for just over an hour, and already was bored out of his mind. Not a single guy in the place had tried to pick him up . . . or even spoken to him. *Might as well go home and beat off,* he thought, and headed toward the stairs that would lead him to the exit door below. He didn't notice the bartender watching him intently and signaling the deejay.

"How's everyone doing tonight?" the deejay yelled into the microphone, his deep voice resonating through the massive room as the music volume lowered a little.

The crowd went wild, and screamed their approval. David groaned and slowly pushed his way through the throng of people that had quickly gathered around the top of the stairs.

"It's time to have some fun now!" the deejay yelled, and suddenly all the lights in the entire bar went out. The crowd roared its approval, and David felt the room get smaller as people began pressing against him on all sides. He tried to continue walking toward where he knew the stairs were, but was steadily being pushed backward toward the back door that led to the patio. There was no exit to the parking lot from the patio, and he cursed as he tried to move forward through the mass of people. But it was useless. They were stampeding toward the back door, and he was blindly being pushed along with them.

The bar was completely dark, and David began to get worried that the crowd would turn violent in its frenzy. In the three years he'd been coming to Tracks, he'd never seen anything like this, and he wondered why all the lights were out. A few feet ahead of him he could see the shadows of the frame of the patio door, and now people were physically pushing him toward it. He felt hands all over his body, pushing and groping at the same time, and he reached down to make sure his wallet was still in his front pocket.

Before he knew it he was pushed through the doorway, onto the patio. The people who had been surrounding him and pushing him forward all quickly retreated and disappeared, and he heard the patio door slam heavily shut and lock. On the other side of the wall he heard the muffled music beating louder again, and saw from the small window frames several feet above him that the dance lights were back on inside the main bar.

But out on the patio it was eerily quiet. This was usually where people came to cool their hot, sweaty bodies after having danced themselves into a frenzy inside. One end of the patio held a small dance floor and had a separate music system that played old disco music and some of the eighties funk that many of the old-timers stubbornly held onto. David had been out there a few times with friends, and remembered laughing and making fun of the lava lamps, old couches and disco queens who didn't fit in with the hip crowd inside the main bar.

The patio was called "Heaven Lounge," and at the moment it seemed very fitting. He was surrounded by pitch-black space and became a little disoriented. Faintly he could hear the music from inside the dance bar several feet away; but out here he began to hear whispers around him, and wondered if the cute bartender had spiked his drink.

A soft, jungle music sound started somewhere above him, and the whispers grew a little louder. Certain he was not out there alone now, he began to sweat a little with fear. The music was slowly but steadily getting louder, and a few seconds later David felt more hands touching him and gently moving him away from the door. He gasped, and yelled out in surprise, swatting blindly at the hands around him.

"What the fuck is going on?" he asked out loud.

More whispers, growing louder by the second all around him, and then a soft blue spotlight lit up the dance floor at the other end. The jungle music was also getting louder, and David saw the dance floor had been transformed into a small stage. On it were trees and vines, and life-size stuffed animals . . . a lion, a tiger, a couple of snakes. He shook his head vigorously, trying to shake off whatever drug the bartender had obviously slipped into his drink, when he was grabbed on all sides by what seemed like a hundred hands. One clasped gently but firmly against his mouth to keep him from screaming, and the others forced him steadily toward the stage. He tripped a couple of times and was lifted back up immediately. After the third stumble, he was lifted off the floor completely and carried effortlessly by the swarm of hands, to the jungle stage.

David struggled against the hands, and the unseen people behind them, and bit at the hand covering his mouth. He heard a whispered "shit" as the hand pulled away, but just as he was about to scream out loud, a piece of cloth was forced across his mouth and tied around the back of his head. His clothes were being carefully removed from his body and he panicked as he struggled in vain against the mob that was carrying him.

By the time he reached the stage, he was completely naked, and his hands had been lightly tied behind his back. The jungle music blared now, completely covering any trace of the house music going on inside the main bar, and David was gently laid on the floor of the stage. He breathed in short, deep breaths through his nose as he felt the hands move from his naked body and heard feet scuffling away.

The spotlight changed to red, and David stumbled to his feet awkwardly, trying to untie his hands. Suddenly, from behind a tree a few feet away, he saw something move, and he stopped in his tracks. His heart raced madly as he had visions of live tigers and lions and snakes, and he thought he would start crying any moment. He heard human whispers and moans a few feet away, out in the darkness, and a moment later saw what had moved from behind the tree.

A man stepped out from the shadows and walked steadily toward David. Easily six feet four inches tall, and well over two hundred pounds of bulging muscles, he wore only a skimpy loincloth. Glowing with a shiny mix of baby oil and sweat, his massive chest was completely smooth, and flexed impressively as he walked toward David. He had long blonde hair that flowed to his shoulders. His legs were long and thickly muscled as they moved slowly and sexily closer. Despite his fear, David felt his cock stir slightly with each advancing step of the stranger. One of his biggest fantasies had always been about Tarzan, but this man was much better than anything he'd seen in his dreams.

The moans from the darkness became louder and mixed with the jungle music blaring from all around him. Tarzan walked right up to David and wrapped one massive hand around the back of his head and pulled the gag from his mouth. No longer struggling, David sighed as the beautiful man gently touched his strong, soft lips to David's own. A hot, sweet tongue licked at his lips and slid inside his mouth confidently.

Tarzan kissed him long and deep as he reached behind David and untied his hands. David relaxed, and when the giant grabbed his hand and pressed it against his firm, muscular chest, David gladly caressed it. He felt the bulging muscles flex beneath his hand, and his cock pounded fully hard as he tweaked the tiny nipples and heard the big man in front of him moan with pleasure.

They kissed for a long moment, Tarzan's adventurous tongue relentless as it probed David's hungry mouth. A high-pitched buzzing sound filled his ears, and he was faintly aware of deep, guttural moans from out in the darkness. But before this could really register with him, the strong, blonde muscular man in front of him planted a hand on each of David's shoulders and firmly pushed him down onto his knees. His face was only an inch or so away from the leopard-skin loincloth, and he swallowed deeply as he inhaled the strong, musky scent of oil and sweat.

He wrapped his arms around the tree trunks that Tarzan called legs, and smiled when he noticed the front of the loincloth bounce in front of his face. He licked his lips and noticed a few blue fluorescent lights starting to blink on dimly from the darkened room in his peripheral vision. He could make out the shapes of several people in the dark. They were all naked, and David started to panic. Tarzan reached down and took the back of David's head and gently but forcefully moved it forward until his face touched the bulging cloth, and David's fear subsided.

Nothing mattered now but getting at the piece of meat that lay under the cloth, and David started sucking on the skimpy covering, his heart racing as he felt the heat and weight of the cock beneath it. In one swift move, Tarzan ripped the piece of cloth from his waist, and a long, heavy, fat uncut dick swung up and knocked against his chin. It wasn't even fully hard yet, only about halfway there, but already it was a monster. Big blue veins ran up and down the length of the pole, and as it pounded harder and bigger with the beat of Tarzan's heart, the silky foreskin stretched and pulled itself back from the shiny head.

David took the cock in his mouth and sucked on it softly, savoring the sweet taste of the precum that was already sliding out of the hole and onto his tongue. His own dick throbbed achingly as he sucked greedily. Tarzan moaned deeply, and slid his cock deeper inside his hot mouth. At the same moment, David felt several hands caressing his legs and ass from the darkness, and a warm, wet mouth slid around his cock, swallowing it deep inside and sucking softly.

He almost blacked out from the pleasure, and closed his eyes as he swallowed all nine inches of the thick cock in front of him. The hands caressing his legs and ass turned to wet tongues, and somewhere along the way the blue fluorescent lights became a little brighter, allowing him to see about forty naked young men standing around him and in various states of fondling one another. Several men were on their knees, eagerly sucking someone else, others were simply holding and squeezing the cocks around them . . . and three or four of them tried unsuccessfully to stifle moans as a cock rammed its way into their asses.

David sucked more eagerly on Tarzan's dick, opening the back of his throat and swallowing as much as he could. He choked as the fat cock swelled against his tonsils, and Tarzan grunted loudly and forced the last inch inside his mouth. David felt himself unable to breathe, but when he tried to pull himself off the giant cock, Tarzan grabbed his head and kept it tight against him as he leaned back and let out his famous Tarzan yell. The first shot hit the back of his throat, and slid down before David knew what was happening. Two or three more slammed hotly against his tongue and tonsils, and David swallowed them hungrily as he tightened the grip of his lips around the fat cock.

He swallowed as much of the hot cum as he could, but there was so much that it began to drip out of the corners of his mouth. David shot his own load deep into the mouth on his cock, and moaned as he reluctantly let Tarzan's huge pole slide from between his lips. Someone yelled out loudly, and a moment later David felt another hot load land on his back just as Tarzan's dick swung wetly away from his lips.

Tarzan motioned to a couple of guys around him, and started to walk behind David as the men pushed him onto all fours and pulled his arms and legs wide apart. Before he could argue, a long hot tongue slid into his ass. When he opened his mouth to moan, another cock slid inside and began pumping his mouth. The cock was smaller than Tarzan's, but not much, and David sucked it greedily as the anonymous tongue lapped wetly at his twitching ass.

The group from the dark crowd started moving closer to him then, and David recognized most of them. Brad and Tom were there; each smiling as they stood above his kneeling body and moved slowly closer. Their hard cocks were buried in the mouths of a couple of guys David remembered meeting, but could not recall their names or where they'd met. When Tom and Brad were directly in front of David, the boys on their cocks moved aside, and the man who had been fucking David's mouth pulled out and moved aside.

Tom and Brad moved to within inches of David and began slapping their hard, slick cocks against his face. Amazingly, another hot load of jizz landed on David's back, and the tongue working his ass was relentless. Tom smiled and grabbed David's jaw as he slid his cock into his mouth. This was the first time David had seen his best friends naked, and he was almost delirious as Tom's long dick slid into his mouth and Brad laid on his back on the floor and swallowed David's still hard cock.

Brad sucked his cock deep and hard into his mouth as Tom fucked his parching lips. Definitely delirious now, David had forgotten about Tarzan . . . until he realized the mouth on his ass had moved away and felt the big, strong hands caress his ass cheeks and spread them apart. He sucked harder on Tom's big dick, and Brad swallowed his dick as David felt his ass hole pierced by Tarzan's hot, fat cock head.

He gasped, taking in a long, slow breath through his nose. Tom's cock slid deeper into his throat and Tarzan shoved the full length of his thick nine inches deep into his ass. David was sure the two big dicks touched heads somewhere deep inside him, and a single tear fell down his cheek as his body tingled with the warmth and pleasure of being filled with cock.

Guys all around him were fucking and sucking wildly, and the room filled with moans and the smell of cum as loads shot in every direction. David specifically felt at least five more loads empty onto his back and ass, and his mouth and ass instinctively tightened and twitched around the cocks occupying them as the hot, sticky jizz hit him. Tom and Tarzan were fucking him with wild abandon, and he could tell they were leaning forward and kissing one another as they plowed his ass and mouth. Brad was swallowing David's cock with equal fervor, and reaching up to tweak his nipples lightly as he deepthroated him.

David's head spun. It seemed to go on for hours, yet at the same time, was all going way too fast. He wasn't sure how long they'd been going at it, but was aware that everyone else in the room had finished and left. He was alone with Brad, Tom, and Tarzan, and that was fine with him. The feeling of having his cock sucked deep inside Brad's hot throat while he was getting fucked at both ends was better than anything he'd ever felt.

He felt his load building deep in his balls again, and couldn't have stopped it if he wanted to . . . which he did not. His big dick grew thicker inside his friend's mouth and pounded uncontrollably as he started shooting his load deep into Brad's slurping mouth. That was all it took for Brad to shoot his own load, and David felt it shoot up and land on his stomach and the base of his cock and balls. His mouth and ass went into automatic reflex mode, and tightened around the huge dicks impaling him, and he knew he would soon be rewarded with even more cum as a result.

Tarzan's cock pounded his ass relentlessly, and the big man gasped loudly for air. His giant dick slid out completely and made an audible "plop" as it left David's ass vacant. Hot cum flew in every direction, landing on his own ass and back, and even flying across him and onto Tom's chest and stomach. Tom grunted loudly and speared his dick deep inside David's throat one last time, leaving it there as it released its load. David didn't even taste it, because the long cock was buried deep past his tonsils; but he felt the cock spasm with each shot, and felt the warmth of the cum as it slid down his throat and into his stomach.

He was in a daze then, almost blacking out. Tarzan picked up his discarded loincloth and walked away, and David fell on top of Brad's quivering body. Tom laid down next to them, and the three friends hugged each other as they caught their breath. They were completely alone in the big room now. Somewhere along the line the music had stopped, and the lights were turned on, but dimmed very low. Inside the main bar, he could hear the heavy bass beat of the dance music and muffled conversations of hundreds of people.

"You didn't really think we'd let you spend your twenty-fifth birthday alone, did you?" Brad asked as he kissed David on the lips. David smiled as he savored the aftertaste of his own cum.

"I mean, give us a break," Tom said, and grinned mischievously, "you're a quarter of a century old. We had no idea what to get you, so we decided to make your biggest fantasy come true. Hope you liked it."

"I had no idea you two were such great friends," David said after catching his breath. "Or so hot."

"Well, now you do. So let's make sure this isn't the last time we get together, okay?"

The three friends laughed and got dressed together.

"By the way, Tom," Brad said as he kissed both of his friends and the three walked arm in arm back into the main bar, "isn't your birthday in a couple of months?"

Plaza del Sol

I had been in Guadalajara, Mexico, for nine months. I had a good job teaching English at a private school. Made lots of money, had lots of friends, gotten lots of sun. Being twenty-five years old, with blonde hair and blue eyes made me more than a little popular with the cute Mexican boys down there, and to my horror, even with the girls. I did my best to put off the girls as much as possible, and to get it on with as many of the cute boys as possible. It wasn't hard. I never dated a student of mine, but once I was no longer their teacher, it was open territory, and there was never a shortage of volunteers. The clubs there were always packed, with lines way out the doors, and I never went home alone unless I wanted to.

Not that it was all about sex. I did make a lot of really good friends. Coworkers, straight and gay friends from the theater and dance groups I went to see often, friends from clubs.

But after nine months I began to become a little bored. That and I was a little homesick. I worked ten hours a day during the week, and five on Saturdays. Though I loved my job, I was getting a little burned out and started thinking about returning to the States.

We had two-hour lunch breaks at the school. There were a number of fast food restaurants right around the school that I visited every once in a while. But I usually went to a little family owned restaurant located in Plaza del Sol, a shopping mall three blocks from the school. Every day they had three homemade meals you could choose from as entrees. They were all cheap, delicious, and served with fresh homemade tortillas and endless glasses of agua frescas, delicious drinks made with water and fresh fruits. After eating lunch I would take a book and sit in the open courtyard and read for an hour or so until it was time to return to the school.

I was always so engrossed in my books that I never realized the intense cruising that went on in that open-air mall. On this sweltering day in July, however, I finished my book very early after lunch, and contented myself with watching the action and scenery around me. Sitting on one of the park benches that surrounded a fountain at the main crossroad in the mall, I was given a fantastic view of the goings on around me. Mall employees rushing back to or leaving leisurely from work; high school kids and working moms getting in some shopping; little old ladies sipping lemonade.

And then there were "the boys." It amazed me how many young men, anywhere from fifteen or so to about thirty, roamed aimlessly up and down the sidewalk, staring each other down. There was nothing subtle about their movements at all. They nodded their heads at one another, raised their eyebrows, licked their lips and groped their crotches. Several of them cruised me very openly, some of them even daring to sit at one of the benches next to mine and flirt with me there. I was amused, but had no place to take them, since I lived quite a ways from the mall, so I pretty much ignored most of them. I watched with fascination as they performed their mating rituals in front of me, and thought about returning to San Francisco.

Then Javier sat down right next to me. I'd seen him a couple of times before, eating lunch at the same little restaurant. He was always wearing a name tag that tattled he was a sales clerk at Suburbia, a Mexican equivalent to Montgomery Ward. He was tall and very solidly built, with straight black hair and hazel eyes accented by long, curly eyelashes. Twin dimples pierced each cheek that were braced by a strong jawline and a clefted chin. He was young, probably about nineteen or twenty, and adorable. I'd stared shamelessly at him when I saw him, trying to get his attention, but whenever I looked at him he was either not looking at me, or he'd look away suddenly. I never pursued it more than that.

But now, here he was, sitting right next to me. He was reading a book and finishing his lemonade. I nodded at him as he sat down, and he nodded back before he began reading. No smile, no licking of the lips or groping of the groin. So I went back to my people-watching trying hard not to think about Javier.

I wasn't very successful. I kept sneaking a peek at him through the corners of my eyes. I could smell his sweet cologne and after a while I swear I could distinguish his body heat from the ninety-eight-degree, humid heat of Mexican summer. I'd sat there for about fifteen minutes when I suddenly felt his knee brush mine. The first time it was just a quick brush, and he pretended to reposition his feet. The next time he let it rest there for a few minutes before moving it. The third time it rested against mine for a moment, and then began applying pressure against my leg.

I looked over at him. He continued reading his book as his leg pushed harder against mine. I looked away quickly and kinda gave my head a quick little shake. I looked back at Javier and this time he looked me right in the eyes and smiled. His beautiful pink lips parted to reveal perfect, pearl-white teeth and those drop-dead gorgeous dimples. My heart did a triple beat and I quickly looked away. With just the batting of his eyelashes and the dimple display he was causing my dick to stir in my jeans.

When I looked back at him, he marked his place in the book he was reading and closed it as he got up to leave. I panicked. My heart dropped to my stomach, I stopped breathing and I felt my face flush hotly. Where was he going? Why didn't I talk to him when I had the chance? Why couldn't I live much closer?

He brushed my leg again as he deliberately walked in front of me rather than going around his side of the bench. I watched him leave, and saw that after a few steps, he turned back around to look at me. He smiled that lethal smile again, and nodded for me to follow him.

I couldn't breathe. This was one of the most gorgeous men I'd seen while in Mexico. He seemed shy and sweet and sexy and mysterious all at once. And now he was motioning for me to follow him. I turned to see which direction he was heading. He stopped right outside a door marking the men's room, made sure I saw where he'd gone, and then disappeared into the door.

I stood up slowly and took a couple of deep breaths before forcing my feet to move one in front of the other. When I reached the rest room door, I saw it was a stairway that went up a narrow hallway, winding around one corner before opening up into the rest room. I took the steps two at a time and walked into the rest room before I could chicken out. Once inside, I had to stop and catch my breath. It was a fairly large bathroom, eight urinals on either side of the room at the far end, with six stalls between the door and the beginning of the urinal section on one side and a bank of sinks and paper towel dispensers across from them.

The doors to each of the stalls were locked and I could hear slurping noises coming from behind them. Javier stood alone at the wall of urinals on one side, and two young guys stood next to each other on the other side. They'd moved their hands back to their own tools when I walked in, but it took them only a few seconds to size me up and move back to jerking each other off in their urinals.

Javier smiled when he saw me walk in, and then moved the shy smile down to his cock. He was standing a few inches from the urinal, showing me his cock. It was still soft, but already long and thick with a soft sheath of foreskin covering its head. He watched it himself as he shook it a couple of times and then looked up at me, still smiling, as he began moving his foreskin slowly back and forth over the shaft.

He nodded at me to take the urinal next to him. I gulped deeply as I noticed his cock hardening in front of my eyes, and walked dazedly to the pisser next to him. I pulled out my half hard dick and pointed it into the urinal, looking straight ahead and pretending to pee.

Javier gave a quiet "psst" and when I looked up he winked at me and raised his eyebrows toward his cock. I ventured a look down there and my knees almost buckled beneath me. His cock was fully hard now, and a drop of precum hung loosely at the head. It was long, maybe nine inches or so, and very thick. When he pulled the foreskin back I saw a long throbbing vein run the length of the top of his dick. My mouth was dry as cotton and I forced my eyes back to the wall in front of me.

I heard some of the stall doors open and their occupants began to meander out one by one. I was getting nervous and started to put my cock back into my jeans when I heard Javier cough conspicuously. I looked over at him and he shook his head no and nodded toward my dick. Another man, about forty, came into the rest room and took the last urinal on our side of the room. He peed quietly as I leaned as far as I could into the urinal so he couldn't see my shriveling dick. Javier didn't seem to care one way or the other, and remained where he was. The older man finished relieving himself and left the restroom along with the last of the stall occupants.

The two boys behind us were still there. The shorter of the two was on his knees sucking his friend, who was leaning against the stall next to him. The sucker kept darting his eyes toward the door, watching out for anyone coming in. They apparently did not think of Javier or myself as a threat.

Javier turned away from me, and with his dick still hard and sticking out of his jeans, walked to the rest room door. He pulled a piece of paper from his back pocket and used a piece of gum from his mouth to stick it to the door. Then he shut the door and stuck the chair which was occupied by a lavatory attendant except during lunch under the handle.

I watched this with stunned silence and listened to my heart pounding in my chest as Javier walked smoothly back toward me, his huge uncut dick leading the way. When he reached me he put his hands on either of my shoulders and slowly pushed me back until I was leaning against the wall.

My cock was fully hard now, and throbbing uncontrollably in front of me. Javier looked me directly in the eyes, smiled and leaned forward to kiss me. His lips were soft and warm. I parted my lips slowly as he licked them and slid his tongue into my mouth. The room grew very hot and I felt a little dizzy as he kissed me passionately. I don't usually precum, but I felt a drop slithering out of my cock head. I was afraid I'd come just from Javier's kiss, but he broke it before I did.

The two kids behind us were moaning and groaning, and Javier and I looked over at them. The kid on his knees was shooting his load onto the floor as he continued to suck his friend furiously. The taller guy let out a loud grunt and pulled his dick out of the shorter guy's mouth. He yanked on it twice and we saw him shoot a huge load onto his friend's face. Spurt after spurt of thick, white cum covered the kid's face. He turned his face away after three or four sprays, and the jizm shot past his ear and onto the floor.

Watching this turned Javier on more than I could ever have imagined, and before I knew what was happening, Javier pushed my shoulders down, forcing me to the floor. Before I could stand back up or figure out what was going on I felt a shot of hot sticky cum land between my nose and my mouth. I looked up at Javier's dick. He wasn't even touching it at all, yet it was shooting a load almost equal to the tall guy across from us all onto my face. He moaned loudly and just let it shoot onto me without touching his dick. I didn't turn my head away, and loved the feel of the hot wet cum as it hit my face.

Javier hooked his hands under my arms and pulled me up to my feet again. He kissed me on the lips, licking his own cum from my face and sliding his tongue covered with his cooling jizz back into my mouth. I sucked on his tongue hungrily, swallowing his cum and making my own cock throb spastically.

The two guys who'd shot their loads just a minute earlier walked over to us and began undressing us both. I looked around nervously and the younger and shorter of the two boys took my chin in his hand and kissed me strongly, letting me know we were safe and wouldn't be bothered. When we were completely naked our two new friends dropped to their knees and began sucking us at the same time.

I can't vouch for the kid sucking on Javier's huge dick, but the one with his lips wrapped around mine must have had a Ph.D. in cocksucking. He swallowed my thick cock in one move and somehow had eight or ten tongues licking the head, the shaft, the balls, all while he moved his mouth up and down the length of it.

Javier leaned over and kissed me while we fucked the boys' mouths in front of us. It didn't take long before I felt the cum boiling in my balls. I moaned softly and sucked harder on Javier's tongue as the kid on his knees in front of me sucked and swallowed my dick like it had never been sucked before. Javier sensed that I was close, and broke our kiss as he pulled the young guy off my dick and onto his feet.

He turned me around so that my back was to him and pushed me gently up against the wall. He told our friends to do the same, and they did as they were told; the older and taller boy against the wall as the younger guy moved behind him. He and Javier bent down and played follow the leader.

Javier began kissing behind my right knee, nibbling and licking his way up the back of my legs until he got to my ass. He kissed and licked my ass cheeks, one by one, then gently spread them apart. I was so hot by then I could barely breathe. I wanted him to fuck me so badly, but when I pushed my ass closer to his face, he just licked it again and blew a cool breath on the exposed hole.

I looked over and saw the short kid was playing the same cat and mouse game with his partner, who was as delirious as I was. His eyes were closed and he was moaning loudly as he pushed his tight smooth ass closer to his partner's teasing mouth.

Javier reached between my legs and pulled gently on my hard cock as his fingers spread my ass cheeks and teased my hole. I grunted my delight, and he finally decided to reward me with what I wanted. I felt his nose press against the small of my back and a second later felt his hot tongue tickling the outside ring of my sphincter. I almost shot my load right then, but tensed up my body and counted to ten to avoid it. Javier moved his left hand from my cock so he could use both hands to keep my cheeks spread open. He slowly worked his tongue around the outside of my ass for a couple of minutes, and then slid it very slowly inside, snaking it in, then out, then back in a little deeper each time. I was going nuts, and noticed the guy next to me was, too.

The younger of our new friends was really getting into licking his friend's ass. I looked down and saw his cock was rock hard and dancing wildly between his legs. He had a nice cock, about my size, but uncut. Huge amounts of precum dripped from the head of his dick, enough to make me wonder if he'd come again.

Javier and his counterpart stood up simultaneously. They must have had some secret code, because they moved together as one from the moment Javier turned me around. The younger kid turned his partner around just as Javier did the same to me, and directed me and my counterpart to kiss. We did, very deeply and passionately as Javier and our other friend dug through their jean pockets for condoms. As we kissed the guy in front of me reached for my hand and placed it on his cock. It was huge, almost as large as Javier's. I wrapped my hand around his dick and began sliding his foreskin up and down his thick pole.

He moaned and gyrated his hips, grinding his cock into and out of my fist. His dick was hot and throbbing strongly. My mouth watered with desire. I wanted to suck him so badly I could almost taste him in my mouth even as my hand pumped him gently closer to orgasm.

Javier leaned forward across my back and kissed my ear.

"*¿Qué quieres, Papi?*" he whispered huskily in my ear. He had his nerve asking me what I wanted as he gently pressed his huge dick against my ass.

I shuddered as my response, and pressed my ass harder against his hot cock. He gave me a tiny laugh and bit my ear softly to let me know he'd gotten the message. Then he moved his head back down to my ass and licked the hole some more, lubing it up to take his mammoth dick. As he stood up again and positioned the huge head of his cock against my twitching hole, he bent me over, indicating he wanted me to suck the guy next to me.

Never one to argue with authority, I leaned over and licked the head of the cock of the guy next to me. It was covered with precum as well, salty and sweet at the same time, and slick as silk. I'd never been with anyone in the States who precame very much at all, and decided at that very moment I was quite fond of the sweet, sticky stuff. I licked the guy's head until it was clean from stickiness, then took a deep breath as I swallowed his cock all the way to his balls.

On my second time swallowing the giant cock, I felt Javier shove the head of his big dick just inside my ass. I tensed up, and knew the boys in front of me were doing exactly the same thing by the deep animal groan escaping my suckee's throat. It took me a moment to relax with Javier's throbbing pole up my ass, but I finally did, and resumed the task of sucking my new friend dry.

I think it may have been a little awkward for the kid fucking the guy next to me, since my guy had to stand up straight so I could suck and swallow his dick. The kid fucking him kept pulling out of his ass and trying to find better positions to fuck him in. He must have signaled Javier, because after only a couple of minutes Javier pulled me into a standing position. He had absolutely no problem whatsoever staying inside me. My ass wrapped itself around his long, thick pole and sucked it further inside. He slid into me in long, slow strides as the shorter guy to my side smiled gratefully, and bent his friend down toward my cock.

I closed my eyes as I felt Javier's cock slide into my hungry ass and a hot, wet mouth envelop my dick. I'd never been fucked and sucked at the same time, but it took no time whatsoever to realize it was my new favorite position. The kid getting fucked and sucking me was every bit the expert cocksucker his friend was. He and Javier found their rhythm with me almost instantly; Javier's thick cock sliding into my ass just as the guy sucking me slid off my cock.

I looked over at the guy with his dick inside my cocksucker's ass. He was pumping wildly, sweat dripping from his brow. He closed his eyes and moaned loudly, just as Javier was doing. I could tell they were both close. I was too, and trying desperately to hold back my orgasm.

I was up to about eight in my silent counting game when the guy fucking my cocksucker pulled out suddenly. He ripped the condom from his cock, and pointed it at his friend's back. The first shot rushed past his friend's head and landed on Javier's chest. Javier grunted loudly and I felt his cock grow unbelievably thicker inside my ass. It started contracting wildly inside me, and I knew that he was shooting a huge load into my ass as the kid across from me shot his hot load all over his friend's back and ass.

Javier kept his cock inside my ass as he came. That and seeing the other kid shoot was all it took for me. I pulled my cock from the other guy's reluctant mouth, shooting my own load in every direction. Some of it landed on the guy's face, some of it on the floor, some in the air and some even on the kid fucking my cocksucker. I'd never shot such a large, wild load, and I laughed a little as it just kept pouring out of my dick. When I laughed my ass muscles squeezed Javier's cock and sent shocks of pleasant pain up my ass and back.

The guy who had been sucking my dick suddenly stood up and tensed his entire body. He cried out loudly as wave after wave of thick white cum shot out of his dick and splattered against the wall in front of him. We all just watched in amazement as it kept coming and coming. It seemed there was enough to fill a glass.

I started laughing first, which caused me so much pain I had to pull Javier's cock out of my ass. Unbelievably, he was still hard. Then the others started laughing as well. We all leaned against a wall or sink and caught our breath. There was cum everywhere; on the wall, the floor, a sink, all of us. The air smelled strongly of it. Pity the next people who came in here to actually use the rest room!

Javier removed his condom carefully and laid it on the sink next to the paper towel holder. It was almost completely filled with his load, and as he laid it on the sink, a good amount spilled out onto the counter. All four of us looked at it and began to giggle again as we got dressed.

We all kissed one another and walked out the door together. As I passed through the door, I pulled off the note Javier had placed there earlier. I wanted a memento of the best fuck of my

life. I stuck it in my pocket and watched as Javier ran back to
his work and the other two friends departed in separate directions. I started walking back to school, and pulled the paper
out to read it on my way.

"Temporarily out of service."

I smiled to myself and doubted the rest room had seen that
much service in quite a while.

Peeping Tom

I have to tell you I was less than thrilled with the prospect of my company transferring me to Denver from San Diego. I didn't want to leave my friends, my family, my beaches. But it would be a big promotion for me if it worked out. So here I was in Denver for a two-week trial period.

I was staying with my friend Paul during my visit. He lived in a high-rise just on the outskirts of downtown. It was so different from where I lived. I had a three-bedroom brick house with a front and back yard, two-car garage, outdoor hot tub and state-of-the-art security system. Paul lived in a small two-bedroom apartment on the fifteenth floor of a plain white stucco building with a tiny balcony, off-street parking, and a dead bolt.

Proving myself capable of a job I really wanted in a city I really didn't want to live in was proving exhausting. I worked ten to twelve hours a day and came home ready to crash. My first week was finally over, and I walked in the door and headed straight for the shower. Paul left town for the weekend and I had the place to myself. A hot bath, a movie while curled up on the couch, and Chinese delivery would be just what the doctor ordered.

I used Paul's bathroom in the master bedroom, since it had a tub and my guest bathroom only had a shower. I sat in the hot water for half an hour before deciding I was getting hungry, and got out to call for some chicken chow mein. I stepped into Paul's bedroom to dry off; the soft carpet in his room was much warmer than the cold tile in the bathroom. As I stood naked in his room, drying my hair, I noticed his bedroom curtains were pulled open, and walked over to close them.

Paul's complex is actually made up of two identical buildings, separated only by a small parking lot between them for those residents who wish to pay an additional forty dollars a month for off-street parking. As I started to close the curtains, I noticed a man standing on his balcony directly across from me. It was dark outside, but there was a light on in the front room of the man's apartment, and he was silhouetted against it. He was shirtless and leaning against the wall of his balcony drinking a cup of something warm. As I pulled the curtains closer together, the man raised his cup and turned to walk into his apartment. As he entered the front room I saw his bare ass. He was completely naked!

He disappeared from sight for a couple of seconds as he turned the lights on brighter in his front room. When he came back into view, I could see him much more clearly. He was tall, about six feet or maybe more, with light blonde hair. He obviously spent a lot of time at the gym; his chest was hard and defined, his stomach hard and flat, his legs long and muscular. I felt my cock stir and remembered I was naked; my towel thrown carelessly over my shoulders. I started to wrap the towel around my waist, but my neighbor shook his head no. I looked around the building to see if anyone else could see me. Satisfied they could not, I dropped the towel to the floor, but half hid my body behind the curtains.

The man leaned against his sliding balcony door and smiled. God, he was gorgeous. He reached down and groped his cock with his hand. My dick was fully hard now and pulsed up and down as the blood rushed through it. My exhibitionist motioned for me to step from behind the curtains. I did so, slowly and shyly, as he stroked his cock to full hardness.

Even from this distance I could see his cock was huge. He stroked it slowly and gently while he sipped on whatever he was drinking. I took my hard cock into my hands and imitated his movements up and down my shaft. I didn't think I was that close to coming, but after only a few strokes of my hand I felt my balls tighten and that familiar chill start at the base of my cock and work its way up my shaft. I was close.

I pulled my hand from my dick and leaned against the window as the man across the parking lot spread his legs wide and slid both his hands up and down his large pole. The glass was cold as I pressed my body against it. It cooled my hot dick and kept me from shooting a load immediately. I rubbed against the window for a few moments while my cock cooled down, watching my neighbor beat his meat.

After a few minutes of stroking his dick, the man walked over to the balcony wall and stood on what must have been a short stool, so that he was standing about knee level at the top of the wall. I saw his strong muscular legs flex as he stroked his big dick right out in the open. My heart started beating faster as I watched him speed up his pounding, and I felt my cock get harder and hotter again.

He leaned back, closed his eyes and moved his hands from his cock just as the first blast of white cum shot out his cock head. It flew easily five feet from his dick and dropped four-teen floors to the ground below. Several other shots of cum spewed from his cock and landed everywhere—over the balcony, on the wall, at his feet.

I love seeing a man come more than anything, and that jizz shot sent me over the edge. I was still rubbing my cock against the window when he came, and my own load came gushing out of my dick before I knew it. Five or six spurts of cum shot out of my cock and splashed against the window and dripped down my shaft in warm waves. It felt so good as I rubbed my cock in it and against the cold window.

I looked across the parking lot and saw my neighbor shaking the last drops of his load onto the floor of his balcony. He looked over at me, smiled, and then waved good-bye as he went inside his apartment and closed the curtains.

The next day, Saturday, I went out and bought a pair of binoculars. I needed to see what this guy looked like up close. I watched for him to appear periodically throughout the day, but didn't actually see him until seven o'clock, just as the sun was going down. He came out onto the balcony, fully dressed, and talking on the phone. I was standing behind the curtains, looking at him with my new binoculars.

He was even more beautiful than I'd imagined. He looked to be in his early thirties. His light blonde hair was short and neatly cut and brushed carelessly to the right side. He had bright blue eyes and short sideburns. A strong roman nose accented a strong jawbone, and his mouth was extremely sexy; full pink lips that parted to reveal perfect, bone-white teeth when he smiled. He had a short stubble on his face that tried unsuccessfully to hide a set of incredibly sexy dimples.

It was hard for me to breathe normally as I took in the beauty of this man. He was wearing a gray suit with a blue tie.

I couldn't wait for him to start taking them off right there on the balcony in front of me. But I was to be disappointed that night. He disconnected the phone, looked right at Paul's bedroom window, and shrugged his shoulders as he pointed to the phone and lifted his hand to his mouth. Apparently he had a dinner date and was not going to perform for me.

Frustrated, I took another hot bath, and curled up on the couch to watch an old black and white movie on television. I dozed off about halfway through the movie and must have slept for a couple of hours when the phone rang. I woke up groggily and looked at the clock above the entertainment center. Two-thirty in the morning. Jesus, who would be calling at this hour?

"Hello," I answered the phone.

For a long moment there was no answer. Then, "Tomorrow night."

"What? Who is this?" I asked, still dazed from sleep.

"Tomorrow night around seven o'clock. Don't disappoint me."

"Look," I started to tell the caller that I was not Paul, when he hung up.

I grabbed my throw blanket from the couch, folded it and put it in the hall closet as I stumbled to bed. I had known Paul about five years, but certainly didn't know all he was into or what he did in his free time. The caller was probably a friend of his who had plans with him tomorrow night and was calling to confirm their date. But, hell, I was too tired to think about that now. I crawled into bed and fell asleep almost immediately.

On Sunday I forced myself to get out of the house. It was a nice day for mid-March, sunny and blue-skied, with barely a hint of a breeze. I decided to hit the park. In Denver there is only one park as far as gay men are concerned. Cheesman Park. An old city ordinance prohibiting nudity in public parks had successfully been knocked down, and now the park was filled with lots of naked sun worshippers every Sunday afternoon there was even a hint of sun peeking through the clouds. Of course, it was mostly middle-aged, balding men who walked around naked. The younger guys wouldn't be caught dead showing their stuff in public. It was only fifty-something degrees outside. Heaven forbid another cute, young guy see him with his pee pee all shriveled! But it was fun watching the volleyball players, so I went.

When the clouds started coming in and the weather dropped a few degrees I decided to go shopping. I bought some clothes and a crystal angel for my collection back home, and then headed back to Paul's place. Feeling only a little hungry, I made a light dinner of salad and fruit, and ate while watching the news. At about six o'clock I ran another hot bath and soaked for an eternity.

I could see the window in Paul's room from the tub. The curtains were pulled back and I had a good view of my friend's apartment across the lot. At about a quarter to seven I saw a light come on in the front room. I jumped out of the tub like I'd been electrocuted, and grabbed the towel as I ran into the bedroom. I quickly dried my body as I ran back to my room to grab my binoculars, then ran back to the window in Paul's room.

The curtains to his balcony window were closed, but I could see his silhouette behind them, stripping his clothes. I focused the binoculars on his balcony and reached down to fondle my cock as I waited for him to go out onto the balcony. I didn't have to wait long. In just a couple of minutes the curtains parted and he stepped out onto the balcony. He was completely naked and drinking a beer.

I took a deep breath as I took in the beauty of his face and body. With the binoculars I could see his nipples harden on his lightly hairy chest. My cock started to fatten as I followed the soft trail of hair down his stomach and to his crotch. He was still soft, and his long thick cock swung heavily as he shifted his weight to lean against the balcony door again as he had the first time I saw him.

I moved the binoculars to his face. He was cleanly shaven and his hair was brushed a little neater than yesterday. He'd probably just gotten back from dinner or something. He smiled that perfect Adonis smile and winked at me. I flushed, and quickly put the binoculars down and pulled the curtains together. I tried to catch my breath for a moment, and then realized how silly I'd been. He knew I was there since Friday, and he was definitely there for a reason, too. I took a deep breath, pulled the curtains back and picked up my binoculars.

He was still leaning against the door, like he hadn't a care in the world, but now he was pulling on his long cock. It was halfway hard now, and I could see the large vein running the length of it. The skin looked so soft, and I imagined the sweet clean smell of his cock after a nice long shower. My own cock was fully hard now, and throbbing as I wished I could taste his dick.

I watched as he carefully slid a metal cock ring on. First he slipped his balls through the large circle, then he squeezed his half-hard shaft through it and pulled the cock ring tight against the base of his cock. His big dick swelled to unbelievable length and thickness, and I saw the large vein pounding wildly against the silky skin of his shaft.

I tugged gently at my dick, loving the feel of the throbbing heat against my hand. Fully hard my dick is almost eight inches, about average thickness. But it is filled with veins that look like a road map coming to life when they are pulsing like they were then. I love to just hold it tightly in my hands when it's hard and just feel the hot blood pounding against my hand.

I jerked my meat slowly as I watched the man across from me doing the same. He was pinching his nipples as he stroked his cock. I watched him do this for about five minutes. Then he turned and walked into his apartment. He was gone for about thirty seconds, and came back holding a cucumber. He held it up for me to see plainly, and began licking it and sucking it into his mouth.

I was so caught up in the feel of my own throbbing hard-on and watching this sexy man try to deepthroat a considerably sized cucumber that I didn't hear the front door open. My hand was sliding steadily up and down my cock and I was moaning sporadically when I felt a pair of arms wrap around my chest and stomach, and a soft cock against my ass cheeks.

I let out a startled gasp, and dropped my binoculars as I turned around to see who was behind me.

"Paul," I searched for an explanation.

"What are you doing here, Randy," he asked as he smiled and looked past me out the window.

"I was just . . ."

"I know what you were doing," he said, and pushed me gently to my knees. "Here, take the real thing."

He was completely naked. I couldn't believe he'd come into the apartment, seen me watching his neighbor, and stripped naked without me hearing him. His cock was still soft, but starting to stir and thicken a little. He reached down and picked up my binoculars as I took his soft dick in my mouth.

I licked around the head for a moment and then slowly sucked the shaft down to his balls. I felt his dick getting hard inside my mouth, and kept sucking on it until it filled my mouth and worked its way deep into my throat.

Paul had an average size dick, about seven inches long, but it was incredibly thick. I choked on it as it filled my throat, and came up for air.

"You been having fun while I was gone?" he asked.

I blushed and looked at him in the eyes.

"Well, I'm glad. But now you'll have some real fun."

He pulled me to my feet and kissed me gently on the mouth. I was acutely aware that the neighbor was seeing all this, and began to get jittery.

"Don't worry about him. He likes to watch as much as you do," Paul said, and turned me around so that I was facing the window again.

The neighbor was smiling and rubbing the cucumber against his ass. He put it back in his mouth, sucked and licked on it some more, and then moved it back to his ass. Paul was rubbing his hard cock against my ass and playing with my dick, which had gone soft for a little while with the surprise, but was now almost fully hard again. He bent me over and knelt on his knees. I picked up the binoculars and watched the neighbor as he alternated sucking the cucumber and rubbing it along his ass crack.

I moaned loudly as I felt Paul's tongue tickle my ass hole. He licked with short, jabbing movements around the pink hole for a minute or so and then slowly slid his tongue deep inside my ass. I felt my ass grip his tongue with spastic movements and moaned as he pushed his tongue deeper inside me while he massaged my ass cheeks. He turned me around a little so that his neighbor could see all the action, but so that I could also keep watching my new friend.

Paul stood up and walked to his nightstand and I watched through the binoculars as the man swallowed half his vegetable and pinched his nipple again. I could tell he was moaning just by the way he arched his body and closed his eyes as he sucked on the cucumber.

I could hear Paul behind me again, rolling a condom on his cock. A moment later I felt the thick head of his dick press against my puckered hole. He'd left it slippery with his saliva, and it slid inside my ass easily as he gently pushed forward. I moaned deeply as his thick cock slid slowly deeper inside my butt until his balls reached my ass cheeks.

"Oh, baby, your ass is so tight and warm," Paul said. "I'm gonna come real quick."

"No," I said, "take it slow."

He moaned and started moving his cock in and out of my ass slowly. I looked up into the binoculars and saw the neighbor was working the cucumber very slowly into his ass. He was watching Paul and me, and was matching Paul's stride beat for beat. I watched in amazement as more and more of the fat cucumber slid into the man's ass. I didn't think it possible, but by the time Paul was pounding my ass with a frantic pace, the guy across the lot from us had all but about two inches of the green veggie deep in his ass.

I felt Paul's dick get even thicker inside my ass as he fucked me. He was moaning loudly now, and I knew he was about to blow his load.

"Look at this guy," I told him, barely able to speak, since I too was close to shooting.

He moaned even louder when he saw the huge pickle buried deep in his neighbor's ass.

The man across the lot suddenly shoved the last two inches of the cucumber inside his ass and stood up. His ass had swallowed the fat intruder and it was completely inside him. He jerked his huge cock frantically, and leaned back with his eyes closed. I knew what that meant, and was ready to shoot my load along with him.

His cum sprayed in every direction; huge, thick, white jets of hot cum covering the wall and chair in front of him. There must have been ten big shots in all. Paul saw it even without the aid of my binoculars, and pulled his dick from my ass with another moan.

He ripped the condom from his cock just before the first shot escaped. He wasn't a shooter, but what seemed like a quart of hot cum poured from his dick. Some of it dripped down the under part of his cock and onto his balls. A lot of it spurted a little ways and landed on my ass. He rubbed his still-hard cock in the cum and rubbed it around my ass, humping my cheeks.

"Oh, man, I'm gonna come," I moaned loudly.

Paul pulled me up and turned me around, falling to his knees as I turned. He moved my hand from my cock and swallowed about half of my dick in his mouth. I tried to pull out of his mouth before I shot, but he held on tight.

My leg muscles tightened as the first wave of cum shot through my cock. I can't remember ever having such an intense orgasm, and Paul choked as it hit the back of his throat. I felt him swallow twice, and it was still shooting out of my shaft. A few drops escaped through his mouth and fell to the floor as he continued to suck me.

When I was drained of my load, we stood up and hugged each other.

"Wow," I said. "Are you okay with this?"

"Sure," he said, and waved at the man across the lot.

"You watch him often?"

"Yeah, you can say that. He'll be over in a couple of minutes. You can ask him yourself."

"What?" I asked, astonished.

"That's Tom. I've told you about him."

"Your boyfriend?"

He smiled and took my hand and led me to his shower.

Managing Adam

Jason was startled awake by the sound of the living room window sliding slowly shut with an ominous creak. He looked over at the clock on the nightstand. Three-thirty in the morning. From the living room he heard a hard thud, unmistakably that of someone who had just grazed his shin on unfamiliarly placed furniture.

"Shit," the man's deep voice grunted.

Jason stared quickly at the phone just a few feet away from him. Would he have time to call the police? Was the intruder armed and dangerous? Should he just get out of bed and slide through the bedroom window to safety?

I reached over and grabbed the bottle of lube from my own nightstand and squeezed a generous amount across the length of my hard cock. My heart was thumping fast and I took in short breaths of excitement as I watched the video. This was my favorite fantasy, and I had known from the moment I saw the cover of the new movie at the video store that I was not going to be disappointed. Produced by one of the top porn companies, directed by a living legend in the business, and starring two of my all-time favorite stars, it was a sure hit with me even before I popped it into the VCR.

As he contemplated his own questions, the bedroom door creaked open. Jason closed his eyes tightly and silently prayed that the burglar would see that the house was not empty, and simply leave. He felt the intruder staring at him for a long moment, then stopped breathing as heavy footsteps walked away from the doorway and across the room. Damn it, he thought, and kept his eyes closed. No such luck. The guy was already searching through the few items on his dresser and from the sounds of things, had found his wallet.

He kept his eyes closed and tried to keep his breathing steady in hopes that the burglar would think he was asleep, and just take what he wanted and leave. But that was not to be the case, either. Suddenly, he sneezed, and cringed as he felt the robber turn around and stare at him.

I slid my hand down the length of my cock, and shivered with the wave of pleasure that buzzed through my head and across my entire body. Not only was the video fantastic, but the new lube I had just bought earlier that day was out of this world as well. My fist slid across the stretched skin of my hard cock, gripping it and squeezing almost with a will of its own. I reached for the remote control with my right hand so that I could pause the action on my TV screen long enough to catch my breath and slow down the inevitable climax that threatened to erupt from my cock. But the remote control fell to the floor instead. Oh, well, I thought, and resigned my left hand to release its grip on my throbbing dick and kept watching the movie instead.

Completely against his will, Jason opened one eye just enough to get a quick glimpse of the man who had broken into his apartment. Even in the dark of the room he could see the man was huge. Well over six feet tall, he easily outweighed Jason by at least fifty pounds. The black sweater and black jeans clung tightly against bulging muscles on his arms and legs. A dark ski mask was pulled snugly over his head.

As the guy approached him, Jason tried to make out what few features he could. It would be important for the police report later. If he lived long enough to file one, that is. He noticed the man had dark eyes, with long, curly eyelashes. A long, strong Roman nose. A patch of darkly stubbled white skin surrounded very full and pink lips. Long, thick legs moved the man closer to the bed quietly.

Of course, Jason could not really have made out all that much detail, having just been startled awake in a dark room in the middle of the night. But I knew who the intruder was, of course, and noticed each of these details. I wrapped my fist around my cock again, and slid it slowly up and down the shaft as I watched the hooded Brent Van Horn move menacingly close to Jason Casper as he lie helplessly on the bed. My heart pounded in my chest as I placed myself in Jason's position, and shivered once again with the heat that pulsed through my cock and up my hand and arm.

"Close your eyes," Brent told Jason in his sexy, masculine voice. "Don't look at me."

Jason quickly did as he was told.

Brent leaned down so that his thick, full lips were no more than an inch from Jason's ear. He pulled the blanket roughly from the bed, exposing Jason's smooth and naked body.

"Roll over."

Jason rolled over, and there, filling the TV screen was the tight, smooth ass that had made him a superstar and broken the hearts of thousands. Twin white globes, silky smooth and hard as a rock, flexed above long muscular legs.

I moaned deeply and squeezed my cock tighter as I slid my hand across it faster, twisting it lovingly across the hard, tight head.

Brent kissed the back of Jason's neck, working his way down the tightly muscled back until he was licking Jason's ass. He ripped his clothes off violently as he went. By the time his tongue had snaked its way into the hungry crevice, he was completely naked. His body was chiseled to perfection, the ultimate vision of strong, muscular masculinity. His chest and arms were lightly covered with black curly hair. The six-pack of abs were rippled and defined so that you saw each one perfectly, even in the moonlit darkness of the room.

He stood up slowly, giving a perfect view of his massive cock as it swung heavily between his legs. It was reportedly ten inches long, thick and heavily veined. Easily the most recognizable cock in gay porn. Throbbing wildly, it oozed a long, thick string of precum from its fat, hard head.

I licked my lips and snaked my tongue around the inside of my mouth, working up what little amount of saliva I could. My hand pumped my cock with long, slow strokes.

Brent reached over and grabbed a condom from the nightstand. Placing it on the head of his cock, he unrolled it roughly down the length of his pole. The condom ran out of rubber about two thirds of the way down, and stretched to near transparency. Brent smiled from beneath the ski cap, and smeared a fistful of spit across his throbbing cock. When he bent over and touched Jason's ass with the big dick, Jason tensed up, flexing his famous ass.

I gasped as my hand pumped my cock faster.

"Please don't hurt me," Jason begged unconvincingly.

"Shut up!" Brent snarled, and slammed his cock deep into Jason's ass in one savage thrust.

"*Owwww!*" *Jason cried out, even as he leaned back to take even more of the giant cock deep inside him.*

"Ughhhh!" I moaned as I caught my breath and jerked off faster and harder.

"*Just shut up and you won't get hurt,*" *Brent said as he slammed his huge dick inside Jason's hungry ass.*

"*All right,*" *Jason moaned, "just please don't hurt me.*"

"*You don't listen, do you, punk?*" *Brent growled, and leaned down to bite Jason softly on the back of his neck as he pounded his thick cock relentlessly into Jason's butt.*

The camera zoomed in for a close-up of Jason's face. Delirious pleasure mixed with a little pain leered back at the camera as he bit down on his pillow. Just behind him, Brent's sexy pink lips nibbled on his victim's ear. Both men moaned with animal lust as the masked intruder fucked the young boy faster and harder.

"Oh, shit." I matched their groans as I felt the cum churning in my balls.

"*Take it, man,*" *Brent groaned. "Here I come.*"

He pulled his giant cock out of Jason's ass with an audible "plop" and ripped the condom from his shaft, throwing it across the room. The first shot of white spunk flew completely out of the camera's range, but was quickly followed with several more that sprayed over Jason's entire back and ass.

I bit down on my own right arm as my cock tried desperately to match the cum shot on the screen. It was nowhere close, but pretty good for me, or any average layman, I thought. I counted six fair-sized squirts and smiled as the hot cum hit my chest and slid down my ribs.

And then there was the knock at my front door.

"Shit," I cursed, as I grabbed the towel next to my bed and wiped furiously at the mess on my chest and stomach.

Should I just ignore the knock, and pretend I wasn't home? No, that wouldn't work. I was the on-site manager of my apartment complex, and my blue Mustang was parked visibly outside the front door. I'd already gotten in trouble with my property management company for not being home enough, and figured I didn't need any more hassle.

A second knock on the front door, louder this time. "Mr. Hoyt," the male voice called out impatiently.

"Just a second," I yelled, and jumped up from the bed. I wrapped the towel around my waist and stumbled to the door.

I looked through the peephole in my door. It was Adam, my new tenant. And from what I could see, he was naked and looking around the hall nervously. I quickly fumbled with the locks on the front door and opened it, waving the kid inside my apartment before anyone else happened to wander by and call the police. He wasn't exactly naked, but damn close. He wore only a pair of skimpy white boxer shorts.

"What the hell are you doing out in the hallways with no clothes on?" I asked as I shut the door behind me.

"I'm really sorry." He blushed. "I was doing laundry, and since the laundry room is right across the hall from my apartment, I didn't see any sense in getting dressed. I guess I didn't realize the doors lock automatically once they're closed, and I locked myself out."

"They don't teach college sophomores to carry their keys with them everywhere they go, huh?"

Adam blushed even deeper. "I'm sorry, Mr. Hoyt."

"Don't call me Mr. Hoyt. It makes me sound old. Shit, I don't even turn thirty for another year and a half. My name's Gary."

"Sorry, Gary," Adam said as he moved uncomfortably from one foot to the other. His southern drawl was thick and intoxicating. "It's just that I was always taught to use Mr. and Mrs. when speaking to my elders. Not that you're that much older than me," he stumbled when I must have looked shocked. "But I don't even turn twenty-one for another six months. It's just habit, I guess."

"Well, break it." I smiled at him. His short, blond hair, blue eyes and deep dimples were getting the best of me. Not to mention his smooth, muscular chest and rippled stomach with the thick patch of golden hair that started just below his navel and disappeared beneath the waistband of his boxers. "It makes me a little nervous."

"Yes, sir," he mumbled, and brushed his big hands through his hair. "I mean, all right."

I noticed he was staring at the skimpy towel that clung around my waist.

"Did I interrupt something?" he asked.

Now it was my turn to blush. "No," I said a bit too quickly, " I was just getting ready to take a shower. No big deal."

"Sorry," he said again. "So, do you think you can let me into my apartment?"

"Yeah, sure," I said as I glanced down to make sure my hard-on was not tenting out in front of me. "I have a spare key in my home office."

"Great. Look, I really gotta pee. Can I use your bathroom while you get the key?"

"Of course. It's down the hall, second door on the left."

As he turned around and ambled down the hallway, I couldn't help but notice his tight ass as the skimpy boxer shorts clung to him. I remembered Adam had told me he played football at the local college when I signed the lease with him last week, and his tightly muscled body certainly showed proof of his dedication to the sport.

"Let me get dressed," I said as I stared at his strong muscular back and smooth, long legs as they walked toward the bathroom. "I'll meet you in the office in just a minute."

"Okay," he said as he closed the bathroom door behind him.

I ran into my bedroom quickly, and threw the towel into the dirty clothes hamper in my closet, hoping to change into something more appropriate. It wasn't until then that I realized I hadn't turned off the video before jumping up and answering the door. Jason and Brent were no longer on the screen, but two new guys were. One of them, a skater punk, was sucking the big dick of the second guy, who was dressed in a suit. They were in a public rest room somewhere.

I reached down for the remote control, but it wasn't on the nightstand. "Shit!" I cursed. Then I remembered knocking it to the floor earlier. I dropped to my knees and looked for it, digging through the pile of the clothes I had been wearing earlier that day. The remote was not in the middle of them, and my heart began to race as I realized I had probably kicked it under the bed when I jumped up to answer the door. I crawled to the edge of the bed and peered underneath. Sure enough, there was the remote, a few feet away, directly under the middle of the king-size bed.

Dropping to my belly, I crawled as far as I could under the bed, reaching out my arm until I grabbed the damned remote control. I pointed it toward the foot of the bed, from underneath, and clicked the Stop button desperately. It was no use. From this vantage point, it didn't work, and the video played on. I heard the businessman encouraging the young skater to swallow his big dick deep into his throat, and the moans of the kid as he tried to do as he was told.

"What the fuck?" It was Adam's voice, and it was directly

behind me. I tried to crawl out from under the bed, but hit
my head as I did so.

"Shit!" I cried out in pain as I crawled backward as quickly
as possible.

"I'm sorry," Adam said, "I guess I turned the wrong way
when I came out the bathroom. I was looking for your office."

"Right instead of left," I grumbled as I sat on my knees and
switched the VCR off.

"What was that?" Adam asked, and nodded toward the television set.

"Just a video," I said, acutely aware of my nakedness.
"Sorry. I was trying to turn it off and get dressed before you
came out. But I lost the remote control."

"That's cool," he said as I stared up at him from the floor.

The outline of his cock pushed against the front of his
shorts, and I couldn't help but stare. It looked long and thick,
and a tiny wet spot appeared halfway down his left leg. I swallowed hard as I felt my own dick begin to swell.

"I thought you were into that," Adam said as he stared at
me, "but I wasn't sure."

"Into what?" I asked defensively.

"You know. Guys."

"Well, yeah, I am. Sorry though." Now it was my turn to
apologize, "I meant to turn it off before you saw it."

"That's cool," he repeated, and massaged his dick inside his
shorts. "You mind?"

"What?"

He continued to pull and squeeze at his dick and nodded
toward the bed.

"Oh. Sure. I guess," I stammered, and stood up as he
walked over and lay down on my bed. "I'll go get your key."

"There's no rush," Adam said as he leaned against my head-board. "I mean, my laundry is still in the washer."

"Right," I said in barely a whisper.

He took the remote control from my hand, turned the VCR back on, and stretched out as the TV screen once again filled with the image of the young kid swallowing the older man's huge cock. Adam's boner was starting to throb and fill even more of his shorts as he watched. Then he looked over at me. His deep blue eyes took in my naked body, and he smiled.

"Wanna join me?" he asked, and patted the bed beside him.

"Sure," I said, and started to walk over to the other side of the bed.

Adam grabbed my arm and pulled me down on top of him. I fell ungracefully, but he caught me and brought my lips down on top of his in one swift move. His tongue darted clumsily inside my mouth. I tried to catch my breath, but was unsuccessful as I felt the hardness of his cock press against my belly and his hands begin to massage my naked ass.

I broke the kiss and looked down into his big blue eyes.

"Suck me," he said, and moved my head down to the front of his shorts.

I reached inside his boxers and pulled out his cock. It was almost as long and thick as Brent Van Horn's, and I gasped even as my tongue reached out to lick him. My fist barely fit around Adam's fat uncut cock. But I didn't let that stop me. I licked the salty head for a long moment, and then swallowed as much of the big dick as I could.

"Damn, that feels good." Adam breathed heavily.

I did my best to take the entire length of his cock into my throat, but barely got half of it down before I felt myself gag. It had been quite a while since I'd had a dick anywhere near that big, and I was embarrassed at my inability to take it all.

But Adam didn't seem to mind, and he pumped himself into my mouth with short, jabbing strokes. After only a minute or so, my jaw began to ache. Just as I was about to come up for air, I felt Adam's big hands tighten around my head, and he shoved his cock deeper into my throat.

The first jet of hot, thick cum splashed against the back of my throat, and I choked as I pulled myself off his impaling cock. Six or seven more streams of his load showered my face as I watched helplessly. His hands were still kneading my ass cheeks and his breath was coming out in short, staccato bursts.

"I wanna fuck you," he said huskily even as the last of his cum dribbled out of his cock head and down his shaft.

"What?" I said dreamily.

He pushed me off him and rolled me onto my stomach. "Condoms?" he asked as he spread my cheeks with his hands and sat up on his knees.

"Top drawer."

He reached inside, grabbed a condom and slid it on his massive cock in one quick move. The latex was stretched every bit as the one that had covered Brent's huge dick in the video earlier, and I buried my head in the pillow as I thought about being fucked by a cock that big. A second later I felt the cold, sticky lube as Adam squeezed it into the crack of my ass. His fat pole rubbed up and down my ass, and he began to push forward.

"Slow down," I said through gritted teeth into the pillow.

"Can't," Adam said. "They don't teach us that in college, either."

The pain was excruciating as his cock speared my ass. I grunted and bit the pillow even harder as Adam shoved his entire length into me. I knew the pain would turn to pleasure soon enough, and began counting to ten. I tried not to think about the fact that each number I counted off could be another inch of fat, throbbing cock inside me.

"Oh, fuck, man." Adam sighed as his balls rested against my ass cheeks. "This is fucking fantastic."

By that time I was a little more relaxed, and the pain had indeed turned to pleasure. I pulled my head from the pillow, turned around and kissed Adam on the lips as I thrust my ass deeper onto his cock.

He began fucking me furiously, first with short, jabbing strokes, then with slow, longer and deeper ones. He kissed me as he slid into me, and before long I could tell that he was getting close.

I sucked harder on his tongue and squeezed my ass cheeks around his cock. That was all it took for me. Seconds later I felt the cum pour from my own cock and soak my sheets and stomach.

"Here I come, Gary!" Adam shouted.

He pulled out of my ass in one painfully emptying stroke, and ripped the condom from his cock. Shots of warm, thick sticky cum showered my back and ass. It seemed like a full minute or more before I felt the last of his cum land on my ass. A few seconds later it began dripping down my sides, and in between my sore ass and across my balls.

Adam rolled off me, and lay down on the bed next to me, catching his breath.

"Sorry, dude," he panted between breaths. "I don't know what came over me."

"Well, I know what came over me," I said as I smiled and leaned over to kiss him again.

"So, you're not mad at me?"

"Uh . . . no."

"Cool."

"Yeah, cool," I said, and cupped his balls in one hand as I rested my head on his chest. "What about your laundry?" I asked several minutes later.

"Laundry? Oh, yeah. It can wait," he said sleepily. A moment later he was snoring lightly.

I got up, cleaned myself off, and then walked to the laundry room. I took his clothes from the washer and threw them in the dryer, then walked back to my apartment. As I turned the doorknob, I couldn't believe it. I was standing out in the hallway in nothing but my briefs, and I had locked myself out of my own apartment.

I knocked and whispered loudly for Adam to let me in.

Next Stop . . . Paradise

I heard the "ding" of the train's door and ran as quickly as I could down the steps, clutching my backpack to my side as I nearly tripped over my own feet and down the stairs. Several people were meandering about with much less rush and haste on their faces than I had on mine. I brushed past them and squeezed onto the crowded subway train just seconds before the door slid closed.

"First time in San Francisco?" the chubby woman next to me asked. I couldn't tell if she was irritated with me for crowding her or not.

"Yes," I answered, and adjusted my bulky bag across my shoulders.

"Thought so."

"How could you tell?"

"Your bag. It's a dead giveaway. Besides, most people know the MUNI system well enough to know that there are trains heading downtown every three minutes or so. We're not usually in such a hurry here," she mumbled as she squeezed her ample body through the sea of people and deeper into the train. She was definitely irritated.

I blushed and stared down at my feet as the train screeched out of the station and began to accelerate. My destination was only four stops away, and I was beginning to think I would have been better off just having walked. It was only about ten blocks. But my bag was beginning to get a little heavy, and I wanted to say I had at least ridden the subway once in my life. So I followed the throng of people deep into the tunnel and rushed onto the already overcrowded train. Now I was beginning to feel a little silly.

If I had given it a little more thought, I would not have started my little sightseeing trip so early in the morning. At a quarter till nine, everyone was on their way to work. But in my defense, I really had no idea there would be that many people, even for downtown San Francisco.

It was my first trip alone, and up to now the largest city I'd ever been to was Wichita, Kansas, where I was currently attending college. Having grown up in a small town of less than a thousand in the Texas panhandle, even Wichita was huge to me. I was on spring break in the middle of my freshman year, and being the spontaneous guy that I was, decided to visit the City By the Bay on my own. Well, kinda. I'd arrived the previous night and spent the night in a shabby, rundown motel just south of Market Street. My cousin lived in Oakland, and I planned on meeting him later that afternoon when he got off work. Until then, I thought I'd soak up the sights of downtown San Francisco, and wanted to get an early start. Like I said, though, I should have thought it out a little more carefully and started after the rush hour. Oh, well.

"Powell Street. Powell Street Station is next," the conductor called out over the speakers.

People began standing up and inching their way toward the doors, squeezing one another and cursing under their breath.

My backpack was obviously getting in their way, and several passengers shot me a nasty glance as they crammed around me, near the door. The train skidded to a stop, the double doors opened, and people spilled out into the station. I heard a few mumbled, "damned tourists" and blushed again.

More than half my train got out at Powell Street, and when I spotted an empty aisle seat, I grabbed it. A few people got on at the station, but not many. I busied myself with staring at the map attached to the wall a few feet ahead of me. When the train took off again, I looked around me at the new people who had just gotten on, trying not to look too much like a tourist.

It was then that I saw him. He'd taken the seat directly across the aisle from mine, and stretched his long legs out into the middle of the now empty aisle. My breath caught in my throat as I stared at him. My heart raced.

He was young, about my age or maybe a year or two older. Latino. Or maybe Filipino, I thought to myself, as I took in his exotic almond-shaped eyes and remembered the large Filipino and Asian community the Bay Area boasted. Either way, he was gorgeous! Almost six feet tall, I guessed as I glanced at his well-muscled body sprawled across the seat and halfway into the aisle. His face was copper brown, and looked like it had never needed a razor. His hair was cut very short around the sides and back, but long, straight black bangs fell over his forehead and across his eyes. He wore black jeans and a white T-shirt. I swallowed hard as I noticed the biceps that bulged enormously as they lay across an equally impressive muscular chest.

A loud shriek filled the train as it ground to a near stop, and then picked up a little speed again. With the movement of the car I felt my cock rub against my own jeans. I was rock hard. Never in my life had I reacted like this to another guy. Sure, I'd noticed a few at school, and even fantasized about one or two of them. But never had I gotten this hard this fast . . . and never just at the first sight of a guy. Maybe it was that he was so different from anyone I'd ever seen before. I was used to blondes and redheads, corn-fed farmers and small-town, Bible Belt boys. I myself have blonde hair, brown eyes and freckles from the summers I've worked on the farms around my small town. Though at five feet five I am shorter than even most guys at school, I am still well-muscled, a result of hard work and good genes. Still, I was taken aback by the long legs, lean and muscular frame of this guy across from me.

"Montgomery Street. Montgomery Street Station is next," the conductor called out as we slowed to a stop.

More people stood up and walked to the doors. The woman sitting next to the beautiful guy I was staring at stood up and tried to step over his sprawled legs. "Excuse me," she said when she couldn't clear them, and the guy sat up in his seat, opened his eyes and moved his legs to his right and into the aisle. His big feet brushed mine as the woman looked at him angrily and stepped past him.

"Sorry," he said to me as the woman followed the group of people out the door. His eyes stared into mine, and again I lost my breath. They were bright blue, almost turquoise, and sparkled.

He continued to stare at me for a long moment. When the train started up again, he slid across the double seat and leaned against the wall, stretching his legs out across both seats and once again kicking me lightly in my own leg. He smiled the most beautiful smile I'd ever seen, causing twin dimples to grace his cheeks. Then he closed his eyes again.

I couldn't help it. My eyes grazed his beautiful face and muscular frame. When they reached his crotch, I took in another deep breath. The bulge was huge, and his left hand was squeezing it playfully, causing it to grow even larger as I stared. My own cock throbbed painfully in my jeans, and I reached down to adjust myself in them.

When I looked up at him again, his eyes were open and looking back at me. He was smiling. Still groping his crotch discreetly but with more pressure. The tip of his tongue peeked out and licked his full, pink lips. Then, with the slowest, slightest close of one eyelid, he winked at me.

The train stopped once again.

"Embarcadero. Embarcadero Station," the conductor said. "This is the last stop."

The guy pushed himself into a sitting position in his seat, stayed there for a moment as he stared into my eyes, and then stood up and walked off the train. I got clumsily to my feet, threw the backpack across my shoulders, and stumbled off the train myself. My eyes never left the kid as he walked slowly to the escalators and began ascending them. His ass flexed as tightly as his big legs against his jeans, I noticed as I stepped onto the moving steps only a few feet below him.

When he reached the top of the escalators, he slowed down and waited for me.

"Where you headed?" he asked. His voice was soft and low.

"Umm, I dunno," I said. "Just walking around I guess."

"Come on, then. I know a place we can go. Follow me."

He walked briskly ahead, and I shook my head to clear the cobwebs. Then I followed him. He walked two blocks, to a large cement building across the street from the Embarcadero Station, and only looked back once, as he walked up a short flight of stairs. Making sure I saw him, he entered the second floor rest room of the building, which I had vaguely realized was an outdoor shopping mall.

As I walked into the rest room, I was assaulted with the

mixed smells of urine and disinfectant. The rest room was clean, but graffiti was scrawled across every wall. Against one wall were two urinals, and next to those, two metal stall doors. No one else was in the room, but I looked around nervously anyway as the door shut behind me. I noticed the black shoes and the bottom of the black jeans under the farthest stall against the far wall. Trying to work up enough saliva to swallow, I quickly walked to the adjoining stall, and closed the door.

I sat on the toilet, trying to force my heart to slow down. In the middle of the left wall was a large, perfectly round, cut out hole. I heard the sound of a belt unbuckling, then the undeniable soft plop of buttons being forced open. I leaned forward and peered into the hole in the wall just in time to see the top of my friend's jeans being pushed down his thick, muscular legs. He was wearing bleach white jockey shorts, and I was amazed at how beautiful and bright they looked against his smooth copper skin.

Then I saw his hands move to the waistband of his shorts, and I sat up straight on the toilet again. *Am I really going to go through with this*, I thought? A second later I was amazed to find myself pulling my own jeans down my legs. Yes, I was.

When I looked back up at the hole, there it was. Very long and very thick, his cock was dangling through the hole. The skin was just as brown and just as smooth as the rest of his body. A sheath of foreskin stretched tightly across his hard cock, allowing about half of the fat head to peek through. A thin drop of clear liquid oozed from the tip of the head, and I licked my lips as my hands reached for his cock.

It throbbed hotly in my hands. I used to have a fairly good sense of self-control, but that was obviously a thing of the past. My heart pounded uncontrollably, my hands squeezed and tugged at the fat cock, and my dry mouth moved on its own accord to swallow its first dick ever. The guy's cock tasted great in my hungry mouth, and I devoured it like it was my last meal.

"Slow down," he said as I slurped clumsily at his cock.

I did. I pulled my mouth off his dick and licked the huge pole with my tongue, swirling it around for a moment. I played with the fat head for a while, licking away all the sweet precum that trickled onto my tongue. Then I became anxious again, and swallowed half of the shaft deep into my throat.

"Oh, fuck, man," the gorgeous kid almost screamed, "I'm coming!"

And he did. Spurt after hot spurt flew from his cock and down my throat before I even had a chance to pull away. I swallowed as much as I could, then slid my mouth off his dick, letting the last few drops dribble onto my chin.

"Shit, that felt great, man," he whispered. "Want me to do you now?"

I stood up quickly and shoved my throbbing cock through the hole before he had a chance to change his mind. A second later I felt the warmest, wettest, tightest sensation I could ever have imagined surrounding my dick. I don't even pretend to believe I have the biggest dick ever; in fact, this guy's cock was easily a couple of inches longer than mine. But mine is the thickest I've ever seen. My fist and fingers barely fit around the hard pink skin when it gets fully hard. This guy had no trouble with it, though. He swallowed my dick as hungrily as I had done his, and I felt myself losing control within seconds.

"Pull back, man, I'm gonna shoot," I said hoarsely.

Suddenly his mouth was off my dick and his hands squeezed the base of my cock.

"Not yet," he moaned. "Not like this."

"What?"

"I want you to fuck me."

A loud, high-pitched ring resonated through my head as the room began to sway and I fought again to catch my breath. No one had ever spoken those words out loud to me. As I struggled with what they meant, and how to deal with it all, his strong hands continued tugging and squeezing my cock. I became dizzy with the idea of actually fucking someone, and lost all track of whatever sensations were happening to my cock. But only for a moment.

Seconds later I felt the tip of my cock pressing against his smooth ass cheeks. Then a quick "pop" and my head was surrounded by intense heat. I knew the head of my dick was now inside his ass, and focused on not fainting.

"Oh, shit, that feels so good, man." The guy in the next stall moaned loudly.

"Are you sure you want to do this?" I whispered huskily.

"Fuck, yeah," he answered, and then began sliding his ass down the length of my cock. His moans became louder as each inch of my dick slowly disappeared inside him.

I heard him breathing heavily as he stopped for a few seconds and then continued. Then I felt the skin just below my belly button and right above my pubic hair touch his smooth ass. His moans increased and his ass muscles began massaging my thick cock. Little dots of bright lights floated in front of my eyes as he slid up and down my cock.

"Fuck me, dude," he said.

I did. I began sliding my cock in and out of his ass, slowly at first, and then with more speed. Once or twice I accidentally pulled all the way out, but he quickly grabbed my dick and pushed it back inside him. That was all it took for me. I began fucking him hard and deep, relishing in the heat of his ass muscles that swallowed my dick. The metal partition that separated the two stalls began to shake and rattle with the force of both of us slamming against it. I held onto the top of it and pressed my face against the cold metal as I fucked with increasing speed and intensity.

"Oh, man, I'm shooting again." He panted, and I felt his strong ass cheeks convulsing stronger around my thick meat.

I speared his ass deep, and rested my hot cock inside the warmth as he shot his load onto the floor in front of him. His ass felt like a hundred fingers massaging my throbbing cock, and I leaned my head back with the pleasure. Then my knees buckled, and I almost fell to the floor.

"Here I come," I said quickly.

I was amazed at how quickly he pulled himself off of my impaling cock. It made an audible "plop" as it left his tight ass, and I heard him dropping to the floor. Then my load started shooting from my dick with a force I'd never imagined, let alone felt. I pressed my body tighter against the wall as I emptied myself, and counted six huge spurts as they flew from my dick. Then my legs did give out from under me, and I slumped to the floor, exhausted. I looked through the hole in the wall and saw the guy's face was covered in my cum. His eyes were closed, and he was smiling.

Then the bathroom door opened, and I jumped up and sat on the toilet seat. I could hear my new friend next door do the same thing. Both of us waited as the new visitor emptied his bladder into the urinals next to us, and then we hurriedly pulled our pants up, tucked our shirts in, and walked over to the sinks.

"Dude, that was great," he said as he washed his hands and looked at me. His bright turquoise eyes sparkled and stared right through me.

"Thanks," I said, a little embarrassed by the compliment.

"Here, you've still got a little cum next to your ear," I grabbed a towel and wiped his face clean.

"You from around here?"

"No. Just visiting. I'm meeting my cousin in Oakland at three o'clock."

"And until then?" He smiled and leaned against his sink.

"No plans, really. I was just going to do a little sightseeing."

"I don't live too far from here. Wanna come over for a while? I could show you a sight or two." He smiled, and his dimples covered his smooth face.

"You want more?" I asked, incredulously.

"Sure. But this time it's my turn." He reached down and carressed my ass as he pulled me into him and kissed me on the mouth.

"Um, I've never been fucked before," I stammered as I hesitantly broke the kiss.

"That's okay. I'll be gentle." He kissed me again and squeezed my ass lovingly.

"Gentle? With that huge thing?"

He laughed. "It's nothing, really. Come on, I'll show you."

He reached down and took my hand in his, and we walked toward the door. When we reached it, he let go of my hand and kissed me lightly on the lips again. Then he opened the door and walked out and toward the escalators.

I followed him, a few steps behind.